CASKET CASE

A Novel

LAUREN EVANS

DELL

NEW YORK

A Dell Trade Paperback Original

Copyright © 2024 by Lucy Books LLC
Book club guide copyright © 2024 by Penguin Random House LLC

Published in the United States by Dell, an imprint of Random House, a division of Penguin Random House LLC, New York.

Dell and the D colophon are registered trademarks of Penguin Random House LLC.
Random House Book Club and colophon are trademarks of Penguin Random House LLC.

ISBN 978-0-593-87375-5
Ebook ISBN 978-0-593-87376-2

Printed in the United States of America on acid-free paper

randomhousebooks.com
randomhousebookclub.com

2   4   6   8   9   7   5   3   1

Interior art by Dava, zolotons © Adobe Stock Photos

Book design by Sara Bereta

CASKET CASE

For all the Rabbittowns

Because I could not stop for Death—
He kindly stopped for me—
—EMILY DICKINSON

CASKET CASE

TODAY

"Thank you for calling Death," a perky voice announces through the car's speakers. "If you know your party's extension, you may dial it at any time, followed by the pound key. For Accounting, press one—"

Garrett presses 1214# on his iPhone's keypad and waits as his call is connected.

"Garrett," Janine answers. "What can I do for you?"

"You can stop sending me to places called 'Rabbittown.'"

"It's *your* region. Why are you calling? I see an appointment on your calendar."

"Yes, I have an appointment, and the address in the file doesn't come up on Google Maps. A little help here?"

"I don't know what you think I can do if Google Maps can't find it."

Garrett sighs and pulls his car into an open parking spot

across from what looks to be a coffee shop. This has been the first semblance of civilization in miles. "You don't see anything in the file?"

"You have the address. That's it."

He leans his head back against the seat. He has never missed an appointment before. He doesn't intend to start today. "I guess I'll ask for directions."

"Thank you for coming to that on your own."

The line clicks, and the screen on his dash changes back to the radio menu. He checks his watch. He doesn't have much time.

As he gets out of the car, he takes a moment to stretch his legs and assess his options. The coffee shop looks busy, and he doesn't have time to worry about bystanders. He glances over his car to the business on the other side of the street.

The old wooden sign hanging over the door says "Rabbit-town Casket Company." He tilts his head, considering. A casket company shouldn't have too many bystanders. Not live ones anyway.

CHAPTER

1

The bell over the door tolls for Mrs. Atkins, Nora's first customer of the day. She marches through the showroom, past the dusty model merchandise dying for her attention, for her affection, for the sinking weight of a decaying body.

Mrs. Atkins hefts her designer handbag onto the counter, ready to be assisted. "Lord, Eleanora, you look just like your mother standing back there."

To be fair, Nora's mother did spend a lot of time behind that counter. She had helped Nora's father paint and install the counter after they found it at a yard sale, freshly ripped from someone else's kitchen to make room for the new and improved. That was the year they painted the walls a blue-tinged eggshell and installed the track lighting to properly show off their new caskets.

"No one wants to buy them if they can't see them," Billy Clanton had said.

Anita Clanton wanted to tell her husband that the models were a bad idea, that this was one of the few retail situations where customers did not want to be near the merchandise. She told him the same thing when he brought in urns and cremation jewelry to display.

Nora Clanton doesn't have an opinion. Not yet anyway.

"How can I help you?" She tries to use her best salesperson tone, but some people don't have one of those.

"I went to Jim Anderson's funeral last week," Mrs. Atkins begins. "And his daughter-in-law, bless her heart, had picked out the ugliest gold casket I've ever seen. When I saw it, I knew I had to pick out my own for when the time comes."

Most customers can describe caskets only in subjective terms. They want it to feel peaceful. They want it to match a personality. They're worried it will clash with a certain outfit. Jim Anderson's daughter-in-law thought the gold was a classy touch.

Marilyn Atkins sings soprano in the choir at the First Baptist Church and never misses a Sunday. She's also healthy as a horse. Some customers are so bothered by the macabre that they choose a casket in the first ten minutes, but not Mrs. Atkins. Nora spends a hefty chunk of her day (one hour and seventeen minutes) pointing out the most tasteful options and listening to Mrs. Atkins's gold bracelets clang against the counter as she finds something wrong with all of them.

"Something like this," Mrs. Atkins says, shoving a stack of printouts in front of Nora's face. The first page has a casket circled in red.

Nora releases a breath from her body, and she wishes she could go with it. "That's mahogany. Just like this one." She flips wearily to the very first casket she showed Mrs. Atkins, back when she still had an ounce of patience.

"Is that one mahogany, too?" Mrs. Atkins squints at both pictures.

"It's the same model. See?" Nora points out the number on both caskets.

"Well, I'm glad I brought these pictures. Otherwise, we never would have found it."

Nora considers the model caskets lining the showroom and if crawling into one might allow her into another world or dimension or place that is not here. But she needs Mrs. Atkins's business, so she leaves that adventure for another day while she finishes the sale.

As she signs her name to the paperwork for a solid mahogany casket with cream satin lining, Mrs. Atkins asks, "Are you still living in that house?"

"Yes, ma'am." Her parents' house has been in Nora's family for a couple of generations.

Mrs. Atkins's family would never be on that side of Rabbittown, but she hears things like everybody else. "It must feel so empty! That house is meant for a family." She slides the paperwork across the counter and gathers her purse to leave. "You haven't found any nice men since you've been back?"

"None that stick." She can't be sure what Mrs. Atkins will say next, but she knows it will be one of the three types of responses everyone says to single women over thirty:

1. You're lucky. Husbands are the worst.
2. It will happen when you least expect it.
3. Don't forget your biological clock.

"It will happen when you least expect it," Mrs. Atkins says. "That's how these things go."

"So I've been told." She stacks the paperwork together with a touch of aggression and attempts to smile in Mrs. Atkins's direction.

Mrs. Atkins doesn't notice; she hasn't noticed other people in years. "You aren't getting any younger," she says, wagging her finger as if scolding a child.

"Thank you for coming in," Nora says, making her way around the counter to shoo Mrs. Atkins out the door. "See you at church."

Mrs. Atkins walks toward the door but stops short in front of the light blue casket at the front of the showroom to run her finger across the top. "You might have a word with your cleaning staff, Eleanora. There's an inch of dust on this one."

"Yes, ma'am, I'll be sure to do that."

"You know, I went to a visitation at one of those Prestige Funeral Homes up in Huntsville, and you might want to stop by one of them." She glances around the showroom, which hasn't changed much since it was first built. "You could use some updating. I'd never buy from a company like that after knowing your mama for my whole life, but it wouldn't hurt to borrow an idea or two from them."

Nora stares at the blue casket as hard as she can to keep from rolling her eyes. Prestige has made a fortune buying up funeral homes and related suppliers in the area. They convince the small businesses that they have their best interests in mind, taking over the "boring" parts of running a business so that the staff can do more to serve customers. In reality, once the sale goes through, Prestige fires most of the staff. Pooling resources is great for the business and not so great for the family who just sold their life's work to someone who turned around and axed them.

"I'll keep that in mind."

Mrs. Atkins nods briskly, and the bell tolls again as she marches out onto the sidewalk.

The administrative part of running Rabbittown Casket Company takes about ten minutes as long as Nora is caught up, and Nora doesn't have much else to do, so she's always caught up. Customers rarely come in without warning, except for the occasional high school kid on a dare.

The store used to be open six days a week, so her parents had mounted a television to the wall to watch Alabama football. Once Nora left for college, her parents decided they might like to have a social life, so they stopped opening on Saturdays, but the television stayed. That television is the reason Nora is now addicted to *General Hospital.*

Nora is sitting with her legs propped up on the desk, watching Carly yell at Sonny for what has to be the millionth time, when a tall man in a suit appears in front of the counter. She jumps, and not gracefully.

"I didn't mean to scare you," the stranger says.

"I should have been paying more attention." Nora's bare feet fumble around underneath the desk to find the shoes they'd ditched. She sinks lower in the chair until her toes hit the fake leather. "I didn't hear you come in."

"Whatever you're watching must be good."

Nora starts to apologize more thoroughly, but he stops her

with something close to a smile. Nora notices that his nose is a little crooked, and he has a faded scar on one cheek. "I get sucked into these shows."

"My grandmother used to record them on VHS in case she missed anything." He gestures to Sonny Corinthos on the screen. "He looks exactly the same."

A mobster points a gun at Sonny, and Carly screams, but Sonny doesn't flinch. Nora hits the power button on the remote.

"You don't have to turn it off on my account."

"I can watch it later. Besides, Sonny will never die."

"Everyone dies. I would think you know that better than most."

Nora is about to ask how he knows about her family, but then she remembers they're standing in her casket store. "I'm sure you didn't come in here to talk about *General Hospital*. May I help you with something?"

"I'm not really a customer. I'm looking for Pearl Drive, and Google Maps brought me here." He holds his phone out to Nora, but she doesn't need it.

"You're close," Nora says, as she walks around the desk and takes in his height and his expensive suit. She can't decide if he's actually handsome or if it's been too long since she's seen a breathing man in a tailored suit. "It's more of a driveway than a road, though. Are you sure you have the right address?"

"I'm looking for Pearl Café."

"Come on, I'll show you." Nora leads him outside into the clear summer day, to the old gravel road that separates the casket store from the fabric store next door, past the silver Mercedes parked on the street that must belong to him. Plenty of folks in Rabbittown have money, but no one would waste it on a fancy car when you could get a truck that requires two parking spots.

"It's right there." Nora points up the hill to an old wooden building just visible through the trees. "The road's not great, so most people walk. Are you here for the food?"

Nora tries to imagine what obscure website or podcast would know about Frank's secret fried chicken recipe. Frank inherited the building from his parents, who ran a general store, but Frank loved to cook, so he and his sister, Ms. Annie, did some remodeling to turn the place into a restaurant. The story is worth telling, but Frank would be too bashful to tell it.

"I'm just here to see the owner. Is the food any good?"

People don't just come to Rabbittown. It's about as far east as you can get in Alabama without hitting the Georgia line. Thirty minutes from Anniston, the closest city of any size, which no one outside of Alabama would recognize. An hour and a half from Birmingham. Something must be going on for a person in a Mercedes to wind up at the Pearl Café.

"You should try the cornbread, if you get a chance."

"I like cornbread. I'm Garrett, by the way. Garrett Bishop."

"Nora Clanton," she says, shaking his hand. His eyes had seemed brown at first, but in the sunlight, they're the color of the leaves on the magnolia tree behind her house. She stares a moment too long, but Garrett stares back with no regard for the silence between them.

Unable to think of anything else, Nora musters, "It's nice to meet you."

"Yeah, thanks for your help," he says, still not breaking eye contact.

"It's no problem." They continue to stare, but neither of them can come up with anything reasonable to say.

"Well, I'll let you get to it," Nora says, choosing this moment to quote her father, certain she'll never see Garrett's face again.

She watches him walk cautiously up the hill in his pristine leather shoes. Nora doesn't know anything about him, including what brought him to Rabbittown, but something tells her she will get the details soon enough. Nothing stays secret for very long, especially when it involves one of Rabbittown's main gossip hubs. The fastest way to spread any news is to make it known at Pearl Café or the First Baptist Church, and the townsfolk know how to take it from there.

Nora stares into space until she can finally close the store and walk up the gravel road to Pearl Café. Nora's grandpa sits at their usual Tuesday night table, facing the front door so he can talk to everyone who comes in for dinner. Frank's sister, Ms. Annie, the waitress/cashier/sweet tea maker/only other employee of Pearl Café, sits at the next table telling what looks to be an exciting story. Nothing happens in Rabbittown without Ms. Annie knowing about it.

When Grandpa sees Nora, he stands in that old-people way that makes you think he might not make it out of the chair.

"Hey, girlie," he says with his trademark toothy grin. All the men in the Clanton family have the same one, and Nora is reminded of her dad.

"Hey, Grandpa. How are things?" She takes her usual seat next to the window.

"Good. I spent most of the day tending to the garden. We're gonna have a lot of squash this year."

"Should you be doing that by yourself?" Nora knows what his

answer will be, but he had one of his knees replaced last year, and he needs reminding.

"I manage."

"Stubborn as ever," Ms. Annie says.

"How are you, Ms. Annie?" Nora asks.

"Better now. We've been slow today." Ms. Annie wears the same blue-and-white ruffled apron every day, with her gray hair smoothed back into a bun. The deacons from the Baptist church also meet here on Tuesday nights. She nods to the table of middle-aged men in the back of the restaurant. "They can't talk about anything but high school football." Ms. Annie prefers gossip over sports.

"Speaking of," Nora says, "I went to see Mrs. Dooley yesterday. She says we're going all the way." Mrs. Dooley used to teach third grade, and now she's the bossiest resident at the Rabbittown Senior Center.

"Mrs. Dooley has always had more faith than the rest of us," Grandpa says. "Where's Frank tonight?" Frank usually waits until the banana pudding course before joining them to push Grandpa's buttons about something in the news. Grandpa knows he's going to do it, but he still gives Frank the reaction he wants.

"He wasn't feeling well, so I sent him up early. Hardly anyone here."

"Hey, we keep this place in business," Grandpa protests.

The whole town keeps it in business, really. It helps that the food is good and that there aren't many other restaurant options without driving thirty minutes into the city. There's also something comforting about the floral wallpaper and spongy blue carpet and the collection of mismatched dining room table sets, which can be pushed together for big celebrations or pulled apart for date night.

A shadow passes the window, and Nora recognizes Garrett Bishop walking back down the driveway toward his silver Mercedes that had still been parked in front of the store when Nora left. "Have you ever seen that guy around here?"

"I don't reckon," Grandpa says, leaning over to get a better look. "He must be passing through with that getup."

"I think he looks nice," Nora says.

"I'll tell him to wait!" Ms. Annie says, moving toward the door like a flash.

"No! I was just saying the suit is nice."

"You sure? Doesn't look like he's wearing a ring."

"I met him earlier," Nora says. "He was looking for Frank, so I gave him directions."

"What'd he want?" Ms. Annie asks.

"No idea," Nora says, knowing Ms. Annie will find out before she goes to bed.

"You're stuck at that store too much. You should take a vacation."

"You could sell the place," Grandpa says.

"Then what would I do?" Nora takes her time unrolling her silverware and placing the paper napkin in her lap, so she doesn't have to look at either of them.

"Go back to your old job," he says. "I'm sure they'll take you."

"I like being my own boss. I'm an entrepreneur." Besides, her old job stopped calling her a couple of months ago.

"You do what you want," he says. "But your mama and daddy didn't want you to spend your life in that store. You should get out and do something once in a while."

"I'm doing something right now."

"Let me set you up!" Ms. Annie says. "Jeff Wilson has a nephew who just got divorced. No kids. Can't remember his name, but I'll call right now."

Thinking of the Wilsons makes Nora think of her parents, so she tries to shut it down quickly. "Adam? We went out in high school. Not a match."

"It's not always about a match," she says. "Let him buy you dinner."

"I would rather buy my own dinner."

Nora used to be a person with a plan. Her parents had raised her that way.

Finish high school.

Go to college.

Find a job that doesn't involve late nights, weekends, or death.

Meet a nice man with a job that doesn't involve late nights, weekends, or death.

Buy a house with a nice lawn in a nice suburb.

Have nice children.

Have nice grandchildren.

Retire.

Rest in peace in a nice casket.

Nora had done what she was supposed to do. She had crossed off one step at a time. She had found a nine-to-five job that paid her rent and then some. She'd had nice friends and a nice boyfriend. She'd had a favorite place for happy hour and tickets to concerts, and Charlie had booked a hotel room in New York City for their anniversary.

Then her parents died.

In other stories like this, an uncle or aunt might step in. But Nora was an adult, so her dad's brother had gone home to Tennessee after the funeral. Her grandparents on the Moore side had died when Nora was a baby, leaving Nora's mother the store. With her mother gone, she was the only one left. She was George Bailey running the Building and Loan, but without hope of anyone else tagging in to give her a break. People in her life had been there for her, especially at first, but no one could fully share the burden of figuring out what comes next. All of the decisions had to be Nora's.

Nora had never thought about the future of the store. Her parents had wanted it that way. She would live her own life. They would take care of everything in Rabbittown. To say she had no desire to run a business would be an understatement. She had never thought of it. No one had ever mentioned it. She wanted to be a basketball player and then president of the United States and then a teacher and then an accountant, and no one ever pushed her otherwise.

So, Nora had to come up with a new plan: handle whatever needed handling in Rabbittown and then to go back to her life. Her normal routine would distract from that lump in her throat and the hollow feeling in her chest. She would jump right back into the regularly scheduled programming.

When it came time to make arrangements to close the store, Nora couldn't do it. Her parents had met on the sidewalk out front. She had learned her multiplication tables in the back room. The store had bought her first car. It had sent her to college. She couldn't sell the house, either. Just the thought of cleaning out everything her parents had owned and loved paralyzed her. How could she stuff her parents' life and work into a storage unit, knowing she would eventually have to throw it all away? So, she sat on it. She told the real estate agent, her bosses, and her boyfriend that she needed time. In a few weeks, she would be ready. She would know what to do.

Then one of her neighbors died from cancer. Her parents had helped the family arrange everything in advance, so Nora opened the store to help her neighbor's son sort through those details. Once he left, she walked the perimeter of the show-room, flipping the same light switches she'd flipped as a child when her parents had signaled it was time to go home for the night. She hadn't left home in days, but now she was thinking about going for a drive or stopping for coffee or taking a walk around the Square. She felt light. She felt useful. She felt she had done something right.

She knows death. It's in her blood. Now more than ever.

Over the past few months, Nora has taken on her dad's morning routine. She scrambles eggs in her great-grandmother's skillet and makes sourdough toast from the loaves her Uncle Ralph brings to the store every few weeks. She was a teenager before she realized that Uncle Ralph wasn't really her uncle. Besides Grandpa, kinda uncles and maybe cousins make up most of her social life. Her friends have a hard time knowing what to say, since the only life she can talk about revolves around her dead family or a casket store, so she's been letting most of their texts go unanswered to spare them the effort. It's a lot to understand, and they shouldn't have to try so hard.

She kept her family's subscription to *The Anniston Star*, and she reads it at breakfast like her dad always did. Her dad used to say the obituary section was good for business. It's like a list of every casket sold in the area, and her dad loved figuring out who they bought from if it wasn't from him. Her mom liked the gossip of it all. If you read enough obituaries, you start to notice the nuanced phrasing of estrangement or peculiar names added to the lists of survivors.

Nora works at the store during the day. She scrolls social media. She watches soap operas. On Tuesdays, she has dinner with Grandpa. On Sundays, she goes to church. There's no Sunday school class for unmarried women over twenty-five, and the lessons in the ladies' class usually involve submitting or mothering or wife-ing, so she's taken up residence in the men's class with Grandpa.

She spends most nights with her TV. Nora tried watching TV right after the accident, but TV families made her sick to her stomach, so she gave it up. Though because she never canceled her parents' cable subscription, it was always there waiting for her. After a few months, she started using it for background noise to avoid the silence. She caught a few minutes of *General Hospital* and decided it wasn't so bad. Those people didn't look or sound like her family. One day, she read an article in the paper about a guy from a neighboring town who played for the Braves, so she turned on the game. She realized she could bear sports, so she started watching anything she could find. She signed up for extra streaming services, so she could have even more options.

After dinner with Grandpa and Ms. Annie, Nora sticks to her usual Tuesday night habits. When she gets home, she pours a glass of the third-cheapest red wine from Rabbittown Grocery into the Crimson Tide glass her dad always used on game days. She knows she should fold the laundry piled on the two easy chairs in the living room, but she doesn't actually care about the laundry or the easy chairs.

She tries to get into a hockey game, but she doesn't understand the rules, so after scrolling Instagram for an hour, she abandons her makeshift wineglass on the coffee table and moves from the couch to watch *Cheers* in her bed. She turns it up a hair too loud to distract herself, because she still hasn't gotten used to sleeping in a silent house. It's like the depression knows she doesn't have her mom to check for monsters anymore. The monster waits until midnight to crawl into bed next to her like a drunk ex-boyfriend, and it's hard to move him once he's comfortable.

SIXTEEN YEARS AGO

The business card is harmless. Boring, even. The woman who slid it across the table is mundane, too. Average. Forgettable.

"We'd like to offer you an internship. Your adviser thought you would be a good fit."

"A good fit for what?" Garrett scans the business card, trying to make sense of it. He was supposed to meet with his adviser, but this woman had shown up instead. He has no interest in an internship. He wants to get out of school quickly and find a real job with a real salary to pay back his student loans.

She squares her shoulders. "We help people going through difficult times."

"Like a nonprofit?"

"Oh, you'll make a profit."

"That's not what I meant." Had she been reading his mind?

"We're an international company that partners with communities to make a difference in the lives of every individual," she recites, like a brochure come to life.

"*Every* individual?"

"You've had your own difficult times, haven't you, Mr. Bishop? I hear you want to make a difference in the world. Is that true?"

He had never mentioned that to anyone. It floats around in the back of his head, like something he might do in a distant future or another life altogether.

"Yes, it's true."

"That's all I needed to hear."

CHAPTER
2

"Everyone dies," Nora says.

"What does that have to do with anything?" Jean asks.

Fifty-seven years ago, Nora's Papa Moore had used this logic to convince her grandma that they should use their savings to start Rabbittown Casket Company and try to make some money off a sure thing. Maybe he was tired of farming, where nothing was a sure thing. Maybe her Papa Moore was just a morbid person. Maybe Death had visited often that year and left the idea as he was passing through. Nora's mom, Anita, wanted to be done with the whole thing, but when Anita's parents died and left her the store, Nora's dad, Billy, convinced her to keep it going. Billy's dad worked a boring office job at an insurance company, so he was excited by the prospect of a family business that would make him feel like he was helping the community with more than just paperwork.

"It's a steady job," Nora says. "Why would I look for another one?"

"Because selling caskets seems about the furthest thing from something most people would want to do. I remember you saying as much."

Nora sits at Jean and Joe's kitchen table watching Jean flip through an old cookbook. The pages are worn and stained with remnants of the recipes inside. She's trying to find a recipe for her grandson's fifth birthday party. Lucas doesn't like cake. He doesn't like bread of any kind. He also doesn't like loud noises or excitement, so this birthday party might not be a great idea, but Nora knows better than to tell that to a grandmother.

"There were some kinks at first, but I'm figuring it out."

"Don't say another word about kinks with the caskets, Eleanora." Jean pauses on a cobbler recipe and examines the ingredients through her dark-rimmed glasses. "What is there to figure out?"

Nora presses the toe of her black ballet flat into the table leg next to her. Joe and Jean have had this square table in the middle of their kitchen for as long as she can remember, and probably much longer than that. "I'm just not as good with customers as Dad was."

Nora's dad remembered everything. He could place everyone, somehow. He knew your cousin or your preacher or your veterinarian. He could recall every conversation. All of the little details that Nora doesn't even notice. She thinks it's the only reason the store has stayed open this long.

Rabbittown Casket Company has always counted on word of mouth as its main marketing strategy. When someone dies suddenly, the family might not know what to do, but they do know they can call their second cousin Billy or Mrs. Anita from church to help them sort it out. The residents of Rabbittown and other places like it are suspicious of any funeral homes that have been taken over by Prestige or big fancy funeral homes like those run by the Chandler family. The Chandlers had started small, and they were owned by a local family, but with every new location they opened, they became more like a big company. More like Prestige.

Nora's parents had no interest in expanding. They just wanted to reach as much of the community as possible. Nora's dad figured the more hands he could shake, the better. Nora's mom used to make sure the doctors and nurses in the area were flush with informative pamphlets and her famous pound cake. Nora has tried to follow those plans exactly, but she can't make her mother's pound cake. It always turns out dry. Anita kept promising to teach Nora how to make it, just like her mother taught her all those years ago, but they never got around to it. You can't predict car accidents. Nora knows she will have to figure out her own marketing techniques, since the "dead parents pity period" feels like it's about to end.

"You're better than you think. It's in your blood. Tell me you've been doing something besides working."

"That's about it."

"What about Ashley and Taylor?" Jean remembers things, too.

"Haven't heard from them."

"Well, call them up." Jean opens another cookbook on the table.

The last time Nora saw Ashley and Taylor, she had just moved back home. They drove to Rabbittown for lunch and to make sure Nora was showering and eating on a regular basis like a functioning member of society. Nora promised to visit them in Birmingham, but she hasn't. They don't push. Nora doesn't blame them.

"We're all just busy right now."

"Busy doing what?"

"Taylor is dating someone. Ashley has a new job." Nora had learned this information from Instagram.

"What are you busy doing?"

"I have a job."

Jean narrows her eyes. Some people would bail from the discomfort of this conversation, but Jean has never bailed on anything, especially when it involves someone she loves.

Even though Joe and Jean are Black, Nora grew up thinking Jean was her aunt until her mother explained that they weren't actually related. Whenever her parents needed help or advice, they called Joe and Jean. Joe had worked at the same insurance company as her grandpa, until they both retired. Joe and Jean were at every basketball game and awards day ceremony Nora can remember. To most other people, Joe and Jean are known for their Christmas lights, which light up the whole neighborhood. Hundreds of people from the eastern half of Alabama drive to the boonies to sit in line to see the show.

"You work at the store from eight to five?" Jean asks.

"Yes."

"You go to church. You see your grandpa. What are you doing the rest of the time?"

"I have things to do at home," Nora says.

"What things?"

"Laundry, the dishes, whatever there is."

"When's the last time you went on a date?"

Sometimes Nora can figure out where these conversations are going, but not today. "I guess sometime before I got dumped."

"Months ago. Single people go on dates, you know."

"Who would I go out with?"

"Whoever you want," Jean says.

"What if I don't want to?"

She smiles. "You'd rather scrub toilets every night?"

"Maybe I need time."

Jean puts her hand over Nora's. "You've been through a lot. Your mama and daddy, moving home, minding that store like a good daughter. But you can't hide there forever."

"I'm not hiding," Nora says.

"You're young."

"I'm thirty. Doesn't feel that young."

"Well, I'm sixty-seven, and you need to be spending time with people your own age."

"No one in Rabbittown is my age," Nora says. She sulks back into the chair and crosses her arms, taking the position of an unruly teenager being lectured.

"Get on Tinder." Jean stands up from the table and slides the cookbook back into its place on the counter next to the stove.

"What do you know about Tinder, Jean?"

"I've got a TV, and it works as well as yours. Maybe better, because I don't run it down watching *Cheers* every night." Jean turns to Nora with her hands on her hips; she means business. "You're going to have to leave the house sometime, girl."

After Nora's parents died, her boyfriend, Charlie, used to drive from Birmingham to Rabbittown on the weekends, and they spent most evenings in the cemetery lying on a blanket near the Clanton family headstones. Nora didn't do it every night, but it was nice to look up at the stars somewhere she thought they might be instead of somewhere she knew they weren't.

She stopped spending nights in the cemetery around the time Charlie stopped being there. Yes, he was technically there, but at some point, Nora started to notice that he was maybe not really "there." Like maybe she was imagining him next to her when he was somewhere else entirely.

Then she found him. She had gone to Birmingham to pick up a few things she had left in her old apartment. She hadn't asked for his help because she wanted to show him that she could leave the house. That she could take care of herself. That things were getting better.

Nora was at a red light when she saw him getting into a car with a woman she didn't know.

She knew things hadn't been great. It hadn't been fun. It hadn't been easy. There was no way for him to be certain that life with Nora would get back to the way it had been. Especially when he'd found someone who still laughed, who didn't ask him to lie under the stars in the cemetery or sleep with the television on. Nora doesn't blame him. It's a lot of work to be the normal one.

She had loved him. She would have married him. They would have been a happy suburban family. Death had changed everything. Ruined everything.

Driving back to the store from Jean's, Nora is reminded of one of the perks of returning to a small town: no traffic. The name Rabbittown is a bit of a misnomer. It's less of a town and more of an unincorporated community, or at least that's what it says on the welcome sign next to the post office as you drive into the Square. "Square" isn't the right word either, but you can't really call it "downtown" if you've ever been to an actual downtown. Rabbittown Casket Company sits between the Taming of the Ewe fabric store and Rabbittown Pharmacy and across from the Chat & Brew coffee shop. The owners of every business on the Square meet once a month as the self-appointed Rabbittown Square Council to ensure that nothing changes in their lifetime. Nora is the newest addition to the group, and she learned pretty quickly that the menfolk will let her know when they want her opinion on anything.

Nora opens the store a few minutes late, but she doesn't care because she has been dreading this particular workday. Nora's dad never liked doing the paperwork right away and generally had trouble making it from point A to point B without getting distracted, so he had an annoying habit of leaving stacks of paper on any surface in the casket shop he could find. She has planned to spend the day sorting through some of the remaining piles, even though she knows it's unlikely that someone would need to see the paperwork for something they've buried six feet under the ground.

A few minutes after flipping the sign from Closed to Open, Nora is sitting on the floor surrounded by yellowed carbon copies of casket orders from the 1980s when she realizes she's not alone. Garrett Bishop stands at the counter waiting to be noticed.

"You scared me. Again," Nora says, unfolding herself as gracefully as she can manage. She runs a hand through her hair and tries to smooth out her clothes.

"I'm sorry. Again."

She lets her eyes wander, taking in his gray suit and white dress shirt with no tie. She can't tell if he's actually in shape or if his self-assuredness just makes him seem like the type of someone who would have a gym membership or one of those apps to find nearby trails. His dark, wavy hair is perfectly arranged. She had doubted her own judgment yesterday, but now she can be sure he's that specific blend of classically handsome with a few interesting peculiarities thrown in to make him the romantic comedy version of hot. She's taking in his long eyelashes when she realizes he's looking back at her with an amused expression, as if he knows exactly the sort of thoughts running through her head.

She clears her throat in an attempt to clear her mind. "Did you find Frank yesterday?"

"I did. Thanks to your help."

"Are you back for more directions?"

"Maybe." He leans down, resting his arms on the counter, so he can meet Nora's eyes. "Where do people go on dates around here?"

Nora's heart beats a little faster, and her stomach fills with something, but she can't decipher if it's hope or dread. She tells herself the question has nothing to do with her. He met her once. It's not going to happen. "I would say the Tasty Dip, but my last date around here was a long time ago." Her last date in general was a long time ago, but he doesn't need to know that.

"That doesn't sound very romantic."

"It's not really, but they have the best ice cream in the county." They also have a back parking lot where teenagers go to make out in their cars. She keeps that to herself.

"Well, I know we just met, but I can only come up with so many reasons to run into you, so I'll be direct. How would you feel about having ice cream with me sometime?"

He seems confident, his forearms propped on the counter like he does this sort of thing all the time, like it wouldn't be a big deal if Nora rejected him to his face, but his jittery hands give him away.

Nora doesn't go on dates. She doesn't go anywhere, really. Her life is stable. Comfortable. Easy. She knows that falling for someone would end all of that. He's attractive. He has a job. He's well-dressed. Why would he want to go out with her? She spends most of her days talking about dead people, and she has certainly looked better.

Garrett drums his fingertips against the countertop, waiting for an answer.

Nora can't imagine how much alcohol it would take to get her to ask out a complete stranger. In person! In broad daylight! Is he an alcoholic? Or a drug addict?

She thinks she should say no and save him from any entanglement with her, but there's something about him. She can't explain it. From what she knows about life-altering soulmate connections, she's supposed to get some sort of signal that the person standing in front of her is the other half of her soul, like when you use the remote to find your car in a parking lot. This doesn't necessarily feel like that, but she feels something. Something as simple as interest, maybe, for the first time in a long time.

"Okay," Nora says.

"Okay?"

"Yes, I would feel okay about the ice cream."

Garrett's lips twitch, but he stops short of a full smile. Playing it cool, he pulls a business card out of his pocket. Knowing where this is going, Nora interrupts.

"Can I give you my number?" She knows that if it's up to her to call, she'll never do it.

Without pause, Garrett hands her his phone and presumably all his secrets, which is refreshing and super weird at the same time. Nora calls her phone, so she has his number.

"Is tonight too soon?" he asks.

"To call or get ice cream?"

"Either. Both. Whatever I can get." Garrett can play it cool for only so long.

"No one has ever been this excited for my company." She assumes that at some point while they're at the ice cream stand where she used to eat dipped cones and push-up pops with her parents, he will ask about her family. No one comes to a first date prepared to offer condolences for dead parents. No one has known what to say ever since she got the call that her parents had wrapped their car around the Wilsons' oak tree half a mile from their house.

"Do I seem desperate?" Garrett asks.

"I work in a casket store. It's probably me who should be desperate."

He laughs, dimples and all, and Nora does her best not to swoon right in front of him.

"I would love to get ice cream tonight. Can you meet me here sometime after four-thirty?"

"Sure," he says, checking his watch. "I'll be here at four-thirty."

Garrett leaves quickly, before Nora has time to change her

mind. She examines the business card he left on the counter. Could his job be as boring as the card looks? It has "Garrett Bishop" and "Regional Director of Logistics" and not much else. There's a strange symbol that Nora doesn't recognize in the top left corner, instead of a company name. It's a circle with two lines coming down like legs from a stick figure, and at the bottom of each leg there are two short lines pointing out. Or maybe it's a key with two stems. Or two keys with their heads overlapped. Maybe she will ask him later. Nora thinks about walking up the hill to the café to ask Frank what he knows about Garrett, but she talks herself out of it. It's a first date. It doesn't have to be that serious.

She is thinking about which ice cream would be the most ladylike to eat—certainly not a cone—when her grandpa calls the store.

"Nora?" His tone doesn't sound right.

"Yeah, it's me. Is everything okay?"

"I hate to call you at work, but I didn't want you to hear it from anyone else."

"Hear what?"

"Something happened last night. It's Frank. He's dead."

TODAY

Garrett reaches the Rabbittown Square thirty minutes ahead of schedule. Even though he had been to Rabbittown before and knew the odds of rural Alabama being hit with a sudden case of rush-hour traffic, why take the risk? He pulls into a diagonal parking spot down the street from Rabbittown Casket Company to wait in his air-conditioned car until closer to the agreed-upon time.

Garrett is always early. He loves it when other people are early, too. He also knows that showing up thirty minutes early for a first date is a red flag. Well, he didn't know that at first, but his sister had explained it after he'd recounted the awkwardness of a date answering her door in a bathrobe with wet hair.

He does what everyone does when they have time to waste. He scrolls. His friend Thomas has a new baby and refers to it as his twin. Garrett doesn't see the resemblance. He thinks babies look like babies, not grown men with beards. But he's genuinely happy that his friend is happy. *Like.*

His ex-girlfriend has posted more pictures from her wedding. Garrett swipes through all of them, even the artsy photos of her shoes. They used to talk about getting married or, more specifically, eloping. His job had been a deal-breaker for her, or at least that's what she said. She couldn't move far away from everyone she knew for him to take a job with so much travel. Didn't he want a family, she had asked. Within a year, she had gotten married to someone else. It didn't last long. Garrett doesn't know the details. He hopes this time will turn out better for her. Next.

There's another series of photos of his sister, Rebecca, and her husband. They're standing next to a waterfall in the first one. In the second they're drinking wine on a patio overlooking a picturesque mountain view. In the third they're kissing, which Garrett could have lived without seeing. Under the photo he types out, "Do either of you have jobs?" He deletes it before posting. It seems like one of those jokes that would be funnier in person, if at all. *Like.*

Bored of everyone else's life updates, he catches up with news on the *New York Times* app. He responds to two work emails. He tries to do anything else on his phone to keep himself from getting nervous about the date with Nora.

Garrett didn't know what he was getting into when he first walked into Rabbittown Casket Company. He had been in a hurry, expecting to run in and run out so he could make his appointment time at Pearl Café. He had not expected Nora. Sure, she was pretty, and it's not like he had never seen a pretty girl in public before. Normally, Garrett tried to ignore them. Women around his age usually weren't single, and if they were, the thought of it going so badly he could never show his face again at Target or the grocery store was enough for him to mind his own business.

It was something else. Something else about her was intriguing before he had even spoken to her. Maybe there was something endearing about the way she was existing in her own world in the middle of the day without expecting to be interrupted. Or the way she jumped when she noticed him standing there. It certainly hadn't been graceful. Somehow, it had struck him as genuine. Unfiltered. Human.

Something catches his eye in the rearview mirror. A man. Two men. Staring at the back of Garrett's car with their arms folded across their tucked-in T-shirts. Garrett is a white man in Alabama, so it doesn't occur to him to be afraid, just curious. He didn't grow up in a small town, but he's been in enough small towns over the years to know that his car attracts attention. Maybe, to them, it's a bit unreasonable or over the top. Garrett figures if he's going to spend the majority of his time in his car, he might as well enjoy it.

CHAPTER

3

The men in the parking lot aren't the only ones who have taken notice of Garrett. Margaret at Rabbittown Pharmacy calls Suzanne at Rabbittown Grocery to ask about the fancy car parked in one of the diagonal spots out front. Margaret assumes the driver must be lost, but Suzanne thinks it's someone's kinfolks coming to visit. They're both disappointed when the car backs out of its spot at 4:25, leaving them without an answer.

Nora could have been ready to meet Garrett out front when he arrived, but she was busy. Not with work. She finished that hours ago. Instead, she spent her afternoon thinking about everything that could go wrong once he got there, and she is surprised to see him drive up at 4:29. He's still wearing his gray suit, but he's ditched the jacket and rolled up his shirtsleeves, easily making him the hottest man she's ever gone out with. She tosses her crossbody over her head and meets him at the front door before she can talk herself out of it.

"We can walk," Nora says, locking up the store and gesturing to the other end of the Square. "The Tasty Dip is a couple of blocks from here."

"Lead the way."

For a moment, they walk down the sidewalk in silence. She doesn't remember how dates are supposed to go.

"So," Garrett says, "have you always sold coffins?"

It's a reasonable question, but it makes Nora laugh. He laughs, too. Maybe this won't be the worst social outing in the history of the human species. But it's only just begun.

"They're caskets, actually," Nora says.

"Is there a difference?"

"Caskets have the hinge on the side. Coffins are the old wooden things where vampires sleep. The ones you see at Halloween."

"I had no idea."

They meander down the sidewalk at a slower pace than either of them is used to. Garrett puts his hands in his pockets, which keeps his knuckles from brushing against Nora's as they walk. Nora considers the Square for the first time in a while. The brick buildings with white-trimmed windows have looked mostly the same for her whole life. A few years ago, the Rabbittown Square Council did allow the Chat & Brew to paint their outdoor furniture royal blue in support of the high school football team, but the change proved quite controversial and is unlikely to be repeated. If Nora weren't using so much of her brain to think about her conversational skills, she might wonder what Rabbittown looks like to an outsider. She might be self-conscious about her sleepy small town, with its cracked sidewalks and faded awnings.

"It's a family business," Nora says. "My grandparents started it, and it's made its way down to me. You can ask whatever you want about it. I'm used to the questions."

"What do people normally ask?"

"Do I have to touch the bodies? No. Is it sad? Sometimes. Is it creepy? Not unless you're creeped out by paperwork."

"Seems like they're thinking of a haunted house."

"Maybe so."

"It didn't seem haunted either time I was there."

"If it is, I don't know about it. Maybe it's a quiet ghost."

"Maybe the ghost likes soap operas, too," he says.

"He probably does by now."

Garrett smiles at her, and she can't help but blush.

They have to walk the length of the Square to reach the Tasty Dip, so they pass all the townspeople who have come together to make sense of what happened to Frank. Nora waves hello to a group of ladies from church who have congregated outside of the post office to exchange information. It will make its way to Nora eventually.

"All of these people are normally at home," Nora says. When she's nervous, she fills the empty space with any words she can get to come out. "Frank, the guy who owns Pearl Café, passed away last night. Everyone is a little freaked out."

"I'm sorry. Were you close?" Garrett asks, reciting the question everyone always asks when they hear about a death. Maybe to judge the mourner's response against what their response should be, Nora thinks. Or to situate the mourner's experience in relation to the questioner's own experiences with death. How much empathy do they require? Will the situation affect their relationship with the mourner and for how long?

"Yeah, I've spent a lot of my life in that restaurant," Nora says. She remembers how quiet the café seemed yesterday with Frank resting upstairs, and maybe she should have gone to check on him. Is everyone who ate at the restaurant yesterday wondering the same thing? If there's something any of them could have done. There in the cluster of memories, she gets a glimpse of Garrett walking past the window and down the hill. "Wait, you were up there yesterday."

"I was," he says, staring down at the sidewalk.

"Did you talk to Frank?"

"I did."

Nora gives him a moment to add to his sentence, but he doesn't. "Did he look okay to you?"

"I don't know." He says this in the same way a petulant child might speak to a scolding parent. "I'm not sure what he usually looks like."

Maybe Nora doesn't understand dating, but she doesn't think it should involve irritation. "Sorry, I'm being nosy."

"You don't have to apologize."

"We can change the subject." She isn't getting anywhere anyway.

They walk in awkward silence to join the group of people lined up on the grass in front of the Tasty Dip. They've been serving ice cream since Nora's grandparents were young and haven't done much in the way of renovations since then. The paint is chipping, but the ice cream tastes fine.

"Popular place," Garrett says, browsing the laminated menu duct-taped to the front of the building.

The group of children in line in front of them alternate between jumping up and down and screaming with anticipation.

"Yeah, there's always a line," Nora says, over the sound of the screaming kids. "It moves fast, though." Parents and babysitters use the Tasty Dip as a reprieve from being stuck in the house with energetic kids, especially when school is out for summer. Some of the parents sit in their cars and read or listen to podcasts or call in to meetings while their children run laps around the building with their faces covered in ice cream.

"I'm not in a hurry," he says.

He looks down to meet her eyes, and her heart stutters. She forces herself to breathe. "What do you normally get?" he asks.

"Depends. I've pretty much tried everything. The dipped cone is a classic. The double chocolate ice cream sandwich. Hot fudge sundae."

"You must like chocolate," he says.

"I do. But they do have things that aren't chocolate, or so I'm told."

"I'll try the hot fudge sundae. I trust you."

Maybe he's falling for her "normal" act.

They sit down at an open picnic table, and Nora tries to eat her ice cream sandwich as gracefully as possible. The dark chocolate ice cream drips down her fingers, and she catches it with a napkin before the mess gets worse.

"What do you like besides chocolate?" Garrett asks.

"I think it's your turn," she says, surprising herself. "You know a lot about me already, and I know nothing about you."

"What do you want to know?"

She thinks for a moment. "The basics, I guess. What do you do? Where are you from?"

"All right," he begins. "I'm in logistics consulting, and it's as boring as it sounds."

"What does that mean?"

"I work for a consulting firm, and they send me to make sure things get from one place to the next without any problems."

She nods her understanding, even though they both know she doesn't fully understand this vague description.

"I grew up in Raleigh," he continues. "My family still lives there. I move around a lot, but I've been in Anniston for about a month."

"How do you like it so far?"

"Seems like a nice town, but this is probably the first thing I've done outside of work since I've been here."

"Have you been downtown yet?"

"I've just driven through it."

"It's grown over the past few years. There are some good restaurants and a brewery, and I think a new bookstore is supposed to open soon."

"Maybe that should be our next adventure."

The butterflies in her stomach test their wings. "I could be your tour guide."

"I want the unauthorized version. The one with all the insider gossip."

"That one costs extra."

He considers this, scooping ice cream into his mouth and sliding the spoon out slowly to collect every bit of hot fudge. "I'm sure we can arrange something."

Nora can't be sure if he's trying to suggest something else entirely or if attractive men just eat in an attractive way, so she attempts to land somewhere in the middle while keeping the rest of her body in check. "You have my number. How's the sundae?"

"A good choice." He scrapes his spoon against the nearly empty plastic cup. He freezes, and a crease forms between his brows. "I'm sorry. I should have offered you some."

She laughs at his expression. "It's fine. I didn't offer you mine, either."

"That's true. You were fast."

"I just didn't want it to melt all over my hands."

He laughs. "I'm sure that's the reason." He picks up a napkin and wipes each finger individually. "Okay, I answered questions. It's your turn."

"What would you like to know?"

"You're from Rabbittown?"

"Yes, I've been in Alabama my whole life. Grew up here, college in Tuscaloosa, moved to Birmingham for a while, and now I'm back."

"How long have you been back?"

"About a year."

"Did you go to school for business?"

"Finance," she says. "I was a financial adviser for a few years."

"Not for you?"

She knows she has to be careful here unless she wants to swing the conversation back to death, which always seems to be lurking. "It was fine, but I like running things myself."

"No boss?"

"No boss." She nods.

A group of high schoolers take over the picnic table next to them, and it's hard to look away from the laughing and the ice cream throwing. Is it appropriate to discipline someone else's kids? Would Garrett judge her for it?

"What do you do when you're not at work?" Garrett asks.

She answers this one honestly: "I watch a lot of TV."

"Like what? Besides *General Hospital.*"

"I never miss *General Hospital*. Otherwise, it's mostly sports."

"Which sports?"

"I'm not picky. My favorites are football and basketball, probably, but I've been getting more into baseball. I like softball. Golf sometimes. Whatever is on."

"Who are your teams?"

"Obviously Alabama," she says.

"Obviously."

"Sorry, is this boring? Do you like sports?"

"Not boring." He smiles. "I'm a Panthers fan."

"You're not an Auburn fan, are you?"

"No. I went to UNC."

"Thank God."

"What would you have done?" he asks.

"Bailed as quickly as possible."

It has occurred to her that she might just be interested in Garrett because he's the only option she's had in a while, but when he laughs, she feels the butterflies flapping around in her stomach like she's in a Meg Ryan movie.

"I get it. I wouldn't go out with a Duke fan."

She laughs. "Neither would I."

He reaches across the table and takes her hand, flipping it over to reveal a swipe of ice cream below her thumb. "You missed a spot." He meets her eyes before using his napkin to wipe it away.

"Thank you. Unfortunately, I'm a messy person. I get the impression you're not."

He smiles. "Why do you say that?"

She examines him from head to toe, leaning down to peek at his shoes under the table. "You carry business cards. Your shiny car. Your clothes."

"What's wrong with my clothes?" He looks down at himself.

"Nothing," she laughs. "That's the point. They're perfect."

"I do like for things to be in order. Is there something wrong with that?"

"No, it's cute, actually." Before she can say anything else, a dirty plastic spoon lands on the table between them.

A teenager with long blond hair appears, retrieving the spoon. "Sorry, Nora. I was trying to hit Theo."

"I think you know what I'm going to say about that."

"That I shouldn't hit anybody?"

"Bingo."

"Sorry!" she calls, running back into the middle of the group of teenagers now throwing anything they can get their hands on.

"Friends of yours?" Garrett asks, watching the scene in front of them.

"I know most of their parents."

"They don't seem worried about that."

Nora turns to him. "Not that I'm in a hurry to leave, but how would you feel about continuing this conversation somewhere away from here? To protect your perfect shoes from flying ice cream?"

"I think that's a great idea. Why don't you test out your tour-guide skills? Give me a tour of Rabbittown?"

"You want to see more of this?" She gestures around them at

the Tasty Dip's surroundings. The unruly kids. The duct-taped signs on the building. The gravel parking lot.

"More of you, actually. But the tour couldn't hurt."

She would love to play it cool, but she can't stop the smile that takes over her face. He answers with one of his own, and she feels it all over her body. She wants to kiss him. To lean across the table and kiss him right here in front of everyone at the Tasty Dip. Is that appropriate for a first date? Could she even pull it off? Sure that she would find a way to make it awkward for both of them, she takes a deep breath instead. "You asked for it. Let's go."

On their walk back to the store, Nora goes as slowly as she can, doing her best to come up with something to say about every building or bench or tree with any kind of significance. They stand in front of the hair salon, and she tries to think of anything she knows about it besides the definition of a hair salon.

"Both of my grandmothers used to get their hair done here on Tuesdays, so they could gossip. It's the first place I would go if I needed information about something in town."

He looks at the building, doing a decent job of pretending to be interested. "I think they might be talking about you tomorrow. It feels like everyone is watching us."

She glances down the street and makes eye contact with the people in front of the grocery store. "I'm sorry about that. They're nosy. They don't mean anything by it." She starts to worry that this might be the deciding factor in whatever happens next between them. That he's probably gotten weirded out by prying eyes on their first date.

"Might as well give them something to talk about," Garrett

says, reaching over to take her hand and bringing her racing thoughts to a screeching halt.

Nora smiles at him. "You're trouble. I can tell."

He shrugs. "I guess you'll have to find out for sure."

Garrett walks her to her car, parked behind the store, and she thanks him for the ice cream. She lets go of his hand to dig her car keys out of her purse, and when she looks up, he's staring down at her. "What's wrong?"

"Nothing's wrong."

"Why are you looking at me like that?"

He smiles. "I'm trying to kiss you, and you're not making it easy."

"Well, that was direct," she says, willing her face to stay its normal color.

"You asked."

Nora puts her purse on top of the car and takes a step toward him. "You can kiss me."

Garrett closes the gap between them and puts his hand on her cheek in one smooth motion. He kisses her once, softly, politely. Before she can think herself out of it, she takes a chance and wraps her arms around him, and then they're really kissing. Like in a Julia Roberts movie.

After a moment of making out in a parking lot like teenagers, he pulls away and takes a breath. "Was that too much for a first date?"

She shakes her head and kisses him again. She doesn't want to stop kissing him. This is what normal women do, isn't it? She's seen it in rom-coms her whole life. They meet someone they like, and the someone likes them back. They smile, they kiss. They live, they laugh, they love. Nora feels like the women she sees on Instagram, the ones who have perfect lives and far too much happiness and positivity for sadness to overtake them.

"When can I see you again?" Garrett asks against her lips. He steps back to give them both space to think coherent thoughts.

"When are you free?" She has no life, but she doesn't want to seem too eager.

"Is tomorrow too soon?"

She laughs. "No, I can see you tomorrow."

"Can I call you tonight?"

She nods, and he leans down for another kiss. As he pulls away, she can see from the look in his eyes that he feels the same way. Like it's way too soon, but there's something here.

CHAPTER

4

The next day, Nora closes the store early to meet Grandpa at the church for Frank's visitation. Nora's dad helped Frank make his funeral arrangements a few years ago, so there isn't really anything for Nora to do except show up. When she'd heard about Frank, she had flipped through her dad's notes to make sure he hadn't forgotten any part of the plans. Of course he hadn't. Frank had been his friend, too. Her dad had expected to be here, to take care of all of this. Her dad would have had something to say beyond the notes in Frank's file, but the notes are all Nora has now.

She has nothing to do to keep her mind from wandering to Garrett. Had he been irritated with her for asking about Frank? Or was that just her imagination?

"Don't you look like somebody," Ms. Owens says as Nora walks up the front church steps. She taught Nora in fourth grade and a couple of years in Sunday school. She's one of those church ladies you don't want to cross.

Nora looks down and hopes she chose the right day-to-night, funeral-to-date black dress. "Thanks. Have you seen my grandpa?"

"He's in line already," she says, as if Nora should know that. "Come on."

Nora follows her past the line of people already forming through the aisles of the church until she finds Grandpa and his usual group of troublemakers.

"Eleanora, you look like a model in that dress," Jean says. "Did you change your hairstyle?"

"I decided to do something with it for once," Nora says. She was happy to find that her straightener still works after months of sitting in the bottom of a bathroom drawer.

She hugs the whole group, saving Grandpa for last.

"How are you, sweetie?" He's wearing the same nondescript dark suit he always wears to formal occasions, even though it's too big for him now.

"I'm okay. How are you?"

"I'm all right, too."

"There are a lot of people here," she says, looking around at the crowd.

"Frank knew everybody," Joe says.

"He took care of everybody, you mean," Margaret says. Margaret is a pharmacist, and she and her husband, Ed, own the pharmacy on the Square.

"Anyone talk to Ms. Annie?" Jean asks.

"I talked to her this morning," Nora says. "She sounded okay. Sad but holding it together."

"He would've liked to see everyone here," Grandpa says.

"He would've had jokes for all of us," Margaret says.

They move through the line toward the front of the church, remembering everything Frank had been to all of them.

"Eleanora, your mama and daddy really loved Frank," Margaret says. "Frank and your daddy used to hold up choir practice because they'd get to laughing."

"I remember," she says. Nora didn't have any brothers and sisters, so many of her friends were adults until she started school. Frank and Ms. Annie would watch her sometimes when her parents had to go out of town for funerals. They taught her to play poker and blackjack, but she wasn't allowed to tell her parents. Those skills had come in handy once she got to college.

"I bet they're all looking down at us right now," Margaret says. They let the thought bounce around in their heads for a moment. They imagine a lot of the same faces staring together, looking down at them and what they've made of themselves.

"So, Eleanora, who's your new friend?" Joe says.

"What friend?" As soon as the words leave her mouth, she realizes he means Garrett.

"We heard you were walking with a man yesterday on the Square," Jean says. She doesn't mention their last conversation, but Nora can tell she's going to ask about Tinder later.

"Do you have a *man*?" Margaret asks, eager to jump on a new piece of gossip.

"I wouldn't go that far. That was our first date."

"How was it?" Grandpa asks.

"Good," she says, hoping they'll take the hint and change the subject. They won't.

"I heard you took him to the Tasty Dip," Jean says.

"I did."

"Well, don't keep us in the dark, Eleanora! What's he like?" Margaret asks.

"He's nice," she says. "We've only been out the one time, so I don't have too much to report."

"Where did you meet him?" Margaret asks.

"Uh, he came by the store. He needed directions." Nora leaves out the Frank part of it because she knows that would cause more questions, and she doesn't have the answers.

"Who would ask directions in a casket store?" Jean asks.

"His GPS brought him there." Honestly, she hadn't thought of that. She forgets that she works with death until someone reminds her.

"He could have come to the pharmacy," Margaret says. "That does sound a bit fishy."

"He's not fishy!"

"Well, is he from around here?" Margaret asks.

"No, he's from North Carolina."

"I'm glad you're getting out," Grandpa says. "You're too young to stay at home."

"Too pretty to stay at home," Jean says. "And too pretty for that other boy. What was his name?"

"Charlie?" Nora asks.

"Yes! Charlie! Catch him in the right light and he looked just like one of Mildred's show horses."

Nora could heat the whole church with her embarrassment. "He wasn't that bad."

"We just know you can find a better one, sweetie," Margaret says.

"I'm seeing him again tonight."

"Sounds serious," Jean says. "Two nights in a row." She shoots Margaret a glance that makes Nora's hands clammy.

"Please don't make me nervous."

"Bring him to us," Ed says. "We'll figure him out right quick like." Nora had almost forgotten Ed was standing there, but that's how Ed is. He sees and hears everything, but he usually lets it play out before he gives his two cents.

"Just take it slow," Grandpa says. "He might be the one. He might not be. Won't know unless you try."

They get through the line to see Ms. Annie and to say their goodbyes to Frank. Nora tries to think about Frank and Ms. Annie and not about her own experience on that side of the visitation line. When her parents died, the visitation lasted for four hours. She stood next to her grandpa, greeting everyone in front of the two matching caskets, until they were the last ones left in more ways than one.

On the way out of the church, Nora hears someone call her name. She turns around to see Johnny Chandler standing in the doorway of an empty Sunday school classroom.

"You can go on ahead," she says to Grandpa. He hugs her goodbye, and she steps into the classroom to talk to Johnny.

Nora wouldn't call Johnny a friend, but she has known about him her whole life. His family owns the biggest funeral home in Anniston, so you could almost call them colleagues. Besides selling caskets, Nora helps her customers talk through their specific wants or needs for arrangements and how to make those things happen. Is anyone coming from out of town? What dates make the most sense? Do you want something religious or something less formal? Something for the whole town or something more intimate? Some people come in advance and have all of these questions answered already. Sometimes death comes before you expect it, and the process is a little more difficult to figure out. Either way, Nora knows how to help and who to call.

Since Nora doesn't run a full-service funeral home, she usually points her customers to Chandler Funeral Home for everything else they need. She does this because they are the closest funeral home to Rabbittown that hasn't sold out to Prestige, not because she has any sort of faith in their customer service.

"Nice service," Nora says. He's pacing the room in his funeral director suit. He's used too much of some sort of product to tame his blond curly hair.

He shrugs. "Pretty standard, but I'll take the compliment. How's the store?"

"Fine," she says. "Business as usual. How's yours?"

"Busy."

This is the way things work with the Clanton and Chandler families. Their parents were always polite to one another's faces. The Clantons owned the redneck casket store, and the Chandlers spent their Sundays rubbing elbows at the Anniston Country Club. Each year, Mrs. Chandler took her daughter to Europe or the Caribbean for spring break, and Nora usually spent that week reading in a corner of the store while her parents worked. Nora's family always understood their spot in the social hierarchy of it all, and in case they ever forgot, the Chandlers were more than happy to knock them down a few rungs with a deliberate snub or a rumor about them.

"Did you want something in particular when you called me in here?" Nora asks.

"I just wanted to see how you're doing. Must be hard doing everything by yourself these days."

"I'm perfectly capable of doing my job, but thanks for your concern."

He huffs. "You know I didn't mean that. What do you take me for, Clanton?" Johnny never uses Nora's first name. She assumes he can't remember it.

"I always know what you mean, Johnny."

He shakes his head but doesn't try to correct her. "You going to that conference coming up?"

"I guess so."

"Aren't they giving your daddy some kind of award?"

"Yeah, some sort of lifetime achievement thing, I think." Nora's dad was very involved with the National Funeral Directors Society. They called to ask her to attend the conference and accept the award on his behalf, and she couldn't say no, even though it sounded both boring and depressing. "Are you going?"

"Maybe," he says. "If Dad doesn't. He loves those things."

"Mine did, too," she says. "It sounds weird to me. What do they even talk about?"

"I think they've got a presentation for gaudy caskets you might like."

She's on the way to being offended, but he's smiling. "Was that a joke?"

"You don't actually think I've looked at the schedule, do you?"

"I guess not. Maybe I'll see you there." She backs toward the door to leave before he can hold her there for more awkward conversation about their fathers.

"Yeah, maybe so. I'll call you if I decide to go. Maybe we can ride together."

She tries not to let the surprise show on her face. They've

never even had a full conversation, and he wants to ride some-where in an enclosed vehicle together?

She manages to say, "Yeah, let me know. Have a good night, Johnny."

"You, too."

Driving into town to meet Garrett gives Nora a chance to put her funeral feelings back into their ever-expanding compart-ment and to locate a more socially acceptable version of herself. She uses the red lights on her route to work on her appearance. She used to love makeup. Growing up, she "borrowed" what-ever her mom had, but when she got to college, she realized there was a whole world of products she hadn't known existed. Sure, she had powder and lip gloss, but Ashley and Taylor, the girls in the dorm room next door, had bags and boxes of bottles and tubes, and Nora had no idea how so many things could go on one face.

Once they graduated and had real salaries with no real obli-gations, they could afford to buy the expensive things they had spent their college years coveting. Nora finally had fancy brushes! She finally had serums! "Had" being the key word. Scraping dried mascara out of the bottom of the tube reminds her how long it's been since she's thought twice about her ap-pearance. Do people still buy mascara? Does Sephora still exist?

As she gets into town, the lights get brighter, and she can see her dull skin tone even more clearly in the light-up mirror on the visor. From the outside, Anniston looks like drive-thrus and chain steakhouses, and it's fine with Nora if the hidden gems stay hidden. One of her favorite restaurants is in the building that used to house the town brothel, but she sensed her mother's disapproval from the great beyond when she thought about taking Garrett there for their second date. Nora chose a small Italian place instead, and he's waiting on the bench outside the front door when she arrives.

"Sorry if I kept you waiting," Nora says.

"You didn't," he says, standing to hug her. "You look great."

"So do you." Garrett can wear a suit, but Nora feels like she can see him better now in dark jeans and a navy button-down. He still looks expensive, but maybe more genuine.

An Italian family owns the restaurant, and since Nora has never been to Italy, she has no choice but to accept this as authentic Italian dining: exposed brick, framed photos of Italian landscapes, more bottles of wine than this restaurant could ever go through. The hostess seats them at a tiny two-person table with a pillowcase-size tablecloth, just enough room for two plates, and not much else.

"How was the service?" he asks.

"Good," she says, and she regrets it immediately. "I mean, as good as these things go. There were people still in line when I left."

He nods. "Are you sure you feel like being out right now? We can do something else."

"Are you changing your mind?"

His eyes go wide. "No! I—"

"I was just kidding. I'm fine."

She tries to remember her posture. Not to fidget. Not to put her elbows on the table. She folds her hands in her lap and tells herself to breathe. The small, nearly empty restaurant and the candlelight—this is intimate. Why are dates like this? Staring at someone you just met while they eat. Maybe it's supposed to be a test. If you can stomach the person's table manners or strange food requests, you can handle whatever they might do or say elsewhere.

"Do you come here a lot?" he asks.

"No, it's a little out of my jurisdiction," she says. She also doesn't have anyone who would eat fancy Italian with her, but he doesn't know that. "Do you live near here?"

"Yeah, my apartment isn't far."

The silence lingers long enough for both of them to wonder if he meant anything by that. Nora runs her hand over her knee to double-check that she shaved in the shower this morning. Of course she shaved. She was too nervous to forget. She shaved, plucked, oiled, and stood naked as a jaybird in front of the bathroom mirror while she pinched every area of her body that she wished were different. Does she intend to sleep with this person she just met? If not sex, then how far?

When Nora started high school, everyone in her youth group at church got *I Kissed Dating Goodbye* as assigned reading. Their twenty-two-year-old youth minister lectured them on the pitfalls of dating and relationships before marriage. God wanted them to be pure for their future spouses, and they would no longer be pure if they gave their first times away to someone else. Some people bought rings and signed purity pledges. Nora didn't have the thirty dollars for the ring, and she was too embarrassed to ask her parents for it. She assumes they were embarrassed, too, because they were sitting in the sanctuary when all of the pledges were read off by the youth minister, and they never said anything to her about her name not being on the list.

Nora gave up on purity culture once she left her parents' house, but those thoughts still come back to haunt her. She is thirty years old with no clue when or if she should sleep with someone. She's had one-night stands, but that was a long time ago, when she had more energy and the body of an eighteen-year-old. Her mother held fast to the "why buy the cow if you can get the milk for free" mentality, and maybe she was right, Nora thinks. Maybe you should wait until you're in love and you know the other person is in love, too. Or maybe life's too short to wait for anything. Maybe there is no right answer. Maybe there are just too many questions.

"Nora?" Garrett asks.

"Hmm?"

He laughs. "I asked what kind of wine you like."

"Sorry," she says, trying to shake the sex out of her brain. "Anything red."

The waitress appears in time to make a few suggestions. Nora assumes all of the wine in the restaurant is better than her usual choice.

"Did you work today?" Nora asks once they're alone again.

"I did. It was a pretty boring day. Mostly office work."

"Do you have an office here?"

"I usually work at home or on the road, depending on the situation."

"I'm still not sure I understand what you do."

He smiles. "No one does. Consulting is pretty vague."

"What did you do today? Specifically."

"Specifically, I updated client files. I'm always behind."

"That does sound boring." Nora decides that leaving it here is the most polite thing she can do. She can prod for more information if he calls again after this date.

"What did you do today? Specifically?"

Nora laughs. "I waited around for someone to buy something, but no one ever did."

The waitress brings the wine, and Nora is thankful for something to do with her hands.

"What's good here?" he asks.

"I don't think anything is bad. I usually have carbonara or something with pesto." Nora's dad loved their lasagna. They used to come here for his birthday, but she doesn't want to mention that. She knows her parents will eventually come up in conversation, but she doesn't have to be the one to bring up the topic. "I've heard the lasagna is good."

"I was thinking about the lasagna."

"Honestly, I'm probably not the person to ask, because I don't like tomato sauce."

"So, you don't like lasagna?"

"It's better than spaghetti."

He looks at Nora for a moment and turns his head a little like he's assessing her.

"What?" she asks.

"I'm trying to figure you out."

Her heart beats a tad faster. "I'm not that complicated."

Of course they're interrupted by the server. This is another problem with dinner dates. You're constantly being bothered by a stranger with questions that have to be answered. They might as well wait until they leave the restaurant to have a full conversation. Garrett orders the lasagna. Nora orders the carbonara. They should have at least eight to twelve minutes alone if the box of store-brand spaghetti noodles in Nora's pantry knows anything.

"If you don't like it, we can order something else," Garrett says. Nora realizes she's been swirling the wine around in her glass without drinking any. So much for not fidgeting.

"No, it's fine. Good, I mean. I don't know much about wine, so I'm not hard to please." She takes a sip to prove her point.

"I'm trying to learn," he says. "My sister is really into it."

"Like she drinks a lot of it?"

He smiles. "Oh, she definitely drinks a lot of it, but she goes to classes and tastings and tries to get everyone else to go with her."

"That doesn't sound too bad. How many siblings do you have?"

"One sister, one brother."

"Older or younger?"

"Older sister, younger brother." He clears his throat. "My brother passed away when I was young."

"I'm so sorry." Most people would feel awkward with this change in topic, but a substantial amount of Nora's conversations over the years had been about death, so she's had a lot of practice with this subject. It's usually easier to talk about someone's life than to remember the facts of their death, or at least it was for her. "What was he like?"

"He was a stereotypical little brother. He was always aggravating my sister and me and following us around. Then he got sick when he was four. Leukemia."

"How old were you?"

"I was eight when he died."

Nora nods her understanding. Of course she has more questions, but with any luck, they'll have more time to talk about it later. "What's your sister like?"

"She's a nurse. She got married a couple of years ago, so she's currently being pressured for children." Now he's the one swirling his wine without drinking any.

"Sorry if I'm interrogating you. I'm a curious person, and it can be annoying."

"It doesn't bother me," he says. "But I think it's your turn. Tell me about your family."

Garrett's family history has taken a little of the pressure off Nora's story. Might as well leave the theatrics for a future date and tell the truth, since he can google it when he gets home, if he hasn't already. She tries to say it as quickly as possible, like ripping off a Band-Aid: "My parents died in a car accident about a year ago. I don't have any brothers or sisters."

"I'm sorry about your parents," Garrett says.

"Thank you," she says, choosing the easiest of response choices. "They were great parents, and I'm lucky I had them for so long. It's just me and my grandpa now."

"What were your parents like?" he asks. "You don't have to answer if you don't want to talk about it."

"I don't mind. My dad was a people person. He could sell anything. He would help anyone. If he didn't know how to deal with something, he knew someone to call. He was a doer. If that makes sense."

"Yeah, it does," he says.

"My mom was more reserved. She could keep a secret. She was funny, too. I look like her. Frizzy dark hair, round face, all the freckles." Nora gestures at her pale arm covered in freckles, still hoping they might join forces one day to give her a tan. "She had blue eyes, though. I got the brown from my dad."

"I assume one of them was tall."

"My mom. She was my height. What are your parents like?"

"They're great. The kind of parents people wish for. I look like my mom, too."

Once again, the server interrupts to slide their plates of pasta in front of them. She asks if they want Parmesan cheese. They do. She asks if they want black pepper. They do. The chef could have just done that in the kitchen, as far as Nora is concerned. She isn't impressed with graters or pepper grinders.

"So, you're close with your grandpa?" Garrett asks when they're alone again. He uses his fork to cut his lasagna into bite-size pieces.

"Yeah, we always have been." She twirls noodles onto her fork as calmly as she can, trying not to fling sauce across the table accidentally. "He offered me a room at his house when I moved back, but I wasn't sure we would be a great roommate match. I took over my parents' house instead."

"How has that turned out?"

"Sometimes I think about selling it, but it seems like it would take a lot of work." She looks over and notices that his plate is half empty. "You must like the lasagna."

"God, yes. Sorry, I could have offered you some." His face turns the color of spaghetti sauce.

"No, I have my own." Nora laughs. "You must have been hungry. Or do you usually eat that quickly?"

"Maybe a little of both. I know it doesn't seem like it, but I swear I have manners."

She laughs again, and they spend the rest of the meal talking about pasta. Nora describes an Italian restaurant she loves in Birmingham. Garrett says they should go sometime. Nora tries not to read too much into his comment. She lets him finish the last few bites of her carbonara. He gives the waitress his credit card to pay without a glance at the check.

"What do you want to do now?" he asks as they leave the restaurant.

"I don't know. There isn't much going on around here on a weeknight."

They take a few steps down the sidewalk, and they're standing in front of an ATM when Garrett says, "Hey."

When Nora turns to reply, he kisses her. They both taste like garlic, but neither of them cares. He's gentle at first, but then Nora wraps her arms around his neck and nothing is gentle.

He pulls away first. "Do you want to come to my apartment?"

She should say no. She's not sure if she's ready for anything more. She's not sure if any of this is a good idea.

But. There's always a "but."

She really likes kissing him.

"Yes."

He takes her hand and leads her to the passenger side of his car, and he opens the door like a true southern gentleman. She tries not to overthink everything as he's driving to his apartment, but overthinking is her specialty. Does she remember how this works? Will she know what to do? She tries to concentrate on the other cars on the road and the song on the radio and the feel of Garrett's hand in hers, figuring that maybe if she doesn't let herself think about it, she can act like a normal person instead of a skittish squirrel trapped in a garage.

Garrett's apartment is more like a townhouse. She walks through the foyer and into the living room, trying to take in all the details. Since she's holding Garrett's hand, he has no choice but to walk with her as she examines the display of photographs on the wall.

"Did you take these?"

"My dad did."

"Is he a photographer?"

He shakes his head. "My dad? No. Not professionally, I mean. As a hobby, I guess."

Garrett doesn't usually stumble over his words.

"Do you not want to talk about your dad?"

"We can talk about whatever you want."

"I feel like you're being weird. Did I say something wrong?"

He tucks a strand of hair behind her ear. "I'm just a little distracted with you here in my apartment."

She takes a step closer to him. "You brought me here."

"I know," he says, closing the remaining space between them. "It's one of my better ideas."

He places a hand against her cheek, and she leans into it, smiling up at him until he kisses her. He's tender at first, but the energy shifts when Nora winds her arms around his neck and pushes her body against his with a groan she can't hold in. He guides her backward until her legs hit the couch. The kisses become long and drawn out, and about the time that she can't take it anymore, he shifts to lie on top of her.

"Is this too fast?" he asks.

"No," she says. "Don't stop." One of her hands finds his hair, and the other reaches across his back, pulling him against her. Garrett's hands move slowly and deliberately over her dress until he finds the zipper.

He pauses to look at her for a moment, and she recognizes the expression in his eyes. "Do you want to go to the bedroom?"

She does. She really does. But even as he asked, her body's overwhelming response was anxiety.

"No," she manages. "Not tonight." She knows it's the right thing to do, but she's disappointed in herself. Why couldn't she just do it? Garrett is hot. He makes her feel like she's hot, too. Sex is a pretty normal way to end a date. It's not her first time. She braces herself for the usual rejection that comes after the guy realizes she's not putting out.

"Okay," he says. "We can stay here." The next kiss and the way his hand slides up her thigh doesn't feel anything like rejection.

It's midnight when she tells him she has to go home. He doesn't ask her to stay. He doesn't even complain about driving her back to the restaurant. Nora's car is the only one left downtown, and Garrett parks his Mercedes next to it.

"You don't have to get out," she says as he turns off the engine and opens his door.

"I want to," Garrett says. He comes around to the passenger side and presses her against the car. "I'm not done kissing you yet." She's the one who wanted to slow down, and she doesn't want to send mixed signals, but it's hard to keep her story straight with his hands in her hair and his tongue in her mouth.

"We're going to get in trouble."

"With who?" he asks against her lips. "There's no one around."

She laughs. "You might be a bad influence."

He rests his forehead against hers. "You seem like a willing participant."

She nods in agreement, standing on her toes to kiss him.

"When can I see you again?" he asks once they're both out of breath.

"When do you want to see me?" she asks.

"Sooner than later."

She smiles. "What about this weekend?"

"I'd like to call you, so we can talk about it."

"I hope you do," she says. She kisses him one last time before getting into her car to drive back to Rabbittown. The last time she drove to Rabbittown after midnight was probably ten years ago. She turns on the radio in time to hear "Cowboy Take Me Away," and she doesn't necessarily feel young, but she does feel alive. Happy, even. Of course, it's Garrett, but it's her, too. She did something she wanted to do, for once. She had fun.

About the time she gets home, her phone rings. It's Garrett.

"Are you home?" he asks.

"Yeah, I just got here."

"I forgot to tell you I had a good time."

"It was implied," she laughs. "I did, too."

"I know I keep forgetting, but I really do have manners."

"You keep saying that."

"You should go to bed," he says. "You have to work."

"I'm trying to." Can he tell she's smiling like an idiot?

"I'll call you tomorrow."

"I look forward to it."

"Good night, Nora."

"Good night, Garrett."

For once, her dreams are not about *Cheers* and Sam Malone.

TWO MONTHS AGO

Garrett's fingers dance rapidly across his keyboard as he types out a missive to one of his direct reports. He hates having people report to him because it means he has to care about things like the dress code and punctuality. He doesn't care for babysitting in any context, but especially when it involves other adults in the workplace.

The items on his desk shake to the beat of Garrett's typing, including the framed photo of his family from last Christmas. The frame used to hold a picture of a former girlfriend, but he replaced that photo after she dumped him for someone else. It teeters toward the edge of the desk. Another paragraph or two will do it.

The sound of knocking alerts Garrett to the presence of someone in his doorway. He doesn't know how long Janine has been standing there; she has that effect on people.

"Am I interrupting? You seem to be in the middle of something."

He lets out a breath. "No, come in. I was just emailing Colin about his Birkenstocks and trying not to go insane in the process."

Janine slides into one of the guest chairs in front of his desk, wearing the same black suit she's worn every day. It's a little more subtle than Elizabeth Holmes's black turtleneck, but Garrett had noticed it early on. He has never seen her wear anything else in all the years they have been working together. "That's what I wanted to talk to you about, in a way."

Garrett crosses his arms. "Okay. What's going on?"

"You aren't happy here."

"Excuse me?"

"Here in this office, I mean. We've worked together for a long time. I've noticed."

Garrett's mouth opens before he has formed a sentence to go with the gesture. "Have I done something wrong?"

"No, not at all." She joins her hands and places them on his desk. He has seen this move many times before. "I think it's time for a new experience for you. To get you out of this office. Away from Colin's Birkenstocks, if you will."

"What kind of new experience?"

"The kind that comes with a pay raise."

He nods. "I'm listening."

"Alabama."

"What about it?"

"Have you ever been?"

"No."

"There's a regional director position opening up. It will be more fieldwork in the beginning. The team is full of new hires, and they need to be trained."

"You don't think I'm getting too old for fieldwork?"

"I think you can handle it. You might enjoy a break from the normal nine-to-five. Besides, I need someone I can trust to train the team."

"And you trained me."

She smiles. "Exactly."

Garrett rotates back and forth in his chair. He thinks of all the other times Janine had given him opportunities like this. He had never hesitated. But it was getting exhausting. Was he really planning to move every two years for the rest of his life? Shouldn't he settle down at some point? "It has to be Alabama?"

"It won't be as bad as you think. Nothing ever is. But I would appreciate you 'taking one for the team,' as they say. It will give you some leverage to move wherever you want in a couple of years."

"You're saying, if I take this job in Alabama for two years, you'll let me choose where to go next?"

She nods. "Don't forget, we're an international company."

He considers the offer. It's a promotion. More money. But he would have to move to Alabama, of all places. A job with more fieldwork will mean more traveling. He hasn't spent any time in Alabama, but he has a lot of experience with hotels in small towns where the only food options were from a drive-thru or a vending machine. Of course, he hadn't been thrilled to move to Pittsburgh when he took this position, and now he's thinking about how much he will miss his apartment downtown.

"What about moving expenses?"

She sits up straighter, ready to negotiate. "Of course."

This job would mean a lot of travel. A lot of living in his car. He decides to push his luck.

"Would you throw in a car?"

"A car of your choice. Done."

He leans back in his chair. "I think we have a deal."

CHAPTER

5

Nora and Garrett make plans to see each other the next night.
When she meets him at his apartment after work, his kitchen
counter is covered with pizza toppings. He has bagged cheese,
bricked cheese, and cheese in plastic tubs alongside peppers,
onions, and meats Nora doesn't completely recognize.

He jitters with excitement. "You said pizza is your favorite,
right?"

"I did say that." Truthfully, fried okra is her favorite, but that's
not a normal answer to share with most people.

"I thought we could make our own. I don't know what you
like—"

"So you bought everything you could find?" Nora says, holding up two of the four jars of pizza sauce on the counter. "Garrett, this might be overkill."

"I was trying to impress you." He's wearing jeans and a T-shirt, and even when he doesn't try, he looks more put together than anyone she knows. How is this man still single?

She laughs. "I'm impressed."

"I'm sure I forgot something obvious." He searches the counter frantically until he locates the cheese pile. "Okay, we do have cheese."

"I think we'll manage," she says, hooking her fingers into his belt loops to pull him toward her. His eyebrows jump in surprise, but they both forget about the pizza until the oven beeps to let them know it's preheated.

"Sorry, I distracted you," she says against his lips.

"I'm not." He kisses her again, and he steps toward her until she realizes he's backing her out of the kitchen.

She reaches out in time to grab the doorframe. "Wait, what about the pizza?"

"I don't care about the pizza right now." In case she's confused, his green eyes sear his meaning into her brain.

"Well, I do. It was really sweet of you to do all of this."

"And we can eat it later," he laughs. He wraps his arms around her, so that their bodies are pressed together.

"Or we can do this later." She hates herself for stalling. Again.

He rests his head against hers for a moment and then presses his lips to her forehead. This gentleness sends the butterflies in her stomach into their own frenzied version of Talladega.

"Fine," he says. "We'll do it your way."

"I'm sorry. I know I started it."

He grabs both sides of her face. "You have to stop apologizing so much."

She starts to apologize again, but he holds a finger against her lips.

"I'm serious. You don't need to apologize to me. Especially not about this."

She nods.

"Unless you're sorry you kissed me."

She shakes her head.

He's looking at her intently, and she can tell he wants to kiss her. She smiles and shakes her head again.

He leans closer and whispers, "I need to do something else with my hands."

She follows him back to his pizza workspace, where he retrieves two sheet pans from a cabinet below.

"I thought we could each make our own. I got a few different pizza crust options," he begins, rifling through the fridge.

"I'll take the first one you find in there," she says. Peering over his shoulder, she notes that he has a very full refrigerator for someone who hasn't been in town long.

He plops a metal-lidded tube into her hand. "Let's go with this one."

She examines it as if she knows anything about tubed pizza crusts before peeling back the label and popping open the can. "Where do you want this?"

A cutting board appears in front of her. She moves out of the way while he cuts the crust in half with an overly large knife. He spreads half on one sheet pan and half on the other. "What do you want on yours?"

She looks over the toppings covering the counter and reaches for the sauce with the title "Pizza Sauce" and the bag of shredded "Pizza Cheese." Behind the peppers and onions, she spots a plastic package of pepperoni and points for Garrett to slide it over to her. "Done."

He tilts his head at her. "That's it? Shredded cheese and pepperoni?"

"And sauce." She waves the jar at him.

"I thought you were a pizza expert."

"I am. I've had every version of pepperoni pizza you can find in the frozen section at Rabbittown Grocery."

His laugh breaks up his gaping expression. "You know what? I will let that go for now, and I will look past this travesty." He points at her pile of toppings. "In exchange, you have to try mine." He begins collecting his own toppings, which include the jar of sauce with the description written in Italian, a clove of garlic, and a green pepper.

"I promise to try it, but I can't promise I'll like it."

"You'll like it."

"You're really going to cut that up?" she asks as he smashes the clove of garlic on a cutting board to remove the papery skin.

He smirks. "That's sort of how it works, yes. Why don't you worry about yours?"

"Fine, I will." She uses a spoon to spread her store-brand sauce all over the crust and tops it with the store-brand shredded cheese. When she checks Garrett's progress, she lets out a gasp. "You cannot be serious."

An anchovy hangs from his fingertips, newly freed from its jar below. He wiggles it toward her face. "You don't like anchovies?"

She takes a step away from him. "No, I will not eat that tiny fish. You need to put it back with its fish family."

"In the jar?" He laughs.

"Away from me."

"You know that pepperoni comes from a pig?"

She plugs her ears. "Don't say that."

"You'll eat that, but you won't eat this? I'm going to cut it up. You won't even know it's there."

"Then why do you need it at all?"

"I'll leave you a section without it. Will that work for you?"

"You better mark that section clearly."

He reaches over for her package of pepperoni. "I will."

While they wait for the pizzas to bake, they put away all the toppings, and Garrett opens a bottle of wine.

"Am I allowed to ask for ranch?" Nora asks as she sits down at his dining room table with her plate of pepperoni pizza and the portion of Garrett's pizza that had been barricaded by a row of pepperoni.

He pulls a bottle from the door of his fridge and hands it to her. "I'm not too good for ranch."

She pours some on the edge of her plate. "All of this really is amazing. Thank you."

"You're welcome." Garrett sits down next to her. "But as a warning, if you say it's not as good as Pizza Rolls, I don't think I'll recover."

She takes a bite of her pepperoni slice. "It's really good. I like the crust."

"So, you would say it's better than Pizza Rolls?"

"I would say, If you can't handle the answer, you shouldn't ask the question."

His jaw drops. "I don't believe that."

She smiles. "I'm just kidding. But I'm not giving up Pizza Rolls."

"I'll save that battle for another day."

After dinner, Garrett finds a soccer game he wants to watch, and Nora admits that she is still trying to understand the sport. She gets the main idea, but the positions and the lines are too much. She certainly can't keep up with all the teams. As he's giving her an overview of the league and why this particular game is important, she realizes that he's really smart. It's not like she thought he was dumb, but he's the kind of smart that lets you skip grades. Nora figures this should probably intimidate her, but he doesn't treat her like she's dumb. He explains things in multiple ways because he wants her to understand them, like he wants to make sure he clears up her confusion. He's one of those teachers who get excited when you answer something correctly.

"How do you know all of this? Do you play soccer?" She has his right hand in hers, massaging her thumbs into his palm and the spaces between his knuckles.

"God, no." He laughs. "I've tried but I'm not great at it. I played basketball."

"So, you just keep up with it?"

"Yeah, I guess. If it's in the sports section, I read it."

"You read the newspaper?"

He nods.

"Like a physical newspaper?"

He laughs. "Yes, I like to hold it in my hand."

"What paper?"

"The *Times*."

This makes her laugh. "Did you just call it 'the *Times*'?"

"That's what it's called!"

"Well, I have a subscription to 'the *Star*,' and by that I mean *The Anniston Star*, because I'm not nearly as worldly as you are."

He tries to hide his smile. "I guess you're caught up on high school football then."

"Hey! They have a decent crossword puzzle."

"You *would* do the crossword puzzle."

"Yeah, I do it at work every morning, thank you very much."

"Do you cheat?"

"Why, you don't think I can do it by myself?" Sometimes she does look up the last few clues, but he doesn't need to know that right now.

"I didn't say that!"

"It was implied."

"I'm sure you're perfectly capable of finishing *The Anniston Star* crossword puzzle," he laughs. He switches hands, and when she presses her thumbs into the fleshy part of his palm he winces.

"Sorry," she says. "Too much?"

He shakes his head and examines the sore spot she found. "I didn't know you could have tension in your hands. How'd you learn to do that?"

"I don't really know," she says. "My mom used to do it. I guess it's sort of a habit now."

"So, you do it to all your dates?"

She narrows her eyes at him. "Just the ones who make fun of my newspaper choices."

He smiles at first, but then his face turns serious. "Can I ask you something?"

She braces herself for the other shoe to drop. "Sure."

"Well." He pauses to gather his thoughts. "I guess really I just want to tell you something." He takes both of her hands and laces their fingers together.

"Are you about to tell me you're married?"

This surprises him. "No. Are you married?"

Nora is mildly distracted by his proximity. The way his lips move when he speaks. The way the pad of his thumb feels against the side of her thumb. "I'm not anything. What did you want to say?"

"I just want you to know that I'm not dating anyone else." He says this with confidence, and not in the same blurting-it-out way that she would have said it. Nora pauses. They are both acutely aware of his eyes searching hers for a reaction and not getting much of anything.

"Okay," she says. She tries to think, but her thoughts don't come.

Garrett tries again with clarification: "I don't know if you're dating other people, but I want you to know that I'm not."

What is the right thing to say here? The truth? That the only other person she is dating is the 1980s reruns version of Ted Danson? She thinks it's probably more attractive if she pretends that she has other options, like she's some sought-after prize that he can win if he tries hard enough. They haven't known each other that long. Shouldn't she try to spare him for a while? Be a little mysterious? He doesn't need to know what her life is really like. The wine and the silence and the fear that everything good will eventually leave.

The more truths she tells him, the closer they get to each other, the sooner he will run. She knows she's supposed to lure him in first, like fishing for catfish with cut-up hot dogs. You're supposed to cover the sharp parts of yourself with the processed-meat parts.

Nora has a house, a steady job, and she thinks your jokes are funny, but surprise! One of the bedrooms in her house is closed off permanently. She only does the dishes every few weeks. She ignores most holidays. She has no friends.

"I can tell by your face that I'm not doing a good job of this," he says.

"I'm sorry. It's not you."

He huffs. "Don't apologize."

"I'm sorry for apologizing."

"Nora."

"What?"

"I'm trying to be serious here." He lowers his head to meet her eyeline.

"I'm listening."

He doesn't look away. "I'm trying to ask if you're dating other people. It's okay if you are. I know it's early, but I really like you, and I just wanted you to know that. I want us to be on the same page."

Nora nods. She doesn't fully know what she thinks or where this whole thing is going, but she's certain she's going to mess it up.

"Can you say something now?" he asks. "You're kind of killing me here."

She sits up straighter to show that she means business. "No, I'm not dating anyone else."

He tries and fails to rein in the huge smile that covers his face. "Well, I would be fine if you didn't. Date anyone else, I mean."

She lets out a laugh, releasing some of the tension in her body. "I'll take that into consideration."

Without warning, he leans across the couch and covers her

mouth with his. She shifts to pull him on top of her, wrapping her legs around him to hold him in place where she wants him. Between his tongue in her mouth and his hand sliding up her dress, Nora loses track of her thoughts. Her hands twist into his hair and move down his back, pulling him closer. When his hand stops at a respectful location, she pauses their kissing long enough to whisper, "Don't stop."

His hand travels up her thigh and under her dress, over her stomach and her bra, and he lowers his mouth to kiss the side of her neck. She arches into him, feeling him against her, and she moans something close to his name. He smiles down at her, and she runs her hand through his hair again, unable to think of something charming to say.

"What do you want?" he asks, his hand skimming down to the lace at her hip.

"Don't stop," she says again. She isn't sure if other words exist at the moment, and she certainly can't call any to mind. She reaches down to guide his hand where and how she wants it, and he doesn't stop until she moans his name a final time and lies back on the couch.

"You're so beautiful," he whispers, kissing her jaw and then her cheek and then her lips.

She kisses him back, snaking her body around his, but he rolls over to lie beside her, creating space between them. "I think we should take this slow," he says.

This is pretty much what she had expected. That she would do something wrong without even knowing. "Okay. Can I ask why?"

He kisses her fingers. "I don't want to mess this up. We don't have to do everything in one night."

"What if I want to do everything in one night?"

A laugh escapes him, so she laughs, too. It's better than crying.

"I'm not immune to all of this, you know." He presses her hand to his lips again.

"It sort of seems like you are."

"I just think we should wait."

"We can wait." Waiting has never killed anyone, as far as she knows. She asks the question floating through her mind: "Are you sure nothing is wrong?"

"Everything is right, I promise." He kisses her gently, as if she might break.

Choosing to believe his words, she burrows into him, wrapping an arm around his chest and resting her head on his shoulder. "Everything is right for me, too."

On Monday, when Nora bursts through Jean's kitchen door, she steps right into the middle of a lecture. Jean and her daughter, Linda, are standing across the room from each other, wearing identical faces of frustration.

"I can come back," Nora says.

"Nope," Linda says. "Your timing is perfect."

Jean had Linda a few years before Nora's mom had her, so Nora spent a lot of her childhood following Linda around and using her hand-me-downs. She's pretty sure that Joe and Jean tried to have more children, but that's not something you talk about around here, so no one knows the details. Nora does know that Linda is as perfect as any child could be. Growing up, she was the smartest person in her class. She never got into trouble. Her dream was to go to Johns Hopkins and become a pediatrician, and she almost made it look easy. She married another pediatrician from Johns Hopkins, and they moved back to Anniston to start their own practice.

"Have a seat," Jean says. "Both of you." Jean slides a child-size cup of coffee across the table to Nora, who sits down next to Linda.

"How are all your tiny patients, Linda?" she asks.

"Passing a stomach bug around at the moment," Linda says, shaking her head. "It's been a rough few weeks."

Nora leans away from her. "Are you contagious?"

"Too late for you if I am. How's the store?"

"The same. I'm thinking about changing things up. Maybe some new paint or curtains or something."

"You should! Paint it something bright."

"When's the last time anything changed in there?" Jean asks.

"Before my time. Before I can remember, at least."

"Let me look through the material I have," Jean says. "I can make you some curtains."

"We should make a weekend of it," Linda says. "You could get some artwork or maybe a new rug. That wouldn't be too expensive."

"I hadn't even thought of artwork," Nora says. "We should find some estate sales or something."

"Do you want help with the painting?" Linda asks.

"You want to help me paint in all your spare time?" Nora takes a drink of her coffee and finds comfort in the familiarity, how she knew exactly what Jean's coffee would taste like before she even touched the cup.

"Oh, I was thinking Lucas. His fingerpainting is getting pretty good."

She laughs. "Actually, I don't hate that idea. What's Lucas up to today?"

"He's upstairs. Tearing something up, probably."

"He won't hurt anything," Jean says. Jean made a deal with Linda after she moved back to Anniston: if Linda would have a baby, Jean would help with the childcare. Once Lucas was born, Jean's house changed overnight into a daycare center. If Lucas gets a new toy at his house, he gets an identical toy at Grandma Jean's.

"So, Nora," Linda begins, "Mom mentioned something about a man in your life. What's that about?"

She tries not to blush. "His name is Garrett. Last night, he said he's not dating anyone else, so I think it's getting serious."

"You're kidding!" Linda says. "That sounds romantic."

"Well, it might have been, but I was surprised, so I probably didn't react in the best way."

"Why were you surprised?" Jean asks.

Nora covers her face with one hand. "I hadn't thought about it. I don't know."

"You hadn't thought about the future?" Linda asks.

"I don't think so," she says, standing up from the table. She takes the carafe out of the old green coffeemaker and refills her tiny cup. She'll never understand why old people can't get normal-size coffee cups like everybody else.

"Well, you're not getting any younger, Eleanora," Jean says.

"Don't listen to her," Linda says. "You have plenty of time."

"I have a question," Jean says, sitting down at the table, which lets Nora know she's getting ready to tell it like it is. "What does your future look like to you?"

"What do you mean?"

"Do you have plans? For your career, maybe? Do you want to get married? Do you want to buy a new lamp? Maybe some new shoes? Those have seen better days."

"I do need to go to Target," Nora says, looking down at her flats.

"Don't pressure her, Mom," Linda says. "She's doing fine, considering the past year."

"She used to have all sorts of plans," Jean says. "That's all I'm trying to say."

"I guess I did," Nora says, swirling the spoon around in her cup. "I was good with numbers, so I became a financial adviser. I thought Charlie and I would get married and have a family, since that's what Charlie said he wanted. None of it happened, so I guess I wasn't too good at it."

Charlie had plans from the day they met. He always knew what his future looked like. He was destined for suburbia and a white picket fence, not dead parents and a casket store. When Nora thinks of kids, she thinks of the tiny caskets she has seen too many times in her life. That wouldn't happen to their kids, Charlie had said. Nora was worrying for nothing. She was always worried for nothing.

Jean gives her a look over her glasses. "Now, that's a load of bull. Excuse me, Lord, but he knows it's true, too. You're just letting life hit you one way or another."

"I'm not letting life do anything."

"That boy wandered into your store and asked you out. I bet he makes all the plans, too."

Nora thinks about it, and even though she would love to contradict Jean, she's not wrong. Garrett has initiated everything so far. "That doesn't mean anything."

"It really doesn't," Linda says.

"Maybe not." Jean shrugs. "Or maybe you won't have to blame yourself for much if something happens."

"Jean, I came over here for gossip, not a lecture."

Jean almost smiles. "I threw it in for free."

"Well, I'm done with that, and now I want gossip."

"Why don't you ask Linda about her gossip?" Jean asks.

"What did you do?" Nora asks.

Linda stands from the table to put her cup in the sink. "I'm surprised you haven't heard. I might have acted out a bit at choir practice."

"It was a mutiny," Jean says. She points at Linda. "You're looking at the new choir director."

Nora's jaw drops. This must have been what they were arguing about when she walked in. Betty Holt has been the choir director at the First Baptist Church of Rabbittown since she appointed herself in the 1970s. "Is Betty dead? Surely I would've heard."

"I didn't kill her, if that's what you're implying," Linda says. She leans back against the counter. "You know Betty wants to sing those same songs over and over, even if they sound terrible. She was telling us what we were going to sing next Sunday, and I simply asked if we could change things up."

"Then Linda pointed out that the choir's rendition of 'The Old Rugged Cross' sounds like the screeching of stray cats," Jean says.

Nora laughs. "That's the Lord's own truth. It also lasts for twenty minutes."

"And I thought everyone already knew that!" Linda says. "It's been terrible since we were kids. Apparently, Betty didn't know.

She said some things and then got upset and stormed off the stage."

"It was time for Betty to retire anyway," Jean says. "No one wanted to tell her."

"Then they voted for the new choir director, and somehow I won," Linda says.

"And you agreed to it?" Nora asks.

"Well, of course she did," Jean says. "Girl needs to fix everything, and apparently it's the choir that needs fixing this week."

Linda rolls her eyes. "How hard can it be, honestly? It's not like I've gotta write the hymnal."

"I can't think of the last time I've been this excited for church," Nora says.

"Join the choir!" Linda says. "We need you."

"No one needs me anywhere near a microphone."

"Do I need to remind you of the screeching cats? You'll fit right in."

"You say that now."

"Your mama never missed a chance to sing in the choir," Jean says. "It's family tradition."

"How about if I say I'll think about it? I want to see what you're like as a director first."

"I give it a month," Jean says. "Betty will be back."

"You don't think I can do it?" Linda asks. She looks at Jean the same way Jean looks at anyone who sasses her.

"I think you can do it," Jean says. "I just don't think you want to."

"I agreed to it, didn't I?" Linda asks.

"In the heat of the moment," Jean says. "You're just like your daddy."

"She's just like you," Nora says to Jean. "Who else could oust Betty Holt? Only someone related to you."

"I didn't oust her!" Linda says. "She just got her feelings hurt."

"Whatever you say." Nora shrugs. "I wasn't there."

Linda narrows her eyes. "I'm going to check on Lucas."

"Be that way," Jean says.

After Linda leaves the room, Jean shakes her head. "I don't know why the two of you have to make things so complicated for yourselves."

"We just want to keep you on your toes," Nora says. She reaches across the table to pat Jean's hand. "You would be bored otherwise."

Jean lowers her chin to look at Nora over her glasses. "I'd like to give that option a try."

Nora only has one appointment this afternoon, so she has plenty of time to think about what Jean said that morning. What does it mean that she's not making plans anymore? Is she really leaving everything up to chance? Up to Garrett? It does take the pressure off Nora, so that nothing will be her fault if things go wrong. Jean is always right, and Nora hates when she's right about something that involves her.

Garrett calls later from a place he claims is past Rabbittown.

"There is nothing past Rabbittown. Your life is in danger."

"I'm safe in my car at the moment," he says.

"What could you possibly have to do out there?"

"One of our clients is out this way, and I have to make an appearance."

"What do you have to do?"

"It's just a meeting. Nothing exciting."

They sit in silence for a moment, and Nora realizes that this could be the time to take initiative. "Hey, Garrett?"

"Hey, Nora."

She laughs and decides to go for it before she makes things weirder. "Can I see you this weekend?"

"Sure. What do you want to do?"

Was she supposed to have something in mind? "I don't know."

"You're not great at this." He laughs.

"I'm trying!"

"You should come up with the plan and then ask me out. That's the general formula." She can sense that he's enjoying her slight discomfort.

"Well, I did it this way. I'm not as smooth as you."

"You're better than you think," he says. "What about Friday after work?"

"I'm free," she says.

"What about Saturday?"

"I'm free then, too. Whichever is better for you."

"What about both days?" he asks.

Is it too eager to agree to a whole weekend? She doesn't want to scare him away. She wants to pull him close. To keep moving forward like a normal couple does. But the closeness is scary, too, in a different way.

"Nora?" he asks, interrupting her thought process.

"Sorry," she says. "Yes, both days would be good for me."

CHAPTER

6

Nora knocks on Garrett's apartment door on Friday, holding takeout from her favorite Mexican restaurant and a jigsaw puzzle she'd found still sealed in plastic wrapping in the top of her hall closet. He opens the door with a grin on his face. When he leans down to kiss her, he immediately starts making fun of the puzzle.

"You really expect us to do a puzzle?" he asks as he transfers the takeout to real plates.

"What's wrong with puzzles?" She crosses her arms and leans against the counter.

"I don't think I've done one since I was a child."

"Well, this is not a child's puzzle."

He hands her a plate of tacos, and they sit down at the table to eat.

Nora waits until he's biting into a taco to ask, "Are you worried it will be too difficult for you?"

He tries not to laugh, to keep the food in his mouth. Once he finishes chewing, he answers, "I'm more worried I'll fall asleep in the middle of it."

"It's okay if you're not the best at something, Garrett. I'll help you."

He gapes at her. "You really think I can't do a puzzle."

She pretends to consider it. "I think there's only one way to know for sure."

"I walked right into that," he says, shaking his head. "Well played."

"Thank you." She smirks.

When they're done with dinner, they take the puzzle to his coffee table and sit down cross-legged on the floor to work on it.

"First, you want to spread out the pieces and turn them all over," Nora explains, pouring the pieces out onto the table. "We need to find the ones for the corners, and we can probably separate any that look like they go on the sides."

He starts flipping pieces over. "You're enjoying this, aren't you?"

"Well, yeah, I brought it, didn't I?"

"What is this supposed to be?" he asks, examining the box. It's a glittery scene of a city on an ocean with small boats docked at the shore.

"I think it's somewhere in Italy, but maybe it's not a real place. I don't know."

"Where did you get it?" He stands the picture against the couch, so they can see it while they're putting it together.

"I found it in a closet. I guess my parents bought it. Or maybe someone gave it to them."

"Did they like puzzles?"

"I don't remember them ever mentioning it, but they might have started after I moved out. I don't really know what they did."

He nods. "I don't know what my parents do, either. I guess I just assume they do the same things they did when I lived there."

"I'm sure they've found new things to do since then." She flips a few more pieces over and gestures at the pile of pieces on his side of the table. "Not that this is a race, but if it were, I would be winning."

"How competitive are you, exactly?" He starts moving pieces around and flipping them over with impressive speed.

"Not very," she admits. "But something tells me you are."

Once they get the border put together and organize the rest of the pieces by color, Nora suggests they take a break.

"We're just getting somewhere," Garrett says, working on the pieces of what he assumes is a red boat.

"Most people do a puzzle over multiple days, Garrett."

"So, we're just supposed to leave it here in piles? What if a piece gets lost?"

She laughs. "I'm trying to give you an out. You didn't want to do this in the first place."

"Well, I'm invested now."

"Fine, I'll work on the yellow ones."

Nora takes a break to close her eyes somewhere around midnight. At one, Garrett sits next to her on the couch and nudges her awake. He's turned off all the lights in the apartment except for the lamp on the table next to her.

"Did you finish?" she asks, sitting up to look over at the table.

"Not even close. Let's work on it tomorrow."

"You do like puzzles." She smiles. "I knew it."

"A pretty girl talked me into it," he says, kissing her slowly.

She winds her arms around his neck to pull him closer, and their kisses grow more desperate. "Stay with me," he whispers.

She nods. "I was hoping you'd say that." She starts to tell him that she didn't want to fall asleep on the drive home, but her mind goes elsewhere when he turns off the lamp and leads her upstairs to his bedroom. He tugs her against him and kisses her with determination, as if he had been waiting all night, or maybe longer. When she feels his hands against her waist, sliding under her shirt, she grabs the edge of his T-shirt and forces it over his head.

"You cannot possibly look like that," she says, barely above a whisper. She runs her hands across his chest to make sure he's real. Maybe healthy food and exercise is less of a scam than she thought.

"I don't know what to say to that," he laughs.

She kisses a spot just above his collarbone. "You don't have to say anything."

He pulls Nora's shirt over her head and unhooks her bra, letting it fall to the floor. Before she can think about it, they're kissing again, their hands roving until he nudges her backward toward the bed. Nora unbuttons her jeans and stumbles out of them, laughing when she has to grab Garrett's arm to hold herself upright.

She points a finger at him, saying, "Now is not the time to make fun of me."

"I'll save that for later." He steps out of his shorts and tugs at the comforter on his bed, making room for them to climb in under the sheets.

Nora rolls him on top of her and groans at the sensation of their bodies moving together. He kisses her jaw and her neck. She slides her hands down his back, pulling him even closer. Her mind is spinning about what might happen next. What she should say. How she should act.

He leans back to look at her, cupping her cheek with his hand. "I don't want to rush this." She wonders how he knows she's not ready, as much as she wants to be. As much as her body is telling her to make a different choice.

She nods. "I feel the same way. But I do want to keep touching you." She snakes a hand between them to show him exactly where she means.

This time, he lets out a groan. "I want that, too."

When she wakes in the morning, she's nestled against his very warm bare chest and wearing his T-shirt. She leans back to look at his face, and he opens his eyes.

"Are you awake?" she asks.

"I am now," he says with a scratchy voice before leaning up to kiss her. "How did you sleep?"

"Like the dead." She kisses him. "Tell me you have an extra toothbrush."

Nora is thankful for the Sam's Club package of toothbrushes under Garrett's sink and less thankful for the soap in the shower she uses to try to scrub off last night's makeup. She puts on a pair of athletic shorts he left out for her and finds him in the kitchen making coffee and scrolling on his phone. She wanders over to see how far he got on the puzzle during her nap, then bursts out laughing.

"What's so funny?" He pokes his head out from the kitchen.

"Your job on this puzzle." She points at an area of the ocean. "None of these are right. These two aren't even close to fitting together!"

He looks over her shoulder. "They're close enough."

"That's not how this works." She laughs. "You're going to have to redo it."

"I was tired, okay."

"Now I know what happens when I leave you to your own devices."

He puts an arm around her. "So it's your fault?"

"Absolutely not."

"Let's work on it later. I'll need caffeine for that."

After they've had coffee, Garrett wants to go for a run, so Nora drives home to shower and change clothes before meeting back up with him for brunch. She also packs a bag in case she winds up staying with him again, even though he hasn't mentioned it.

Garrett and the mimosas at brunch convince her to go to the movies to see some three-hour western that he swears will win awards. She sleeps through half of it, drooling on his shoulder.

They don't finish the puzzle on Saturday night either, because they can barely keep their hands off each other. Nora turns on the Alabama football game, but it's difficult to pay attention since Alabama is winning by three touchdowns before halftime. They wind up in bed before the sun is fully down, and neither of them is bothered by it. She can't believe Garrett is real and that he likes her, and she can't stop touching him to make sure she's not imagining it, but also just because she can.

Garrett makes her feel like she can be herself, no matter what that is. Her past relationships had been fraught with potential and expectations, and she was always afraid that she was doing the wrong thing. Like she was always walking a tightrope. Garrett doesn't make her feel like she's being graded by an unwritten rubric. He seems to want more of her, whatever that might turn out to be.

Garrett asks Nora to stay again on Sunday. And again, after he cooks dinner for her on Monday. Every night when they go to sleep, he pulls her into him and wraps an arm around her waist. He whispers, "Good night" into her ear, and he doesn't pull away until the next morning. Nora sleeps more soundly than she has in a while. The room is not too quiet or too dark, and she doesn't have to sleep with the TV on.

"Good morning," Garrett says, kissing Nora on the cheek as she walks into the kitchen already dressed for work.

"Good morning," Nora says.

She leans against the countertop while Garrett continues tossing frozen fruit into his blender. He tops it off with a handful of spinach, a splash of oat milk, and some sort of protein powder before pressing the blend button. Nora winces at the sound, and in response, Garrett puts a coffee pod into his Keurig and hits the start button.

"Sorry," he says, turning off the blender. "I forget you're not a morning person."

"I thought I was until I met you, but I can't handle this much noise before eight A.M. Is the sun even up all the way?"

"Yes. It's a beautiful day," he says, his voice sounding eerily similar to the birds chirping in *Cinderella*.

"And you know this because you went for a run already?" she asks.

"Did you think I just wake up sweating?" He laughs. "Please drink some coffee before you hurt yourself." He hands her the mug of French roast, and the smell alone helps her feel more whole.

"You act like I'm the crazy one, but it's definitely you. No one in this time zone is as awake as you are right now."

She sits on a barstool while he pours his smoothie into a cup with a reusable straw. Her eyes travel from his grassy Nikes up his calves to his basketball shorts and to his T-shirt with the sleeves cut off, presumably to show off his biceps. He catches her eyes once they make it to his face.

"Why are you looking at me like that?" he asks.

"Because I feel like it," she says. "Is that okay with you?"

He joins her at the bar. "Is it okay if I kiss you?"

She nods, pressing her lips to his. They taste like strawberries.

"So, I have to tell you something," he says, pulling away. He takes a sip of his smoothie, and Nora's mind goes to every worst-case scenario she can think of.

"Are you married?" she asks.

He tilts his head. "Why do you keep asking me that?"

She tilts her head back at him. "Why did you answer the question with a question?"

"No, I'm not married. I've been with you for the past four days."

Nora decides to ignore the second part of that answer. "What did you want to tell me?"

"I have to go out of town for work. We've had some turnover, and I have to train a new employee."

"Oh," she says, grateful for a survivable scenario. "Where do you have to go?"

"I just got the assignments this morning. It looks like I'll be all over the state. Well, not here, but everywhere else. Montgomery first, and we end up near Huntsville."

"When do you leave?"

"This afternoon," he says. "I'll get back on the twenty-fourth."

Her heart sinks. "Wow, that sounds like a long time."

"Fourteen days."

"Weekends, too?" she asks.

"Weekends, too. We're short-staffed."

"Can I ask a stupid question?"

"You can ask whatever you want." He puts a hand on her thigh, and the butterflies in her stomach almost distract her.

"Does this mean we won't see each other for fourteen days?"

"Yes, that's what it means."

She takes a preemptive deep breath, but the anxiety comes anyway.

"Hey," he says. "That's all it means. We're going to talk every day. I promise."

She nods. "I'm sorry. I know it's not a long time. I'm being crazy."

"Don't apologize. You're not crazy." He takes her face in his hand. "I don't want to leave you, either."

"I'll be fine." She feels the guilt seeping in around the panic. He's working. He said he doesn't want to leave. She shouldn't make him feel bad about it. "Is it something you'll enjoy doing?"

"I'll mostly be watching the new guy talk to clients and then telling him what he does wrong."

"You'll get to see new places," Nora says.

Garrett sighs. "I'd rather see new places with my girlfriend."

"Your girlfriend?" Nora asks with a smirk. "Is she around? Can I meet her?"

He takes her hand, lacing their fingers together. "I guess that's something we have to discuss."

"Discuss away."

He glances down at their hands, and Nora wonders if he's embarrassed or nervous. It's an interesting shift in their dynamic when she's not the one feeling anxious about something. When he meets her eyes, a smile covers his face, and she can't help but smile in response. "I want you to be my girlfriend."

"Does that mean you would be my boyfriend?"

He tilts his head as if considering it. "I think so."

"I accept those terms."

"Yes?" he asks.

"Yes. Obviously." She laughs and leans over to kiss him.

"Can I tell you something else?"

"Sure."

"Work has been a problem for me in the past. In past relationships, I mean. I have to be away a lot."

"You told me that when we met," she says.

"I don't want my job to mess this up. I like you."

She smiles and rests her forehead against his for a moment. "I like you, too. We'll be fine. It's just fourteen days."

When Garrett leaves town, the anxiety shows up in his place. Nora knows their relationship is fine. She's happy. A level of happy she had forgotten about. She has no reason to doubt him. But the thoughts start to creep in on day two. What's he doing? Why hasn't he texted back?

On day five, Garrett tells her the fourteen days will actually be fifteen. Even though she knows it's not that long of a trip, the thoughts get worse. If he said he would call, but he hasn't yet, maybe he won't. She doesn't even know exactly where he is. He could be lying about all of this. He could be at his apartment. He could be with someone else at his apartment. Should she drive by?

The Instagram therapy accounts Nora follows say that she needs to get out of her head, so that the thoughts don't control her, but that's easier said than done. She can't seem to find anything to take her mind off of her worries. Television won't do it. Reading is too passive. Instagram makes it worse.

Nora turns to her usual coping habits: wine and *Cheers*. On day eight, she crawls into bed with a bottle of red wine, a plate of reheated leftover pizza, and a pudding cup for dessert. She starts *Cheers* where she left off: the episode where Sam and Diane get engaged after sorting through the usual high jinks of a sitcom.

After she's eaten all of the pizza and the pudding and drunk most of the wine, Garrett calls. Nora lets the phone ring twice before answering, as if she hasn't had the phone next to her since the day she met him.

"Hey, what are you doing?" he asks.

"Watching *Cheers*. Drinking wine. What are you doing?"

"The same thing."

"You're watching *Cheers*?" she screeches.

He laughs. "Yes, you convinced me."

"You must really like me." She barely recognizes the sound of her own giggle, a side effect of drinking one glass too many.

"I was getting a little jealous of this bartender you were spending all your nights with."

"If you'll come home, you can spend your nights here, too,"

she says. A very small, more sober part of her wonders if this is a step too far, considering that he has never even been to her house.

"Is that the wine talking, or are you serious?"

"I'm serious! The wine is only whispering."

"'Whispering'?" He laughs. "What does that mean?"

"You know what it means!" They both laugh, and then they keep laughing because they're both laughing, as if they're in the same room instead of more than a hundred miles apart.

"How's Montgomery?" Nora asks.

Garrett groans.

"That's our capital, you know. You should have a little respect."

"Montgomery is fine. This hotel is a different story."

"What's wrong with it?"

"It smells weird."

Nora laughs. "What does it smell like?"

"Bleach."

"Well, at least it's clean."

"Too clean. You have to ask yourself why they need so much bleach."

"Murder, probably."

"That's not comforting, Nora."

"Do you want me to come and protect you? From the bleach?"

"That is exactly what I want."

Nora sinks down in the bed and hugs the pillow next to her. "Is the bed comfortable?"

She hears him rustling around. "Not particularly."

"Do they have free breakfast?"

"Yes."

"And you're complaining?"

"I don't eat the breakfast."

Nora gasps. "Why not? It's free!"

Garrett laughs. "I stop for coffee and eat then."

"The hotel has coffee."

"Not decent coffee."

"Don't take this the wrong way, but you're lucky you're handsome, because you're kind of a snob."

"I'm not a snob!"

Nora laughs. Then she thinks about Garrett in his bleached hotel room, and she laughs again.

"It's not funny. Take it back."

"The truth hurts sometimes. Don't worry. I still like you. I wish you would come home, though."

"I wish I would, too."

On day eight, Nora is driving home from work when she gets the urge to roll down her window. Summers in Alabama begin without warning, after two weeks of spring that can be difficult to recognize as the only chance for picnics or riding bikes or any other outdoor activity without bugs and clothes soaked with sweat. Fall arrives in a similar fashion, as if someone has opened the oven door to let a breeze in after months of constant convection.

Since the summer heat is fading into fall, maybe, Nora thinks, she can use her house as a way to distract herself. This idea hits her while sitting on the back porch in the dark being eaten alive by mosquitoes. Normal people invite their boyfriends over to their houses, but Nora can't do that because she lives in an early 2000s time capsule, and no one needs to see that. She hasn't changed anything since her parents died, and they never changed anything if they could help it. She could at least change the light bulb on the back porch. Are there light bulbs in the house? Do light bulbs go bad after an extended period of time? These are the sorts of things her dad would know. Or he would pretend he knew and ask her mother for the answer.

After work the next day, Nora drives into the city to go to Home Depot. She comes home with light bulbs, a few boxes of outdoor string lights, citronella candles, and cleaning supplies that the salesperson swore would work on any back porch. She unwraps new scrub brushes and a new broom and cleans every inch of the porch until the cobwebs and dust are gone. Once she changes the porch light bulb, lights the candles, and hangs the string lights, she feels accomplished. Like she could have someone over without embarrassment. The inside of the house needs the same treatment, but that's a whole other thing to tackle, on another day. She pours a glass of wine and sits down at her newly cleaned patio table to take in all of her effort. That's when she notices the garden. Or the jungle where the garden used to be.

The next afternoon, she opens the storage building in the backyard, which her dad painted to match the house. She hasn't been out here in months. No one has. There are cobwebs every-where. Possibly spiders. Probably snakes. Someone could be liv-ing out here, watching *Cheers* and drinking wine, and she wouldn't know. She doesn't want to think about that right now. She just needs a shovel.

She grabs any and all tools with a long handle and chucks them through the front door of the building and out onto the ground. She has no idea what half of these things are because she's not usually an outdoorsy person. She doesn't have memories of helping her dad in the yard, since they were both fine if she just stayed out of the way.

Her mom's floral-print gloves are still in a drawer in the garage, so she takes a pair, assuming this is what they're for. She steps over the railroad-tie border of what used to be the garden, immediately waist-deep in tall weeds. This would be a good home for a snake. A snake family, even. Some of the weeds are loose enough that she can pull them out by hand, so she makes a little progress before she has to turn to actual tools. She's sure someone in the neighborhood has some sort of machine that will do this—what exactly is a Bush Hog? But the destruction is cathartic. She might almost call it fun.

She's using a post-hole digger like a giant pair of tweezers when she senses movement behind her.

"What's going on out here?" Grandpa asks, eyeing the mess. Half of the yard is covered in dug-up weeds and roots. She thinks about what she is going to do with all of the remains once they're out of the ground. Maybe set them on fire. That feels right.

"I'm being productive," she says, wiping sweat from her forehead.

"Are you digging to China?"

"I'm trying to get the garden in order," she says. "I'm sure I'm not doing it right." She removes her gloves and sits down on the nearest railroad tie to wait for the lecture.

"There are easier ways," he says. "You know, your mama used to come out here when she had something on her mind."

"Is it that obvious?" She laughs.

"Ginger thought there was a stranger in your yard, then she realized it was you having some sort of tantrum, so she called me." Nora's next-door neighbor has always paid a little too much attention to what everyone else in the neighborhood is doing, and she feels a sense of duty to share everything she knows with parties who might be interested.

"It's not a tantrum," Nora says, eyeing her dirt-covered tennis shoes. "I'm not having a tantrum."

"Do you want to talk about it?"

"It's really nothing," she says. She looks down at her hands; they're disgusting even though she's been wearing gloves. She doesn't know the last time she had actual dirt on her hands, under her fingernails. "I'm just overthinking things."

"About that boy?"

"Sort of. I guess." When she and Grandpa had dinner last, Nora refused to say much about Garrett. The more she talks to the people in her life about her relationship with Garrett, the more she will have to come to terms with how strong her feelings are, and she knows it's too soon to have feelings like that. In the same vein, the more people she tells about her relationship, the more she will have to tell about the breakup. People feel sorry enough for her already. "He's out of town, and I'm just antsy."

"'Antsy,'" he says, testing the word. He grabs a plastic chair from the patio, positions it next to the garden, and sits down. "Have you heard from him?"

"Yes. He's fine. Great, actually. He's the most reliable person I've ever dated. It's me with the problem."

"Well, what's the problem?"

She has to be honest with her grandpa. He knows her too well to accept anything else. "I'm just waiting on the other shoe to drop. I like him and he likes me, but he could easily find someone normal instead of me."

He nods. They sit in silence for a few minutes, and Nora notices that the lightning bugs are out. She catches one in her hands and watches it crawl around on her palm. She wills herself to feel the tiny feet as it moves, but she can't. When she was little, she used to catch them in Mason jars and seal the metal lids to keep the lightning bugs inside. After many jars of dead bugs, her dad used it as an opportunity to teach her about oxygen. Nora stares at the bug on her hand until it flies away, ensuring its own safety.

"I don't know," she says. "I have no reason to doubt Garrett, but I do anyway. Or maybe I doubt myself. He'll find out how crazy I am."

"You're not any crazier than anyone else."

"Oh, really?" She gestures to the mess around her, truly seeing it for the first time. The garden looks ten times worse than it had when she started. It would take days to fully clean it up.

"Home improvement doesn't make you crazy," Grandpa says. He's always given her too much credit.

"I just wanted it to look like it used to look. Mom worked hard on it, and I let it go to weeds. I can learn to garden, can't I?"

"Do it how you want," he says. "It doesn't have to be her way."

"Can I burn this when I'm done?" she asks, holding up a long stalk of something she can't identify.

He arches an eyebrow. "I wouldn't."

"You think I'll burn the house down."

He shrugs. "Do it how you want. Once you get all this dug up, it'll be easier. This is the hard part."

"I hope so. At least it keeps me from wondering where Garrett is."

"Where is he?"

She starts to pick the dirt out from under her fingernails. "I don't know. Somewhere near Jasper or something. I can't keep up. He's training someone."

"Training them for what?"

"Honestly, I still have no idea, but there's only so many times you can ask."

"Have you heard from him lately?" Grandpa asks.

"Yeah, this morning."

"That's not so bad. You should give him a chance."

"You haven't even met him," she says.

He shrugs. "I have a good feeling. He's got you out here doing yardwork. He has to be worth something."

She laughs. "I probably won't tell him about this. I'm still trying to keep the crazy to myself."

"Gotta let it out sometime. Rip the Band-Aid off. You'll feel better."

TODAY

Garrett follows a path around his hotel room, bouncing a pink rubber ball as he goes. He had found the ball outside a school playground, across the street from a construction accident he had managed a few weeks ago. He had let the ball drop from his hand to the sidewalk, and the satisfaction of catching it on the way back up had been a surprise. Since then, he's kept the ball in his suitcase, not knowing he would use it on so many nights like this. Nights after he met Nora.

Usually, Garrett spent his nights at hotels eating takeout and watching crime shows while catching up on work. There are always emails to send and forms to file. Sometimes, he tries out the hotel gym, but this is not that kind of hotel.

Instead, he bounces the ball. Around the bed and over to the tiled floor next to the sink and back to the front door. The circuit takes only a few seconds, but it gives him something to do while his brain cycles through all of his thoughts of Nora.

Before Rabbittown, he never really thought about dating again. He figured it could be something he did after he was done working for Death, once he had helped rebuild his parents' savings, since they'd spent all of what they had and gone deeply into debt paying for his brother's cancer treatments. He also wanted to set aside some money for their retirement. He could have a normal job and a normal dating life then.

Garrett knows he fell for Nora the second he saw her, even if he tries to tell himself otherwise. He really did want to take it slow, but he couldn't help himself. The more he had seen her standing in that room filled with caskets, the more a little voice inside told him she could be the one to understand. He likes making her laugh and kissing her and watching the funny Tik-Toks she sends him while he's on the road and listening to her talk about *Cheers*, which he finds himself watching regularly on his own now.

Nora is complicated, but maybe not as complicated as she thinks she is. She would understand why he wants to help his family. And why he wants to help other families. He and his sister didn't get to say goodbye to their brother. He was just gone. His job has allowed him to heal from that pain by being with others in that moment. Surely she would see that, too.

In his younger days, maybe he had enjoyed the secrecy. It had protected him from getting hurt by keeping him from getting too serious with anyone. He could always leave, and they would have to understand.

This is how he knows he's in trouble. In the past, the leaving had been a welcome escape from someone wanting to share more of his life. Now the leaving hurts. He's seen his friends obsessed with their partners, but he never really understood it until now. He wants to know where Nora is and what she thinks about where she is and what she's doing. He bounces the ball harder. How did this happen?

He's no longer content with a life of hotel rooms and a constant stream of work appointments. He wants candlelit Italian dinners and walks to get ice cream and kisses in the car. But what if she doesn't understand? If she can't forgive him for the secrecy? Or the things he's done for Death? The things he would keep doing for Death?

He bounces the ball a final time and stares up at the popcorn ceiling, accepting the obvious. None of the questions matter, at least not in the face of reality.

He's falling in love with Nora, and he has to tell her the truth. The right time will come. Eventually.

CHAPTER

7

The bell above the door rings; after a moment, Nora recognizes Mr. Sanderson. It's been years since she's seen him. His older son, Ben, was in her class at school, and his younger son, Ethan, was only a few years behind. They lived down the street, and they used to invite Nora over to jump on the trampoline with them during the summer. Their families had gone to many of the same community events and church barbecues over the years.

"Hey, Mr. Sanderson," Nora says as he approaches the counter. "It's been a while."

"I almost didn't recognize you, Eleanora, but you look so much like your mother."

She hears the crack in his voice, the telltale sign that they aren't planning for a future funeral.

"How can I help you?" she asks.

He looks away to gather himself, so Nora tries again.

"If you'll just tell me who we're planning for and when it happened, I can walk you through it from there."

"It's Ethan."

This information knocks the breath out of Nora's chest. She had assumed it would be a grandparent or even Mrs. Sanderson, but her mind hadn't gone to the boys. She freezes, unsure of what to do next and certain that her dad could have handled this moment better.

"My God," she says. "I'm so sorry. I hadn't heard."

She fiddles with her necklace in lieu of showing emotion, since someone has to be in control, and it should never be the parent of a dead child. She knows how to hold herself together. She gives him a moment to compose himself.

"Car accident near Fort Payne late last night," Mr. Sanderson explains. "He was on his way home from Ohio."

Nora tries to remember why Ethan would be in Ohio. Had he moved there at some point? The information was jumbled up in the odds and ends Nora had accumulated about people she hasn't seen in a decade and might never see again. Ethan had gotten a scholarship to Kent State and met an Ohio girl and stayed after graduation. Nora's mom had told her that before her own car accident.

"I'm so sorry to hear that. I know everyone was really proud of him." Nora hears her dad's voice reminding her that Mr. Sanderson is here for a purpose, not for comfort. There isn't much comfort in a situation like this anyway. "I'll go through some common options, and we'll figure this out together."

Mr. Sanderson chooses a simple casket, black with a sage interior because Ethan liked green. Nora usually handles only the casket part, but she walks Mr. Sanderson through some ideas for the burial and any services he might want to have and puts him in contact with the right people to take care of it.

"I'm sure I'm forgetting something," he says as they're wrapping up. "Melanie usually handles things like this."

"That's what I'm here for," Nora says. "If you have any questions, please call me. If I can't help, I have an arsenal of phone numbers."

"I appreciate your help. I didn't know where to start. No one prepares you for this."

"I'm glad I could help." She gives him a folder with copies of forms and business cards for florists, churches, and anything else she can think to include.

Mr. Sanderson stops on his way to the door. "I wonder if they're together now, Ethan and your parents."

"I'm sure Dad is showing him around," Nora says, hoping this is the right answer. She has no idea where anyone is, and that reminder lands on her chest like a stone falling down a well. "See you at the service."

He tips his head in her direction and walks out onto the sidewalk.

Once the door closes, Nora sinks to the floor behind the counter. She doesn't usually react this way when someone dies, but her parents' faces are in the front of her mind now. The memories are flooding in, and she knows she has to get a handle on herself. If she gives them a yard, they'll take the whole field.

Instagram therapists have taught her how to calm herself down. She needs to clear her mind. She concentrates on breathing. She thinks about nature. A tree. Leaves. Roots stretching out underneath. Stretching farther than any of us can see.

She puts herself back together and calls her grandpa. This is what small-town people have been raised to do. They call the next person in the chain.

"That poor boy," he says. "His poor mama."

"Mr. Sanderson was holding it together. I don't think it's hit him yet."

"You all right?" he asks.

"Yeah," she says. "I'm fine, I guess."

"Why don't you come over tonight?"

"You have Bible study," she reminds him. Grandpa never misses the men's Bible study class, mostly so he can say he never misses it and for the hour they spend discussing college football after the lesson.

"We can have our own Bible study at the house," he says. "I've been wanting a closer look at Leviticus."

She laughs. "I'll pass. But thanks."

Nora closes down the store and heads home for the day because entrepreneurs can do that. As soon as she walks into the house, she feels it. The sense that someone else is there. The same feeling she gets when someone walks up behind her. She's felt it before, and it has never amounted to anything. But the chance is always there. The chance that she'll open her parents' bedroom door and her mom will be sitting at her vanity swiping blush onto her cheeks. The chance that her dad will be watching some old football game in his recliner. The chance that the whole thing has been a dream or hallucination.

The house is empty. The rooms are empty. She knows this. Still, she finds herself in the hallway, running her fingertips along the wallpaper below the row of family photos and dragging her feet to postpone the inevitable. She pauses at her parents' door, hand on the cold doorknob, giving herself the opportunity to snap out of it. When she opens the door, the room is empty. As empty as it's been for a year. She notices her mom's things on her vanity. Her brush full of dark hair with strands of gray still wound into the bristles. Makeup spilling out of her makeup bag. Two necklaces and a pair of earrings next to a monogrammed Tervis tumbler of water.

The floor creaks when she steps across the threshold, and she remembers how these stupid floors always let her dad know when she was trying to sneak out of bed in the middle of the night. The room is mostly clean, except for a solid layer of dust that she should probably take care of at some point. She remembers when her dad begged her and her mom to let him paint this room crimson, and now she realizes he was probably just doing it to make her laugh, and she did.

Her parents hadn't gone to college, but her dad was obsessed with the University of Alabama. He thought Tuscaloosa was the greatest city on the planet. He was so excited when she got her acceptance letter. He told anyone who would listen. Her dad had done so much to make sure she was able to go there, even if he hadn't been able to, and she had taken it for granted. She had taken everything they did for her for granted.

A tear falls down her cheek. Nora doesn't like the way crying feels. Like she can't control her body. Being sad is one thing. She can still work or attend social functions while sad. Crying makes a thing into *a thing*. Here she is, making her parents' death *a thing*. Again.

She's still sitting on the edge of her parents' bed when Garrett calls.

"When will you be back?" she asks after the small talk.

"In an hour or so," Garrett says. They haven't seen each other in fifteen days, and she's worried that the distance has made things weird between them. She's worried that the worrying about it makes it weirder.

"Can I see you?" she asks. She knows this question reeks of desperation, but she can't care about that right now.

"Yeah, I'd offer you dinner, but I don't have anything at my apartment. We can go out if you want."

"You can come to my house," Nora says. After she blurts that out, she remembers he's never been to her house. She had always volunteered to meet him at his apartment, afraid he would judge her for living at her parents' house in her thirties.

"I'd like that," he says. "Will you text me the address?"

As she sends him the information, Nora's anxiety reminds her that Grandpa is the only other person who has stepped foot in her house in the past year. The adrenaline wakes up and takes over. She wipes down counters and lights candles. Does the house stink? What if it does, and she's become conditioned to it? She makes her bed for the first time in months. Nora's version of laundry usually means she washes and dries her clothes and then forms various piles around the house to avoid folding and putting them away. She tosses one pile at a time into the back of her closet for Future Nora to address.

Her bathroom could be worse. Nora had spent one of her recent lunch breaks browsing Rabbittown Pharmacy to restock her dwindling beauty supplies, and she had deposited all of these new purchases in a pile on her countertop. She slides what she can into cabinets and drawers and organizes the most normal products into some semblance of a display on the back corner of the counter.

Nora's fears about the state of the house make her forget about something else she needs to straighten: herself. She catches a glimpse of her unbrushed hair in her bathroom mirror and freezes for a moment at the thought of greeting him after fifteen days in her dad's Alabama sweatpants and an oversized, stained T-shirt.

She crawls into the closet to sift through the piles and grabs the first thing that feels like jeans and the first shirt she can find that smells like laundry detergent.

Strip. Airplane bath. Deodorant. Underwear without holes. Clothes. Hairbrush. Powder. Mascara.

As she makes a final sweep, she sees headlights across the front of the house. He rings the doorbell, and the butterflies in her stomach wake up from hibernation. She's excited and nervous, and she forgets about the shape of her house and her clothes, and she can't get to the door fast enough.

When she opens the front door, Garrett is standing there on the porch with his hands in his pockets. He must be the person magazines are referring to when they describe a day-to-night look: suit pants but no jacket with his top two shirt buttons undone. Have his eyes always been such a vivid green?

Garrett's face looks a bit haggard at first, like his trip has been exhausting, and maybe more than just physically. Once he sees Nora, he smiles and his face brightens as if he's finally reached the finish line of a race.

"Hi," Nora says.

"Hello," he says, his smile growing.

She gestures for him to enter the living room while she holds the door open.

All of the feelings she has carried for the past couple of weeks are replaced by relief and excitement, and she can't wait any longer to touch him. She stands on her toes to wrap her arms around his neck and press her body against his. "I missed you."

Garrett tilts his head to touch his forehead to hers, and then he kisses her so gently Nora thinks her heart might stop. She pulls him closer, as if maybe they can fill all of the space that formed between them while he was away.

He kisses her with more feeling. "I missed you, too," he says. "I forgot to say that."

If Nora could smile any bigger, she would. "How was your trip?"

"Too long," he says, pulling her into a hug, as if he has been gone forever. "You smell good."

She laughs nervously, remembering where her clothes have been. "Don't smell me."

"Too late."

"Where were you today?" She pretends to smooth out the front of his shirt, but it's just an excuse to touch him.

"Scottsboro this morning, I think. God only knows at this point."

Slightly alarmed by his tone of voice, she examines him closely to find that his hair looks less than perfect, and there are bags under his eyes.

"Is everything okay?" she asks.

"Yes. Why?" he asks. He kisses her cheek and her jaw and her neck.

"You seem—I don't know." She gasps when she feels the tip of his tongue. "Not your normal self."

"I'm just tired," he says, raising his head to kiss her lips. "Are you going to show me around?"

"Oh yeah, I forgot." She turns and gestures like Vanna White. "Welcome to my house. This is the living room." She leads him through to the kitchen and the dining room and back to the living room. Besides cleanliness, she hadn't had time to think about what it might look like to him. How it might feel when he got the full picture of his thirty-year-old girlfriend living in her childhood home with everything just as her parents left it.

"Is this you?" he asks, pointing at a framed photo on the wall of a dark-haired little girl pulling a baby doll in a wagon.

"Yeah, that's me. I used to pull that wagon around the neighborhood."

Garrett turns his attention to the other photos in the room, examining them one by one. "Your parents?" he asks, picking up a framed photo from the edge of a side table.

"Yeah, that was maybe five years ago. It was their anniversary," she says.

This part of the "after" is new for Nora. She has never had to talk about her parents to people who have never met them and now can't ever meet them. She has to carry their stories on her own, and hope she gets all of the details right.

He nods. "You do look like your mom. What was her name?"

"Anita. My dad was Billy. Well, William, but that's his dad's name. My grandpa."

"Is Nora a family name?"

"Eleanora," she says. "Technically."

"You never told me that." He laughs.

"Are you making fun of me?"

"No," he says, putting the frame back where he found it. "I like your name."

"It was my grandmother's."

"I told you I like it," he says. He takes one of her hands and laces their fingers together. "Are you trying to pick a fight?"

"No," she says, but she sort of is. She's ready to defend her space and all the things in it.

"Good," he says. "I'm tired. And hungry."

"We can eat." In her rushed preparation for his arrival, she never thought to check the fridge. Other than shredded cheese, she has no idea what is in there. She knows she has a pantry full of boxes and cans and God knows what else that she's never cleaned out. The freezer is full of bags of vegetables from years past, and the deep freeze one in the laundry room is full of casseroles from when her parents passed.

As she starts toward the kitchen, she knows she should probably communicate this issue before he sees it for himself. "Listen, I should be honest."

"What?"

"I invited you over here because I wanted to see you—"

"And now you don't?"

"No, I do! I just didn't think it through." She was too busy worrying about what he would think of the potentially expired store-brand face wash on her bathroom counter. "I don't know what food I have to offer. I swear my mom raised me better than this."

He exhales. "You scared me."

"What did you think I was going to say?"

He massages his temples. "I don't know. It could have been anything."

She pulls him into the kitchen and points to the counter where she had thought to put out two actual wineglasses next to the bottle of fourteen-dollar cabernet she'd bought at the pharmacy. She had purchased this slightly nicer bottle instead of her usual choice in hopes that Garrett would come over and drink it with her when he was back in town. "I do have wine."

She has started peeling the foil off the top when Garrett steps up behind her and loops his arms around her waist. She leans into him and kisses his cheek. She notices that he's still somewhat droopier than usual. "Are you sure you don't want to talk about it?"

"I'm fine," he says. "Let me see that before you hurt yourself."

"I'm very good at opening wine bottles," she says. Still, she slides him the bottle and the electric wine opener, because she will always let someone or something else do manual labor on her behalf, as evidenced by the automatic corkscrew.

"I know." He smiles. "I like talking to you after you've opened one."

This surprises her. "What do you mean?"

He shrugs, and she can tell he's trying not to laugh. "Your voice is different."

"What's wrong with my voice?"

"Nothing is wrong with it." He pours two glasses and hands her one.

"Can you elaborate?" she asks.

He purses his lips while he's thinking. "What is that magnet?" he asks, pointing toward the refrigerator.

"Don't change the subject."

He laughs. "I was trying to think of how to describe it. You're just more . . . I don't know."

"You don't want to tell me."

He's rubbing his temples again.

"Why are you doing that?" she asks.

"Doing what?"

"Rubbing your head."

He covers his face for a moment, but she can tell he's laughing. "I think drunk you likes me more than sober you. That's all." He crosses his arms, waiting for her response.

She thinks back on their late-night phone calls; she has never said anything outrageous. She didn't even drink that much, and she knows this because she didn't take her glass or the bottle to her bedroom except for that one night. When she wakes up next to a wine bottle, she knows she's going to have a hangover even before she feels it. The whole time he was gone, she was sober enough to turn everything off and to remember to lock the doors and to switch to drinking water sometime before bed.

She reaches out and touches his face, and he leans into her palm. "You're cute when you're exasperated," she says.

He kisses the palm of her hand. "I'm not exasperated."

"You're tired."

"Yes, I'm tired." He picks up his wineglass and holds it out to her. "And I need a drink."

She clinks her glass against his. "To needing a drink."

They both take a sip. "This isn't as bad as I thought it would be," he says.

"Well, thanks." She rolls her eyes. "Sorry I'm not as fancy as you." She sets the glass on the counter and starts rummaging through the fridge.

"I didn't mean it like that. I just wouldn't have picked it out." To be fair, the label is a skeleton wearing a top hat while riding a unicycle. Garrett steps behind her, watching her dig through the produce drawer. "Hey, whatever you were going to eat is fine."

All at once Nora feels stupid, and she's sure he thinks she's stupid, too. Like her house is stupid and her life is stupid. She feels a lump in her throat. She closes the fridge and crosses her arms. "Maybe we shouldn't do this."

Garrett tilts his head, and Nora's face heats. She wishes she could be anywhere but here.

"Do what?"

The lump in her throat grows, and she looks away, willing herself to be normal.

He puts his hands on her arms softly, as if he's trying to calm a feral animal. "Nora, I'm sorry. The wine is fine. More than fine. Can we please talk about it?"

The apology in his voice sets her off, and she starts to cry. She tries to stop it, but she can't. Once again, her body is in control, and she has no say in the matter.

"Please don't cry. Look at me."

She does, and his green eyes search hers, wanting to help, wanting to understand. That does it. Nora is full-on *Bachelor*-contestant-crying in the middle of her kitchen. Garrett winds his arms around her, and she sobs into his shoulder.

"Baby, please don't cry," he says. That's the first time he's ever called her that, which feels important in the moment, but she won't remember it later. "Please talk to me."

Finally, around her sobs, she says what she's known all night and what she should have said when he walked in the door: "I'm sorry. It's been a bad day."

They stand there in front of her refrigerator, and he holds her while she cries. He doesn't say anything. He doesn't know what to say. Nora is positive he's retracing his steps, trying to figure out how he wound up dating a lunatic. He rubs her back and waits for her to calm down. Eventually she does.

She pulls away, sniffling and wiping the tears from her face. When she looks up at him, he's waiting patiently for an explanation. "I'm sorry. I feel like a jerk. Please just go. You don't deserve whatever this is." She gestures at her ugly cry face.

"Do you want to talk about it?" he asks. He runs his hands up and down her arms, unwilling to pull away completely.

"You don't have to do this. You can really just go. I'll be fine."

"I don't want to go," he says firmly. "I want you to tell me what's going on."

Nora stares at him for a moment, trying to decide what to do next. She figures she's ruined everything already, so she might as well be honest. "You didn't do anything wrong. I found out today that a guy I grew up with died last night. His dad came in and bought a casket, and I guess I've been upset ever since. I'm sorry. I thought I was fine, or I wouldn't have invited you over. Clearly, I was wrong."

Garrett hugs her then, tightly, and she hugs him back, waiting for whatever happens next. He pulls away but only far enough to rest his forehead on hers for a moment. "I want to be here with you," he says. "I want you to tell me these things."

So, she does. She tells him about Ethan's accident and how their families used to be close. How he had a whole life planned, and now it was gone. "I guess it was just a surprise. It made me think of my parents. And how things used to be. I don't know. It was a long day."

Garrett holds her in front of the refrigerator for who knows how long. She prays to God and whoever else is listening that she hasn't ruined everything.

She whispers, "I'm sorry, Garrett," because she knows she'll cry again if she tries to say it any louder.

"Don't apologize," he says. "You didn't do anything wrong."

She decides to will her composure to come back by changing the subject. "Yes, I did. Do I have mascara all over my face?"

His brows furrow. "No."

"Can I trust your judgment?"

"Yes."

"Are you going to leave?" she asks, examining his face for some sort of clue on how fast he plans to run away.

"Do you want me to?"

"No," she says.

"Then I'll stay."

She nods, trying to think of a way to change the subject. "Do you want a grilled cheese?"

He smiles, and some of the tension leaves his body. "Yes. Please."

She shows him her tried-and-true procedure: real butter, homemade sourdough from her Uncle Ralph, a Kraft Single, and shredded cheese of a fancier variety (tonight they have Monterey Jack). After dinner, they move to the couch and start a movie on Netflix that everyone on the internet has seen except for the two of them. Garrett pulls her close to him, and it doesn't take long for her to realize that neither of them is in the mood for the movie. On his third deep sigh, she leans up so she can see his face.

"We can watch something else," she says.

"Watch whatever you want," he says. He looks what Nora's mother would call "ragged."

She turns off the television and shifts, so they're facing each other. "I can't tell if you're upset about something or if you're just tired."

He laces their fingers together. "I'm mostly just tired."

"Do you want to talk about the rest of it?"

They stare at each other for a bit. Nora doesn't mind the silence, but she can tell he has more to say, whether he'll decide to or not.

He takes a breath. "Sometimes my job is just hard."

"How so?"

"It's a lot of moving parts and moving people and figuring out all of that."

"Isn't that what logistics is? I looked it up."

He smiles. "Let me rephrase: sometimes I have to work with multiple parties, and it can be frustrating trying to make sure the moving parts are moved correctly."

"And you were training someone?"

He nods. "I had to slow everything down, which wasn't always ideal."

His description is vague, but she can tell that's how he wants it, so she leaves it alone. She has caused enough drama tonight.

"I also hated being in hotels for so long." He rubs his thumb over the back of her hand.

"Why? Hotels are fun."

"These weren't exactly five-star."

She crinkles her nose. "Did you have bedbugs?"

He laughs. "No."

"Thank God. You're as good as done once you have them."

He rolls his eyes.

She squeezes his hand. "It's true!"

"Have you had them before?" he asks.

"No, but I've read about them."

"Of course you have."

"Well, the tiny bottles of shampoo are nice, right?"

"I just wanted to be in my bed."

"That's fair."

"I missed sleeping next to you." He says this confidently, but she can tell by his stare that he's waiting for her reaction.

"Were you lonely?" she asks.

He nods. "And cold."

"I was lonely and cold, too." She slides closer and tucks herself under his arm, and he wraps her up with both arms. "I'm glad you missed me."

He kisses the top of her head, and maybe that's not an erogenous zone, but she still feels it from there to the tips of her toes. She barely knows him, so she's probably rushing it. She's probably just trying to latch on to this warm body that has inserted itself into her solitary life. He's here for work and has no reason to stay, and Nora doesn't intend to leave. Maybe the depth of her feelings doesn't make sense as far as logic is concerned, but she can't help it. She wants him here, and she wants to take care of him, and she wants him to take care of her.

Before she can overthink it, she asks, "Do you want to go to bed?"

He nods, and she leads him to her bedroom.

FOURTEEN YEARS AGO

"Another hurricane?" Garrett asks. He holds his phone up to show Janine across the car. "Are we hurricane experts now?"

"You'll get used to it." She doesn't take her eyes off the road. The sky has darkened since they crossed from Georgia to Florida, but they haven't hit the rain yet.

He runs his thumb over the screen of his phone, scrolling past emails from restaurants and clothing stores to get to the ones about his newest work assignments. The assignments populate on his calendar at the same time he receives an email with the details. Janine says the best thing to do with questions about those details is to forget them. Whatever the system doesn't handle, your gut will. Garrett has learned to keep moving forward, no matter what the situation is. In fact, he tries to know as little about the situation as possible. The end result would be the same either way.

"Don't think too far ahead," Janine says. "We've got a few to handle before we get there." She takes the next exit for Lake City and follows her GPS to the parking lot of an Aldi.

"An Aldi, really?"

"More of a Whole Foods guy?"

"No," he says, thinking of the dark chocolate peanut butter cups at Trader Joe's. "I just think it will be . . . a scene."

"It's always a scene. That's the job."

"What are we looking for this time?"

She turns around in the Ford Focus they rented to look out the back windshield. "A red Camry and a black coat."

They both watch the parking lot for a few moments before a red Camry pulls into the lot and parks farther down the aisle. A woman gets out of the car, trying to keep her purse strap in place on the shoulder of her black coat. Her blond hair is twisted up into a clip on the back of her head.

"She's young," Garrett says.

"Forty-two. That's something we forget." She examines her Rolex. "Two minutes."

Garrett drums his fingertips against the door handle, waiting for the word.

"You can try one on your own tomorrow."

"Really? By myself?"

"I think you're ready," Janine says. She has found that people take up whatever container she gives them. If she says he's ready, he will be ready. "Now, what do we need to remember?" She gestures at the front door of the Aldi, where a man and two children are trying to get their coin into the slot on the shopping cart.

"The bystanders."

Janine nods.

Both of their phone alarms sound at the same time.

"Follow my lead."

CHAPTER
8

Elaine Gardner eyes Nora across the counter while running the espresso machine at the Chat & Brew in Rabbittown Square. She's known Eleanora Clanton as long as Eleanora has been alive, and she's never heard that girl hum anything, but here she is. At the counter. Humming a tune from God knows where. She has always been polite, and she tips well, but she's . . . Elaine tries to think of the right word. "Careful" is what she comes up with. Even when she was a child. All of the other kids would run around the Square screaming like heathens, but not Eleanora.

Elaine starts to feel guilty for judging her like that. People are allowed to hum. This is a free country, after all. Then Nora starts nodding her head to whatever she's humming, and Elaine can't help herself.

"What's gotten into you?"

Nora jerks her head up. "Me?"

"I don't see anyone else carrying on their own concert." Nora's cheeks redden, and Elaine feels like she's looking at Anita Clanton. Like she's serving coffee to a ghost.

"Sorry," Nora mumbles.

"No apology needed," Elaine says. She pours steamed oat milk into Nora's cup, places the plastic lid on top, and slides the cup across the counter to Nora. "Seems like you're in a good mood."

"I guess I am." Nora smiles. "Have a good day."

"You, too."

Nora laughs to herself as she crosses the street to open the store. The sun is shining, the birds are chirping, and everything is going her way. In her head, at least.

Nora's good mood goes out the window with the sound of the first storm siren before she even makes it to her desk. She spends the day watching the local news, trying to understand the timing and locations of the storms sweeping through the state of Alabama. The meteorologist gives warning after warning to be cautious, and so do Jean, Margaret (stopping by on her way home from the pharmacy), Ms. Annie, and Grandpa.

She texts Garrett to make sure he's paying attention to the radar. She hadn't been fully awake when Garrett left her house that morning, but he had promised to come back over once he was done with his appointments for the day. Or did he say meetings? She still didn't know what he did all day.

No one is shopping for a casket in the rain and with a tornado warning, so Nora has all day to obsess over the weather, just like everyone else in town. Rabbittown's biggest storm threat should hit later in the evening, so Nora gets the store ready before she packs up. This means pacing through every area of the store and sliding everything from the top of her desk down into the drawers, as if drawers would stop a tornado. It tricks her into cleaning up the back room and filing the papers she has left strewn about. She rolls the model caskets to the back of the store and unplugs the electronics before locking the door to head home.

Nora wanders around her house nervously. She gathers pillows and cushions and tosses them into the hallway in case she needs them later. She makes sure all of the windows are closed and locked, as if they had been opened in years. Eventually, she gives up on the preparation and forces herself to sit down. The meteorologist on TV points out a swath of red and green heading straight for the Rabbittown area.

Nora reaches for her phone to call Garrett but fumbles, her phone clattering to the floor. The noise brings her wandering mind back to the present moment.

"What are you doing?" Nora asks once he answers.

"I'm working. What are you doing?"

"Watching the weather." She leans back on the couch, letting her head hit the top of the cushion. "You know there's a tornado coming, right?"

"Yes, I know." A door closes on his end of the call.

"Where are you?"

"I'm about to go home."

"You're getting in a car right now. I heard the door." For a moment, an image of him at some secret place enters her mind, but she doesn't let it take over. It doesn't matter where he is. He shouldn't be in a car. "Did you not hear the part about the tornado?"

"Are you worried about the storm? Everything is going to be fine."

"I didn't call so you could help me feel better. I wanted to make sure you're paying attention."

"I'm paying attention."

"People die when tornadoes come through Alabama."

"I know that."

Lightning draws Nora's attention to the living room windows as a clap of thunder sounds, startling some of her mom's porcelain knickknacks on a shelf in the corner. It startles Nora, too, even though she had known it was coming. Thunder has always startled Nora, despite the fact that lightning is a pretty good indicator that you can expect thunder.

"Can you at least tell me you're driving home?" she asks, her voice coming out higher than usual. "Your car is the worst place you can be. I don't care how fancy it is."

"I promise I'll go straight home."

"Right now?"

"Soon."

"You're going to get yourself killed."

He sighs. "I'm not dying tonight, and neither are you."

"You don't know that."

"I do know that. I'm going to call you in thirty minutes, okay?"

"We're going to talk about this. You better not be a second late. I'm not kidding."

"I won't be."

Nora curls up with a blanket to watch the local news coverage and to wait for the thirty-minute timer on her phone to go off.

The meteorologist has ditched his jacket and tie, signaling that he has a long night ahead of him. Nora has never fully trusted meteorologists—she can't even count how many times she has gotten caught in a rainstorm that was nowhere to be found on the radar—but when he zooms in to follow the storm's path, she recognizes the communities that are usually too small to be picked out on the weather maps. None of them are that close to Rabbittown, so she has no reason to worry about her own safety, although faces and names of those who might be in danger come into her mind.

Nora tries to stop worrying about Garrett, but her mind wanders to her parents. They had been in a car, too. So was Ethan. It hadn't even been raining either of those times. Is this what death has done to her? Is this her life now? Worrying every time someone she loves is in a car?

But this isn't about the car, is it? It's about the tornado tearing through the area with no rhyme or reason. This had been death, too. She was following what she knew after spending most of her life in Alabama. Watching the weather and waiting for the meteorologist to say, "If you're in Rabbittown, you need to be in a safe place." Her safest place was the basement, where she has stashed her laptop, chargers, pillows, candles, flashlights, and an old bicycle helmet. Tornadoes really do kill people. Nora has seen it her whole life, and Garrett had just blown it off like it was no big deal.

Nora thinks of confidence as something you put on from the outside, like a jacket hanging in her closet. She can't fathom what it must feel like to have confidence bubble up from within, to feel like you were well equipped to handle whatever was coming. Surely she's felt it before, but the older she gets, the less she trusts the world around her to be predictable enough to let her be confident about anything.

She opens Facebook, and as usual, she immediately regrets it. Reports about the storm are everywhere. There won't be photos until morning, but the maps of the storm's path and the descriptions of people's experiences are enough. The news outlets seem sure that there will be deaths. There always are.

Another flash of lightning. A clap of thunder. A flash of light closer to her window. Suddenly Nora is sitting in the dark. She turns on the flashlight next to her and scans the room. She should have gone to her grandpa's or Jean's or even to a neighbor's house. She isn't usually afraid of the dark, but there's something different about the power being out. It's like the dark has you trapped, and you have no idea when you'll get out. The usual things that go bump in the night are compounded by the not knowing what happens next.

Nora lights an old lantern of her mother's and moves into the hallway, onto a pile of cushions, just to be safe. If the storm were closer, she would go to the basement, but it's scary down there. Always has been. Listening to the sounds of the rain and wind outside, she wonders if she will be able to sleep tonight. If the storm will be over soon. If it has already done its damage. She thinks about phoning Garrett, but she doesn't want to be that anxious girl calling her boyfriend to rescue her, especially when her thirty-minute timer hasn't gone off yet.

If she was honest, what she really wants is the same thing every heroine in this sort of story wants: for Garrett to want to be with her in intense moments like this without her having to ask. If she asks, there's a chance that he'll say no. There's a chance that things aren't the way Nora thinks they are with Garrett, and this isn't the way she wants to find that out. By being too much. By confirming that their relationship can't withstand the weight of her needs.

As a modern woman, she feels guilty about this. Shouldn't she be able to take care of herself without the help of a man? But she does take care of herself. All the time. Does it really set humanity back if she wants the person she loves to be around when she's having a hard time? And, if so, how does she change that part inside of her?

TODAY

Garrett drives through the pouring rain, directed by the voice on his phone's navigation system. Two more blocks. He pulls into a driveway as the wind picks up, and his car starts to rock back and forth.

He takes a deep breath and waits for his watch to strike 7:17. It's been a long time since he's had one of these jobs. But he feels his training kicking back in.

Follow the steps. Stick to the script. Everything goes how it's supposed to go. The alarms on his phone and watch go off at the same time. He reaches around to grab the bag in his backseat as the power in the neighborhood goes out. He steps out into the rain and makes his way toward the house in the dark.

CHAPTER

9

Nora remembers another storm when she was younger, when her parents were still alive, when she felt normal. Nora's mom didn't like going into the basement in the dark, so the three of them gathered in the hallway under the row of family portraits lining the walls. Nora's dad brought sleeping bags, pillows, and a lantern to make it feel like camping. It did a little bit, from what Nora remembered.

Her dad told stories about the weirdest funerals he had ever attended, and her mom pretended to be appalled, as if she hadn't been right next to him when the events occurred. Seven-year-old Nora giggled as if drunk aunts tripping over gravestones were the silliest thing she had ever heard. This was how their dynamic worked. Her dad said silly things until he made Nora laugh, and she could be a tough audience. Nora's mom would be the one to answer questions to clean up the mess. Nora's dad had been a fun person, and sometimes there's a lot of cleaning up to do around fun people. Her parents weren't the lovey-dovey types, but Nora remembers nights like that when they seemed as happy as any couple could be, even while waiting for a tornado to pass.

This one should have passed by now. She had once again waited out another storm alone, and the slimy feeling in the pit of her stomach told her that it wouldn't be the last. Maybe she would always be here in the dark in the hallway of her dead parents' house. Maybe there was nothing else. She had tried to embrace it, hadn't she? Maybe there was more she could do to make it her own, since it was her own now. Replace the thirty-year-old wallpaper. Replace the family portraits in the hallway. Etsy probably has a lovely print of Sam Malone she can frame. He's the other resident of the household, after all.

A thunderclap makes Nora jump. Rain hammers on the roof and against the windows. Nora picks up her phone and opens the podcast app. She scrolls through episodes before tossing her phone out of reach. She should have thought to charge it before the power went out. She isn't one of those people with a porta-ble phone charger ready to go. Well, she has one somewhere, but it had become useless fairly quickly because she lost the charging cord first, followed by the charger itself. Instead, she is one of those people who knows that there's a fifty-fifty chance that the power will go out and she'll choose to do nothing to prepare for it.

She did think to buy a box of wine on her way home to make sure she wouldn't run out. With the lantern lighting her path, she goes to the kitchen and manhandles the cardboard until the plastic nozzle appears and releases the wine into her glass.

The rain and wind begin to die down outside, so Nora relocates from the hallway floor to the couch. Just before her timer goes off, Garrett calls.

"Are you trying to give me a heart attack?"

"How are things there?" he asks, ignoring her question.

"The power is out. I'm sitting in the dark."

"Do you want some company?"

She would have loved some an hour ago. "If you mean you, then yes."

"I'm on my way. I'll be there soon."

Nora lights another lantern and fills another glass with wine, assuming he'll be in the mood for a drink. She wants to be a normal person and forget about his behavior earlier tonight, but she also wants to yell at him for being negligent. Maybe she should flip a coin.

She takes her mind off this debate momentarily by calling to check on her grandpa, Ms. Annie, Jean, and Margaret. They're all fine. None of them want to talk long, so they can save their phone batteries. Nora almost asks them when any of their phone batteries have gotten below eighty percent, but she doesn't.

Garrett pulls into the driveway, and Nora takes a lantern to meet him at the door.

"I'm very happy to see you," Garrett says, wrapping his arms around her.

Nora jumps back. "You are soaking wet! Were you just standing out in the rain?"

He shrugs out of his raincoat. "It was coming down pretty hard earlier."

"Garrett," Nora starts. She doesn't know what to say, and she really doesn't want to fight, so she shakes her head and leaves him standing in the foyer by himself.

He follows her through the dark living room to the couch, where she hands him his glass of wine. He takes a sip. "Go ahead."

"Go ahead what?"

"Say whatever you want to say."

"I don't *want* to say anything." She takes a drink of her own wine.

"I know you're mad."

"I'm disappointed."

He barks out a laugh. "In my experience, 'disappointed' has always been worse."

"Well, what were you thinking, Garrett? Maybe a tornado doesn't mean anything to you, but you shouldn't be in the car. That's like the most basic rule."

"I was perfectly fine."

"Thank God. Literally." She clasps her hands together and closes her eyes. "Thank you, God, for sparing my idiot boy-friend's life tonight."

He puts a hand over hers.

"My parents died in a car accident. It was not easy to sit here while you drove into a tornado. If your boss expects that from you, you need a new boss."

"I'm sorry I worried you, but I was not driving into a tornado. I was safe."

She intertwines one of her hands with his. "I don't know that I'll ever believe that in these sorts of situations. I want to ask you to refrain from putting your life in danger."

"You're going to have to trust me sometimes."

"It's not you I don't trust. It's the universe."

Garrett pulls her closer to him. "I really don't want my job to come between us."

She can't read his face very well by lantern light. Nora wouldn't have made it in any century without electricity. "Why do you think it could?"

"Nights like tonight." He leans his head against hers and kisses her softly above her ear. "Sometimes I have to go places and miss things. I'm good at my job. It means something to me. I feel like it's what I'm supposed to be doing, as weird as that sounds when I say it out loud."

"It's not weird to like your job."

"And honestly, I'm not willing to give that up so I can go to a random birthday party in the middle of the week or make it home by a certain time or whatever else might come up."

She considers this.

"What are you thinking?"

"I'm trying to decide if it should bother me more than it does. I don't like you putting yourself in danger, but the rest of that isn't a huge deal to me. I don't have much going on that you would miss. I'm usually just sitting on the couch."

"See, I can't tell if you mean that or if you're actually saying something else."

"What else would I be saying?"

"That you're sitting home alone, and I should feel bad about it."

"I'm sorry—"

"You have to stop apologizing for everything."

"But what if I really am sorry?" She sits up to look at him. "I'm not manipulating you. You asked me to trust you, and you need to trust me, too, even though I'm not the one driving into tornadoes."

"You don't have to worry about me."

"Well, I do worry about you. That's the whole point of this conversation. I spent hours worrying about you."

He takes a deep breath. "Can we back up and start over?"

"Start over from where?"

"I don't know. Whenever it was in the conversation that you started getting mad at me. I would like to go back and redo it."

Nora laughs. "I don't think it works like that."

"Says who?"

"Most people."

"I don't want to fight."

"Neither do I. Look, I'm glad you like your job. We can figure all of that out. But I'm never going to be fine with you risking your life when it could be avoided. I don't think you would like it if I did that."

"I'm a better driver than you."

She leans away from him and crosses her arms. "Will you please take this seriously? Maybe this is what happened with your other girlfriends. I'm trying to have an honest conversation, and you're ignoring my side of it."

He tries to take one of her hands, but she doesn't let him. "I'm not ignoring you," he says. "I'm sorry about what happened to your parents and everything that came after that. I'm sorry you've had to do it alone. It's not fair, and you didn't deserve it."

Her cheeks redden. She hates this feeling. Like she's one of the dogs in a Sarah McLachlan commercial. "I don't need your pity. Once it runs out, you'll be bored with me. I've seen it before."

"Look at me, please."

She does as he asks, and he stares into her eyes, willing her to see the truth. "Do you honestly think I'm with you because I feel sorry for you? Is that what you really think?"

"I don't know what I think."

He startles her by taking her face in his hands. "Is it not obvious that I love you, Nora? I *am* sorry that you've had bad things happen to you. But I'm pretty sure I loved you before I knew any of that. I know this is way too fast, but it's how I feel. I can't help it."

Nora watches enough soap operas that she should have known this was coming, but she's caught off guard. With her mouth open.

"You don't have to say anything back," he says. "That's really not how I planned to have this conversation, but I'm tired, and, well, it's the truth. I'm not going anywhere. I do hear you, and I promise I'll think about your feelings next time."

She lunges forward to kiss him. To keep him from changing his mind. She wraps her arms around his neck to pull him closer. His hands are in her hair before she realizes she forgot to respond. "I love you, too, Garrett. It's way too soon, but I feel it, too."

Nora didn't know that she's been waiting for a conversation like this, for Garrett to tell her how he feels, to be ready for the next step. Other boyfriends have said that they loved her in the past: one in high school, a guy in college who said it only when he was drunk, and then Charlie. She doesn't doubt that they loved her in those moments, but something always happened for them to change their minds. Drifting apart, sobering up, death.

She prays to anyone listening that this time, things will be different. That he'll be the one who stays.

She climbs onto his lap, straddling him against the couch, trying to get closer to him. She pauses long enough to unbutton his shirt and toss it aside, so she can touch his bare skin. She can't see him in the dark, but something feels different. Maybe she should have noticed the night before, but she was too preoccupied with him being in her house and in her bed and finally sleeping next to her after all of the nights apart.

"Have you been working out?"

He smirks. "Yes. I had some angst from missing my girlfriend that I needed to get out."

"I dug up the backyard."

"What?"

"I'll show you tomorrow. Could you kiss me, please?"

He pulls her shirt over her head, and they're kissing again. His hands travel up her back and down past her waist, pressing her against him.

Nora can't take it any longer. She stops long enough to snatch the lantern off the table a little too harshly, leading him down the hallway through piles of pillows to her bedroom and onto her bed. She runs her hands over his body, and she can't believe he's hers.

Garrett reaches for her bra, then hesitates. "We still don't have to do this now."

"I want to."

"I'm not trying to pressure you into anything—"

She puts a finger to his lips. "Trust me."

They take off one piece of clothing at a time, until there's nothing between them. His lips are on her neck, and her mind is running away with itself. What if she doesn't remember what to do? Or if she does something weird? Or if she's not enough after all this waiting?

She pulls his face to hers and kisses him deeply, silently begging him to distract her. She groans when he presses his body against hers, and then his hand is there, making her forget anything that had worried her in the first place. When she looks at him, she still can't believe he's real. He is hot, but it's more than that. He loves her.

"Will you hurry up, please?" she asks as he reaches for a condom in the drawer of her nightstand. She had purchased them when she bought the box of wine without knowing she would need them so soon.

He laughs as he rolls back to her, tearing open the package. "No, I will not be hurrying at all anytime soon."

True to his word, he's slow and sure, and every time Nora starts to disappear in her head, he finds a way to bring her back. During the less romantic parts, like when Nora's calf starts to cramp or when Garrett's hand gets tangled in her hair, they laugh at each other and at the weirdness of it, and Nora is amazed that she can reach this level of joy, something she thought was lost after everything that had happened.

Afterward, Garrett holds her close and runs his fingers up and down her arm.

"I love you," she whispers.

"I love you, too." By the sound of his voice, he's falling asleep. She had been angry at him earlier, and she tries to arrange that in her mind next to the happiness inside her now, but she can't quite remember what they were fighting about in the first place.

CHAPTER

10

Nora wakes up early and rolls over so that she and Garrett lie nose to nose. He looks young when he's sleeping, or at the very least innocent. She had just wanted to look at him, but she can't stop herself. She places her hand against his jaw and glides her thumb across his cheek.

"Hey," he says. He opens his eyes, and they stare at each other for a moment.

"Hi."

"How did you sleep?"

"You're like sleeping with a heater." She had known that already, but a night without air-conditioning made it harder to ignore. The power had come back on in the middle of the night.

"I'll sleep on my side of the bed next time."

Should she care that he has already claimed one side of her bed? She runs her hands over his chest and his shoulders and around his neck until she has some leverage to pull him on top of her. He's still half asleep, but he complies with her silent request without much ado.

"How did *you* sleep?" she asks.

"Good," he says. He presses his lips to hers.

"Looks like the power is back on."

"Uh-huh." Garrett kisses her cheek and her jaw and her neck. She moves her hand down his body until she finds what she's looking for, and he kisses her soundly.

A couple of hours later, Garrett whispers, "I have to go."

She opens her eyes. He's sitting fully dressed next to her.

It takes her a moment to understand what's going on. That he is ready for work, and she is very much not. "What time is it?"

"Seven forty-five."

She sits up and rubs her eyes. "I don't know the last time I slept this late."

He kisses her forehead. "You wore me out, too."

"Hey!"

"It's not a complaint."

"Maybe you should go to work now."

Garrett's face has shifted subtly overnight. His eyes seem brighter, and the corners of his mouth point upward. She kisses him; he tastes like toothpaste.

"Did you use my toothbrush?"

He tilts his head. "Does it matter?"

She thinks for a moment, while he laces their fingers together on top of her grandmother's quilt. "I'm not sure."

He laughs. "I found an extra in the cabinet."

"You went through my cabinet?"

"Yes, I know all of your secrets now."

He kisses her again, gently, like she's made of glass. Nora pulls him toward the bed, hoping for more, but it's no surprise that he's stronger than she is.

"I have to go to work," he says against her lips.

"Fine."

"I love you."

"I love you, too." She says it without hesitation because it's the truth.

"I'll see you later," he says, getting up from the bed.

"Later, when?"

"Tonight? We'll figure it out."

"Okay."

"I'm not going anywhere," he says from her bedroom doorway. "You can trust me."

"I trust you," she says. She has no idea if it's true, but she holds on to it anyway.

Nora and Garrett become more obnoxiously obsessed with each other as the day goes on. He calls her at lunch. He brings a bouquet of flowers and a bottle of wine (without a unicycling skeleton on the label) to her house after work. Everything is right. Everything is settled.

Nora wakes up on Saturday morning to the sound of Garrett breathing in her ear. She rolls over to face him and feels him stir as their bodies fit together. He grabs her hips and shifts her on top of him. His eyes are barely open, but she can tell he's waiting for her to take the lead. Taking the lead in bed has always given Nora anxiety, because she figures it's likely that she's doing something wrong—or, at least, not as good as she could be doing it. She's not hot enough or bold enough or anything enough. Garrett senses her hesitation.

"Is this okay?" he asks in a sleepy voice.

"Is it okay for you?"

He smiles. "I'd say so."

She leans down to kiss him, and he rolls her over so that he's looking down at her.

"You're beautiful," he says. He kisses her again, so she doesn't have to come up with a response.

Nora is getting ready at her sink when Garrett appears in the bathroom doorway.

"Do you have plans today?" he asks.

"Yeah, I have to go to a work thing. The services for Ethan start at two, and I want to get there early to make sure things go okay."

"Do you want me to go with you?"

She concentrates on her mascara. "You don't have to do that. I'm sure you have something better to do."

"That's not what I asked," he says, crossing his arms like he means business.

"I'm going with my grandpa. It's fine. Really."

"Okay, I won't push."

She shoos him out and closes the door, so that she can change into one of her standard funeral dresses in peace. When she opens the door, he's still standing there with his arms crossed.

"When do I get to meet your grandpa?" he asks.

Nora laughs, brushing past him to get to her dresser. "I thought you weren't going to push?"

"Well, this is different."

"When do I get to meet *your* family?" she asks. She takes a tangle of jewelry from a dish on her dresser and attempts to retrieve the pearl necklace she wants. Garrett takes the pile out of her hand and starts working on the knot himself.

"I'm glad you asked," he says. "I'm going for my mom's birthday in November, and I want you to come with me."

"To North Carolina?"

He nods but doesn't look up.

"Your mom won't care?"

He smiles. "No. She's on my case every day about meeting you."

"You told your mom about me?"

"Yeah, is that weird?" He holds out his palm with all three necklaces untangled. She takes the pearl necklace and fastens it around her neck, while he puts the other two back in the dish.

"I guess not." Nora wonders what her mom would think of Garrett. For a moment, she imagines introducing them, before remembering that it will never happen.

"She asked if I would send a picture, so she could see what you look like. I told her absolutely not."

She laughs. "You can send her a picture, Garrett. I don't think we have one, but we can take one. You should have just told me."

"She can meet you in person."

"If that's what you want, but make sure she knows that's your decision."

He pulls her close to him. "I wouldn't worry about it. She'll like you."

"You don't know that. Don't start us on the wrong foot." She puts her hand on his cheek and runs her thumb across his stubble.

He kisses her quickly. "Fine. I'll call her right now."

"Now?"

He darts across the room to grab his phone. "Yeah, it'll take five minutes and will get both of you off my case."

Before Nora can show him what being on his case would actually look like, she hears the FaceTime ring followed by his mom's voice.

"Hey, Mom." He stands in the middle of the room with the phone a few inches from his face.

"Hi, sweetheart. Is everything okay?"

"Yeah, why wouldn't it be?" His brow furrows.

"I'm usually the one calling you."

He rolls his eyes and sits down on the end of Nora's bed. "Well, you've been asking all kinds of questions about Nora—"

"I wouldn't put it that way," she says. "We're all just curious."

"I figured I would call, so you can talk to her yourself."

He glances at Nora to check for her permission, as if she could say no at this point. She lets out a sigh and collects her manners before sitting on the bed next to him.

Garrett adjusts the phone so that Nora and his mom can see each other. Nora could have picked her out of a crowd. She has Garrett's green eyes and his mouth and a very familiar surprised face.

"Mom, this is Nora," Garrett says. "Nora, this is my mom."

"Hi, Mrs. Bishop." She smiles with teeth and tries to summon some of her dad's energetic persona.

"Please call me 'Jo.' I'm glad I'm finally getting to put a face with the name. He talks about you all the time."

Nora raises her eyebrows at Garrett, who's the color of an Alabama jersey. "A normal amount," he says, giving his mother a look Nora's sure she's seen many times before.

"She knows what I mean, Garrett."

Nora smiles at him.

"This was a bad idea," he says.

"No, it wasn't," Nora says, reaching over to place her hand on his leg.

"How did you meet Garrett?"

"I already told you that, Mom," Garrett says.

"Maybe I want to hear it from Nora."

Garrett is tense all over. Nora didn't know he could be nervous.

"I'm happy to tell it," Nora fibs. "I work at a casket company, which I know is strange, but it's the family business. Anyway, it's not the sort of business where people come in to look around, and I guess I didn't hear the bell over the door because all of a sudden, Garrett was standing there at the counter. I never get handsome men in suits wandering in off the street, so I was having a hard time keeping it together."

Garrett's mom laughs, and Nora takes this as a sign that she's doing a decent job.

She continues: "He was looking for directions to the restaurant next door, so I helped him. Then I was eating dinner there with my grandpa that night, and we saw Garrett as he was leaving. Everyone in the restaurant wanted me to chase him down, but I chickened out. I really didn't think he would be interested."

"You never told me that part," Garrett says.

"I was really surprised when he came back the next day. Well, not as surprised as the first time, but you know what I mean."

"You have to come meet the family in person," his mom says. "My birthday is in a couple of months, and I'm not taking no for an answer."

Nora glances at Garrett, but he doesn't meet her eyes.

"I would love to," Nora says, hoping she might mean it later. "You're kind to invite me."

Garrett and his mom say their goodbyes, and Garrett tosses his phone across the bed.

"Was that okay?" Nora asks.

"More than okay." He kisses her with feeling. "Can I drive you to the service? I can come back and pick you up afterward."

"I guess," Nora says. She had almost put it out of her mind. "But you don't have to. I can drive myself."

"I want to," he says.

"You want to drive me to church, then drive all the way to town, and then drive all the way back?"

"Yes."

"Why?"

"I'll do a lot for a pretty girl."

She rolls her eyes.

"I want to take you out afterward. On a real date. Is that so ridiculous?"

"A little bit, but I'll let you do it anyway."

Sometimes Nora forgets that his life is different from hers, but it's pretty evident as she slides into his Mercedes. She had never been in a Mercedes before she met Garrett.

"How do you keep your car so clean?" she asks as he backs out of the driveway.

"I clean it," he says.

The black leather looks brand-new. "You practically live in here. There should be a wrapper or something somewhere." She turns around to examine the backseat; even the floorboards are pristine.

"I don't leave things in here." He reaches his hand across the console, and Nora holds it in both of hers.

"Don't ever look in my car." She thinks of the coffee stains, receipts, wadded-up napkins, and God knows what else piled in her passenger seat. "Unless you want to clean it."

"I'll think about it," he tells her, smiling.

She stares out the window for a minute, thinking back on the conversation she had with Garrett's mother. She turns the words over in her mind. "Can I ask you something?"

"Sure," he says.

"I sort of feel like you called your mom like that so I would agree to go with you to North Carolina."

"That's not a question."

"That's not a no," she says.

"Not completely."

"I would have said yes. I want to meet your family."

He squeezes her hand, and she assumes that's the only response she's going to get. She's not in the mood to push it.

When they pull up to the church, Nora's grandpa and his friends are standing on the sidewalk. She sees them turn to one another, and she knows they're trying to guess who might be in the fancy mystery car.

"Thank you for the ride," she says to Garrett, leaning across the console to kiss him.

"Let me know when I should come back," he says. "Are you sure you don't want me to go in with you?"

Nora has been able to postpone thinking about Ethan, since she's been preoccupied thinking about Garrett. She hopes she can postpone it altogether, but if not, she's not ready for Garrett to have to deal with it. He's already seen her cry this week.

"I'll be fine," she says. "It's part of the job."

"I'm not buying that," Garrett says. "But we can talk later. I love you."

"I love you, too."

When she climbs out of the car, Grandpa raises his eyebrows.

"Well, well, well, look who it is," Joe says as she approaches the group. Joe, Grandpa, and Ed are all wearing black suits. Jean wears a long black skirt with a matching sweater set. Then there's Margaret, who cannot resist a floral-print dress, even at a funeral. If you were to ask her about it, she would point to her pair of black shoes, which is all the black she owns.

"Is that your new boyfriend?" Jean waves at the car as Garrett drives away.

"Lord, she's smiling like a tomcat—of course it's the boyfriend," Joe says.

Her grandpa hugs her more tightly than usual. "How you doin'?"

"I'm fine," she says. "You?"

"Fine, fine."

"You didn't want to introduce us?" Jean asks.

Nora knows she won't let go of the Garrett thing until she responds. "Maybe later," she says. "Maybe not at a funeral."

"Y'all," Margaret begins, "I saw Pamela at the pharmacy this morning, and she looked just awful."

"I can't imagine losing a grandbaby like that," Jean says.

"Ed said the accident was terrible. One of the worst he's ever seen. You could hardly tell it was a car," Margaret says.

Nora realizes that Ed has been quieter than usual. "Did you have to pick it up?" she asks. He drives a wrecker for the county, and he's usually the first to know about car accidents in the area.

Ed nods. "You know, I've seen that car before." He points toward the parking lot. "That Mercedes with the UNC plates."

"You mean Garrett's car?" Nora asks.

"Garrett," Ed says. "That was his name. He was there, too. I heard him talking to the police."

"He was where, honey?" Margaret asks Ed.

"At the accident."

Everyone looks at Nora for an explanation, but she doesn't have one. "What accident?" she asks.

"Ethan's accident," Ed says. "The other night. He was telling the police what he saw, and then he left in that Mercedes."

Margaret leans in to whisper to Nora: "He's taking this one hard, honey."

"I know what I'm saying, Margaret," Ed insists. He ambles away from the group and into the parking lot without another word. This is southern-man code for "I'm feeling feelings."

"Wasn't he gone last week?" Grandpa asks, and for a moment Nora is back in the yard digging up the garden.

"Garrett?" Nora asks, as if he could mean anyone else. "He was out of town for work, but I don't know why he wouldn't mention this to me." Ed disappears in between rows of cars, and part of her wants to chase him down. To demand every tidbit of information he has. Part of her prefers not knowing.

"What does Garrett do?" Jean asks.

"He works in logistics," she says. Her brow wrinkles as she tries to fit the puzzle pieces together in her mind.

"Honey, I wouldn't pay Ed any mind," Margaret says. "Between you, me, and the fence post, he hasn't been himself the past few days."

"So, you think Ed imagined it?" Nora asks. She's seen grief do a lot of strange things, but she doesn't think it made Ed dream up this scenario out of thin air.

"It was dark." Margaret shrugs. "I'm sure it was another silver car. Yesterday, while I was at work, he forgot to turn off the hose and turned our garden into a swamp. He put his ramen noodles on to boil and forgot about those, too, bless his heart. Had to throw out a perfectly good pot when I got home."

"He was probably in shock," Joe says.

"It's been a long week. First this accident and then the tornado. Did you see the pictures of that house near Anniston? Everything blown away but that one closet. Somehow the little boy found his way in there, but he doesn't remember how. His parents are gone. It's the saddest thing."

"Had to be the Lord," Jean says. She looks at Nora over her glasses, "And if *you* go looking for a problem, you're likely to find one."

"Ain't that the truth," Margaret says. "Don't go getting ideas in your head. That Garrett's cute from what I heard."

"I'm hoping for more than cute, Margaret."

"The truth will come out," Grandpa says. Everyone recognizes this as the final word of the conversation.

"I should probably head inside," Nora says. "I want to make sure everything is running smoothly."

"Oh, you better," Margaret says. "Lord knows the Chandlers could use the help."

"They're not that bad off," Jean says.

"Remember my Aunt Ruby's funeral? They didn't reserve enough pews for the family, and I had to sit in the back."

"All of Rabbittown was kin to your Aunt Ruby," Joe says.

"Well, they should have known that," Margaret says.

Margaret is the oldest of eight siblings, and Aunt Ruby was one of ten. They all lined up with their spouses and kids and grandkids at the front of the church, and it took forever for everyone to get through the line. The service started an hour and a half late. All because Johnny Chandler was too scared to tell Margaret it was immediate family only. To be fair, Nora is scared of her, too, but she would never admit that.

"I'll see you all inside," Nora says.

She walks up the church stairs and straight into Johnny Chandler.

"Nora Clanton," he says in lieu of an actual greeting. He runs a hand through his curls, which are a little more unruly than usual. She would wait for him to use the manners his mother taught him, but she's not sure any of the Chandlers hold manners in high regard.

"Hi, Johnny. How's it going?" She gestures to the sanctuary behind him, where she assumes the family is having a few private moments before the service.

"Run of the mill," he says with a shrug.

She tries not to scoff, but it happens anyway. "Run of the mill" is not what she wants to hear when the situation involves people she cares about. She steps past him toward the closed doors. "Excuse me."

"Where are you going?"

"To check on the family, since you don't seem to care."

He steps in front of her, and she gets a whiff of his expensive cologne. "No, you're not."

"Yes, I am," she says. "Move."

"This isn't your job, Clanton. You got your cash for that piece of tin in there, so you can go home."

"If you were any good at your job, I wouldn't have to come in here." She slides past him and into the room.

"Nora!" he whisper-shouts, but he's not in charge of her.

Nora sits in a pew toward the middle of the room, watching the proceedings, until Ethan's uncle notices her and invites her to the front. She tries not to intrude, but no one keeps a go bag for funeral services, and families usually need things if they're going to be on their feet receiving guests for hours. In the past, she's brought in water bottles, ordered lunch deliveries for people who needed to be reminded to eat, retrieved sweaters from cars, entertained restless kids, and done almost anything else imaginable. Her mom always said you can't help with the grieving, but you can help with everything else.

She's enveloped in hugs from everyone in the family, and Ethan's mom brings her up to the casket to say goodbye. The funeral home did a good job with him, but she doesn't intend to tell Johnny that.

After walking them through the plans for the rest of the afternoon (Johnny's job, not hers), Nora reminds them to eat a snack, drink water, and take whatever pills need to be taken.

She sees Johnny step into the room, and he gestures to his watch before propping the doors open to let the line start moving.

Once the visitation is flowing smoothly, Nora joins Johnny in the back of the room.

"I don't need your help, you know," he says.

"Looked like you did."

He shakes his head. "I have to say, as much as it annoys me, you really aren't bad at all this."

"Wow, is that a compliment?" she asks.

"Something like it."

"I'm going to go find my grandpa," she says. "I think you can handle it from here."

"You're going to let me do my job? What a treat."

Johnny smiles at her before she goes, and she almost thinks they could be friends. Almost.

Once she makes it through the visitation line and takes her seat for the service, her mind starts to wander. First, it's the memories of her parents' service. She stood with her grandpa where the Sandersons are now, the two of them more exhausted than they'd ever been, listening to all of Rabbittown try to come up with the right thing to say, when everyone was too shocked to make much sense at all.

Garrett keeps popping into her mind. She tries to concentrate on the service, but she can't keep the thoughts out. She knows that her grandpa is right. The truth will come out. If there's anything to know about Garrett, she'll figure it out eventually. In the most likely scenario, Ed is just confused. It was dark. He saw a similar man in a similar car. In the worst-case scenario, Garrett was at the scene of Ethan's wreck but then pretended he didn't know anything about it when Nora brought it up. If he helped at the scene of an accident, why would he want to hide that? Why would he lie about it?

After the service, she stands next to her grandpa outside on the sidewalk. Neither of them says anything, but they both know they're thinking about a couple of patches of grass down at the cemetery. It's sort of the state of her life that she's almost numb to funerals, but numbness is not an adequate substitute for feelings. There's that page in cookbooks that tells you what to do if you need to replace the milk or oil or eggs or anything else you might need for a recipe, but no amount of numbness can replace the feelings you're supposed to have. You'll always come up short, and your cake will never rise.

"You look a thousand miles away," Grandpa says.

Instead of harping on about the same sadness they're always harping on about, she starts on another subject: "I'm trying to decide if I should be mad at Garrett on the off chance Ed is right."

"Take it a step at a time, Eleanora," Grandpa says.

"What would you do? I talked to Garrett about the wreck, and he never said anything about being there. Do you think Ed is lying?" She crosses her arms over her chest, as if that might ease the icky feeling growing there. She wishes she could un-know the whole thing.

"I don't think it would cross Ed's mind to lie about something like that. I know there's more to it, though." He shakes his head. She imagines the puzzle pieces not quite fitting into place in his mind, either.

"What do you think?" she asks. Her fingers drum against the

side of her arm. She could use instructions from an adult right about now. Do this. Say this. Think this.

He shrugs. "Don't matter what I say, really. You're gonna ask your questions, but you can't do all your knowing about a person all at once, Eleanora."

"So, what's your advice?" Her hands jolt out in front of her, demanding an answer they can hold on to.

"Just be easy," he says. "Don't jump all over him as soon as you see him."

"So, you think I'm overreacting?"

He shakes his head. "Not as such. But remember you're not Sherlock Holmes. This is not a murder mystery."

"It might be!"

Grandpa laughs, so she laughs, too. "I knew your mind was running in circles. Give the man a chance to explain himself."

She huffs and crosses her arms again. "Why are you taking up for Garrett? You haven't even met him."

Grandpa stares at her for a moment, as if she's missing something obvious and he's giving her a second to catch up. "I'm taking up for that girl carrying on in the yard a couple of days ago. Let him have enough rope to hang himself."

"That's your advice?" she asks. "Let him hang himself?"

"Most people are capable of doing that without help from anybody else. None of us use the sense we were raised with."

"You know, you probably shouldn't mention a hanging so close to a funeral." Nora rocks back and forth on her feet, hoping the motion will settle the rest of her.

"I'm old. I get a pass," he says. In that moment, he reminds her of her dad. Something about the look in his eye. The crinkle between his eyebrows. Nora wonders if her father would know what to do. If he would give the same advice. She pushes that thought into the ever-growing pile of things she'll never get the answers to.

Everything shifts when Garrett's car drives into the lot, and Nora feels less certain about her doubts from the past couple of hours. She had no doubts when she left the house this morning. He's done everything right. More than right, really. She knows the doubts started in the same place they always start: Why would someone like him be with someone like me? There must be something wrong with him.

Garrett's door opens, and he steps out, presumably to meet Grandpa. He's clean-shaven and dressed in serious date clothes, tucked-in shirt and all. He smiles, and she remembers what it feels like for his mouth to be on hers, and her heart starts to run away with itself.

"Hi," she says casually, as if nothing has ever been wrong. Or that's how she means to say it, but it comes out with the same swoony tone teenagers use when they talk about their crushes.

"Hello," he says. His smile is a little swoony, too.

"This is my grandpa, William Clanton," she says as Garrett joins them on the sidewalk. "Grandpa, this is Garrett."

"Good to meet you, sir," Garrett says while shaking her grandfather's hand. "I'm sorry for your loss." Nora had almost forgotten about the funeral. Self-absorption is the most direct way to move past death.

Grandpa nods his thanks. "When you get to be my age, you see the Lord take a lot of folks, but the young ones are never easy."

"I thought the service went well," she says, trying to give

them both an out. Death's not a great conversation starter, even if it does cut through most of the nonsense.

"Oh yeah, the preacher did a right nice job," Grandpa says. "I could tell Johnny Chandler wasn't too happy with you."

She rolls her eyes and turns to Garrett. "His family runs Chandler Funeral Home in town."

"Johnny ain't got the sense to get in out of the rain, so he's probably lucky you were willing to help," Grandpa says. "I wouldn't want to cross Melanie Sanderson on a good day."

"He hates when I get involved, but I can't not get involved sometimes."

"Somehow that doesn't surprise me," Garrett says.

"What is that supposed to mean?"

"I just mean you like to take care of people." He smiles.

"Eleanora comes from a long line of nosy women," Grandpa says.

"Thanks, Grandpa," she says. "We're going to leave before you start telling stories."

"I'll save those for next time."

"I'd like to hear them," Garrett says.

"I'll think of some good ones. You two get outta here." Grandpa reaches out to hug her, and he adds, so low that only she can hear, "Take your time, Eleanora."

"I will," she says.

The Rolling Stones fill the silence when Garrett starts the car, and he turns down the volume so they can hear themselves think.

"Do you like the Rolling Stones?" she asks.

"You can change it," he says.

"No, I just realized I don't know what kind of music you like."

"Doesn't everyone like the Rolling Stones?"

"I guess," she says. Is he being evasive? She should stop reading so much into everything, because some things are nothings.

"Do you want to talk about it?" Garrett asks, reaching over to take her hand.

"About the funeral?"

"You don't have to if you don't want to."

"It was sad," she says. "Funerals for young people are the worst."

"How do *you* feel about it?"

"I just told you," she says. "It was sad."

"We can talk about something else."

"What do you want me to say?"

He squeezes her hand. "I'm just trying to be here for you."

She holds up their linked hands. "You are here for me."

"You know what I mean, Nora," he says in the tone of an impatient parent.

She takes a deep breath. If she's going to give him a chance, she has to give him a chance. "It reminded me of my parents. When Grandpa and I were the only ones left to stand at the front of the church."

They drive for a few miles in silence while Nora sorts through the thoughts in her head. The truth is, she doesn't know what she's feeling. It's never just one thing. How do you pinpoint it to one or two words? It's like a cocktail—you taste all the ingredients at once, but unless you're an experienced drinker you probably couldn't break it down into its parts. She wants to tell Garrett that she'll get over it and that she's not sad all the time, but it's always there in some capacity. She will never be wholly one thing.

"I wish my life weren't like this," she says. "It seems like I'm always going from one funeral to another. There's death everywhere. Partly the nature of my job, I guess."

"I'm sorry about Ethan," he says. "And about your family. But death is inevitable. A different job wouldn't change that."

"Maybe so," she says. "I just—I want to tell you I won't always be this sad. I'm sorry you're having to deal with it. I'm sorry—"

Garrett squeezes her hand. "I told you, you don't have to apologize for having feelings, Nora."

"I just meant I'm sorry you're always having to listen to them. You shouldn't have to deal with me all the time."

"Well, I want to *deal with you,* so you're going to have to get over it."

"You know what I mean, Garrett."

He nods and looks over at her. "I know exactly what you mean."

He turns next to the car wash where no one would actually get their car washed because it's always crowded with teenagers hanging out in truck beds. He pulls into a spot in front of Dean's, which has the best steak in town but the worst service. The waitresses are known for throwing condiment bottles and silverware across the room to customers. A waitress once told Nora's dad where to find the sweet tea pitcher if he wanted a refill. It doesn't bother Nora because she's used to it, but she needs to warn Garrett.

"Have you been here before?" she asks.

He turns to her. "Don't try to change the subject. I want to talk about this."

"Talk about what?" she asks.

He takes both of her hands into his across the console. "I

don't know who made you feel like you're a burden, but I'm not that person. I want to know everything you're thinking and feeling, if you want to share it with me. It's not too much. I feel lucky you give me the time of day."

"That's the weirdest thing I've ever heard," she says before she can stop herself.

"Which part?"

"You do not want to hear everything that goes on in my head. I don't even want to hear that. At the risk of ruining my chances, you could do better."

He rolls his eyes. "I can't tell if you're fishing for compliments or if you really feel that way. You're beautiful and smart. You're a good person. It's probably too soon for me to say this, but I hate being away from you. Even just this afternoon, I wanted to know what you were doing."

Nora's cheeks redden. "You could have come with me."

"I didn't think you wanted me to!" Garrett's eyebrows almost reach his hairline for a moment. "Don't change the subject."

"I'm not! I don't even know what the subject is at this point."

"If you want to talk to me about your family, I want to hear it. I don't want to push you, but I want to know, okay? Whatever you're feeling, I want to know."

"All right," she says. "I hear you."

"You don't have to do everything on your own. You don't have to shut me out." He reaches across the console to tuck a piece of hair behind her ear.

"I already said okay. You also told me not to apologize, so I don't know what to say."

"You don't have to say anything," he says. He leans forward to kiss her.

"Actually, I do want to say something. I'm right about you being out of my league."

He leans back with a huff. "How do you figure?"

"Look at you!" she says. "Normally, I'm freaked out by hot people, but somehow you're also a good person. Look at this car! You have a job. You don't seem to have an ounce of baggage."

"I have baggage. Everyone has baggage."

She rolls her eyes. "Whatever you say. You're practically a Disney prince."

"Is that a compliment?"

"It's the truth. There has to be something wrong with you. What is it? I thought you might be bad in bed, but that's not the issue."

He smiles and kisses her hand. "I'm sort of enjoying this progress report."

"That probably means you were good in school, too."

"I got by."

"What are you doing here, Garrett? How did you find me?"

"Luck? God, maybe? I don't know. Why do we have to question it?"

"I question everything."

He laughs. "That's an understatement."

They stare at each other for a moment, both of them smiling like idiots. He sees her. He knows her. He's still here.

"I love you, Nora," he says.

"I love you, too." Nora leans across the console, and they kiss for a while, long enough for her to forget what they were talking about in the first place.

"Should we go inside?" she asks. "Or do you want to keep kissing in the car?"

"I guess we can't do both."

She smiles. "No, we can't."

"This is supposed to be a proper date," he says. "I'm not supposed to be kissing you before dinner."

"I want to be kissed before dinner. And after dinner."

He laughs. "Well, good, because that's what you're going to get."

Garrett meets her in front of the car and wraps his arms around her. "I'm sorry you had a hard day."

She sinks into him. "Thank you. I'm sorry, too."

He takes her hand and leads her to the door.

"Have you been here before?"

"No, I just heard it was the place to go for a steak."

"It is a good steak, but it might be a culture shock."

"'Culture shock'?" he asks, holding the door open for her.

She doesn't have to answer because the restaurant answers for her. If they hadn't walked straight in from outside, she might think they were in a basement. The windows are covered by dark curtains. The carpet is dark. The walls are dark. It still smells like cigarette smoke years after smoking was banned. Everything is laminated, including the hostess's name tag.

"We have a reservation for two under Bishop," Garrett tells her. She holds up a finger and disappears into the dining room. Nora sees a group she went to high school with sitting at the bar; Lord willing, they'll already be too drunk to notice her.

Nora loops an arm around Garrett's waist, and he wraps his around her shoulders. She starts to tell Garrett that she would feel better going home, because he just said he wants to know how she's feeling, but he speaks first.

"How would you feel about eating at home?" he asks. "It's

been a long day, and I'm not sure I can handle whatever is happening at that back table." She looks behind her and sees a banner with penises on either end to celebrate a bachelorette party. The table is covered with neon drinks, and the bride can barely hold her head up.

"I would like that very much. Thank you."

They order their food to go, pick up wine from Winn-Dixie, and eat their steak and baked potatoes at Garrett's dining room table while watching the last quarter of the Alabama football game.

"I know this isn't very romantic," he says. "I wanted to do something nice for you."

She laughs. "I get to watch the end of the game and avoid people I don't want to talk to. That's about as nice as it gets."

He scrapes his fork around the inside of a tiny plastic cup of butter to get the last bit of it onto his potato. "Wait until we go to Raleigh. There are so many places I want to take you."

"I don't need you to take me anywhere," she says. "I don't fit in at fancy places."

"You don't fit in at Dean's, either."

She stabs a piece of steak onto her fork. "It's an acquired taste. Like everything else around here."

"I don't know—I liked you when I saw you," Garrett says, raising his eyebrows.

"I think you were just happy to meet someone who enjoys soap operas as much as you do."

"Yes, your legs on the desk had nothing to do with it."

This time it's Nora's eyebrows that go up.

He raises his hands in defense, still holding his knife and fork. "I'm just telling the truth."

"Can I ask you a serious question?"

"Shoot."

She takes a deep breath and tries to still the apprehension in her chest. "When will you have to leave again? Like permanently."

"Well, I can usually negotiate, but probably two years from now."

"Do you like it here?" she asks.

"I've been in worse places. It's not somewhere I would have chosen myself."

She nods, letting his answer bounce around in her head, trying to figure out if it's what she wanted to hear. It's what she had expected. It's what most people would say. She doesn't know anyone who's spread out a map of the world, weighed the pros and cons of every city, and chosen to move their life to whichever won. Cities are always in context. People are always moving to someone or something that might make their lives easier or better. Rabbittown tugged Nora home, and that was set in motion by whatever ancestor decided to move here in the first place. She has to assume that Garrett feels a similar tug from Raleigh. Or any other town that stays open past nine.

"If you're wondering if I'm going anywhere," Garrett says, "the answer is no. I meant that when I said it."

She lets out the breath she'd been holding when she recognizes this as the answer she wanted to hear, the one that settles into the alarmed spaces of her brain like a security blanket. "That's what I was asking. I guess I could have been more direct."

He reaches across the table and takes her hand. He brings it to his mouth and kisses her palm. "You're stuck with me."

Nora thinks they're finally going to finish that movie on Netflix when they move to the couch after dinner, but she curls into him closer than normal, so that they're touching in every way possible. Garrett brushes his hand up and down her back and through her hair, and she lets herself relax. She lets the tension fall out of her shoulders and snuggles closer to his chest. He brings her hand to his mouth and kisses her palm again and then the inside of her wrist.

"I don't think this movie is as good as everyone thinks it is," he says.

"We're not paying that much attention to it." She tips her head back, so she can kiss the soft skin underneath the side of his jaw.

"I'm more interested in what you're doing right now."

She sits up, so they're nose to nose. "I can move to the chair until the movie is over."

He bands his arms around her waist, holding her in place. "Not happening."

She leans in to kiss him at the same time something in the movie explodes. Nora and Garrett both jump, sending their foreheads crashing into each other.

"Why is your head so hard?" Nora asks, clutching her head.

"I think I might have a concussion," Garrett says, head in his hands. "I really hate this movie."

Nora laughs as Garrett searches the couch for the remote to turn off the television.

"I'm glad you think my concussion is funny."

"You don't have a concussion."

He considers her point. "You are not a doctor."

"I can make the expert assessment that you are not in need of a casket."

"I *will* take your word on that."

"I would be happy to show you some options if you want to be prepared."

"Now you're turning my injury into a business opportunity." He puts his hand over his heart. "That hurts worse than the concussion, Nora."

"Let me see it." She reaches for his head and stares at his pupils, trying to remember how people on TV check for concussions, but his eyes look normal to her. "You're fine."

"You didn't even shine a light in my eyes."

She laughs. "Oh yeah, I forgot."

He laughs, too. "You're not allowed to make any medical decisions for either of us from now on."

"Stop talking," she says, pressing her mouth to his. She kisses him for what she hopes is long enough that he'll forget about his Netflix injury, and she takes it as a sign of success when he grabs her thighs and shifts her to sit on top of him.

When she moves against him, he groans, "Nora, you drive me crazy."

"Will you take me to bed, please?"

"Remind me where that is. I'm concussed."

She laughs and climbs off him. "I'm going to take off my clothes in the other room. Maybe you can figure out what to do from there."

"I'm willing to try."

TEN YEARS AGO

Garrett zones out. He's supposed to be updating his files in the system, but he's distracted by the snow falling outside. Or maybe it's something else entirely. His phone vibrates against his newly assembled IKEA desk.

"How's Minnesota?" his mom asks.

"Cold. It's snowing."

"I don't know about you being up there for the winter. Are you sure you have warm enough clothes?"

"Yes, Mom."

"And the right stuff for your car?"

"I think so." He stands from his desk to pace around the room. The furniture still surprises him, even after a few weeks. He had gotten used to a mostly empty apartment with a mattress on the floor.

"It's seventy degrees here today."

"Did you call to rub that in my face?"

She laughs. "No, I did have a reason for calling. Your dad got a weird email—"

"I already told him he shouldn't open a message if he doesn't know who sent it."

"No, it's not that. It was a receipt for making a payment on one of the loans from your brother's treatment. But he didn't make the payment! Someone else did."

"What do you mean?" He moved to look out the living room window, to feel the cold through the windowpane.

"We don't know. All he can find out is that it came from a PayPal account. I hope someone didn't make a mistake. It was a big payment. Ten thousand dollars."

"Well, if it was a mistake, I think they would have realized that the payment didn't make it to their account. Maybe it was someone from the church."

"Who at church would have that kind of money? Or know what PayPal is? I wouldn't know how to do something like that."

"I don't know, Mom, but I wouldn't worry about it too much. It sounds like someone's trying to do a nice thing." He rests his head against the window.

"That's what your sister said."

"Don't tell her I agreed with her."

His mom laughs. "I won't hold you up. I know you're working. I just had to tell you that."

"Yeah, I have to go. I'll call you later."

"Love you."

"Love you, too."

Garrett exhales, tossing his phone onto the couch. He grabs his wallet from his back pocket and takes out a folded piece of paper with his parents' names at the top. Ten thousand dollars wouldn't make much of a dent, but he would keep trying, no matter where he had to move.

CHAPTER

11

Nora and Garrett shift into a calmer relationship rhythm over the next couple of weeks. He leaves town for work for a few days at a time, and he shows up at Nora's house when he's finished. She doesn't know what to make of it at first. No one is chasing or ghosting or calling at two A.M. Garrett doesn't forget about their plans or when he promised to call or that she exists.

She had spent her early twenties waiting on text messages or calls or attention of any kind from the men she liked, and who had claimed to like her. After dark, the situation was always completely clear, especially after midnight. They liked her so much. They needed to see her again. They made plans for weekends in the future. They had never met anyone like her. Like werewolves, when the sun came back out, these men would revert to the way they were before, as if they couldn't remember what had happened. As if everything they had said or done could be explained away by the presence of the moon.

Then she met Charlie. The connection didn't knock her over, but he did want to hang out with her more than once, and even during daylight hours. He was kind. He was smart. He was funny. They wanted the same things. They were planning a future together before Nora realized it was happening. She spent time with his family, and he spent time with hers. They fell into a comfortable routine over the four years they were together. Nora had no complaints. It was easy. Everything was good. Until it wasn't.

With Garrett, there was no slow build. He had almost quite literally knocked her out of her chair when she first met him. His passion had been clear from the beginning. He wanted to be with her, and he wasn't afraid to show it. He didn't need time to get to know her or to figure it out. He didn't want to date around to consider other options. He wanted her, and she wanted him, too. Sure, it was becoming more routine as time passed, but it was never boring.

He brings her flowers and tiny souvenirs from his travels. They let each other complain about work. He listens to her talk about whatever moderately large animal keeps stomping through her garden at night. She listens to him talk about the fighting couple staying in the room next to his at a hotel in Gardendale. Nora starts buying groceries for healthy people. They cook pasta and grill steaks. She eats vegetables. He finds a trail near Nora's house for early morning runs. She explains that the trail is for hunters, not runners, so he decides to run through the neighborhood instead.

Nora would categorize herself as hesitantly optimistic. In the back of her mind, she fears that something will come along to kill this relationship, that it will die like everything else. But it can be difficult to remember that feeling with all of the flirty love stuff floating around.

Nora invites her grandpa over to have dinner with her and Garrett. She closes the store on time and rushes home to make sure everything will be perfect, or at least won't send anyone to the hospital. Grandpa has enough to deal with without having to worry about her, too, so she will show him that she is the responsible and mentally stable adult he has helped raise her to be. She will do this with barbecue chicken, mashed potatoes, green beans canned by her mother from her own garden, and rolls from a package she found in the back of her freezer.

"It smells good in here," Grandpa says as he walks in the door.

"I told you I knew how to cook," she says.

He's wearing one of his short-sleeved button-up shirts, which might make anyone else look like Dwight Schrute, but Grandpa can pull it off. She gestures toward a chair at the kitchen table; he sits down slowly at first, but he lands in the chair with a thud. He might not be able to get up again. Maybe they should just eat in the kitchen.

"How's the store?" he asks.

"Fine," she says. "It was slow today." She drains the boiling water from the potatoes and adds milk and butter to the pan. The potato masher is buried in the bottom of the utensil drawer, and she has almost decided to use a fork when she finally feels the blue plastic handle and wrestles it out.

"What did you do today?" she asks Grandpa as she starts mashing.

"Tended the garden," he begins. "It was outright hot. Hotter than it should be."

"You're not supposed to be doing that in the heat. You should wait a few days for it to cool off again."

"I did it in the morning," he says. "I spent the afternoon on the phone with your cousin Mavis."

"What did she have to say?" she asks. Technically Mavis is Nora's dad's second cousin, but she lives in Georgia, so they don't ever see her. She's always seemed like an old lady, but Nora has no concept of how old she really is. Mavis is the person with all the family gossip, even though she lives the farthest away.

"Oh, the usual. Her sister has glaucoma. Her kids don't go to church enough. One of them smokes."

"Well, cigarettes aren't the worst thing to happen to a person." Once the potatoes are the right consistency (the moment she is tired of mashing them), she adds salt and pepper. She sticks a teaspoon into the pot for a taste test, and she thinks they're good enough. "Actually, I guess they could turn out to be the worst thing, so I'll take that back."

He shakes his head. "You know what I always told your daddy and what I always told you."

"Don't put anything on fire close to your face," she recites.

"It's bad news every time."

Nora stirs the green beans and removes the chicken from the oven. People in her family have always been really particular about barbecue sauce. Her special blend involves a mixture of sauce from the barbecue stand at the Texaco down the street, hot sauce made by someone at church, and an ever-so-slight spoonful of mayonnaise. She uses a grill brush to apply it liberally to the chicken. She hasn't gone to this much trouble for a meal in a long time. Maybe ever. Maybe the proper southern lady inside her is finally taking charge, or maybe it's something else.

"So, your man is coming over, too?" Grandpa asks.

"Yep," she says. "He should be here any minute."

She digs out the bag of yeast rolls from the freezer and drops a few onto a sheet pan and slides it into the oven. Her mom always said not to look at expiration dates on food in the freezer. Probably bad advice, but she died in a car wreck, not from food poisoning.

"And he's being good to you?" Grandpa asks. He leans back in his chair, and Nora refrains from making a joke to lighten the mood.

"He is. Things are going really well. I am taking your advice."

"I need to go out and look at the garden before it gets dark. See if you've been destroying it again."

"I hope you do go look at it," she says. "I've spent the past couple of weeks trying to clear it out, so it can be usable again."

"Does that mean you're going to start planting?"

"I think so."

He considers this for a moment. "You're staying for a while?"

"Well, yes. I live here. Why are you always trying to get me to leave?" This almost sounds like a joke, but she hears the truth in her own voice.

"I just want you to be happy, Eleanora. That's all. I don't want you moping around for the rest of your life."

"I'm not moping!" She flings a kitchen towel across the counter by accident.

He smiles. "You do have more pep in your step than usual."

"Maybe so," she says. To keep Grandpa from having to move again, she sets the kitchen table with three of everything: forks, knives, plates, glasses. The junk drawer rewards her with just enough brown paper fast-food napkins. She knows that some other people's families have cloth napkins and matching sets of dinnerware, but Nora has never seen the Clantons use anything like that. She was too young to remember when her mom packed up all the china to store in the attic.

"What's this?" Grandpa asks, reaching across the table toward the business card and salt packet that tumbled out with the napkins.

"It's Garrett's business card," she says, handing it to him. "He gave it to me when we met. Don't tell him I put it in the junk drawer."

Grandpa examines it and points to the symbol at the top of the card. "Do you know what this thing is?"

"No, not really. I don't fully understand what he does. Don't tell him that, either."

"Hmm," Grandpa mutters, handing her the business card, which she tosses back into the junk drawer.

"What does that noise mean?"

"Just thinking. Do I need to have the talk with him?"

"What talk?" She sits down next to him to wait on the rolls.

"Well, I don't know. Your daddy's not here. Seems like I should be looking out for you, but I know you're not a kid anymore."

She doesn't usually care for displays of masculine bravado,

but it's sort of nice to have someone around to offer it. In truth, she's not sure how Grandpa plans to protect her if he can't get up from a chair. Her mom's side of the family is the one with all the fancy guns. "You can say whatever you want, as far as I'm concerned, but I don't know that it's necessary."

"I'll try not to embarrass you."

"That's not possible." The sound of a car door out front interrupts them. "I do want your opinion."

The creak of the screen door has her out of her chair and on the way to the door before the knock sounds.

Garrett stands on the front porch holding a bouquet of sunflowers. At first glance, she thinks he came straight from work, but maybe his button-down is tucked into his pants to make a good impression.

"You look nice," she says, taking the flowers from him as he walks through the door.

"So do you," he says. He puts a hand on her waist and leans in to kiss her cheek. "You smell good, too."

"Like chicken?" She cringes.

"Like Nora." He smiles.

"Thank you for the flowers," she says on the way to the kitchen.

"You're welcome. I noticed the others were dying."

"Grandpa, you remember Garrett?" she asks.

She lets them greet each other, while she replaces the dying flowers in the vase on the table.

"This looks good," Garrett says. "Can I do something?" He pretends to assess the food, but he's really examining the damage she's done to the kitchen. None of which is permanent.

"I want to put all of this on the table," she says, pointing to the kitchen table.

"In here?"

She nods.

"Eleanora is worried I can't make it to the dining room," Grandpa says.

She rolls her eyes. "Maybe I just like eating in here."

"Two things can be true at once," Grandpa says.

Garrett laughs under his breath.

"You don't start," she says, handing Garrett a couple of serving spoons.

"I didn't say a word." His smile makes her want to kiss him, but she doesn't. This is one of the few times she and Garrett have been around other people like this, so she's not completely sure how to act.

Grandpa clears his throat, and she looks over to see him pointing at the oven.

"The rolls!" she shouts. When she opens the oven door, nothing is on fire, but the rolls do not look like the photo on the outside of the three-year-old package. "Oh, shoot. They're ruined."

"They're not ruined," Garrett says, leaning over with a spatula to flip one over. "Look, they're fine."

"They're very done," she says. She takes the spatula from Garrett to tap the top of one. The dark brown crust doesn't give.

"Bring them over here," Grandpa announces.

"You can't even see them from there," she says. "You might not want them."

"If it's cooked, I'll eat it. No need to fuss about it."

"I'm sorry," she says, tilting the pan to slide the rolls into her mom's wood-grain bread basket. "I wanted everything to be right."

"Everything is right," Garrett says. He tugs her elbow toward the table. "Let's eat."

"I'll say grace," Grandpa says. Nora concentrates on her breathing while he prays for their family, their friends, the church, the president, and the food on the table before them. Her nerves will settle once they start eating. Or that's what she tells herself.

Garrett takes a piece of chicken and passes the rest across the table to Grandpa. She dollops a pile of mashed potatoes onto her plate, hoping they will at least be edible. Grandpa hands her the plate of traitorous rolls, and for a moment she considers launching them across the room.

"Y'all see the Braves last night?" Grandpa asks.

"We caught the last few innings," Garrett says. "I really thought they were going to pull it out." They had watched the end of the game in bed, and Nora slept through part of it even though she was the one who had turned it on. Garrett had been riveted, watching intently, following the commentary from other fans on Twitter, and reading some of the better jokes to Nora.

"You a Braves fan?" Grandpa asks.

"I'm learning to be," he says.

"Who's your team?"

"I don't really have a baseball team. I'm from North Caro-lina, so I'm more of a basketball fan."

Both of them slice into their chicken, and no one freaks out, so Nora assumes it's done. She samples the mashed potatoes and the green beans, and they taste fine to her. Edible at the very least. Her roll can sit in the green bean juice and rot for all she cares.

Grandpa nods. "Which side are you?"

"UNC," Garrett says. "There's not much choice in my family."

"Those Duke folks are a bit much for me," Grandpa says.

Garrett laughs. "Some might say that about Alabama fans."

"Not in this house," she says, surprising herself. It comes out sharper than necessary, but it releases some of her angst about the situation.

"*I* would never say that," Garrett says. He grins at her in the purest way, and she can feel his joy in the space between them. She lets it seep into her pores, arching an eyebrow as if she could ever be truly irritated at him.

"Shoot," Grandpa says, raking a green bean onto his fork. "You've never watched anything with Eleanora then."

"I'm not that bad!"

"Breaking a window might be crossing a line," he says.

"That was an accident."

Garrett's eyes widen. "I have to hear this story."

"No, you don't," she says.

Grandpa sets his fork down, going into full storyteller mode. "When Eleanora was little, she would come spend weekends at our house. One Saturday, we were watching Alabama play basketball. She had a little basketball with the Alabama A on it," he says, holding his hands out to mimic the grapefruit-size ball. Her dad had bought it for her the year before when they went to a game in Tuscaloosa.

"Next thing you know, the referee called a foul on a player she liked."

"Antoine Pettway," she mumbles.

"Yep," Grandpa agrees. "Foul on Pettway and Eleanora throws a ball through our living room window."

"I bounced it!" she says. "It bounced into the window! I didn't throw it!"

"I can't believe you broke a window," Garrett laughs.

"I'm surprised she didn't break more than that," Grandpa says. "She was rough as any boy I've ever seen. She used to get going as fast as she could down the street with a basketball, and as soon as I would get the words 'Be careful' out of my mouth, she would fall and skin up her whole leg. She'd be fine and back on the move again before I could get off the porch."

"That should have been my cue to stop with the basketball," she says.

"You did fine," Grandpa says, picking up his fork to swirl his potatoes. "More to life than sports, or that's what I tried to tell your daddy."

A silence falls and lingers, and she needs to fill it. She turns to Garrett to say, "I liked math."

She tries to come up with more words: "I was better at math than sports."

"Oh, yes, we went to our share of those competitions, too," Grandpa says without looking up.

"I don't think I know anyone who likes math," Garrett says.

"Yeah, I don't have many friends." She means this as a joke, but no one laughs because it's currently true. "Not a lot of party tricks."

"She won all kinds of trophies and stuff for that brain of hers," Grandpa says. "I'm sure it's all out in the garage."

"I want to see," Garrett says.

"I think that's enough of this conversation," Nora says. "No more stories about me."

"That's fine. I've gotta save some for next time," Grandpa says.

They finish their meal, without any indication of food poisoning. Nora tries to clear the plates, but Garrett does it instead. He piles everything into the sink and covers the food on the stove.

Nora retrieves the box of Klondike bars from the freezer, her grandpa's favorite dessert.

"Now, this is the main event," Grandpa says.

Nora bites into hers, and chocolate and ice cream start to melt onto her hands. Garrett passes her a napkin. Is she the only one thinking of their first date? Her nervousness. The way she had worried about getting ice cream on her hands. The way he kissed her in the parking lot.

"Eleanora says you work in logistics. What does that mean, exactly?" Grandpa asks.

"Well, I take care of moving parts, basically. I make sure things get from one place to another," Garrett says.

That's the same thing he always says, and Nora hasn't been able to get much else out of him, even after all this time.

"I know a little bit about logistics," Grandpa says, a smile creeping onto his face. "You do a lot of traveling?"

"Right now I do. We have clients all over the place. I've also been doing some training, and then I have to hang around to make sure the new guy doesn't mess up. Or new girl, I guess."

"This is the first time I'm hearing about the new girl," Nora says.

He holds in a laugh. "We're not an all-male company. That's probably illegal."

"So, you've been traveling around for weeks at a time with another girl?" She's kidding at first, but maybe there's a reason she doesn't know anything about his job. Maybe it's on purpose.

"Oh, boy," Grandpa says.

Garrett has the gall to smirk right there at the dinner table. "My female co-worker drives herself."

" 'Female co-worker,' " Nora scoffs. "As long as she knows that's all she is. I do come from a long line of rednecks, so I can set her straight."

"She tells the truth there," Grandpa says.

"You don't have anything to worry about," Garrett says. "The redneck stuff sounds interesting, though."

"It ain't for the faint of heart," Grandpa says.

"I'll remember that," Garrett says.

"Well, I think I'm going to head out to catch the game," Grandpa says. "Thanks for having me over." He braces himself against the table to stand.

"You can watch it here," Nora says. She stands to walk him to the door because she knows what his answer will be.

"No, I've got to get home. I've got an early day tomorrow. Good to see you, Garrett." He reaches out his hand, and Garrett returns the handshake.

Nora walks her grandpa to the door. She hugs him before he steps out onto the porch.

"So, what do you think?" she whispers into his ear.

"I think you're gonna be all right."

"That's all you're gonna give me?"

"That's all for tonight."

She closes the door to find Garrett standing in the living room behind her.

"I think he likes you," Nora says.

"I hope so," he says, as he wraps his arms around her waist. "Because I like you."

She rests her palms flat on his chest and stands on her tiptoes to kiss him. She whispers against his lips, "Are you trying to distract me from your traveling companion?"

He sulks. "This isn't worth a conversation, Nora. There's nothing to talk about."

"I trust you," Nora says. She has decided that she means it, for the most part. "I'm just giving you a hard time."

"I would prefer an easy time, if possible."

She laughs. "I'm sure you would. Speaking of, how was work today?"

He deflates and leads her to the couch. "It was fine. I'm just tired."

"Do you want to talk about it?" She leans into him, knowing it might be easier to share his feelings if she isn't staring at him.

"It's not that interesting."

She ignores his assessment. The man thinks basketball games from twenty years ago are interesting. "Was it tiring because you had a lot to do or because what you had to do was difficult?"

He sighs. "I don't know. The first one, I guess."

"Are you a drug dealer?"

"What?" He sits up so he can see her face and determine if she's serious. "Why would you ask that?"

"You won't say anything about your job, so I figure it must be illegal or something."

He laughs. "It's not illegal. I just don't like to talk about it at home. I have to think about it all day."

"That's probably what a drug dealer would say."

"You should have picked a better question, then."

Nora laughs, and Garrett pulls her into him, kissing her mouth, her cheek, then her jaw.

"I know you're trying to change the subject." She winds her arms around to thread her fingers into his hair. "But you're going to have to talk to me eventually."

"And I will. Eventually."

A few days later, instead of sitting around waiting on someone to die, Nora closes the store in the middle of the day to run errands. Nothing in Rabbittown is open after dark, so really, it's necessary. She picks up pasta and wine at Rabbittown Grocery. She also grabs a bag of pepperoni Pizza Rolls to bury in the bottom of the freezer for nights when Garrett is traveling.

She steps into the pharmacy to see if Margaret is around, but Margaret had to go into town for a dentist appointment. The staff tells Nora it was her annual cleaning, because that's what Margaret told them. Really, she broke a crown eating caramel corn from a big tin she got for her birthday from her cousins in Tallahassee, according to Jean.

Nora wanders the aisles, remembering the days when she would leave a hard day of work in Birmingham and spend an hour in CVS. Drugstore products calm her. Maybelline's Great Lash and Dr. Teal's Mineral Soak were waiting in the same familiar places when she would wander down from the store on afternoons after school. Or when she had a hard day at her first job and needed an hour to settle down before putting on a happy face for girls' night and *The Bachelor*.

She stops by the Rabbittown Senior Center because she hasn't seen Mrs. Dooley in a few weeks. Her granddaughter Sharon had been one of Nora's best friends growing up, and they had kept in touch after they both left Rabbittown. Sharon lives with her husband and two kids in Virginia Beach and can't visit often, so Nora looks in on Mrs. Dooley from time to time. She knows Sharon has other family in town to do that, but she would want Sharon to keep an eye on her grandpa if their roles were reversed.

Mrs. Dooley spent her life teaching third grade, and somehow, at ninety-four, she still remembers everyone she taught. Her room is decorated with photographs and artwork from her kids, grandkids, and former students.

"Lord, Eleanora, you look just like your mama," she says, hitting a button that makes the bed rise until she's sitting up.

"How are you, Mrs. Dooley?" Nora asks, leaning down to hug her.

"I feel just fine. You know I'm ninety-four?"

"I knew it was slightly past finger counting."

"Well, I don't feel it. I don't feel a day past sixty. I don't even know why they've got me in here." Mrs. Dooley has had three heart attacks and both knees replaced. She knows why she's in here.

"Maybe you'll get out of here soon." It's not true, but it's what she wants to hear.

Nora shows her all the pictures she can find of Sharon and her sisters on Facebook, plus a video Sharon sent of her kids playing in the yard last week.

"That boy needs a haircut," Mrs. Dooley says, pointing to Sharon's six-year-old, who has shoulder-length brown curls.

"I think he likes it long."

Mrs. Dooley shoots Nora a look, and Nora doesn't have to press for its meaning. "Well, you tell her to give her grandmother a call once in a while. I got a phone in this place, you know."

"I'll remind her."

"How are you doing?" Mrs. Dooley asks conspiratorially, like Nora has secrets to spill.

"Good. I'm still working at the store and hanging out with Grandpa."

"I see him from time to time. Jean and Margaret, too. I hear things."

"What does that mean?" Nora laughs.

Mrs. Dooley leans closer and considers Nora for a moment. "You better get out of this town, girl."

"What if I like it here?"

"You're still young. You don't realize what you're doing."

"What do you mean?" This could be going somewhere worthwhile, or it could be a bout of old-people confusion. Sharon did mention that her grandmother had been more out of it lately, but Nora didn't realize that this could be what she meant.

"You're like one of those criminals on TV who go back to the scene of the crime." She shakes her head as if Nora is the dumbest of them all.

"I don't know what you mean, Mrs. Dooley. What crime?" None of this makes sense to Nora, but she is willing to hear her out.

"Far as I can tell, the bad stuff that happened to you happened around here."

"I don't know about that."

"Well, I do. I'm an old woman, and I know these things. You need to get outta Dodge."

"What am I dodging?"

"Your whole life here is death."

Nora has spent the past year convincing herself that the death in her life feels bigger than it is. That, logically, there are more people alive in her life than people who have died. That she's no different from anyone else. She never thought that the death could be related to geography. That Rabbittown could be cursed. She clears this from her mind with a shake of her head.

"You need to get away from that store, girl. I can feel it. Something's fixin' to start up." Mrs. Dooley leans forward in her bed to examine Nora from head to toe. She pauses on her face and looks into her eyes for a moment too long. "Or maybe it already has."

The remaining bit of Nora's patience seeps out with a deep sigh. She changes the subject. "Here, I brought you something." She hands Mrs. Dooley a plastic bag from the pharmacy, filled with magazines, a couple of paperbacks, and all the junk food she could find that wouldn't break Mrs. Dooley's false teeth.

Her eyes light up. "You're a good one, Eleanora."

"Thanks. Now I have to get back to work. I've got caskets to sell."

"You better visit me again," Mrs. Dooley says. "And tell that granddaughter of mine the same thing."

"I will. You try to stay out of trouble with the nurses."

"No fun in that."

Nora winds through the hallway toward the front door. She's texting Sharon an update when a familiar face appears in front of her. A startled face with raised eyebrows.

"Garrett?"

"What are you doing here?" he asks. He's wearing a gray suit that probably costs more than Nora's entire wardrobe.

Nora lifts her mouth to his out of habit, and he kisses her back, but without his usual warmth. "Are you visiting someone?" She tries to think of someone he would know in this nursing home in Rabbittown, but no one comes to mind. Garrett has never mentioned knowing anyone else in Rabbittown.

Garrett looks past her and down the hall. "I'm here for work. What are you doing here?"

Nora's brain can't make logistics and a nursing home go together. "I was visiting one of my old teachers."

"That's nice of you," he says, without taking his eyes off the hallway behind her.

She turns around, expecting to see something or someone lurking there, but the hallway is empty. "It seems like you're busy. We can talk later."

He looks down at her then. "I'm sorry. I'm distracted. Can I see you tonight?"

"Sure." Between now and then, she can make a list of the one thousand questions she has about his job to ask him one by one.

"I'll come by when I'm done here." He kisses her cheek before disappearing down the hallway.

On the way to her car, Nora's thoughts spin, and she can't make herself go farther than the sidewalk just beyond the front doors of the building. What could logistics have to do with a nursing home? He's mentioned moving parts, but what moves around in nursing homes? Equipment? Patients?

She trusts Garrett, although the less he will tell her about his job, the more she suspects something nefarious. He said his job wasn't illegal, but would he tell her if it were?

Nora knows where she can find the answers to at least some of these questions. Inside the double doors behind her. Garrett wouldn't even have to know she's there. She just needs a minute or two to figure out exactly what he's doing or who he's meeting.

She slips back through the front doors and tiptoes quickly down the hallway, pausing to peek around every corner until she sees the back of Garrett's head as he ducks into a room. Is he meeting with a patient? She slinks down the hall in that direction, unsure if she should slow down or hurry up. Anyone could see her at any moment and ruin the whole thing.

He's in Mrs. Dooley's room. She checks the numbers on the doors to be sure, but it's the same room she left a few minutes ago. Nora gets as close as she can to the edge of the door, until she can hear Mrs. Dooley talking to Garrett. No matter how hard she strains, she can't make out the words. The hum of their voices doesn't tell her anything. What would Mrs. Dooley have to do with logistics?

Nora leans into the outside of the doorframe while they talk, but she still can't decipher anything. The sound of Garrett's voice gets louder, so she steps into the room next door. She turns around to apologize to the patient there, hoping she can convince them not to scream until she figures out what to do next. It's Mrs. Moss, the lady who used to play the organ at church when Nora was little. Nora didn't know she was still alive, but here she is sitting in a leather recliner next to her bed, staring at the television.

"I'm not eatin' till after my stories," she says without breaking her concentration.

"Uh, that sounds good."

Has Nora really learned no spy skills from watching *Alias*? The only thing she can think to do is hide, so she does. Behind Mrs. Moss's open door. Now she can't hear anything. She stares through the gaps between the door hinges, until she sees Garrett leave Mrs. Dooley's room. He moves quickly down the hallway, and Nora sticks her head out in time to watch him slip around the corner toward the front door.

From the other end of the hallway, people are running. Alarms are sounding. She turns to see a group of nurses racing toward her, pulling a cart of equipment. Nora assumes they're coming for her: Mrs. Moss must have hit some secret panic button on her recliner. She opens her mouth to try to explain, but they aren't looking at her at all. They run into Mrs. Dooley's room instead.

Nora steps into the doorway. One of the nurses is hovering over Mrs. Dooley, calling her name and getting no response. A doctor slides past Nora and instructs her to wait outside.

Nora knows they have to do their jobs, but she also knows Mrs. Dooley. By the look on her face, she's not coming back.

CHAPTER

12

Nora drives back to the store without making the decision to do so. She doesn't remember unlocking the door. Flipping the sign from Closed to Open. Starting work again as if the things that made sense this morning still make sense this afternoon.

Garrett is a murderer.

It's basic logic. It's Occam's razor. Sherlock Holmes would agree.

Three people in Nora's life have died since she met him: Frank, Ethan, and Mrs. Dooley.

Garrett was there all three times: with Frank at the restaurant, at the scene of Ethan's accident, and in Mrs. Dooley's room.

Of all the casket companies in all the world, of course a murderer would walk into hers.

He's had numerous opportunities to murder her, too. He always knows where she is. She sleeps next to him. He could easily poison her food or slip something into her glass of wine. He killed Mrs. Dooley in broad daylight, so he doesn't seem scared of being caught.

Did Garrett kill Mrs. Dooley? Nora didn't actually see him do it. She's ninety-five percent sure. The timing could have been a coincidence. Or maybe he didn't kill her directly. Maybe he got her worked up. He confronted her. He revealed a secret. What if he's her long-lost grandson?

General Hospital is getting to Nora's brain, but people in Port Charles get murdered in hospital beds all the time, so maybe it's a good place to start.

The bell over the front door rings as the door swings open, and the time it takes for the person to enter tells her who to expect.

"Hello, Mr. Roy," Nora calls, as the old man plops the front two wheels of his silver walker over the threshold. She would try to help him, but she knows from experience that he'll put up a fight.

Mr. Roy has been old and crotchety for as long as Nora has been alive. He certainly wouldn't let a woman hold the door for him. Mr. Roy believes that women should be confined to the kitchen, even though his wife, Eustice, God rest her patient soul, was in every room of the house while he pretended to be confined to his recliner. She brought him his meals on a tray. She told him when to go to bed. She laid out his clothes for him. After she died, he needed to find a new way to exert his power, which is why he comes to the Square to bother local business owners from time to time.

"Hey there, girl." He's wearing the same denim overalls and

red flannel shirt he wears every time he leaves his house. What's left of his white hair is sticking out all over his head. He squints to see Nora across the room through his thick, metal-framed glasses.

"What can I do for you?" she asks. He doesn't answer. Instead, he uses his walker to make his way to the counter.

He clicks his walker forward, and his feet slide along after it. Click of the walker. Left foot. Right foot.

Click of the walker. Left foot. Right foot.

Nora's boyfriend might be murdering the people of their town, but sure, she has time to wait for the oldest person in Rabbittown to demonstrate his masculinity.

When Mr. Roy finally makes it to the counter, she repeats the question she feels like she asked two days ago: "What can I do for you?"

He takes a second to catch his breath. "I want to see my papers."

"Do you want to change something?"

"I want to see my papers."

Nora didn't bother to refile the hard copies after the last time he came in with the same demand, but she makes a show of opening a drawer in the filing cabinet and searching through folders until she locates his in the front of the drawer. She slides the folder across the counter, and he stretches his neck out to see it.

He sorted all of this out with Nora's parents, but he still comes in and drags his middle finger across every word of every page, particularly the part that specifies where he wants to be buried. Even if the hard copy disintegrates, the copy stored in the cloud disappears, and the same thing happens at the funeral home and at his lawyer's office, Nora thinks, someone in town will have sense enough to bury him next to his wife under the tombstone labeled JAMES ROY. None of it matters anyway, because this man is over one hundred years old, and he's not going anywhere anytime soon.

Nora's fingers drum on the countertop, and the toe of her right shoe taps out a similar beat on the floor. "They should be the same as the last time you came in, Mr. Roy. I haven't changed anything."

He will believe this once he reads it on the paper copy. Nora needs to find out who at the church is responsible for giving him rides to the Square, so she can tell them to stop. After he leaves here, Mr. Roy is going to click and slide on down to talk to the pharmacy staff about his prescriptions and then to the grocery store to ask questions about the same grocery order he gets every week.

Mr. Roy licks the tip of his thumb and rubs it against the tip of his index finger, so he can flip to the second page of the twenty-year-old file. Nora would prefer this man to be in his recliner rubbing spit on his own belongings. She needs to find Garrett. Or maybe she doesn't. Maybe she needs to find the police station. Maybe she needs to leave town and hope he never finds her.

Mr. Roy makes a clucking noise under his breath as he gets to the part about the burial plot. She's told him before that Rabbittown Casket Company doesn't do the burying.

"You can check all that with the Chandlers," she says. "I can have Johnny call you at home."

He ignores her presence, running his crooked middle finger across the words on the page in front of him.

"Do you have a question?"

Still nothing.

"I think you handled all of this with my dad. He was the one who processed it. The notes in the back are in his handwriting." She hopes that the thought of a male church deacon filling out his forms will assure him.

Before Nora realizes it, she is openly pacing behind the desk. Maybe if she told him it was a matter of life and death, he would click on to his next victim. Actually, since he's made it to one hundred, maybe he has some advice on the situation. If he mentions what she tells him to anyone, no one will believe him.

"Can I ask you something, Mr. Roy?"

He looks up at her for the first time, his light eyes staring through his silver-rimmed glasses. He makes a noise that sounds like "Huh?"

"If I think, but I'm not sure, that my boyfriend might be involved in something he shouldn't be, you know, like breaking a commandment, do you think I should ask him about it?"

Mr. Roy's eyes squint ever so slightly.

"It might be nothing."

He looks down at the file and then back up at her.

"Mr. Roy?"

The bell over the door rings again, and in walks Garrett, looking much the same as he had earlier. Was that just today? He smiles at Nora without reserve, so she knows he doesn't know she knows. She smiles back out of habit, or because it's hard not to smile at the person you love.

"Hi. Mr. Roy and I were just finishing up."

"Take your time," Garrett says.

He smirks at the frustrated look she gives him in return.

"Do you have any questions, Mr. Roy?" Nora asks again.

Mr. Roy turns his head far enough so that he can see Garrett looking at one of the display caskets. He looks back as if waiting for an explanation.

"That's my boyfriend." She is fully prepared to paint him as senile if he refers to anything he shouldn't.

Mr. Roy claps his hand down on top of the file. "This is fine."

"I'm glad to hear it. I'm going to put it back in the cabinet for safekeeping."

"I want to make sure me and Mrs. Roy wind up in the same place."

"You will," she says, holding up the file. "It's all here."

"See, girl, the only thing to do when you're not sure is to get sure." He widens his eyes enough that Nora knows he's not just talking about Eustice.

"Yes, sir. Thank you."

He gives a single nod, signaling that the matter is settled, and then he clicks his walker around in a circle until he's facing the door.

Click of the walker. Left foot. Right foot.

Click of the walker. Left foot. Right foot.

Mr. Roy pauses halfway there to take a deep breath, and Garrett takes a step toward him. She waves her hand to get Garrett's attention and shakes her head to discourage any assistance. Sure enough, Mr. Roy is clicking again in no time. When he's a click or two away from the door, Garrett approaches.

"Let me get that," Garrett says, swinging the door open wide enough for the walker to fit through.

"I can manage, boy."

Once he's gone, Garrett steps back in and asks, "Is he okay by himself like that?"

"He's off to torment someone else. He's fine."

"That was sweet. What he said about his wife. Did he call me 'boy'?"

"He's like one hundred and two, so I wouldn't worry about it. Will you flip the sign?"

He turns the sign to Closed and walks across the store toward her. She still has no plan. She doesn't want to upset him in case he does skew homicidal, so she attempts to go through the usual motions of their greeting. Instead, when he drops his head to kiss her, she hears Mrs. Dooley telling her to run. Nora pulls away as soon as their lips meet.

"What's wrong?" he asks.

"Nothing. What are you doing here?"

"I thought we could go to dinner once you're done."

She takes a step back to organize her thoughts. Should they go to dinner, so she can question him in public?

"You look a million miles away," Garrett says. "What's going on?"

Nora is a terrible actress. No point in trying to put it off.

"I saw you today. At the nursing home."

He hesitates for the briefest of moments, but it's enough.

"I know." He smiles. "We spoke, remember?"

"After that, with Mrs. Dooley. I saw you."

All of the emotion leaves his face, and she takes another step away from him. She doesn't have weapons stashed anywhere, but if she can catch him off guard she might be able to make it to the door. She just needs to get out onto the street to scream for help.

"Nora, whatever you saw, it's not what you think."

He holds his hand out toward her as if she's a stray animal. Like he doesn't want her to do anything rash. It's one thing to know that someone has lied to you, to know you can't trust that person. To feel the hurt and the betrayal. Nora can handle those things fine. She's done it before. She can't handle the not knowing, the confusion, the gray area. She's opened the door, and now she has to walk through it.

"Why don't you explain it to me, then?" She crosses her arms over her chest, the classic body language of an angry girlfriend, but what she feels is beyond anger.

He runs his hand over his face without saying anything.

"If you can't explain what happened with Mrs. Dooley, maybe you can tell me what you did the day we met when you went to see Frank. Or how about the night Ethan died? It was a Tuesday. Do you remember?"

"I was working that night," he says, his face void of any emotion, as if he's reading his lines from a script.

"That *Wednesday*, you came to my house after your work trip, and I told you all about Ethan dying, and you stayed at my house for the first time. Do you remember that?"

"Of course I—"

"When you got to my house that night, I could tell you were upset about something, and you acted like you were just tired from work. I want to know what that was about."

He stands there for a moment, trying to figure out what to say.

"You can't just answer the question about where you were? I'll tell you exactly where I was at any point in time you want to know."

"Why don't you believe I was working?"

"'Working' is not a real answer. What does 'working' mean? What were you doing?"

"I told you already. I had to train a new person in the middle of nowhere. Then I had to stop in with some clients in Huntsville, and then I came to your house. That's it."

"You do see that's not telling me anything, right?"

"I'm trying." His defeated tone breaks Nora's heart a little.

"What do you do for work?" she asks. "Literally, what do you do?"

"I told you, logistics."

"So, what do you do when you meet with a client?"

"We move things from one place to another. That's all."

"Honestly, are you five years old? What sort of 'things' do you move, Garrett? Name one 'thing.'"

He rubs his hand against his temple. "Depends on the client."

"This," Nora says, gesturing to his face. "*This* is what I mean. You're lying to me. I can tell by your face you're hiding something."

"I'm not lying. It's just not simple to explain."

"So, I'm too stupid to understand your job?"

"No! I never said that." His eyes beg her to believe him.

"Then explain it to me. What happened with Mrs. Dooley today?"

"Do you not trust me?"

"Don't piss down my leg and tell me it's raining. Something is going on here. I knew it was too good to be true. I never should have let it get this far."

"Don't say that."

"I think you should go."

"Can we please just talk about this?"

"I gave you a chance to talk, and you didn't take it. This is over."

"Don't say that," he says, taking a step toward her.

"Don't take another step," she says, holding up her hand, as if she could possibly stop him if he really wanted to close the gap, if he really wanted to convince her not to do this. "I just want this to be over. I won't tell anyone anything. Please just leave."

"Are you afraid of me?"

"Yes." Tears pool in her eyes, and a lump rises in her throat.

"I won't hurt you, Nora. You can't think I would do that."

"How could I think anything else?"

"Please just give me five minutes."

Nora makes the mistake of looking at him when he says this. She doesn't want to be involved in any murdery, vigilante bullshit, but she doesn't think she'll be able to sleep again without knowing. Without fully understanding what sort of person he is.

"Five minutes," she says. "If you hesitate one time, I'm finished. The clock is starting."

"Can we sit down?"

She points to one of the chairs in front of her desk and sits across from him in her desk chair. Whatever is coming is not going to be good, and she doesn't want her mind to be clouded by his proximity or by the memories of his skin on hers. He sits down in the chair and wrings his hands for a moment. She can't wait any longer for him to put words together.

"Are you some kind of drug dealer?" she asks.

He seems surprised by the question. "No, I'm not a drug dealer."

"Are you an assassin?"

His mouth drops open. "I'm not doing anything illegal."

"I was with Mrs. Dooley right before you were, and she was fine. Then you went in, and she died. Circumstantial, maybe, but it's not nothing. You need to start talking."

"It's hard to figure out where to start." He takes a deep breath. "First of all, Nora, I meant what I said. I love you. I want a future with you. I never meant to hurt you by keeping this from you, but I hope you'll understand why I did.

"When I was a junior in college, I met a recruiter, and she offered me an internship. I think she must have known about my experience with my brother. I don't know. She said we would be helping real people in a tangible way, and I had been sort of floundering and didn't know what I wanted to do, but when she said that, it just clicked. I couldn't think of anything that sounded better, so I took the offer and moved to Kentucky for the summer. I moved back there after graduation. I've been with the company ever since. It was a lot of travel at first. After a few years, I got transferred to Minnesota. Then a small town in Texas. Then my boss got promoted to a position in Pittsburgh, and she promoted me out of the field to an analyst job there. A couple of months ago, she offered me regional director of logistics for this region, so I moved here."

"You're still not telling me anything tangible."

"I'm trying." He takes a break from wringing his hands to rub his temples. Then he places his hands in his lap and squares his shoulders, his green eyes boring into hers. "I really do work in logistics, but the things that I move from one place to another are human beings. I help human beings get from the living world to the other side."

He clears his throat. "I work for Death."

Nora assumes this is some sort of metaphor, so she waits for him to continue. He doesn't. He's waiting for her to respond. She takes a deep breath as she processes what she just heard. Then she laughs. She can't help it. After a few seconds, she's doubled over laughing in front of a sociopath or psychopath or whatever sort of path would do this.

"I'm not kidding, Nora."

"I don't doubt it," she says through tears. "It's not even surprising that this would happen to me, you know?"

"I swear I'm telling you the truth."

"You can leave now. I don't know if you're having some sort of psychotic break, but I need you to do it somewhere else."

"I swear it's true, and I'll answer whatever you want to know."

"I want to know why you're still here."

He runs his hand through his hair. "I'm ready to answer questions. Ask me."

"Fine. Are you trying to make killing people into some sort of reputable job?"

"I don't kill anyone. I'm just the person who explains that they're dying when they're dying. It's easier if someone is around to guide you through the process."

"And you claim there are more of you?"

"Yes, I work for a global corporation."

"Death? Death is a corporation?"

"I know it sounds crazy—"

"I was with my grandmother when she died, so why didn't I see you? Why doesn't anyone see any of you? Wouldn't Death Helpers be a known fact by now?"

"They do pop up in literature from time to time—"

"Cut the shit, Garrett." Nora gets up from her chair.

"Someone was there when your grandmother died. You just don't remember."

She slams the palm of her hand onto her desk in one of the more dramatic displays of her adult life. "You think I could forget something like that?"

He stands, but he doesn't move any closer. "Death protects itself. It's not that you don't remember, it's that you've been made to forget."

"Like *Men in Black*?"

"The same principle, but no. It's closer to some kind of hypnosis. I'm not sure how it works, science-wise."

"Do you not perform it?"

"Yes, but I'm not a psychologist. Or a neurologist. I just follow the procedure."

She starts to pace around the store, circling the display of caskets. "Explain it, then. Walk me through an example."

"I show up to an appointment."

"An appointment? So, it's scheduled?"

"Yes."

"You know in advance when a person is going to die?"

"Yes."

She stops in front of the brown casket in the middle. "Do you know when I'm going to die?"

"No, I don't have the security clearance to search the database. Only senior directors can do that."

"Senior directors of what? Of Death?"

"Yes."

She continues to walk in circles, as if it might encourage her brain to go into overdrive and understand all of this nonsense.

"I have a scheduler at the main office in North Dakota."

"Death is based in North Dakota?"

"Yes, Dickinson, North Dakota."

"As in Emily? Is that a joke?"

"No. Well, it might be someone's joke, but it's not mine." He shakes his head as if to clear his mind. "Let me finish."

She crosses her arms over her chest.

"I go to the appointments on my calendar. It depends on the situation, but I usually go in and tell the person it's time. Sometimes, they have questions. Sometimes, I just wait with them until it happens."

"Until what happens?"

"Well, I can only communicate with this side of things, so it's hard to say exactly, but the heart slows, and they see, for lack of a better term, a door to the other side, and they go through it."

"That can't be true."

"It is true. I promise. All of this is true." He takes a few steps forward, so she walks around to the other side of the casket in front of her. A few steps closer to the door.

"What about the people who die suddenly?"

"Someone is there with them."

"That cannot be true, Garrett. My parents drove their car into a tree on a backwoods country road. No one was there."

"Someone was there, Nora. Someone is always there."

"Who pays you?" If she's learned anything from TV, she knows that to find the answers, follow the money.

"What do you mean?"

"Who pays your salary?"

"The same people who pay your salary," Garrett says. "Death is an industry."

"Don't try to bring me into this."

"Look at your invoices, Nora. There are fees for everything. Death always gets its cut."

"This is insanity."

"It sounds crazy, but you know me. You know I'm telling the truth." He walks toward her until they have only a dusty brown casket between them.

None of this can be real, but why does it feel like he's telling her the truth? "This is why you were looking for Frank when I met you."

"Yes." His eyes light up.

"You got so weird when I asked you about it when we went to get ice cream."

"I couldn't tell you anything, and I didn't know you yet."

"You needed to know me better so you could lie to me properly?"

"Do you think I could have told you this on our first date? Is that what you would've done?"

Nora thinks back on everything he's said about work. Every place he's claimed to go. The whole relationship spreads out like puzzle pieces in her head, and she starts putting the corners together to force it into the proper shape.

"How do you not get caught? If I knew something was going on, surely someone else must have suspected it."

"Like I said, I don't know the science of it, but I imagine it's like a haze settling in the area, and it becomes pretty easy to convince someone to remember things a certain way."

She knows the answer to this already, but she needs him to say it: "Where were you that Tuesday night?"

He takes a breath before he answers: "I got called in at the last minute to a car wreck. I was with Ethan."

She doesn't know why, but this, after everything, fills her eyes with tears. "You were with him when he died?"

"Yes."

"Was he in pain?"

"No. It happened fast."

"You stayed until the ambulance came?"

He nods. "He wasn't—he had been thrown from the car. It was dark, and I wanted to make sure they found him. I don't know. That's not part of my job, but young people are hard."

"Yeah, they are." She lets out some of the tension she's been holding in all night. "My grandpa's friend saw you there. He drives a tow truck and had to pick up the car."

"I guess I was bound to slip up somewhere."

"Why didn't you erase their memories?"

"I don't like doing it. I didn't think about them being connected to you. I didn't know you knew him until you told me."

"This is Alabama. You should assume everyone is connected until you find out otherwise."

He shrugs, exhaustion plain on his face.

"Why didn't you erase mine?"

"What do you mean?"

"You let me know all of this. About Frank. Running into you

at the nursing home. You could have erased all of it, and I wouldn't have anything to put together."

He shakes his head. "I wouldn't do that to you."

"That doesn't make sense. If you wanted to keep it a secret, you aren't doing a good job."

"Yeah, I've noticed."

"I'm really trying to understand this, Garrett." She leans down to rest her head on her arms on the brown maple casket.

"I know. It's a lot. But I don't want to keep secrets from you. I was always going to tell you. I just didn't know how."

She lifts her head to see him leaning on the other side of the casket, his forehead a few inches from hers. She knows he wants to touch her, and honestly, she wants that, too. It's been a terrible day, and she wants him to tell her everything is going to be fine.

"If you have more questions, I want to answer them," Garrett says. "If not, I have a question for you."

"I have a thousand questions, but you can go first."

"Will you tell me what you're thinking?"

"I don't know whether my boyfriend has serious mental issues or if he's the Grim Reaper."

"A little of both."

She rolls her eyes and takes a few steps away from him.

"I remember what it was like when I got dragged to the middle of nowhere, Kentucky, to have this conversation. I didn't believe it until I saw it."

"Please don't say you want to show me."

"I'm not allowed," he says. "I'm not even allowed to have this conversation."

"Then why are we having it?" Her eyes fill with tears again. "Why are you doing this to me?"

He comes to her then, slowly, and she knows she should tell him no, but she doesn't. He puts his arms around her, and the feelings pour out. Garrett made her think soulmates could be real, and that maybe he could be hers, but what if it's not Garrett? What if it's Death?

"I'm sorry," she says, wiping her eyes. "I don't know what to make of all of this."

"Nora, this is my job. It doesn't have to change things with us. Nothing has to change."

"I think it already has."

He tenses. "What does that mean?"

"I just need to think. Say all of this is true, and you're not having a psychotic break." She gestures at the room full of caskets. "I used to be a normal person with a normal life. Now every day of my life is about death, and you're telling me you're responsible for it."

"You're giving me a little too much credit."

"You walk into a room full of people begging for a miracle, and you end a person's life."

"Everyone dies, Nora. It's how life works." He says this gently, willing her to believe that he's a good person. "I'm there so they don't have to go through it alone. Being there with someone in a moment like that is hard to put into words, but it's important that no one has to go through it on their own, no matter what your family is like or how little or how much money you have. Being able to provide this for people is a gift for them and for me."

"My parents had half their lives left, and someone like you sat next to them and watched as it ended. What kind of job is that?"

"Would you rather someone die alone and scared?"

"I would rather you be a drug dealer."

He takes her face in his hands. "You know you can trust me, Nora."

"I'm trying," she whispers.

"You want me to go?" The pain in his eyes and in his voice almost changes her mind. She wants to get over it. She wants to apologize for doubting him. She wants to forget this ever happened and go back to how they were. She wants to do anything except what she does next.

"Please go."

"I want you to promise you're not shutting me out."

"I need some space right now." They stare at each other for a moment too long, long enough for her heart to break a little more.

She kisses his cheek, and a tear escapes, trickling down her face until she catches it with her knuckle.

He walks toward the door and turns back. "I hate leaving you alone knowing you're upset."

"I'm used to being alone and upset."

"Nora, please. I love you. Don't give up on me."

The bell over the door rings, and he's gone.

CHAPTER
13

When Nora gets home, she unzips her dress and lets it fall to the floor in her bedroom. She puts on one of her dad's old Alabama T-shirts and throws her hair into a bun on top of her head. Scrubbing the smeared makeup and maybe an extra layer of skin from her face is cathartic. She's a professional mourner, and she knows it's more efficient to let her true self and her feelings take over as soon as possible. Her true self drinks wine with no pants on. The feelings will follow.

Nora keeps a Sharpie and a legal pad on her coffee table for occasions such as this.

She settles into her recliner under a blanket. Her wineglass settles onto its coaster. She takes the legal pad and writes "PRO" on one side and "CON" on the other with a line down the middle. Might as well start with the main issue.

CON: More death and dying

This is the crux of it all, isn't it? How would she feel if she were someone else? Death has taken over her life without her consent. It stole her parents. It broke her relationships. It took her job and her future. It made sure that she would spend her days and nights steeping in death itself. Death robbed her of any opportunity for a normal life. A life like everyone else gets.

How can she be with someone who helps Death do this to other people? When Garrett is traveling, and she feels the urge to dig up another garden, she'll know that this, too, is Death. Can she keep Garrett in her life knowing that she's adding more Death? Knowing that she'll be spending her days at the store trying to clean up Garrett's mess?

CON: He might be crazy.

This whole thing is the craziest idea she's ever heard. She doesn't know why she believes him, but she does. She's also been wrong about people before. Is she ready to deal with that scenario? Will she need to be committed because she believes him? How much will that cost and will her insurance cover it?

If his story is true, what kind of person chooses this job? Nora was born into a family with a casket store. Garrett chose to work for Death. What kind of person willingly does that?

CON: The lying

No way around it. He didn't tell her the truth.

CON: More lying

They'll have to tell more lies. She's going to have to explain to Grandpa and his friends that Garrett just happened to be passing through when both Frank and Ethan died. What if they have children? Will they lie to them, too?

CON: The travel

He's always moving. Is she going to relocate across the country for Death? Are they going to break up anyway because she owns a store in Alabama and he needs to be elsewhere to do his job? Doesn't she want him doing this particular job far away from everyone she knows?

CON: The work

Everyone says things are supposed to be easy with the right person. Nothing about this is easy, so how can this be the right person?

Her phone lights up, Garrett's name on the screen. She's debating whether or not she should read it when it lights up again.

I'm home. I love you.

I'm not going anywhere.

PRO: I'm in love with him.

This is the only one she needs to write down.

After a night of tossing and turning and a few too many episodes of *Cheers*, she decides to go for a run. Is she a runner? Not in the traditional sense. All right, not in any sense. She hasn't done more than a leisurely stroll since college, but she needs to do something that involves movement. How hard can it be?

The layer of fog waiting outside her front door almost changes her mind. With Harry Styles blasting through her headphones, she makes it to the end of her street before she has to admit that this is a terrible idea. Maybe walking is fine. Walking is good. Walking takes place outside of her house and away from her laptop. Of course, she had googled the whole thing. She'd waited until she got into bed, which isn't the best idea if you're going to google things like "Death North Dakota" or "Death Dying Logistics." She'd even found Garrett on LinkedIn and stalked some of his connections, but she hadn't turned up anything useful. Everything about Death on the internet was either from medical journals or folklore. There wasn't much in between.

Nora does believe Garrett. She realized this at about two A.M.: he's telling the truth about Death and his job. She doesn't know what it says about her that it took only a couple of hours for her to believe that the world is different than she thought it was. That she has spent so much time thinking and talking about death, and she has no idea how it really works. That there are people in the world walking around with this huge secret.

She doesn't know if the question was ever about believing him. People lie all the time. Other people get over it. The question is if she can get past it. Can she date someone who helps take the people she loves? Can she accept that when he leaves the house every morning, he'll be going to end the lives of real people? Or help end their lives? Does the difference matter?

She knows there are plenty of people in relationships with someone whose job they wouldn't do themselves or don't understand. There are people with high security clearance or doing top-secret experiments who have spouses at home. People marry soldiers, firefighters, and police officers all the time, knowing that their jobs could put them in danger. They get past it. According to Facebook, some of them embrace it. Can she do the same thing?

Nora walks through Rabbittown for a while, even though she shouldn't. No one walks in Rabbittown. Everyone drives. The roads don't even have sidewalks. The sun is rising over the southernmost end of the Appalachians, and she has one of those moments where she remembers that she's lucky to be alive and to be in this place to experience it. This thing with Garrett isn't the worst thing that's ever happened to her, and she keeps coming back to that. She *can* get past a lot of things. She always has. But does she want to?

The church parking lot is empty, so she cuts through on her way to get some advice. She stops to say hello to her grandparents. Her mom's parents are first, and then her dad's mom is a few markers down. Seeing Eleanora Clanton on her nana's tombstone had always been entertaining—freaky at first and now a little funny. Maybe she could request to be buried in the same grave to save money. Maybe they could share the same casket, too. They have a lot to catch up on.

Her parents have a nice view: they're under a dogwood tree and next to the woods, so they're not crowded on all sides. The dew soaks through her leggings when she sits down next to the gravestone.

"Hey, y'all," Nora says aloud. She doesn't know if she has to speak out loud, like in a real conversation, or if they can hear all the crazy inside her head. "I don't know what to do."

She wishes she could see or hear some kind of biblical miracle taking place in front of her, but she doesn't. She's tried it before.

She explains the situation as best she can, but surely wherever they are, they've been watching it play out. Have they been yelling at Nora like she yells at the TV screen when someone on *The Bachelor* is making a stupid decision?

"I love him," she says, once she's finished her summary. "You probably already know that. But what if he's a bad person?"

She waits. She gets nothing but silence. A vehicle pulls up behind her, and she turns to see her grandpa parking his old truck in the driveway. Coffee in hand, he walks past the other cemetery residents until he gets to Nora. This isn't the first time they've run into each other here, and it won't be the last.

"You're up early," he says as he hugs her hello.

"Couldn't sleep."

He nods. "About that boy."

"It's complicated."

"Always is. What do your mama and them say about it?"

"Nothing. As usual."

"Did you ask him all your questions?"

"I did. I couldn't wait."

"That don't surprise me." He smiles. He's wearing a windsuit jacket that he's had since Nora was a little girl and an Alabama hat with the old logo.

"He was there with Ethan," she says simply. She doesn't want to try to explain everything else to someone with a heart condition. They're already standing in a cemetery. "He didn't want to upset me."

Grandpa nods. "I thought that might be the case."

"It's not supposed to be this hard, is it? But it always is for me."

"You're young yet."

"I'm thirty, Grandpa."

"Well, you're just settling down. You never picked a good one until now." He tucks his hand into the front pocket of his pants like this is the simplest thing he's ever said.

"What makes you think Garrett is a good one?"

He shrugs. "I trust you."

She laughs. "You probably shouldn't. I have no idea what I'm doing."

"Now, Eleanora, I was born at night, but it wasn't last night."

"What's that supposed to mean?"

"Use the sense the good Lord gave you." He puts his hand on her shoulder. "This boy's got you staying up all night and talking to gravestones at seven A.M. There's something to it."

"I've finally lost my mind. It's been a long time coming."

"You ain't done it."

"I'm out here asking gravestones for relationship advice. Call it what it is."

"You're just working yourself into a tizzy. Can't nobody tell you what to do. Life doesn't give yes or no answers."

"How did you know, then? With Nana?"

He considers this for a moment, and Nora swears to give up on love if he comes back with an answer from a Nicholas Sparks book. "We didn't know any better than you know. We were kids, but we knew we loved each other, so we just decided."

"You're saying I just need to decide? And that will fix everything?"

"Not until you're ready. But marriage and all that is just deciding you're gonna do it and then doing it every day. God's not gonna call you on the telephone and tell you if you're doing it right. If you want to try, then try."

"What if I don't think it's right?"

"You wouldn't be out here at seven A.M."

She ventures a partial truth: "I'm not sure I'm okay with his job. He's not going to be in Alabama forever, and he's gone all the time. I don't think I want to move around all the time."

"You're putting the cart before the horse. You don't need all these answers right now, but I'll tell you what, you can't hide out in Rabbittown forever."

She rolls her eyes. "I already told you. I'm not hiding. I have a house and a job."

"Those belong to these folks." He gestures at the gravestones in front of them.

"They're mine now."

He shakes his head. "I'm not gonna tell you what to do, but you need to think about having something that's yours. You're just biding your time here until you won't have any left."

"I don't know if you should talk about death in front of dead people."

"What else is there to talk to them about? No new business around here."

The early morning fog has started to lift, and the sun is taking her place in the sky. "What brought you here at seven A.M.?" Nora asks.

"I like to come by early and check on things."

She can't imagine what things an eighty-five-year-old would need to check on in the cemetery, but she doesn't ask. "I guess I can head home now, since none of you will help me."

"I'll give you my two cents, and I think I can speak for the others. You need to get in your car and go talk to that boy. You're not gonna sleep until you do."

"His name is Garrett."

"I'll learn it if he sticks around. Bring him to supper on Tuesday."

"Your house?" Pearl Café hasn't reopened since Frank died, and neither of them is ready to start a new tradition.

"Yep, I'll cook."

"Are we having beanie weenies?"

"I guess you'll find out on Tuesday."

Nora leaves her grandpa to have his own time with the family and starts her walk home. People are always talking about how a walk can cure anything, but Nora is certain they never mention the walk back. By the time she gets home, she looks like she could be next on Garrett's list. She showers off the morning exercise, but there are no highfalutin shower products that can negate a sleepless night of crying.

As she gets dressed, Nora reminds herself of her responsibility in this whole thing. To his credit, Garrett told her something difficult that he didn't have to share. He could have made her forget his whole existence, and he didn't. She doesn't need to overthink the situation. She needs to ask questions, get the answers, and decide. She needs to be logical. She needs to be kind. She needs to hear exactly what he's saying, nothing more and nothing less.

Although a mantra or breathing technique might work for most people, the only thing that helps Nora calm down is country music, but, like, the good kind. Sometimes she wonders if country music was just a ruse to get Garth and Trisha together, because that's about the time the wheels fell off the wagon. Nora remembers when country music used to show you your heart before stomping all over it.

Nora gets in the car, starts her 911 playlist, and is coming out of the "I Can Love You Like That" feelings when she notices she's about to show up at Garrett's apartment unannounced before nine A.M. She'll feel better once they talk things out, but he could be on his own morning run, and she deserves caffeine before a serious conversation. She winds up at Jack's instead.

Jack's is sort of a catchall between six and eleven A.M. because they have the best fast-food breakfast in town. To be fair,

Nora can't think of another place to get breakfast in Anniston besides Cracker Barrel. A lot of people would still rather have Jack's. It's an Alabama institution known for chicken, biscuits, and the regular gathering of retirees having coffee as the sun comes up. The Jack's in Tuscaloosa rescued Nora from hangovers more often than she would care to admit. This Jack's is known for the police officer who stops by every morning to collect biscuit orders for the inmates at the city jail.

Nora places her usual order at the counter: a sausage biscuit with grape jelly, hashbrowns, sweet tea, and a black coffee with a handful of creamer packets. She requests a little plastic container of their fry seasoning salt, which she hasn't done in years because she has been conditioned to believe that that salt is bad for your heart, and real adults worry about stuff like that. At this point, though, who cares? Dying seems unlikely if she's dating the man in charge. How does that work, exactly? Is he immortal?

A group of retirees sit in the back of the restaurant at tables that have been pushed together and cluttered with copies of *The Anniston Star* and Styrofoam coffee cups. They've all turned to listen to a man in an Alabama baseball cap in the middle of the table tell a story about football. It must be something they've heard before, or maybe they were all there, because they take turns correcting the time on the clock or emphasizing details like the unbelievable size of a defensive lineman. Before long, Nora is invested in the story, too. There's something comforting about it, about old folks reliving their glory days. Or maybe it's just the fulfilled expectations. She knew there would be a group of old men drinking coffee in Jack's, because this happens in every Jack's every day. She has always hated surprises. They're usually loud and obnoxious and require immediate and undivided enthrallment. Nora prefers the quiet peace of normalcy that settles in when no one is paying attention.

Once she finishes eating, the anticipation arrives. Maybe it's the double dose of caffeine or the sugar in the sweet tea. But she's nervous. She winds the straw's paper around her finger until it holds a perfect spiral shape on its own. She knows better than to overthink a conversation. It's impossible to account for the other person, no matter how many times you run it through in your head. She keeps reminding herself to be calm. To be patient. This is easier said than done as she sits alone in a red vinyl booth watching cars pull into the drive-thru line and pause at the speaker.

A familiar silver Mercedes drives into the lot and parks in one of the empty spaces. Sure enough, Garrett climbs out. He's dressed in shorts and a Nike T-shirt like he's been running. This is the main breakfast place in town, so it's not completely out of the ordinary that they would both be here at the same time, but maybe it's not a coincidence at all.

Garrett walks in the door and straight to the counter to order. Nora's heart starts its fluttering as soon as she sees him. She wishes she could control it, but she can't. He has his back to her, and she watches his hands and feet fidget like he could start running through the restaurant at any moment. She lets her mind wander to a few places it probably shouldn't wander in Jack's this early in the morning. How is it possible to be unsure about someone's morality and intentions but completely sure that you'd like to get behind closed doors with them?

Nora's mind has taken up residence with Garrett in her bedroom when he turns around with his red plastic tray full of food. He's looking around for a table when he spots her. He hesitates, confused, but she motions him over.

"Hi," he says, holding his tray tightly.

"Hi. Would you like to sit down?" She gestures to the empty seat across from her.

"Uh, sure." He sits down. "I didn't expect to see you here."

"So, you're not stalking me, then?"

He laughs. "No, I decided against it."

"I feel like I should apologize for not waiting." She looks down at her tray of wadded-up papers and napkins.

"That's not necessary. What are you doing here?" He starts to unwrap and arrange his food.

"Breakfast. Same as you."

"Don't you have one of these closer to your house?" He squirts strawberry jelly on his bacon, egg, and cheese biscuit. She doesn't feel great about that move, but the jelly situation is a good way down the list of things that need sorting.

"I didn't really sleep last night. I wanted to talk to you, but I realized how early it was, so I stopped here."

He stares at her while he chews. His eyes are bright green today, like treetops in spring. "Do you really think I slept after last night?"

"You don't usually seem to have trouble."

"I don't usually upset you enough to be sent away."

"Do you really want to talk about this here?" She glances around the restaurant and realizes that no one cares what the two of them might be talking about.

He shrugs. "It might be better this way."

She cocks her head to the side. "How so?"

He takes a drink of his coffee. "I won't be as tempted to touch you."

"Fair point. Do you want to start?"

"You talk. I'll listen."

"Okay." She rubs her hands together to stop them from clamming up. It doesn't work. "I'm sorry I kicked you out."

He shakes his head. "Don't be."

"I needed space to think."

"I know that," he says with his mouth full.

"You're supposed to be listening."

He holds his hands up in surrender.

"I thought about it. I made a pro and con list."

"On your legal pad?" He raises an eyebrow.

She narrows her eyes. "Yes, on my legal pad. I guess the most important thing is that I do love you. I meant it when I said it. I'm still not sure about the rest of it. Nothing about this is normal. You can talk now."

He takes a drink of his coffee first. "I know asking you to understand it is asking a lot."

"Does your family know?"

"It sounds like a boring job, so they've never really asked questions. I haven't had to lie."

"But I would have to lie. That's how this would work, right?"

"No, you could say I work in logistics. That's not a lie."

"I'm not crazy about having to explain this to you, but yes, that is a lie. You're misleading people on purpose."

"Well, you're the first person I've told, and look how well it's going. This hasn't been a problem until now."

"Because you got caught."

"Honestly, yes," he says. "I would have told you, but not like this."

"What were you waiting for? Our wedding night?"

"I thought I might do it at the altar."

"This isn't funny, Garrett. You're sitting here telling me that you were planning to lie to me for as long as you could get away with it. What am I supposed to say?"

He wads up the wrapper from his biscuit until it's a compact ball of papery foil. "I don't know. I don't know what I would say if our roles were reversed."

"Well, our roles aren't reversed. This is where we are. Discussing the future of our relationship at Jack's."

"Do you want to leave?" he asks.

"I want to figure this out."

He sighs. "I don't know what to say, Nora. I want to answer your questions, but this discussion seems to be making it worse."

It's her turn to sigh. "I'm really trying."

He reaches across the table to put his greasy hand over hers. She asks, "Would you ever quit your job?"

"Would it matter at this point if I did?"

"I don't know." She tries to force her scattered thoughts into coherent questions, but she can't seem to grasp their edges and make them behave. "I think I need more time. I don't even know where to start."

They sit in silence, their hands still clasped in the middle of the table. She stares down at her Styrofoam cup. She can't meet his eyes, because she isn't sure what she'll see. Or what she wants to see. Is this the same man she fell in love with? Or someone else entirely?

"What do you mean by 'time'?" he asks.

"I need to process all of this."

He takes a deep breath and shifts in the booth so that he's sitting up straighter. "Does that mean you want to break up?"

Her heart jumps into her throat. "No. But do you want to break up?"

"No, I'm trying to understand what you're asking."

"I just need a couple of days. Then I'll be ready to talk about it." She thinks. She hopes.

"Can I see you again on Friday?"

Her heart falls, even though she's the one asking for time. "Friday seems far away."

He squeezes her hand. "I have to go out of town today. I get back Friday. Trust me, I would rather be with you."

"That was the right thing to say."

He laughs. "I finally got one right."

"Friday works for me."

"I promise I'll tell you whatever you want to know."

"I'll work on a list," she says.

"Bring your legal pad."

"Are you really making fun of me right now?"

"I don't know what I'm doing anymore."

A child shrieks across the restaurant, and Nora and Garrett are surprised to remember they aren't alone. There's a crowd at the register and a line of people out the door. Everyone is trying to get breakfast before Jack's starts serving lunch.

"We should go," Nora says. "Someone else can use this table."

"Yeah, I have to leave soon, and I haven't even unpacked from the last trip."

He follows her out of the restaurant, and they walk to her car, a few spaces over from his.

"I don't know how I missed your car when I pulled in," Garrett says. "Lack of sleep, I guess."

"I was sort of hoping you were stalking me."

"I'll remember that for next time." He takes both of her hands.

She might not understand how to decipher all the thoughts swirling in her head, but she recognizes the feeling in the pit of her stomach and her thundering heart. It's fear. She's afraid to get in the car. Afraid it will change things between them.

"Can you tell me where you're going?" she asks.

"Near Montgomery. I'll tell you whatever you want to know." She nods.

"Am I allowed to hug you?" he asks.

"I could use it."

Garrett pulls her close, and she wraps her arms around his waist and lays her head on his shoulder. She breathes. The pressure in her chest ceases long enough for her to remember that she was happy a few days ago, truly happy.

"I'm sorry, Nora. I wish things weren't this way."

"Me, too."

He pulls back far enough to see her face.

"I'll call you," he says. He kisses her cheek and walks to his car without looking back.

CHAPTER
14

He doesn't call.

Nora wonders. She wanders. She waits.

She goes to work every day and sits at her desk, staring at her phone. At night, she drinks whatever red wine was on sale at Rabbittown Grocery and pretends to watch TV while staring at her phone. Some nights, she cries. Some nights, she gets so angry she can't sit still. She writes texts of all varieties and never sends them.

On Tuesday, she shows up at her grandpa's house in full mope.

He hugs her as she comes through the door, and without another word, he pours two glasses of sweet tea and sits down at his kitchen table.

"Why don't you sit a spell and tell me what's going on?"

She resists the urge to wilt until she's lying on the kitchen floor because it does strike her as a little dramatic.

"Well, I talked to Garrett on Saturday and asked him for some time to think. He said he would call, but I haven't heard from him since. I know he's doing what I asked him to do, and he's giving me space, but it's making me anxious."

"Time's not a bad thing. Can't always say the same for thinking."

"I never should have gone out with him in the first place. I knew it was a mistake."

"He'll call." He stands so slowly that Nora almost reaches out to help him. He opens the oven door, and the smell of Mexican cornbread fills the room. She knows he must have pintos and a ham hock in the Crock-Pot. It's one of the simplest meals on the planet, but it's also one of Nora's favorites.

"You don't know that." She grabs the bowls and spoons and puts them on the counter next to the stove.

"He said he would. You asked for time. Give the boy a chance to sort himself out."

"I don't want to have to give him a chance. I don't want any of this drama."

"Too late for that now, girl."

She watches as he places a piece of cornbread into the bottom of each bowl and then spoons the beans over them. He slides the bowls onto the table and reaches into the fridge for the pepper sauce. He blesses the food, and they dig in.

"How's the store?"

"It's good. I've actually been pretty busy the past few days."

"Anyone we know?"

"No, just people making arrangements ahead of time."

"Always happens after a big funeral, doesn't it?"

She nods. "Oh, I'm going to Birmingham in a few weeks to get that award for Dad."

"I forgot about that. Do you want me to ride with you?" he asks, as if his back could handle the drive to Birmingham and back.

"You don't have to. It's not that big of a deal."

"You've got my number if you change your mind."

After dinner, they take their sweet tea to the back porch. Nora has spent half of her life on her grandparents' back porch. When she was little, she would sit next to her grandmother and name the birds in the yard. Her grandmother had learned from her own grandmother to identify them based on their colors and their calls, and she taught the same ones to Nora. Blue jays. Chickadees. Whip-poor-wills.

They sit opposite each other at the green metal patio table, which has been on the back porch for as long as Nora can remember. Her grandparents used to sit at this table every morning with the sound of their teaspoons clinking against their mugs, dissolving the scoop of instant coffee granules into hot water.

Nora tucks her ankles underneath her chair like she always does. She watches the condensation drip down her glass and onto the table.

Without a word, Grandpa points at a bird perched on the porch railing. A cardinal with its head slightly cocked, sussing out the humans on the porch.

"Joe and Jean asked after you yesterday," Grandpa says.

"She called me earlier today. I need to call her back." Jean will want to know what's going on with Garrett, but Nora has the same question. Why hasn't he called? Why would he say he would call if he wasn't going to call? Is he in trouble at work? Did Death find out he told someone? Is he in some interrogation room with a bright light shining in his face? Or worse? After these thoughts come the other thoughts, the ones about Nora's plain face or frizzy hair. Or the way she talks or the way she kisses. Maybe the sex wasn't as good as she thought. Maybe he didn't want to date someone who had a problem with his job. Maybe he would never call again.

"I think she wants you to help with some kids' thing at church."

"Not like I have other things to do."

"You've gotta snap out of this attitude, Eleanora."

"I'm trying," she says, using the tone of a scolded child.

"You know as well as anybody that the Lord does what he wants to do when he wants to do it. It's not for us to understand."

"Well, I don't like being confused."

"No moping around here. That's your nana's rule, and we stick to it."

The next day, Nora writes Garrett a letter. It starts off innocently enough, but by the end, she's cursed him in every way she can imagine. She rips it up into tiny pieces and puts it down the garbage disposal. She wishes she could forget that anything between them ever happened.

Sadness is terrible, but it's happiness that's the problem. She doesn't lie awake at night thinking about her parents dying. She's remembering her tenth birthday, when they went to see the Braves play. Or the way the house always smelled like her mom's cooking. Or feeling Garrett next to her as she falls asleep.

"When did you talk to him last?" Jean asks the following day when Nora returns her call.

"Saturday morning," she says. "Nothing since then. He left town again for work."

"What exactly did he say before he left?"

Nora can't tell her the whole truth, which reminds her of the problem with this whole thing. She paces a circle around the caskets at the front of the store. "Well, we got into an argument about his job. He works a lot. He's gone a lot. Ed was right about Garrett being at Ethan's accident. He just didn't tell me about it. So, I asked for time to think about things, and he said he would call. He also said he wanted to see me on Friday, but that doesn't seem likely anymore."

"Why isn't it likely?"

"Because that's tomorrow."

"He might call tomorrow."

"He won't," Nora says. She stares out the front window, watching the people on the sidewalk. People who go on about their days without wondering if Death has deathed their boy-friend.

"How do you know he won't call?" Jean asks.

"Why hasn't he called before now? He clearly doesn't care."

She thinks back to Garrett's work trip earlier in their relation-ship. She had moped around then, too. But this is a different brand of mope. Before, she had worried that the absence would show him that he didn't want her around, after all. A clean break. This time is different because of everything they have said to each other. There's nothing clean about it.

"Or he's giving you the space you asked for. Did you think about calling him?"

She had thought about calling and begging him to come back, reminding him what he had said about his feelings for her. She had thought about calling and cursing him out, specifying all the lives he had ruined, including hers.

"Of course I did. I also thought about blocking his phone number and moving to Alaska. I've thought about a lot of things this week."

"Have you thought about being patient?"

"No."

"Maybe you should."

"You're supposed to be on my side."

"Of course I'm on your side, Eleanora." Her tone is gentle. Jean could easily tell Nora that she got exactly what she wanted. Time to think. But she doesn't.

"You think I should call him?"

"If you want to call him. I don't think you'll get anything but heartache if you keep letting your thoughts run off on their own. But I think he'll call. Maybe he needed time, too."

"I think he and I both need to get it together."

"That's one thing we can all agree on."

Garrett calls Nora on Friday at 1:08 P.M.

"Hello?" Nora answers. She's still at the store, and his call interrupted her spinning around in her desk chair to distract her from the clock.

"Hey. Is now a good time?"

Nora narrows her eyes but wills herself to settle down. To play it cool as a corpse. "Yeah, I'm not busy."

"Are you still free tonight?"

"Well, I agreed to a date with you already, so I didn't think I was free." Nora has never played it cool in her life.

"I was just making sure that you . . . that you still want to."

"What's wrong with you?" She stands to add emphasis to whatever comes out of her mouth next, but he can't see her, so maybe the emphasis is for herself.

"What do you mean?"

"Why are you being so weird?"

"I'm not being weird."

"You haven't called me for days, and now that you finally called, you're talking to me like you're trying to make an appointment with your dentist."

He sighs. "I'm sorry. I'm not trying to be weird."

Nora has agonized over this all week, and Garrett pretending that nothing happened is pushing her to her limit. Maybe he's not pretending. Maybe he hasn't thought about Nora at all. "Don't do me any favors, Garrett. If you just want to be finished with all this, we can be finished."

"Why would you think I want to be finished?"

"Because you obviously don't want to talk to me, or you would have called."

"I was giving you time. You asked for it, remember?"

"I also remember you saying you would call."

"This is me calling. The literal definition of the word."

"I'm not in the mood for any nonsense." She can hear him trying not to laugh, but that doesn't make her mean it any less.

"I can tell. We can talk about it tonight. Can I pick you up at the store?"

"I'll be here."

Nora figures the dead can wait a couple of hours for her to go home to get what she needs for her date. By the time closing rolls around, she looks as good as she can possibly look. She has on one of three new dresses she bought from a sketchy online boutique a couple of weeks ago. She's wearing actual makeup. She straightened her frizzy hair. She did all of this at the store, strewing her belongings around the showroom like she owns the place. But she does own the place. So it's fine.

Garrett's Mercedes pulls up in front of the store, and she decides to stand next to her desk, so maybe it wouldn't look like she has been waiting on him. He opens the door, and she notes that he's also decided to look his best. He's wearing a dark gray suit and a maroon tie, and he's holding a bouquet of red roses.

"Hi," he says.

"Hello." She picks up her bag from the desk and approaches him as casually as she can manage. He's handsome. She's weak. It's a perfect storm for her to forget that she's been despairing for days because of him. She stops once she gets a few steps away. He can do the rest.

"You look beautiful." He pushes the bouquet toward her. "These are for you."

"Thank you." She can tell they're expensive. "You didn't have to do this."

"I wanted to."

"I have a vase in the back." He follows her past the desk and into the back room, where she locates a dusty glass vase hiding on one of the shelves. She washes it out in the sink before filling it with water and the bouquet. Then they're both standing there, unsure of what to say.

"So, I made reservations somewhere," he says, finally. "But I can cancel them if you want to do something else."

"What kind of reservations?"

"It's called 'Miller's on Main.' I've never been, but it has good reviews."

He really must be sorry. Miller's is what everyone uses for weddings and fancy old-people anniversary parties. It will be very private because no one else Nora knows would be eating there on a Friday night. "Yeah, the food is great. We can go there."

She follows him out to the car, and they're stuck in silence again. He doesn't turn on the radio. He doesn't reach for her hand. She doesn't reach for his. Why are they even doing this?

"Do you want to talk?" he asks.

"Sure."

"You can start your list of questions."

"I do have a list." She pulls out the Notes app on her phone. She made a few drafts on her legal pad and then moved the final choices over to her phone. "Are you allowed to tell me all of this? Or is this some big secret that's going to get me killed."

He smirks. "It's not going to get you killed. It's not special ops."

"It sort of seems like it if you have the power to erase my memory."

"I wouldn't do that to you. I told you that."

"Maybe you already did."

"If I had done that, you would like me again."

"If I didn't like you, I wouldn't be here."

He reaches across to take her hand and glances over for permission. She laces their fingers together in response. "Next question."

She looks down at her phone. "A lot of people die every day, right? And you help them all? It sounds like a Santa Claus–type job."

"It's a big company."

"Do you have magic reindeer?"

"No reindeer. We contract out the high-volume jobs, which helps."

"Can you dumb that down?"

"It wouldn't make sense to have us in and out of hospitals all day, for example. We have logistics coordinators on staff there."

"That's what they're called?"

"Yes, that's what we're all called."

"And they report to you?"

"The ones in my region do."

"So, if you're not working in hospitals, what do you do?"

"I usually handle the more complex situations."

"What would you call 'complex'?"

"Accidents, usually. That's where the logistics part comes in."

"What if people die at home?"

"There's a whole vertical and specialized training for that, since it can be delicate."

"You went to Frank's house."

He shrugs. "He was a remote one-off, and it made sense in my schedule."

Nora's eyes widen. "Jesus, he was more than a 'remote one-off' to me, Garrett."

"I didn't mean it that way. I'm sorry. That's just how he got on my schedule."

"What was it like, with Frank?"

He looks over at her. "Are you sure you want to know?"

"Wouldn't you want to know?"

"Frank was a pretty easy client."

"Wait, why do you call them 'clients'? That doesn't really make sense."

"We're helping them."

She hopes her look conveys the "are you kidding" that she's feeling.

"We *are* helping them, Nora. I know it's hard to see it that way, but, trust me, it's better that someone is there to at least tell them it's happening."

"Tell me about Frank."

"It was a heart condition. Those are easier than others. Most people aren't surprised to hear they have a heart condition, and once they feel it, they know you're telling the truth."

"Was he in pain?"

"It was fast." This means yes.

"Do you have something specific you say every time?"

"There are scripts. I've been doing the job for so long, I usually say whatever seems best. I tell them they're going to the other side. Most people assume I mean heaven."

"What do you mean?"

"I mean the other side."

"You don't believe in heaven?"

He smiles. "That's a separate conversation, isn't it?"

She accepts his diversion. "So, you just wait until, what, a sign that they're dead?"

"I have a sensor that tells me."

She laughs, despite the dark feeling in the pit of her stomach. "You'll need to explain that."

"I have one right here." He reaches into the center console and pulls out a plastic case with his initials on it. He opens it and extracts a device that looks like an infrared thermometer. It makes a *bloop bloop* sound when he turns it on; then he points it at Nora, and it makes a sad video game sound.

"You're still here," he says. He shows her the screen, which is red except for a number in the center. "That's your heart rate."

"If it can sense my heart rate from over there, why are nurses still using their fingers to check for pulses?"

"I don't need as much accuracy. It's pretty obvious when it happens. You don't need the little green light to tell you."

"So, your assignment has never been wrong? The person always dies when they're supposed to?"

"It's never wrong."

"Who has that list?"

"That's above my pay grade. Above my boss's pay grade. Above her boss's pay grade."

"Who's your boss?"

"Her name is Janine. She's the director in charge of the eastern half of the country."

"Is she in North Dakota?"

"No, our eastern field office is in Kentucky."

"Why are all of your offices in the middle of nowhere?"

He laughs. "Says the girl from Rabbittown. I would think you would understand."

She rolls her eyes. "I guess there's no one to tell your secrets."

"I assume so. Above my pay grade."

The trees passing outside the car window start to disappear as they get closer to town. They're replaced with AT&T stores and Burger Kings and run-down strip malls with nail salons and a TitleMax and the Mexican restaurant that used to be a Shoney's. Nora's dad always gave her a hard time when she wanted to go into town with her friends, as if she were headed into the streets of a big city like Atlanta or D.C. He used to say Anniston was just big enough to get people in trouble. Maybe he meant high cholesterol and loans you can't pay back. Maybe he meant Death.

"That's an easy answer," she says.

"It's the truth."

"Has this always been a thing?"

"Death?"

"People working for Death."

Garrett thinks for a moment. "They're called 'logistics coordinators,' and there are a lot of stories, depending on what you believe. Hermes and Charon in Greek mythology. Azrael in Islam. Saint Michael in Catholicism. Jesus giving Peter the keys to heaven. Elijah and Elisha. I guess you could also say Jesus, in a way. Or maybe God himself was the first example when Moses died.

"I've heard there are really old records in China that might signal the beginning of the business side of things. It's not really something they tell you at orientation. As far as America goes, the Native Americans had their own way, other countries and their settlers had their own ways, and Theodore Roosevelt thought his ranch in North Dakota could be the right place to bring everyone together."

"You're telling me Theodore Roosevelt was part of this? That presidents work for Death?"

"They don't work *for* Death, but it is a huge undertaking happening in their country," he says, smirking at Nora. "No pun intended. Technically, Roosevelt wasn't the president yet, but his mother and his wife had just died on the same day, which made him a likely candidate to want to help other people."

Images of the Grim Reaper in the Oval Office float through her whirring mind. She feels a whole world opening up under this one, with lifetimes of knowledge she could never fully understand. She had been here, missing everything happening around her.

He pulls into a parking space in front of the restaurant, and Nora's nerves show up. She looks down at her dress, unsure if she chose the right one. It's a dark green wrap dress with flutter sleeves that might be a little too short and a little too low-cut for a place like Miller's.

"Are you ready?" he asks.

"Sure," she says, opening the car door.

He meets her on her side of the car and holds out his hand, so she takes it. "You look beautiful. I don't know if I told you that."

"You did, but I don't mind hearing it again."

Once they're inside, the hostess leads them through a mostly empty restaurant to a table in the corner of a back room. The only other people are couples who could be their parents. Miller's has low lighting and soft music, but the décor is not much different from what you would find in a cruise ship dining room. Still, it's as upscale as you can get without going all the way to Birmingham.

"Did you request this table?" she asks once they're alone.

"I asked for something quiet."

"She probably thinks you're ashamed of me. Or that I'm a prostitute."

This is the moment the waiter arrives to explain the specials and take their drink orders. He acts as if he didn't hear her, but all three of them know he did. She holds in her embarrassed laughter while Garrett orders a bottle of wine and whatever appetizer the waiter is trying to sell.

"I'm sorry. I don't get out much," she says, once the waiter has gone back to the kitchen.

Garrett fiddles with his tie, examining it for nonexistent flaws.

"Are you nervous?"

He sits up straighter, letting his tie fall back in place. "Something like that."

They stare at each other until it becomes too much, and Nora can't take the tension anymore. "Tell me about your trip."

He describes the weather, the trip to Montgomery, and the bagels at his less than ideal hotel. The waiter brings the wine and a fried green tomato appetizer. He places a small white plate in front of each of them and fills their glasses. When asked if they're ready to order entrées, Nora and Garrett both answer, "I can be" even though they haven't opened their menus. Nora orders scallops, the first item on the list. Garrett orders the steak.

"Would you like a glass of white wine to go with your scallops?" the waiter asks.

"I'll be fine," Nora answers, handing him the menu. She has too much on her mind to make another decision. She doubts she will notice the taste of anything on her plate anyway.

"What do you do at the hotel at night?" she asks Garrett when they're alone again.

"Work, usually. Watch *Law & Order*." He gestures at the appetizer in front of them, encouraging her to go first.

"Like *actual* work?" She stabs a fried green tomato slice with her fork and drops it on the plate in front of her.

He smiles. "No, like paperwork. I have to write everything up."

"Okay, this I don't get. Feels sort of like a done deal. Why do the details matter?"

He uses his knife to cut his tomato slice in half and then into fourths. "Well, we don't want to get sued."

She laughs. "A dead person can't sue you. Who would sue Death?"

"If you can sue McDonald's, you can sue Death."

"Do you get sued often?"

"Probably. I assume the legal team takes care of it."

"What do you mean 'takes care of it'?"

He tilts his head. "You always jump to dramatic conclusions. I don't work for Tony Soprano."

"Do you hear yourself, or should I repeat it back to you? I'm pretty sure . . ." She glances around to make sure no one is listening to them, and of course no one is listening because they're practically sitting in the alley behind the restaurant. "Your whole job is 'taking care of it.'"

"Fair enough. What did you do this week?"

She thinks back to despairing on the couch. "Nothing interesting."

"It's interesting to me."

She rolls her eyes. "I doubt that."

"Well, talking about my job all night is certainly not interesting."

"Fine. If you want to know, I'll tell you." She takes a large gulp of wine. "I opened the store every day. Rabbittown has been pretty uneventful this week, so I wasn't busy. I had dinner with my grandpa on Tuesday."

"Where did you go?" he asks.

"His house. We haven't ventured out since you took Frank." His eyes widen.

"Am I not allowed to joke about it?"

He holds his hands up in surrender. "You're allowed to do whatever you want."

"You did take my fried okra supplier without any warning."

"We can go to KFC when we leave here."

Her mouth drops open. "KFC? Listen to this accent. Do you really think I am talking about fried okra from a drive-thru?"

"I'll learn how to make it."

"That might be worse."

"Stop deflecting. I want to hear about your week."

"Well, since we're telling each other the truth now, I mostly spent it waiting for you to call, and you never did. I watched TV. I drank wine. That's about it."

He runs his hand over his hair, which she recognizes as a sign of frustration. "I'm sorry."

"Don't be. It's my prerogative to be pathetic."

"You're not pathetic, but you are the one who asked for time. I gave you time."

"You caused this whole situation, Garrett. Don't come at me with that shit."

"You're really mad at me, aren't you?"

"Yes." She's feeling so many things, and one of them is anger. None of this is fair, and most of it is his fault.

Thanks to God or the kitchen staff or a little of both, at that moment the entrées arrive, saving Nora from a righteous tirade. They're supposed to be talking about everything, but she doesn't want to fight about it. There's no point in yelling at each other about the past. She wants to figure out where to go from here.

The waiter slides Nora's plate in front of her on the table. Maybe it was misguided for her to order seafood when the restaurant is six hours from the ocean, but the scallops on her plate are obviously for fancy people. They're stacked perfectly on top of a bed of rice and roasted vegetables, and it looks like someone has used a paintbrush to swipe a red sauce around the edge of the plate. Most of Nora's usual sauces come from tiny plastic tubs. Could someone like her get used to living like this?

"That looks amazing," she says, gesturing to the giant steak on Garrett's plate.

"Yeah, it does, but you're not changing the subject."

She rolls her eyes (again) and turns her attention to her food.

Garrett adds, "I'll wait until you're ready to talk about it."

"What if that never happens?"

He shrugs. "Maybe I'll keep pushing your buttons until you start talking."

She flips a scallop around her plate, trying to pin it down so she can cut it with her knife. "I just don't like this situation. I don't have any control over it."

"You do have control." He cuts into his steak, and red juice runs all over his plate and into his potatoes. He doesn't seem to notice.

"I thought I did until you disappeared for days."

"I swear I had to work." He puts his utensils down and takes her hand, fork and all, so that he has her full attention. "You can't think it was easy for me to leave when things are like this between us?"

Does she really think he was lying about work? No. Does she want him to hurt a bit? Yes. "Seemed easy enough to me."

"It wasn't. I was thinking about you the whole time. I couldn't sleep for thinking about you."

"Will you please eat your food now?"

He huffs his disapproval but goes back to cutting his steak.

She doesn't want to eat in silence, so she thinks of some of the questions from the list. "Do you have meetings?"

He nods. When he finishes chewing he says, "I usually call in from the field."

"Who do you meet with?"

"Depends. I have a one-on-one with Janine every Monday. I have one-on-ones with my direct reports."

"Who are your direct reports?"

"A few district managers. I stop by the district offices a couple of times a year, but it's usually just a phone call."

"They have offices?"

He takes a drink of his wine and points at her meal. "If I have to eat, you have to eat."

She looks down at the two scallops remaining, along with everything else on the plate. "Fine. But answer my question."

"Yes, they have offices. Desks, copy machines, the works. We have local offices that take care of everything in their area and report to the district offices. Then the district offices report to people like me."

"You don't have an office?"

"No, I gave it up when I took this promotion."

"Would you want an office? It seems like that would be a good thing."

He thinks for a moment. "I would probably want to settle down eventually, but I would have to move to one of the main field offices or to North Dakota."

"Probably a dumb question, but that would be a promotion?"

"Yes."

"Is that your goal?"

He puts his fork on his completely empty plate and picks up his wineglass. He swirls the wine around a bit before answering. "I don't know what my goal is. I don't want to move to North Dakota."

Nora laughs. "I can't imagine why not."

"Would you ever move?" he asks.

"Would I leave Rabbittown?"

"Yes."

She thinks of a few flippant responses, but she knows she should be honest tonight of all nights. "Do you mean in general or do you mean with you to North Dakota?"

"Both. Either. I don't know."

She puts down her fork and gives up on whatever is left on the plate. As if he had been lurking in the corner, the waiter appears to clear plates and refill glasses with the wine left in the bottle.

"I do have the store and the house to think about, but it's not a no. North Dakota might be a no, but I've never been there, so I probably shouldn't judge prematurely."

"That's a logical response."

"Sometimes I'm a logical person."

"This is going to sound like a different question than it is, but could we go somewhere to talk? I don't care where."

She smiles because she can't help herself. The feelings haven't gone away. "Yes, to talk. I guess your apartment is closest."

On the way there, she keeps working down the list of questions, and the answers are boring and unhelpful. She wants to get a full sense of the company so she can understand, and Garrett has no problem telling her all about staff meetings and orientation and company picnics. Death seems as dull as any other corporation.

When they get to his apartment, he says, "This might help." He holds up a finger, then gestures to his work bag, lying on the dining room table, and retrieves a packet of papers from it. He rifles through until he finds a large sheet of paper that has been folded to fit into the stack. When he spreads it out, it's an organizational chart bigger than the table. It's the size of a bedsheet. She points at the symbol in the corner, the same one she had seen on his business card.

"What does this mean?"

"It's a logo," Garrett says. "I heard it used to be the staff with two snakes that Hermes carried, but that became too popular in regular culture, so they started using the keys of Hades."

Nora traces the lines from the executives at the top to logistics coordinators, analysts, and administrative assistants at the bottom. There are dotted lines that disappear over the edges of the page, indicating other teams and employees not listed. The font is almost too tiny to read, but she can tell that many of the rectangles have the word "Vacant."

"What happened to these people?"

"They went somewhere else or retired." He points at a section in the middle of the page. "This whole team is new, so they have to hire everybody."

"What do you mean 'went somewhere else'?"

"Got a new job offer."

"So, you wouldn't, like, off them?"

He laughs. "No, Nora."

"How do you list Death on a résumé?"

"Our offices have signs out front with business names other than Death. It depends on where you're located."

"Where do you work after Death?"

"Another Fortune 500 company usually. Airlines, pharma, sometimes the government. A guy who started with me is running for state senator now."

"I thought this was a big secret."

"I bet you don't know what half the companies on that list do. No one does."

She's too fascinated by the map in front of her to go down that rabbit hole. "Wait, what are all these departments? Communications, HR? Why do you need those?"

"Same reason anyone else does."

"Death has Human Resources?"

"Well, yeah. We have to hire new employees. They also handle the disciplinary stuff, like write-ups or sexual harassment or whatever."

"Death has sexual harassment training?"

"I think you're imagining a Grim Reaper convention. We're like every other company in this country: a bunch of old white men at the top making decisions that don't make a lot of sense or affect them in any way, while the rest of us down here"—he gestures to the bottom half of the paper—"wait patiently for them to retire so we can update things."

She nods as she tries to take this in. She also notices that the squares at the top don't have names in them. "What is this?"

"Board of directors. No one knows who they are. You could probably make some accurate guesses, though."

"What do you mean?"

"Well, you're a pretty smart girl who reads the physical newspaper every— Ugh," he grunts when she pokes him in the ribs. "You pay attention to things, and you didn't know the company existed. We must have some friends in high places."

"It doesn't bother you?"

"I don't really think about it."

"You don't care who you're working for?" There's too much happening in her head to keep standing, so she sits down on the couch.

"I like my director and my team. I'm good at the job. The rest of it doesn't really affect me."

"It affects everyone on the planet, Garrett."

He walks across the room to stand in front of her. "I think you know what's really bothering you about this, and it's not the secrets. Can we please talk about it?"

She takes a breath to try and collect her thoughts. "You're right. My problem is with the job itself."

"These people are dying, Nora. You know me. You can't think I go around killing people for a living."

"No one is dying until you get there. That's how you explained it to me. It's not a coincidence, so stop acting like you're just an innocent person stumbling into it."

"I am an innocent person."

"You know for a fact that a person is going to die, and you don't do anything to try to stop it." When it comes out, she knows this is the truth she's been tiptoeing around in her brain.

"I couldn't if I wanted to." His voice is pleading, and he sits down next to her as if his nearness would change her mind. "I don't control death."

"When Frank was dying, you had all day to call a doctor, and you didn't."

"It's not that simple."

"You get a list every day of people dying around you, and you let them."

"You really think I could stop Death? No one can do that. It wouldn't work."

"My problem is that you've never tried. How have you never tried?"

He runs his hand through his hair. "Say I did try. How many do you think I would save before the company realized they were short on deaths? One? Two, tops?"

"I don't know."

"What would that do? They would replace me with someone else and keep going. This is bigger than me."

"'What would that do?'" she repeats, standing up from the couch. "It would save one person! It would save their family and their friends and everyone else who loves them. It could change everything. Multiple people knew my parents were going to die, and not one of them called to say not to get in the car. And you think that's okay."

He stands up next to her. "I have a dead brother, remember? No one can change fate, but at least someone helped him understand what was happening to him."

"Why does it have to be this job? There are so many jobs out there where you could help people."

"I wasn't there when my brother died. Our parents didn't want my sister and me in the room, as if that would make it easier for us. I never forgave myself for not asking more questions so I could understand what was going on. I knew they were keeping something from us, but I also understood that they didn't want me to press it, so I didn't."

"You were a child, Garrett."

"That doesn't change how it feels. I should have been there with him. When Aaron got sick, I started sleeping in his room with him. We would talk about everything. The leukemia, the chemo, whatever movie we had just seen, the funny things our dog would do every day. I should have been there at the end, too.

"My job is not to end someone's life. My job is to make a really hard thing easier. To be a calming presence or someone with the answers or a shoulder to cry on. Whatever they need in that moment when they have to leave everything and everyone behind.

"I didn't get to be with my brother, but I'm glad someone else was. I'm glad this job exists. I'm proud to be part of it, even if it means I have to keep it from the people in my life."

"That feels like an idealistic answer."

"It's the only answer I have."

"Or do they just pay you enough to have that answer?"

He shakes his head and turns away from her.

"Say whatever you want to say to me. Might as well get it out now," she says.

He turns back. "You judge me for taking money from Death when you do the same thing. Your parents did the same thing."

"You don't know anything about my parents. Don't pretend that anything I do is the same as what you do. I sell a box for the bodies you leave lying around. Actually, why doesn't Death just take the bodies, too? Line your pockets with more money."

"I'm not going to apologize for the money. You don't know what my life has been like or my family's life. I help people move on as peacefully as possible, and then I take the money I'm owed for the service. Leukemia treatments weren't cheap. College wasn't cheap. You took over the store for your family, and I do this for mine."

"Do you really think your parents would be fine with that arrangement?"

"I don't need their permission." He pauses for a breath. "This is getting out of hand. I don't want to fight with you." He holds up his hands in surrender and sits back down on the couch.

"What if it were me? You know eventually someone you work with will know I'm dying, and they won't do or say anything to stop it. Is that fine with you?"

"No, I wouldn't be fine if you died, but you can't stop Death, Nora. It doesn't matter what I want. You're going to die anyway. So am I. It's part of life."

She feels her head nodding as she takes in what he's said. She sits next to him on the couch and puts her hand on top of his. "I've spent my whole life around grieving people. I know you said you get used to it, but I guess I haven't. I love you, but I can't be part of this."

He grabs her hand, and she can tell he's not planning to let go. "Please, give me a chance, Nora. Please. I'll change whatever you want. I'll do whatever you want."

Looking into his pleading eyes, Nora knows he's telling the truth. She knows he would change everything for her. She also knows what the answer to her next question will be. "What if you had gotten my grandpa's name over the past couple of months? What would you have done?"

He glances at the floor and back to her, and that's all she needs to see. "I've never been in that position before. I've never thought about it."

"Can you take me home?"

He doesn't protest. As they drive out of the city toward Rabbittown, the lights get fewer and farther between, and eventually they're in the dark except for his headlights.

They don't say anything for a while, until Garrett clears his throat. "I would have told you, Nora. I just had never thought about it. Of course I would have told you."

"We both know that's not true."

"Please, give me a chance. You said you loved me."

His voice breaks her a little more inside. "I do love you. I just can't do this."

"What about more time? Take some time to think about it."

"I don't need time."

"Please, don't say that."

"It's the truth, Garrett."

He doesn't say anything else until he pulls into Nora's driveway. He turns off the car and the lights. "I know you've made up your mind, but I want to say something first."

She nods because she can't speak.

"I heard everything you said, and I respect your decision. But I'm not going anywhere. I know we're supposed to be together. I'll wait as long as I have to wait for you to see it, too."

The tears Nora has been holding in for the last few hours start to fall, and Garrett takes one of her hands and laces their fingers together. She looks up at him and sees the same person she's always seen. The man she's loved since she laid eyes on him. She sees everything with him: marriage, kids, growing old together. She leans forward and kisses his cheek the way she's done so many times before.

"Don't make this any harder," she whispers.

He lets go of her hand and sits back in his seat. "You'll see, and I'll be here when you do."

TWENTY-SEVEN YEARS AGO

Garrett and his sister, Rebecca, wait impatiently in a hospital lobby just beyond the cafeteria. They had been there for hours, and this wasn't the first time. Their brother Aaron spends a lot of time in the hospital, ever since their parents told them he has leukemia. Garrett always knew things were bad with Aaron when they weren't allowed in the hospital room. Usually, they could sit on the bed with him and watch TV. Today, after a few minutes in Aaron's room, their parents had sent him and Rebecca downstairs with their Aunt Heidi. They liked this better than the waiting rooms upstairs, which were somber and had no televisions or windows. The lobby is near the cafeteria and has huge windows where they can watch all of the families coming and going.

They sit in a row of three chairs, Rebecca swinging her feet out into the aisle. "Do you want something to eat?" Aunt Heidi asks.

They shake their heads.

"I want to go up there with Mom," Rebecca says.

"You just have to wait a little while longer. She'll come down and get you." Aunt Heidi has been chewing her fingernails all day, but there is nothing left to chew.

"I want something to drink," Garrett says.

Aunt Heidi perks up. "What do you want? Do you want something, Rebecca?"

"Coke."

"I want a Coke if he's getting a Coke."

"I'll be right back. Stay here, please."

"Yes, ma'am," they say in unison.

Once Aunt Heidi turns the corner, Rebecca asks, "How much longer do you think it will take?"

Garrett shrugs. "We haven't seen them in a long time."

She huffs. "I wanted to go to school today. I had a math test."

"Maybe we can go tomorrow, after Aaron leaves here."

A woman in black sits down in Aunt Heidi's seat. Rebecca is alert and ready to protect her brother from the inevitable kidnapping she has been trained to expect.

"Is Aaron your brother?" the woman asks.

Garrett and Rebecca nod.

"Who are you?" Garrett asks.

Rebecca elbows him. "That's rude."

He tries again: "My name is Garrett. This is Rebecca."

"Hello, Garrett," the woman says, reaching out her hand to shake his. "We're going to be great friends. You'll see."

Rebecca eyes the woman's black suit suspiciously. "How do you know our brother?"

"You can trust me. I'm going to take care of everything."

"What do you mean?" Rebecca asks. But the woman is already leaving before Rebecca can finish the question. They watch her walk around the corner toward the elevators.

"Let's go outside," Garrett says, his Coke and the woman forgotten as soon as he sees two boys racing each other down the sidewalk.

"Aunt Heidi will be mad."

"We'll just go right there," he says, pointing at nothing in particular. "Please?"

Rebecca rolls her eyes, but her parents have specifically asked her not to make a scene in the hospital, so she starts toward the glass doors without a word, and Garrett follows behind.

They head down the sidewalk to a small courtyard surrounded by benches in front of the hospital. He sees a pebble lying in the grass and picks it up to examine it.

Rebecca knocks it out of his hand. "Don't pick stuff up off the ground. That's gross."

"It's just a rock."

He reaches down to pick it up again and show it to her. After she looks it over, he winds up and throws it as hard as he can, over the birdbath in the middle of the courtyard.

"You could have hit someone!" Rebecca says.

"There's no one out here!"

"There could have been!"

In the years to come, Garrett will wonder what he was doing when his brother died. What he was thinking about, or if he knew somehow that something big and terrible was happening.

He won't remember that he and his sister were yelling about a rock they had found and never seen again.

He won't know that anything has happened until later that night. His aunt will drive them to her house, where they'll eat McDonald's and watch TV. His parents will finally come to pick them up, and they'll race to the door only to find different people from the ones they had seen earlier that day. Their parents will take Garrett and Rebecca by the hand and lead them into their aunt's living room and tell them that Aaron will not be coming home.

The next time Garrett sees Aaron, he is in a tiny blue casket. He had left without his toys or his blanket and without giving his older brother the chance to hold his hand and tell him everything would be okay.

CHAPTER
15

Nora spirals. The days run together. She drinks a lot. She cries a lot. She eats a lot of macaroni and cheese. Sometimes she opens the store. Sometimes she sits on her back porch instead. Sometimes she tries the running thing again. This is the worst sort of breakup. Nora could see perfect life right there in front of her, but she couldn't reach it.

She decides to go to church, mostly because she doesn't want her grandpa showing up at her house for a wellness check but also because she feels a little guilty for the Sundays she missed when she was with Garrett. She wears one of her black dresses and a cardigan, along with a swipe of mascara and her hair pulled back into a ponytail.

Her grandpa is helping greet people at the door, so Nora gives him a hug and continues past him without much conversation. She sits down next to Jean in her usual third-row seat.

"Girl, you look like death."

"Thank you," Nora says, flipping through the program. "That's the look I was going for."

"No word from Garrett?" Jean wears a lavender pantsuit to match her lavender nails.

"Nope."

"It's not 1950. Call him yourself if you want to talk to him."

"Who says I want to talk to him?"

"That hairdo. When was the last time you brushed it?"

Nora narrows her eyes. "I'm going to sit somewhere else."

"No, you're not. You wouldn't risk having to talk to someone else."

Nora sighs. She looks around as the choir walks single file down the center aisle, led by Linda in a bright pink dress with bright pink heels to match. She glows from either the pride or the power of leading the First Baptist Church of Rabbittown Choir, or maybe from a little of both.

Nora notices Betty Holt sitting in the back of the sanctuary with her arms crossed, trying to look anywhere else but the choir. "I see Betty is still mad."

"She'll likely die that way," Jean says. She shakes her head. "Linda is enjoying this too much."

As the choir files into the rows of the loft, they take the white binders from their seats and flip to the first song. Linda moves into her position at the front and waits for the pianist to start playing.

"She looks hot, though," Nora whispers to Jean. "That has to be worth something."

"This is church, not a nightclub," Jean says, swatting Nora's leg with her program.

Nora pretends to wince. "Maybe we should turn it into a nightclub."

"Hush."

Nora's grandpa takes the seat next to her, and she forces a smile as the pianist begins to play "Take My Hand, Precious Lord." Why had she chosen to attend a Baptist church today? She should have gone to the megachurch in the city, so she didn't have to hear a word about Death. It would have been all hope and joy and perseverance through troubles.

Through the storm, through the night

Lead me on to the light

Nora makes it to the second verse before she lets herself think about Garrett taking people's hands and leading them home. Is she really going to do this for the rest of her life? Think about Garrett every time anyone mentions death? It's going to be a little annoying, since she sells caskets for a living.

Take my hand, precious Lord

Lead me home

Linda waves her hands in the elegant way that would tell a person with musical talent how to sing this song. Nora has no musical talent, but she gets a little lost in the rhythm of Linda's arms, in the gentleness of their motion. Maybe Linda was just proving a point when she took the job as choir director, but she is made for it.

Nora doesn't know where her mind is when Jean reaches over and places her hand on top of hers.

"It's going to be all right, you know."

"How do you know?"

"Trust an old woman when she tells you something."

Nora smiles. "Whatever you say, Jean."

Sometime the next week, Nora starts going into work more regularly. Eventually, she gets the store back on schedule and decides to throw herself into work for a change. She's heard it helps other people. She organizes the back closet. She picks up some paint samples from Home Depot. She's staring at a wall that she's swiped with four terrible options when the phone rings.

"Rabbittown Casket Company, how can I help you?"

"Hey, this is Johnny."

"What's up?" He's usually calling to give Nora a hard time about something she suggested to a customer. She thinks he would be the happiest person of all if she closed the store and left Rabbittown for good.

"Are you still going to the conference this week?"

She pauses for a moment to think and to remember what week it is. "Uh, yeah. I am. I'm going Wednesday and Thursday."

"Are you staying in Birmingham?"

"Where is this conversation going?" She's not in the habit of sharing personal information with rude people.

"I was calling to see if you wanted to ride together."

"Oh."

"I'm just trying to be nice, Clanton. You can say no."

"Sorry, I'm just surprised." She can't imagine that being in a car with Johnny would be very pleasant, but this is one of those things she knows her parents would have encouraged, and she doesn't think she can say no. "Yes, I am staying in Birmingham, and I would like a ride. Are you offering to drive?"

She can hear his mocking grin through the phone. "I sure ain't calling to beg you for a ride. Will your car even make it to Birmingham?"

"My car will be alive long after all of us are gone."

"Whatever you say. I'll pick you up at your little shop Wednesday morning at seven. Don't be late."

"I'll see if I can manage it."

Nora hadn't thought too much about the conference, mostly because it doesn't involve Garrett or her broken heart. She's sure Johnny has some sort of agenda for wanting to spend time with her, but maybe it will be nice to be around a man who has made his distaste for her existence abundantly clear over the years. She'll already know where she stands and what he means, and she can leave the magnifying glass and decoder ring at home.

Packing for the conference, she remembers why she doesn't go to these things. What professional clothes should she wear to sit in rooms while other people make her feel bad about how she does her job? What notebook should she use to jot down notes that she will likely never look at again? She settles for simplicity: black on black.

Nora pours a glass of wine and lies down on the couch to watch television, but her mind drifts to her dad's award. If he were here to accept it on his own behalf, he would have a whole speech prepared. It would probably start with a joke. It would be self-deprecating. He would manage to take no credit for anything while thanking everyone else individually for everything they do. She doesn't think her dad cared too much about awards, but he did like attention. He would have enjoyed this. They would have gone as a family. Her mom would have packed a bag full of snacks for the car ride, even though it only takes an hour and a half to get there.

Being on a stage is pretty much the worst thing Nora can imagine. Right up there with speaking on someone else's behalf. She figures she should probably jot a few words down, so she doesn't look like a deer in headlights, but she can't imagine the audience will expect much from her. It's not lost on anyone that she's no Billy Clanton.

A dream about Garrett wakes her up at three A.M. on Wednesday, so she is plenty able to get to the store before Johnny. She and her bag sit outside the front door to wait. This gives her just enough time to dissect the dream: Garrett shows up to her house in one of his suits and says everything she needs to hear before it turns into a run-of-the-mill sex dream. She's trying to remember the details when she's interrupted by a honk.

"Let's go, Clanton," Johnny calls through the open window of his truck. He drives what Nora would describe as a big black truck, but it probably has some sort of magical powers that only rich people can access.

"Good morning to you, too," she says as she takes the passenger seat.

"Last chance to back out."

"Just drive."

They make it to the interstate before she decides she can't stand it anymore. "What in God's name is this music?"

"I didn't think Rabbittown would be too good for country."

She starts pushing buttons on the radio before he swats her hand away.

"Hey, my car, my music."

"What if we just turn it off?"

"You want to drive in silence?"

"We could talk. Like normal people."

He glances at her as if she might be trying to trick him into something. "Fine. What would you like to talk about?"

"I don't know," she says. "How's your family?"

"Fine. Next question."

"You could put in a little effort."

He drums his fingers on the steering wheel. "Parents are fine. They're all but retired and spend most of their time at the country club or on vacation."

"How are Missy and Danny?" His younger siblings are both older than Nora, but she used to hear about them from her parents. Danny dated a few of the cheerleaders in Nora's grade at school.

"Missy is good. Lives in Birmingham with her husband and is about to have a baby. Danny is always a wild card. I'm sure you've heard."

Danny got injured playing football in high school and wound up with an addiction to pain pills. "I haven't heard much. My gossip comes from old people at church."

"I think he's doing all right. He's in some sort of halfway house. He has a job."

"That must be a lot to deal with," she says. "I can't imagine."

"It is what it is."

"So, you've got the store to yourself?"

"Just me and the dead folks. Your turn to talk."

She laughs. "Not much to tell. I'm sure whatever you've heard is true."

"I heard you have a new boyfriend. Some dude with a Mercedes."

Is this what it feels like to be stabbed? A sharp pain followed by a dull ache that feels like it will last forever.

"We broke up, so there's not much to tell."

"What happened?"

"We liked each other fine, but all the other stuff got in the way. He travels a lot for work. I live in the boonies."

"I'm sorry."

"It is what it is."

He smirks, and for a brief moment, she understands how he gets so many pretty girls to like him. The curls, the asshole personality, that smirk. Nora figures he has girls in their twenties waiting in line to be the one who can melt his cold heart.

"Do you date a lot?"

"Who would I date?" she asks. "Small-town casket lady doesn't exactly attract most men. If there were any single men around."

"That's what Tinder is for. Or Bumble. I've never seen you on there."

"And you never will."

"So, you have something against all dating, or is it just the apps?"

"I have something against meeting someone like you who pretends to be super interested in everything about me until you get me into bed and then never calls me again."

"You're thinking too hard about it."

"What do you mean?"

"It's just meeting people. You don't need to have an agenda."

"I don't need any more terrible experiences with men, and I'm too old to spend my nights in bars."

"But surely you like to have sex. You can use it for that."

This catches her off guard. "I do like sex. I don't like to have it with strangers."

He nods. "I guess I understand that."

"I doubt you do, but that's okay."

"What's that supposed to mean?"

"Nothing. You just have a reputation for lovin' and leavin', if you will."

He rolls his eyes. "Two sides to every story, Clanton."

Johnny changes lanes to pass an eighteen-wheeler at high speed on a bridge over Logan Martin Lake. Nora didn't expect to fear for her life this soon.

"Well, we've got time. What's your side?"

He takes a deep breath. "Look, sometimes I'm just not interested. Why should I have to pretend to be interested? How long do I have to drag it out?"

Nora thinks about this for a moment.

"I made you mad, didn't I?" he asks.

"I'm just thinking. I feel like the problem is when you pretend you're interested in the beginning. Why do you do that?"

"I am interested in the beginning. She's pretty. She can take a joke. Whatever the case may be. Then we go out, and it's not right."

"So, why do you sleep with her if it's not right?"

"Sometimes it takes the sex for me to realize it's not right."

"Sometimes?"

He smirks. "Sometimes I want to sleep with her, but I don't want to talk to her again. You can't tell me that you've been ready to marry every person you've ever slept with."

"No comment," Nora says.

"All right, I'll put it this way: I bet you've met someone who was attractive enough or fun enough to sleep with, but not all *there* up here." He taps the side of his head with his finger. "I think it's fine if you see the situation for what it is and then move on sooner than later."

"I'll agree with you to a certain extent. I just think it would be easier if you didn't come on so strongly in the beginning. What happened to that last girl? The blond one who used to come to services sometimes. She seemed nice."

He shrugs. "She was nice. She wanted to get married, and I didn't."

"To her or in general?"

"Are you a shrink or something?" he asks with a laugh. "I didn't want to marry *her*. Can we change the subject? Or do you have any other exes you want to talk about?"

"No," she laughs. "We can change the subject. How's work?"

Nora and Johnny spend the rest of the drive talking about work, which isn't the worst thing, since most people would prefer talking about anything *but* her job. Johnny gets it, though. Neither of them has to explain anything. She didn't realize how lucky her parents were to have each other until she was running the store alone.

Signs for the National Funeral Directors Society Annual Conference begin as soon as they enter the parking deck. There are stickers on the ground, giant posters on the walls, and arrows on every surface, pointing to the entrance to the convention center. Nora isn't sure if it's because people who work in the funeral industry need extra help with directions or if the organizers want to encourage the general public to join. All of the signs use the acronym "NFDS," which seems less enticing than the actual conference of funeral directors. Maybe there are people in the world who are interested in joining the world's most boring-sounding cult. Weirder things have happened, particularly to Nora.

The acronyms stop when they step into the convention center. Nora and Johnny walk past six full-size caskets and past the smattering of vendors pushing flyers and business cards into their hands before they even get to the reception desk. They each give their name to the personable women at the desk, and they are handed two MarketingFunerals.com lanyards so they can wear the name tags where everyone can see them.

"Get your ribbons over here," Margie (according to her name tag) says. She leads them down the table to a row of tiny ribbons to attach to their name tags; the bits of cloth denote things like "First-Time Attendee," "Presenter," or "Officer."

"We're good." Johnny ushers Nora in front of him and away from the table. He takes the pamphlets of vendor information she has accumulated and drops them into the first trash can he sees. "I hate these things."

"Why did you come?" Nora asks.

"These are my people, obviously." He gestures to the crowd of sixty-year-old men ahead of them, all holding to-go coffee cups and laughing as if someone has just told the world's best joke.

They manage to find seats for the welcome ceremony pretty quickly, and Nora scans the program for sessions that might be interesting.

"Too bad this isn't online so you could search for 'caskets' and be done with it," Johnny says with his signature smirk.

"I know that's a dig at me, but you're right. It should have been online. For the environment."

"Killing people *and* the environment. When will we be stopped?"

Nora looks around the room the way she always does at these things; as Johnny just pointed out, they're surrounded by old white men. There are a few women and fewer people of color sprinkled through the crowd. Johnny and Nora are two of the youngest people in the room.

"Searching for your next one-night stand?"

She gives him a look. "I don't think anyone here is having any sort of stand tonight."

"People hook up at these things all the time. We'll have to check out the hotel bar later."

Nora doesn't really know how to respond to this, because she knew Johnny was her ride to the conference, but she did not know they would be spending the day together. They've already spoken more words to each other today than they have in their whole lives.

"I might be too tired from all of the festivities."

"I actually think you'll be needing a drink if you attend 'Embalming: Thriving Beyond Surviving.'"

"That's not real," she says.

He points it out in the book. "And here is a panel about decorative urns."

"Maybe you should go to some of these intense ones. 'Five Keys to Facial Reconstruction' or 'Cremation for Dummies.'"

"I should really go to some of these about finance. I don't know shit about all that. And I don't care to."

"I actually know a lot of shit about finance, if you ever want to compare notes. It's the rest of it that I don't know."

"I'm probably going to take you up on that."

"Well, if we can help each other, then we can go ahead and leave. This is useless."

"Nope," Johnny says. "One of us has an award to accept. I'm as shocked as you are that it isn't me."

Nora rolls her eyes.

"Did you write your speech?"

"Do I really have to give a speech?"

He cocks his head to one side. "Hell yeah, you have to give a speech. It's what everyone came for. Give the people what they want, Clanton."

"Speeches are not my thing."

"You're lucky I'm here."

"Since when are you a public speaker?"

"Since I'm the only hope you've got and the most charming person in this room."

"I'm sure," she says.

He leans in to whisper: "Once these people hear you're Billy's daughter, they'll be done for. I'd probably hide that name tag, too, unless you want a fan club."

Nora flips her name tag over. She knows he's probably messing with her, but just in case, she would like to avoid the attention.

The welcome ceremony lasts about thirty minutes longer than needed. They hear from every member of the board of directors. A bald man in a chestnut suit makes a speech to remind the group that the customer is always right. A man with a Santa Claus beard gives a few tips on how to put the "fun" in "funeral." When he suggests that they should play popular music like Usher and Pitbull, Johnny squeezes Nora's arm.

Once they're finally free, they both decide to attend some

marketing workshops. Nora tries to take it seriously, but Johnny mocks everything the instructors suggest.

"Why did you come if you weren't going to listen?" Nora asks after they leave the second workshop and pick up the sandwich boxes provided for lunch. Johnny locates two easy chairs in the hallway so they don't have to make conversation with other people during their break.

"The better question is: Why did I pay money for them to tell me things I already know? That lady didn't have a lick of sense. Maybe I should have put the money for this conference into our marketing budget."

"You should be more open-minded," Nora says, even though he's right in this one instance.

"She legit said to put up signs. Signs. As if anybody at this conference doesn't have a sign."

"Which one are you going to next?" Nora asks, holding the booklet open so he can see the options.

He huffs out some of his frustration. "I need to go to the cremation one, probably."

"I think I'm going to go to the customer relations one."

He scoffs. "You don't need any help with that. You go to the cremation one and take notes for me and let me go to the customer relations one."

"What is that supposed to mean?"

"All I ever hear is how good you are with customers: 'Nora is so sweet.' 'Nora helped us so much.' 'Maybe I should call and ask Nora.'"

"News to me. I'm not that good with people. Maybe I'm just better than you are."

"That's not a surprise to anyone. Okay, time to find out how long to smoke the meat."

"Johnny!"

He stands up. "I'll find you later."

As Nora watches him disappear into the crowd, she tries to wrap her head around the past few months. She never thought any of this could happen. She never thought she would be happy again after she moved home. She never expected to meet Garrett or fall in love. She didn't think she would ever move on. Now she's in some sort of weird friendship with someone who has always hated her. This is probably what those greeting cards mean when they say: "God works in mysterious ways." "Everything happens for a reason." "Make plans and God laughs."

Nora attends a couple of seminars on how to deal with grieving families and decides that Johnny was a little bit right. "Grieving and Spiritual Hygiene" is a tad too woo-woo for her taste. She doesn't think she'll be burning sage or speaking words over a customer anytime soon, but she's glad to hear there are options out there. "Customer Retention in the Funeral Space" provides a few good suggestions on how to follow up with customers, but her parents did that the old-fashioned way—by calling them on the telephone. One perk of a small business is that Nora can reach out to all of her customers directly. Most of the time, she actually cares to find out how they're doing. It's not a ploy for more business. She doesn't need to pay a vendor to set up mailings or email lists. Does anyone really want a postcard from a casket company?

Coming out of the bathroom, she runs into Johnny.

"You look like you've had a rough day," she says. His hair is all over the place, and his whole body droops as if it's slowly melting.

"I didn't realize how boring my job was until I heard these people talking about it."

Nora and Johnny follow the crowd of people, assuming they're all heading toward the exit.

"Johnny Chandler!" someone shouts over the crowd.

"Hey, Larry," Johnny calls, as a short, balding man comes barreling toward him. Johnny reaches out a hand, but Larry pulls him in for a hug instead.

"I better see you at the driving range tomorrow."

"I'll be there. I figured you'd come find me if I didn't sign up."

"You're right about that. It's tradition." When he turns to Nora, she can make out the Prestige logo on his polo shirt. "You can't be here with this guy."

"And yet, here I am," Nora says.

"This is Nora Clanton," Johnny says. "We carpooled."

"Wait, you're Billy's daughter?" His tone is almost accusatory.

"That's me."

"I was so sorry to hear about that. I'm glad to see you here."

"We all are, Larry." Johnny cranes his neck as if looking for someone. "We've actually gotta go meet someone, but let's catch up tomorrow."

Larry pats him a little too intensely on the back. "You've got the first round."

"You can count on it."

"Who are we meeting?" Nora asks after Larry disappears into the crowd.

"Anybody but him."

"How do you know him?"

"He's at all these things. Knows my dad. The usual."

"And he works for Prestige?"

"Yep. Loves it. Makes a ton of money."

Nora rolls her eyes. "I'm sure he does."

"Can we leave now?" Johnny asks.

"Sure. You look like you need a nap." Nora follows him toward the door, moving along with practically everyone else in the building.

"I need more than a nap."

"Do you need a casket?" she asks, gesturing at the six caskets ahead of them, next to the registration table. "That blue one looks like your taste."

He smirks. "You trying to make a sale, Clanton?"

"Always be closing, Chandler."

They walk between the caskets to get out the door, and Johnny stops to run his hand over the pale blue casket. "Make your case."

Nora holds in her laughter. She knows how to sell a casket. "This model is top of the line. From far away you might think it's metal, but it's actually high-quality wood that's been primed and painted this sky-blue color. Personally, I think this color skews a bit too gray if you're going to use the gold hardware. Good news is that this whole thing is custom, so we can do better."

Nora walks around to examine the interior. Some people in the crowd pause curiously, but no one cares enough to stop completely. "We can do better here, too. The ivory color makes sense, but this is not real velvet. This is also a dated design. The ruching is a little much. You might bury a founding father in this."

"You don't like the French design?" He runs his hands over the velvet on the lid.

"I prefer to support American designers, Johnny."

He smiles beyond a smirk this time, using his whole face for once.

"What?" Nora says.

He shakes his head. "I've always wondered how you get so much of my business, but I've never had a pretty girl try to sell me a casket. Now I understand."

"Was that a compliment? From you?"

"Don't let it go to your head. Let's go."

They walk down the corridor to the parking deck to get their bags to take to the hotel, which also connects to the parking deck.

"How did you know that velvet was fake?" Johnny asks.

"Some of the smaller hardware was plastic. It was mostly a guess."

"This is what I get for not having models in the store."

"I can teach you about caskets, and you can teach me about cremation. How was that session?"

"I didn't know there could be so many questions about burning a body."

"I'm imagining you in the back of the room, mumbling under your breath."

"By the end of it, I was ready to volunteer to be the example." Nora laughs.

"You know," Johnny says, "you're the only person I know who laughs at these jokes."

"You're the only person I know who would make these jokes."

They smile at each other as they reach the truck. He hands Nora her bag.

"What do you have in here, Clanton? It's one night."

"None of your business."

He passes her the handle of the smallest rolling suitcase she's ever seen. "I can't let you carry that."

"I can carry my own bag, Johnny. I packed it."

He takes the bag off her shoulder and puts it over his. "Get over it. I've had a long day."

Nora rolls her eyes, but he doesn't see because he's already walking toward the hotel entrance. There are more NFDS signs leading them inside, as if otherwise they couldn't find the hotel's reception desk. Johnny and Nora wait in line behind other conference-goers wearing their MarketingFunerals.com lanyards. Johnny yanks his lanyard over his head and then does the same to Nora's. He slides both of them into the side pocket of her bag. They check in and head to the elevator.

"What floor did you get?" Nora asks.

"Eight. You?"

"Nine."

"We should have gotten adjoining rooms." They slide into a car with what feels like half the conference attendees.

"That doesn't seem like a great idea."

An older man they do not know replies, "Seems like you should get her in your actual room, not the adjoining one."

"Jim!" says a woman in an extremely southern accent.

"What? She's a pretty girl. What happens in Birmingham stays in Birmingham, Julie."

Nora forces her mouth closed and prays for the elevator to make it to nine without ceasing. The doors open on the fourth floor, and all of the other passengers besides Julie and Jim shuffle away from this situation as fast as they can.

"You're ruining my chances," Johnny says to Julie when the doors close.

Nora looks at him as if he's lost his mind. "Excuse me?"

"No use denying it, Clanton."

The elevator dings for the eighth floor.

"Go to your room." She shoves his suitcase toward him and takes her bag from his shoulder. He struts into the hallway and out of sight.

"He's cute," Julie says.

"He's something," Nora says.

"I sense the chemistry between the two of you." She and Jim give each other a knowing glance; Nora has never been more thankful for elevator doors to open on her floor.

"Johnny has chemistry with everybody. Have a good night."

"You, too!"

Nora finds her room, and she's comforted when she sees the two queen beds waiting. She could have gotten a king, but she likes having the extra bed so she can lay out all of her things. It's sort of like the chair in the corner of her bedroom, but big enough to display multiple outfits at one time. Nora unpacks her toiletry products and spreads them along the counter in the bathroom. Her skin-care regimen will be ready when she needs it. Hours from now. Is it only five?

She lies down on the bed closest to the window and soaks up the silence. This is the first moment of the day when she really thinks of Garrett. What is he doing? Who is he with? Has he thought of her at all? She feels that emptiness in her heart, claiming the spot he used to fill. She wishes he were lying next to her.

Nora has been through this before, and she knows that these feelings will go away. She doesn't think about any of the other guys she's dated. This one feels different, though. Worse. But don't they all? She knows that one day she'll make it through a whole day without seeing his face in her mind. A whole day without remembering what it was like to kiss him or to feel him next to her at night. Eventually, it will be like it never happened.

Someone knocks at the door. She gets up and looks out the peephole: Johnny is standing there with one hand in his pocket like some sort of model in a cologne ad.

Nora opens the door. "How did you know which room was mine?"

"I knocked until you answered," he says, strolling in like he owns the place.

"Really?"

He plops down on the bed closest to the door and rearranges the pillows so he can lean against the headboard. "No, I saw the number on that thing." He gestures to the room-key envelope on the desk.

"Are we going to bed at five, or can we get a drink?" he asks.

"What did you have in mind?" She wants to tell him to get his shoes off the bed, but it's not her bedspread, so she tries not to care.

"I'd like to go to a real restaurant with a real bar, but I'll settle for downstairs."

"Are you asking me to go out with you?"

"In a literal sense, yes. Go out from this boring hotel."

"I guess that's fine."

"You have another date I don't know about?"

She looks over at him, and of course he has that smirk. "Nope. I'm stuck with you."

He nags her while she touches up her hair and makeup, but she takes her time. Nora hasn't been to Birmingham in so long, and she misses it. Or she misses the person she was when she lived in Birmingham. Either way, she wants to look her best. She wants to eat trendy food and stay out late and regret all of it in the morning. She wants to step back into her old life as if she never left it.

"Where do you want to go?" she asks, as they step out of the hotel and into the waning light.

"I want to walk around for a bit." He turns to the left and starts walking. She tries to keep up, but he doesn't seem to care either way.

"I forgot it was still early," Nora says. The streets around them are full of rush-hour traffic; Nora can't think of the last time she's needed to honk her car horn.

"Because we've been stuck inside with people in terrible suits who make funeral jokes."

"You've been making funeral jokes."

"And I am the worst."

"You're telling me."

They walk for a few blocks in comfortable silence until Johnny stops in the middle of the sidewalk.

"What about here?" He nods toward a nondescript brick building with a black front door.

"This place? I thought you wanted to go to a bar?"

"It is a bar." He points to a tiny metal plate above the door that reads: BAR.

She scopes out the building for a moment. There are a few windows, but all she can see is her reflection.

"Where's your sense of adventure?"

"You're buying." False confidence is key in these situations, so Nora brushes past him and flings the door open. She steps into a dark room, but once her eyes adjust, she realizes it's not scary at all. The brick wall behind the bar is the only decoration in the room. The other walls are taupe. The bar, tables, and chairs are shiny dark wood.

Two men sit at the bar drinking beer, but not together. Nora walks up between them, and the Sam Malone wannabe—aren't they all?—places a napkin in front of her.

"What can I get you?" he asks.

"I'll have an old-fashioned. He's paying," she says, pointing her thumb in Johnny's direction.

"I'll have a gin and tonic," Johnny says.

The bartender tells them to sit wherever they like, so Nora chooses a booth against the windows. Johnny slides in across from her with a weird look on his face.

"What?"

"I never thought I'd see you in a place like this."

"In a bar?"

"In a bar like this."

"What does that mean?"

"I figured you for a girl who likes pink drinks with weird names."

"Maybe you don't know me that well."

"Maybe not."

The bartender brings their drinks to the table.

"I'm sure he could make you something pink if you want it," she says to Johnny. The bartender looks confused but not un-willing.

"I'll pass," Johnny says. "Maybe later."

"Sure thing," the bartender says before walking back to the bar.

"Why did you suggest this place if you thought I wouldn't like it?" She swirls her straw around the one giant ice cube floating in her glass.

"Trying to keep you on your toes."

"Well, I prefer the quiet. For future reference."

"I'll file that away for the next time we're at a death conference."

Nora laughs. "What was your favorite part?"

"Probably when we were in the marketing session, and you wrote 'update signage' in your little notebook."

"I came to this conference to learn something."

He leans back in the booth. "Your store has been there for a hundred years. You sell one product—"

"We sell a variety of products, I'll have you know."

"It's a box for a dead person. It goes in the ground, and you never see it again. Most folks want to know as little about it as possible."

"Maybe one day we'll have a sale or something. Buy one, get one."

He laughs. "Have you ever had a sale?"

"We're under new management now. Anything is possible."

"How are you finding it?"

"Running the store?"

"Yeah. Being back in Rabbittown and all."

"It's fine." She could leave it at that, but she goes on: "It's not where I thought I would be, but it's in my blood, I guess."

"I don't know if I ever actually said sorry about your parents. I am sorry. Truly. They were good people."

"Thank you. Them being gone might've helped your business a bit."

He looks stunned for an instant before the smirk takes over his face. "I'd rather beat you fair and square."

"I don't cater to your demographic, so you shouldn't have any trouble with sales."

"Well, let's hear it, Business School. What's my demographic?" He downs half of his gin and tonic, then sits the glass back down on the ring of condensation on his napkin.

"People on your side of town. The ones who play tennis at the country club while the help watches the kids."

"What's your problem with money, Clanton?"

"I don't have a problem with anything."

"My family worked hard to get where they are. I'm not going to apologize for it."

She laughs. "Are you not the 'Chandler' in Chandler Farms?"

"What does that have to do with anything?"

"I don't think anyone would pay top dollar to get married in my family homestead unless they're looking for dirt floors."

"Say whatever it is you're trying to say."

She leans back against the booth. "It's just difficult to take your hard-work mentality seriously when you've got a plantation down the road. That's all."

He rolls his eyes. "I'm not going to justify my work ethic to you."

"I didn't say anything about your work ethic. You seem to be running the place on your own."

"Is it my turn?"

"Go for it."

Johnny crosses his arms. "This probably works against my own interests, but why haven't you thought about expanding?"

"I don't think I want to."

"I'm no scholar, but seems to me, the more you can charge, the more you'll make. You've got a ceiling now. They buy the one thing and leave."

"Maybe I should copy you and start upcharging for things like starting a PowerPoint or pushing play on a CD player?"

He holds both hands up. "Look, I'm just telling you the truth."

"I don't think I'm cut out for it." She takes a sip of her drink to mask the icky feeling of telling the truth.

"Then why keep the place? Why not sell it?"

"Who would buy it? Prestige?"

"I might," he says.

Nora puts her drink back on the table with a little more force than she meant to use, sloshing some of it down the side of the glass. "What?"

"I'd have to see numbers, but it's worth looking into if you're trying to get out."

"Where's the punch line?" Nora asks.

"I'm dead serious," he says. "No pun intended."

Selling the store has been in the back of Nora's mind for some time, but the nature of the thing has always taken care of itself. If she didn't have an offer, she wouldn't sell. She wouldn't get an offer if she didn't put it up for sale. This might not be a real offer, but it's enough to make her really think about the possibility.

"What would you do?" He waves at the bartender to bring another round, so she sips from the tiny red straw in her glass until it makes the slurping noise her mom had once forbidden her from making.

"If I didn't have the store?" She feels the whiskey settling in her mostly empty stomach. Maybe she should have grabbed extra food during lunch, but at the time she hadn't known she would be drinking liquor before dinner.

"Yeah, where would you go? You lived here for a while, didn't you?"

She nods. "I guess I could sell the house and go wherever I want. I just don't know that I want to go anywhere."

"You could stay on," Johnny says.

"Run the store for you?"

"Best-case scenario for me. You do what the Clantons do best, and I get the profits."

She rolls her eyes.

"Think about it. We could talk about updates and renovations. Whatever you want."

"And you'd be my boss?"

"Something like that," he says with the smirk.

"I don't know if that's a good idea."

"I think we could be a good team."

Nora doesn't fully trust anything Johnny Chandler says, so she expects him to take all of this back at the exact moment she convinces herself to go through with it.

"Look," he says. "I didn't mean to turn this into anything serious. We can talk about it later. We'd have to figure out the details."

"There's no expiration date on this deal?"

He smiles. "I seem to be the only one interested, so I can be patient for now."

"What would you do if you could do something else?"

"No clue. Maybe sell cars?"

"Sell cars?"

He shrugs. "I've always liked going to car shows and watching those guys on TV who rebuild old cars. I think I could be good at selling them."

"Interesting. I wouldn't have guessed that."

"What was your guess?"

She tilts her head for a moment, examining him. "You do sort of look like a car salesman. I think you could do corporate life, too. One of those jobs with a vague title no one understands." This image makes her think of Garrett. It's like a pinprick.

"I think I'll stick with what I've got," Johnny says.

During their second round of drinks, the bar starts to get busier. The main clientele seems to be middle-aged men drinking beer, which perhaps explains the lack of décor.

During their third round, they decide they should probably eat something. They make it as far as a trendy Mexican restaurant on the next block before giving up the search.

"What is a plantain nacho?" Johnny asks once they're at yet another booth, waiting on the pitcher of margaritas he ordered.

"If you have to ask, you won't like it," Nora says, scanning the menu for something that can soak up the alcohol she's already had and the alcohol she's about to add to it.

"I thought a plantain was a banana?"

"It looks like one."

"Banana nachos?"

She laughs. "They make them into chips."

"You think 'banana chips' sounds better? Bananas and jalapeños?"

"You don't have to order it, Johnny. Look, they have a bacon quesadilla you can order."

"I know you're making fun of me, but I might get it anyway."

"Maybe you should. I'm getting tacos."

The waitress brings salsa and the margarita pitcher.

"What kind of place charges you for chips and salsa?" Johnny asks once she's left the table.

"People love this place."

"Did you come here a lot when you lived here?" He fills both of their glasses without making too much of a mess.

"I lived a few blocks from here, so we went to a lot of these places. There's a good bar a few doors down."

"Would you move back?"

"I don't know. I miss parts of it, but things are different now. I'm different now, I guess."

"How do you mean?"

"Well, I used to go out a lot, and I can't tell you the last time I've been out past nine."

"Not a lot happening in Rabbittown?"

"My TV gets a lot of use."

"Well, drink up. We're about to change that."

Nora should know not to count anything out when tequila is involved. By the time they've finished dinner, Johnny is ready for something else. She is, too. She never expected to have a night out with Johnny Chandler, but she's having fun. She had forgotten what it was like to have friends. To wander wherever the drinks take you.

The bar down the block is almost exactly as Nora remembers it. Young people everywhere. Games at every table, but it's too dark to play them.

"What do you want?" she shouts into his ear.

"You're not paying."

She takes a step closer to the bar. "Tell me or I'll order you something pink."

"Miller Lite. I'll find a seat." She almost tells him there are no seats, but he can figure that out himself.

After getting the drinks, Nora looks for him in the crowd and finds him leaning against the back wall.

"I think we're the oldest people in here," he says, taking his beer.

"No doubt," she says. "That's how I spotted you. The creepy old man in the back."

He smiles a real smile instead of the smirk, so he must be drunk. "Would it kill you to be nice to me for five minutes?"

"It might."

He shakes his head.

"You're not nice to me," she points out. A dancing couple almost falls into her, but Johnny grabs her arm to yank her out of the way.

"I think that was nice," he says.

"I'll give you that one."

"I just didn't want you to spill your drink all over me."

"I figured you had a motive. You always do." Nora is pretty drunk, too.

"What's that supposed to mean?"

She stares at him for a moment to steady herself. "Are your eyes blue or gray?"

He tilts his head. "I don't know. A little of both, I guess."

"Mine are brown."

"Obviously. You're drunk."

"So are you."

"Are you going to throw up? I don't want any part of that."

"No, I can hold my liquor."

"Your accent comes out when you drink."

"Your accent is always out."

He shrugs and drinks the rest of his beer. Nora watches him as he looks around at the crowd and then back at her. "Why are you staring at me?" he asks.

"Is all this so you can sleep with me?"

"What?"

"Are you trying to sleep with me?"

He laughs. "If I were, you'd know."

"How?"

"We'd be at the hotel already."

She rolls her eyes.

"Are *you* trying to sleep with *me*?" he asks.

She considers it for a moment. "I don't think so."

"That's not a no, Clanton."

"It's not a yes either, so don't let it go to your head."

He points at a guy near the bar thrusting both hands into the air without any regard for the beat of the song she's too old to recognize.

"He's drunker than we are," Johnny says.

"So is she," Nora says, pointing to a girl with her head down on the bar.

Over the next three beers, they take turns finding people drunker than they are. When they're the two drunkest people left in the bar, they decide to go back to the hotel. Nora's conscience tells her they probably shouldn't walk back, but she doesn't think she can effectively call an Uber. She hasn't opened the app since she moved back to Rabbittown.

Johnny walks a step or two ahead, as usual. He's singing

"Strawberry Wine," and Nora tries to fill in the words he can't remember. He holds his arms in the air, but not like the boy in the bar. Johnny's arms extend as far as they can go, as if he can touch every person in his imaginary crowd, as if the people in the nosebleeds can remember the hot July moon at his grandpa's farm.

This is the moment when Nora realizes she is attracted to Johnny Chandler. He's not hiding behind pride or sarcastic pretenses. Like anyone screaming '90s country in downtown Birmingham, he's vulnerable and exposed for the person he is. He's not what she thought he was. He's not like anyone else.

As soon as this thought crosses her mind, she knows she needs to go to sleep. She needs to get back to the hotel as fast as she can and into her room before she can do anything stupid. She starts to run. She passes Johnny in the middle of his encore, and she hears him shout, "Nora!"

"Come on!" she yells. Somehow, she hits the crosswalks perfectly, and she runs through three straight before she remembers that she's not a runner. She's barely a walker.

Johnny is right behind her and grabs her around the waist as she bends over to catch her breath.

"I shouldn't have done that," she says, gasping for air.

"You had it, Flo-Jo," Johnny says in between breaths. "The hotel is right there."

She looks up from her crumpled position and sees that he's right. She only had one block to go.

"I shouldn't have stopped."

"Maybe you shouldn't have started." He's in the same position she is, trying to catch his breath, too.

"Why are you tired?"

"Chasing you!"

"You didn't have to chase me." Nora straightens and puts her hands on top of her head like the athletes at her high school used to do.

"My mom did say not to chase girls," he says. He stands and takes one of her arms and pulls it along with him. "Let's go."

Nora lets him take her hand, and he leads her to the hotel at a speed she can barely match. "Could you slow down?"

"Keep up, Clanton." He drags her through the hotel lobby and doesn't let go of her hand as he pushes the elevator button. "You made it to eleven fifty-six."

"It's midnight?" she asks.

"Eleven fifty-six."

The elevator dings, and a woman wearing sequins and stilettos comes out into the lobby, pulling a man in a black suit behind her.

"Going out?" Johnny asks.

"Something like that," the woman says. They almost miss the elevator watching her walk out of the hotel.

"Where are they going?" Nora asks as they get on the elevator.

"I don't think we want to know." Johnny pushes the buttons for both of their floors.

He's still holding her hand, and she doesn't hate it. She likes the feeling of someone else taking care of her instead of having to take care of herself. When they get to his floor, he pushes the "door close" button instead of getting off.

"That was stupid," he says.

"What are you doing?"

"Well, I'm not just going to leave you on the elevator."

"I know where my room is."

The elevator dings, and the doors open. "Good, you can lead the way."

They make it to her door, and she stares at it for a moment. "Do you think I have a key?"

He laughs. "You better have a key."

She looks down at her dress. "I don't have pockets."

"You have a purse."

He's right. It's slung across her body. "Oh."

"Let me see." He unzips it and finds the key card.

"I can do it."

He hands it to her, and she does her best to push it into a slot at the top of the lock.

"Not like that, Clanton. Jesus." Johnny takes the key card out of her hand and waves it in front of the lock, and the light on it turns green.

"Oh, this is a fancy lock."

She doesn't open the door fast enough, so he has to wave the card in front of the lock again. This time, he reaches past her and turns the handle to push the door open.

"You're drunk," he says.

"I know." She takes her purse off and throws it on the second bed. "I need to wash my face."

"Go ahead," he says.

"You don't have to stay."

"So you can bust your head open and blame it on me? I don't think so."

She washes her face and brushes her teeth, and when she walks out of the bathroom, she's surprised to see Johnny standing there.

"You didn't leave."

"Are you finished?" he asks.

"Well, I have to change, but I'm not drunk enough to do that in front of you."

"I'll leave. Come and lock the door behind me."

She walks with him to the door, and he turns to face her.

"Johnny?"

"What?" He's holding the door open with his foot.

"I don't want to be weird, but this was the most fun I've had in a long time. I know you're being nice to me because I'm sad, but I don't care at this exact moment." He stares at her for long enough that she wonders if what she had meant to say had come out of her mouth right.

"I'm not sure if you're aware, but I own a very successful funeral home. Sad doesn't faze me."

She rolls her eyes. "Whatever you say, Johnny."

"Hey, Clanton?" he asks.

"What?"

He takes a step toward her and lets the door close. "I'm going to kiss you now."

"Okay."

Nora leans back against the wall, and Johnny presses his body into hers. He raises his hand and tucks a strand of hair behind her ear as his other hand wraps around her waist. He leans forward, and as his lips touch hers, Nora stops breathing. Before she can have the thought, her palm is against his chest, creating space between them. She squeezes her eyes shut, as if that could make the situation go away.

"I'm sorry," she says. "I'm so sorry."

"Don't apologize."

She takes a deep breath before meeting his eyes. His face is blank, as if he's waiting to see her reaction. "I'm just not ready, but I wanted to be."

"I understand," he says, but she can't tell if he really does.

She opens her mouth to continue, to explain that it's not him and that he hasn't done anything wrong, but he holds up a hand to stop her.

"Let's talk about this when we're sober and when it's not the middle of the night."

"I don't want to leave it like this."

His mouth quirks, revealing a bit of his usual self. "I promise to let you talk in circles all the way home, if that's what you want to do."

"You're not mad at me?"

"My ego is a little wounded, but I'll bounce back."

They smile at each other, and Nora feels their connection from earlier slipping back into place.

"I'll see you in the morning," he says. "Good night, Clanton."

"Good night."

She closes the door behind him, then changes her clothes and jumps into bed as fast as she can, knowing that sleep is the only thing that can keep her from thinking of Garrett.

CHAPTER

16

Nora's head throbs to the beat of her alarm. Light streams through a small gap in the curtains, and she has no idea where she is. Then it all comes back to her. The hotel. The conference. Johnny Chandler.

She drags her near-lifeless body into the shower, somehow mustering up the strength to reach her arms over her head to wash her hair. For some reason, she feels like an errant teenager, like someone is going to discipline her for almost kissing Johnny. Like Garrett is going to run into the room and tell her everything was a huge misunderstanding and that she should have waited for him to explain. She scrubs her hands over her face as if Neutrogena can remove the guilt and shame and embarrassment of the whole situation. How could she manage to make things worse than they already were?

As she's brushing her teeth in front of the bathroom mirror, the logic starts to return. Nora is single. Johnny is single. She hasn't heard from Garrett since they broke up, weeks ago. She's allowed to kiss whoever she wants, whenever she wants. If she's honest with herself, she likes being with Johnny. Garrett had always been a mystery. He was new and exciting. Johnny is familiar and comfortable. They had grown up in the same place with the same people. Johnny understands her job. He understands the pressure of running a family business you never wanted to run.

Nora puts on her nicest black dress with her mom's pearl earrings and necklace. Drying her hair takes so much effort that she has to sit down for an intermission. No makeup in the world is enough to cover up a hangover for someone in their thirties, although this could be the one place where looking like a corpse will be acceptable.

There's a knock on the door as she's putting on her shoes, and her heart flutters. She wishes it would stop doing that. She opens the door to Johnny holding two coffee cups.

"Hey, there."

"Hi." She moves back to let him inside the room.

"Here," he says, handing her one of the coffee cups.

"You're a saint." Nora takes a sip, noticing that Johnny doesn't look hungover at all. He's wearing a black suit with a black tie, and his blond curls are still wet. He pushes them back away from his face and looks around the room at her mess.

"Please don't rush the dead." She takes her coffee into the bathroom to start packing her toiletries.

Johnny leans in the doorway with his usual smirk, like the villain in a CW show. "How are you feeling?"

"I can't feel much of anything but this headache. How do you feel?"

"Like shit."

"You don't look like shit. I look like shit." She combs through her hair with her fingers, but it's not helping. She gathers all of her things from the bathroom and pushes past him into the bedroom.

"I'm faking it."

He watches as Nora collects the clothes she's thrown all over the room and stuffs them, unfolded, into her bag. She's trying to force her toiletry bag to fit into the few remaining inches when she feels Johnny next to her.

"Let me see it, Clanton."

She huffs and hands over the bags. While he adjusts her meager attempt at organization, she sits on the edge of the bed drinking her coffee, trying to come up with some banter. Her brain refuses to participate. Instead, it reminds her of why she came to Birmingham in the first place. Dead people. Dead Dad. Dead Dad award.

Johnny puts the bag next to the door and sits down beside her.

"I can't give a speech today," she says.

"Sure you can."

She shakes her head. "There's one thing I can do for my dad, and I can't even do it right."

"It's going to be fine."

"I didn't even write anything." She's holding back tears, likely caused by the hangover, or at least that's what she tells herself.

Johnny puts his arm around her shoulders. "You need breakfast. We'll work on the speech after that. It can't be that hard. The award's won already."

"Easy for you to say." She lays her head on his shoulder, and they're silent for a moment. Nora knows he'll sit there as long as she wants. She also knows he's the same Johnny who has been rude all of her life. Maybe he's different than she thought. Maybe he's grown up. Maybe it's possible for a person to be two things at once.

"I guess we should go," she says. They stand, and he gives her a once-over.

"You sure?"

She nods. "No use putting it off."

"Before we do," he begins. "I just wanted to say I'm sorry. About last night."

Her love life could use its own casket.

"You really don't have to apologize," she says, forcing herself to make eye contact with him when all she wants to do is hide from her own embarrassment.

"I was drunk. It was stupid. I know you just got out of a relationship, and I'm pretty sure you hated me before yesterday."

"I've never hated you, Johnny."

"Well." He pauses to gather his thoughts. She's never seen him do that. "Either way. I don't want it to be weird."

"I agree."

He takes a step toward her and reaches out to tuck a hair behind her ear, just like he did the night before. "Don't get me wrong: I still want to kiss you. But I'm willing to put it on hold."

She opens her mouth to respond, but he holds up a hand.

"Let's get through today, all right?"

She releases the breath she didn't realize she had been holding. "Thank you."

She gives the room one last check for any forgotten belongings, and they walk to the elevator.

"Wait, where's your stuff?" Nora asks.

"I put it in the car already."

"How long have you been up?"

The elevator arrives with no one else on it.

"Long enough." He takes one corner, and she takes the other. "I know what I said, but can I just say one last thing, and then I swear I'll shut up?"

"Uh, sure."

"You look really pretty."

She rolls her eyes. "I look like it's time for you to plan my services."

"You calling me a liar?"

"I'm not calling you anything."

He shakes his head. "It gets a little tiring having to be the voice of reason all the time."

"Have I mentioned that I have a headache? You're not helping."

"I kinda like a little hangover on a woman. It's charming."

"Shut up, Johnny."

He smiles as the elevator doors open in the lobby. "Yes, ma'am."

They take her bag to the truck and try to find a seat in the hotel restaurant, but they're all filled with undertakers. She was supposed to have breakfast and work on her speech, and now she can't. She starts to lose her grip on reality, so Johnny steers her shoulders out of the restaurant and into the street. They walk, taking in the fresh air, until they find a diner on the next corner.

A perky young waitress brings the food. Nora picks at her scrambled eggs until she realizes Johnny is looking at her.

"You gotta eat something," he says.

"I know. I'm nervous."

"The food will help."

She gives him a look, and he hands her a piece of toast from her plate.

"Eat this, and I'll shut up," he says. "I swear."

She bites into the toast and chews it slowly. She knows it will make her feel better, but she doesn't have to like it. Johnny doesn't have any problem getting through his "whatever you've got back in the kitchen" omelet.

"How can you eat that right now?"

He shrugs. "I'm hungry."

She holds up a second piece of toast for his approval and takes a bite.

"You want a bite of this?"

"God, no. You don't even know what it is."

"It's an omelet."

"Whatever you say."

She eats a few bites of her own eggs, but she can't do much more. Maybe it's the texture. Or the smell. Or the multiple types of alcohol from last night bubbling up. She shoves her plate to the middle of the table and steals a piece of bacon from his.

"Hey, get your own breakfast meat."

"You'll live."

He finishes his plate of nonsense and pushes it to the center of the table.

"Now let's get to work on that speech."

"We're going to miss the opening session if we don't leave now."

"I think we can put the 'fun' in 'funeral' right here in this diner."

"If you're sure."

"I'm sure. What do you want to say?"

She thinks for a moment. "Well, I suppose I should introduce myself and thank them for the prestigious award."

"Yes, I would start there. Lead with flattery." She can tell he's taking this seriously, and it's endearing.

"I don't really know what to say about my dad. It's hard to sum up a whole person."

"I wouldn't shoot for that. You don't owe these people anything. You certainly don't owe them your whole dad. Focus on the work parts."

"His whole business model was people, not product. No one is happy to have to come into a casket store, and Dad was always prepared for that, no matter the situation. He was good at his job, and he loved it. He loved helping people he knew through hard times."

Johnny nods, sliding his coffee cup across the table from one hand to the other.

"Is that enough?" She can't think about it much longer without having to actually think about it. She shouldn't even be doing this. Her dad should be here.

"I think so. You don't have to overdo it."

"Should I write it down?"

He thinks for a moment. "Nah, leave it unscripted."

"What if I forget what to say? I'm not good at this."

"You won't. If the worst happens, I'll pull the fire alarm, and you can meet me at the truck."

She laughs. "Promise?"

"Yep."

"Thanks, Johnny."

"Anytime."

They walk back to the conference, Nora one step behind Johnny, and they make it to the exhibition hall with a few minutes to spare. They're standing with the other latecomers just outside the main doors, waiting for the first session to finish.

"Are you Nora?"

When she turns around, she recognizes the woman's face. "Yes."

"I knew you must be! You look just like your mama. I'm Leann. I think you spoke to my husband, Brian, on the phone?"

"Oh, yes, ma'am, I did." Brian is the man who called and guilted Nora into doing this.

"This is going to be short and sweet. You'll want to sit near the front. We're going to show some old clips and pictures of your dad. Some of our leadership team will say a few words, and then we'll explain the award and call you up to accept."

Before she can say anything, the doors swing open and Leann says, "Come with me."

Nora grabs Johnny's arm and drags him along. Leann leads them to the front row of seats and points out two seats near the middle. "I've got to go check on some things. Will you be all right?"

"I'll be fine."

Leann walks away as a slideshow of Nora's parents projects onto the screen in the front of the room. Nora hears faint instrumental music start to play.

She turns toward Johnny and speaks low into his ear: "I don't want to be weird, and maybe I just have it on the brain, but does this sort of seem like—"

"A funeral?" he asks as if he doesn't care who hears him. "Seems like Leann might be a one-trick pony."

"This is weird, right? He's been dead for more than a year."

"What do you expect? Says a lot that we're the two most normal people here." He picks up a program from the seat beside him. "These folks are having a silent auction later to give away an autographed copy of an album of funeral music and some kind of antique coffin once owned by Marilyn Manson. Nothing here is normal."

"Let me see that." Sure enough, there's a whole list of prizes to be won, including a gift basket of industrial candles and odor neutralizers from a crematorium and a trip to the National Gravestone Museum in Ohio. "Oh, this one is normal. A weekend at Leann and Brian's lake house with Leann and Brian."

"Somehow, that is the creepiest one."

The lights dim, and the music stops for an awkward moment of silence before a new song begins. The crowd seems to recognize this as a sign to find their seats. Is Leann going to make Nora march out and back in like families do at funeral services?

Johnny leans over. "Remember to breathe."

She takes a deep breath. "I will."

The slideshow she had been trying to ignore starts over. When Brian called about the award, he asked Nora to send a few family photos, and she did, but it wasn't enough for a slideshow. She's never seen the majority of these photos. Most of them are candids—her dad giving a thumbs-up over an overfilled plate of wings, her mom and dad sitting in easy chairs in front of a fireplace, her dad standing onstage and talking with his hands.

Nora senses the mood in the room changing before her brain can catch up. People here had sent these photos. The reason this feels like a funeral is because, in a way, it is one. Hadn't they come to the actual funeral? It's hard for Nora to remember who she saw that week, but she knows some of them were there. A few of them sent flowers and cards. A few of them offered to help with the service. A few of them brought casseroles and restaurant gift cards because sometimes that's all you know to do.

Nora has never thought of anyone else's grief about her parents' deaths. Everyone has focused on her and her grandpa, since they're the two leftovers. If life is like a puzzle or a tapestry or some other object that represents the way everyone fits together, Nora has a few gaps that keep it from being whole.

It's hard to remember that her parents were real people. She always envisions them behind the counter at the store or in the living room watching television, but that wasn't the totality of their lives. They had lives before she arrived. They had lives once she moved out.

Maybe the people in this room also have a Billy-and-Anita-shaped gap in their lives. Maybe it's not as big as Nora's, but maybe it's there.

As more and more photos pass across the screen, Nora notices the people around her lighting up with recognition. She sees the memories surface in different pockets of the room as people laugh or point at the pictures they recognize. The clasped hands and tissue boxes. The happy memories blending with the sad reality to create that bittersweet taste of grief.

Nora's parents have belonged to her since the day she was born, but they belong to a lot of other people, too.

Then there's a photo of her family on the screen: her dad, her mom, and Nora sitting on a blanket, eating watermelon off paper plates. They're all wearing Alabama T-shirts with the old logo. Her mom's hair has been teased to high heaven. Nora must have been seven or eight.

Johnny reaches over and puts his hand over hers, and she intertwines their fingers.

"I don't remember that."

"It was at the fall festival in town," Johnny whispers.

Nora's eyebrows draw together in confusion.

"My mom had it, for some reason."

"You sent it in?"

He shrugs. "They asked for pictures, and I had a picture."

For so long Nora had wanted to get away from these people and this life, to create her own place in the world without the baggage of the past, to be free of the expectations that come with it, but there's something to be said for the people who can remember the things she can't. The people who don't require explanations because they've known every iteration of her.

Two gray-haired men take the stage after the slideshow. Nora figures she has probably met them, but she has no clue who they are. The first one, wearing a black suit slightly too big for his body, welcomes the crowd and gives a brief rundown of Nora's dad's life, the kind you would find in an obituary. Maybe it is his obituary.

The second man must be the entertainment, based solely on his bright blue tie covered in tropical fish. He tells a few stories about Billy Clanton; they're filled with inside jokes that Nora doesn't understand, but by the end of it the crowd has completely dissolved into silliness and laughter.

Brian and Leann are next, and Leann nods at Nora to signal that it's about to be her turn.

"I should have written something down," she whispers to Johnny.

"If you can't think of anything, just ask them to stand for the Pledge of Allegiance. They'll do it, and it will buy you some time."

Brian is going into detail about the importance of the award and its past recipients.

"That's your advice?"

"No one is expecting the Gettysburg Address."

"I don't want to look stupid."

"Well, you're not stupid, so that's not possible."

Leann steps to the microphone to run through the many things Billy Clanton did for the organization. Nora didn't have a clue about any of it.

"Many of us are old enough to remember Anita's parents," Brian says when it's his turn again, "and when they passed, we weren't sure what would happen to their store, but now most of us know that Billy could have talked anyone into anything, so he talked Anita into putting everything they had into it. He started showing up at our meetings, and before we knew it, he was running things on our leadership team and had become a friend to all of us.

"So, for everything that's been mentioned up here and all the things we can't put into words," Brian concludes, "we would like to present the National Funeral Directors Society Lifetime Achievement Award to Billy Clanton. And here to accept on his behalf is his daughter, who is following in his footsteps, Eleanora Clanton."

Everyone in the room stands to applaud. Nora freezes in her seat.

Johnny pulls her to her feet and leans in to whisper, "You know what to say, Clanton. Just do it."

Nora nods and smooths out her dress before walking toward the stage. Her adrenaline makes her take the steps too fast, and she trips slightly, but she tells herself that maybe no one noticed. Brian and Leann both pull her in for a hug, and she tries to pretend that it's normal to hug people she just met in person. Nora's eyes widen as Brian hands her the award: a rectangular chunk of granite engraved with her dad's name and sitting on a granite base, not unlike his gravestone. She holds it up for the crowd, and for Johnny in particular, who covers his mouth to stifle his laughter.

Nora waits for everyone to sit down and for the room to fall silent, which is what everyone does on every awards show, but it's not great for her nerves to be standing in front of a silent room with no real plan for what to say.

"Like Brian said, I'm Eleanora Clanton, and I'm Billy and Anita's daughter."

Lead with flattery.

"I can't thank you all enough for all of the kind things you said about my dad today. His work and this organization were important to him, and I know he would be proud to receive this prestigious award. All of you meant a lot to him, too. He would have been tickled pink to see the pictures and hear the stories, and those of you who knew my dad know you would have had to hear about this day forever."

They laugh, so maybe she's on the right track. She looks down at Johnny, and he nods his encouragement.

Focus on the work parts.

"Most of you probably know that Dad and Mom inherited Rabbittown Casket Company from my grandparents. On paper, a small-town casket company is not a great business idea." A few people laugh, even though she's not joking. "But Dad spent most of his life making it work. Beyond that, he made it successful. He set an example for me and for anyone else who was paying attention by putting people before profit. Dad loved helping people. As most of you know firsthand, we see customers on some of the worst days of their lives, and Dad helped shoulder a few of those burdens, if only for a little while."

A few people in the audience are wiping their eyes, so she decides to wrap it up before the emotion gets to her.

"I wish he were here to accept this award instead of me, since he did all of the work to deserve it, and he loved any opportunity to be on a stage with a microphone." This gets more laughs, so they definitely knew her dad well. "Thank you to the National Funeral Directors Society for your generosity and support for so many years."

Nora raises the miniature gravestone—a toast, of sort, to her parents—and steps back from the podium, and the crowd gives another standing ovation. She understands that this applause is for her dad, but it still makes her feel weird. Her heart races and sweat pools under her feet, inside her shoes. She takes a deep breath and focuses only on making it to the seat next to Johnny. When she gets there, he hugs her with one arm and takes the award to examine it.

"These people need to be stopped," he says under his breath. "You were great, by the way. Didn't faint once."

"Thanks."

"You've got some fans." He nods to the aisle to her left. Sure enough, a single-file line has formed, with Brian and Leann in front.

Much like at a visitation, everyone cycles through one by one to pay their respects. This takes an excruciatingly long time, but Nora is used to visitations. She recognizes what these people are feeling. They need to do this for themselves, not for Nora.

Halfway through the line, she turns to say something to Johnny, to get a break from the grief, but he's lying across three chairs with an arm draped over his face, using his jacket as a pillow, sound asleep. She will have to get through this on her own. She's done it before.

"Wake up," Nora says, after shaking the last hand, nudging Johnny's elbow with her knee.

"Is it over?" he asks, dropping his arm.

"I think so."

"Nora?" someone calls from behind her. She knows who it is before she turns around, but she still doesn't quite believe it when she sees Garrett standing there.

"What are you doing here?" Not the most polite she's ever been, but they're past that.

"I'm here for the conference." He's wearing a dark gray suit, white shirt, and emerald-green tie. The green in his tie makes his green eyes stand out even more than they normally do, and Nora realizes that her knees could buckle at any moment.

"Why?"

He tilts his head, confused by her confusion. "We always have a representative at these things, and I volunteered. You told me about the award."

Her brain spins, trying to understand. "I guess that makes sense." Actually, she doesn't think it makes much sense at all.

"You did great," he says. "Really."

"Thanks—I was nervous."

He smiles. "I thought you might be, but they're going to be asking you to lead a committee or something after that. I know your parents are proud of you."

Nora had forgotten that Johnny was in the room, so it's a surprise when he appears beside her, his jacket folded over his arm. With his tie loosened and his sleeves rolled up, she's once again reminded that he should be in a catalog.

"Johnny, this is Garrett Bishop," she says. "Garrett, this is Johnny Chandler."

"As in Chandler Funeral Home?" Garrett asks.

"That's me."

"I live a few blocks over from it."

"Hope you're not downwind," Johnny says.

Nora elbows him. "Don't be gross."

"Yes, where are my manners?" Johnny asks as he reaches across to shake Garrett's hand. "It's nice to meet you."

Nora remembers Garrett's hands. She remembers his mouth. Then she remembers her night with Johnny, and she forces herself to stay in the present moment.

"Nice to meet you, too," Garrett says. Nora can tell he's trying to understand if something is going on between her and Johnny; maybe if he figures it out, he could let her know. "Are you going to other sessions today?"

"I think Johnny is going to the golf thing, and I'm going to a session about pre-sales. What about you?"

"I'm not sure yet," Garrett says. "I've seen a couple I'm interested in."

"Well, I guess I'll take my trophy to the meeting rooms down the hall."

"I'll let you know when I'm back from the golf course," Johnny says. "Hopefully it will be sooner than later."

"Have fun with Larry," Nora says.

"Enjoy your very exciting seminars on things you already know how to do. Nice meeting you, Garrett."

"Nice to meet you, too."

Once Johnny is out of earshot, Garrett leans over to ask, "Mind if I tag along with you?"

"To a seminar about casket pre-sales?"

"Maybe I'll learn something. I'm not ready to let you go yet."

He smiles, and Nora melts. Being in his presence has cleared her mind of everything that happened before now. The secrets. The fights. The breakup. She straightens, pulling herself together, as if better posture might do the trick.

"I hope it's okay I came," he continues. "I've missed you."

"I've missed you, too." She hadn't realized how much until she saw him. She hadn't let herself think about him being there for her, but she needed him. "I think the room is in this direction."

"Lead the way."

As they walk through the convention center, Garrett breaks the silence: "Can I ask you something?"

"Uh, sure."

"Johnny Chandler?"

Nora laughs. There's nothing else to do when someone is that straightforward. "What about him?"

"Are you really here with him?"

"Well, it sort of looks like I'm here with you."

"You know what I mean."

"He offered to drive me here."

"I'm sure he offered more than that."

"Garrett!"

"Tell me I'm wrong."

Nora sees the room up ahead and pulls Garrett aside in front of a row of windows in an attempt to keep the whole conference from hearing about her drama.

"It's not your business either way."

"Well, *either way*, you're better than him."

"You don't even know him."

"I know enough. People talk. And last I heard, you didn't like him and neither did your grandpa."

"Oh my God, he drove me to a conference we were both going to. It's not like he proposed."

Garrett turns to stare out the window. "I don't care for this situation."

"And you think it's fun for me?"

"You're the one moving on like nothing between us mattered."

"That's not true. I'm not with him. Did you just come here to yell at me?"

"No, I didn't want to talk about this."

"Then let's not talk about it."

Nora assumes that going to the seminar will give her a chance to clear her head. "Come on, let's learn about casket sales."

Nora is often wrong.

Garrett sits in the chair next to her, their bodies not at all touching, and that's all Nora can think about for forty-eight minutes. He fidgets. She fidgets. She squeezes her hands together, trying to think of anything else. It doesn't work.

When the session is over, they walk back into the hallway, back to the not-at-all-private area in front of the windows.

"Well, that was enlightening," Garrett says.

Nora leans against a window. "You didn't have to come. I'm sure there was another session you could have gone to that pertains to your . . . particular set of skills."

Garrett looks at her sideways. "Do you actually think I came here for this conference? Let me take you to lunch."

Nora starts shaking her head before her brain can make words. "I don't think that's a good idea."

"Lunch or lunch with me?"

"The second one."

"What's the worst that can happen? We eat food? You miss a session? I'll email them for the slides."

"I don't trust myself." She didn't mean to say it out loud, but there it is.

"I trust you. If you decide it's going terribly, you can leave."

He leads her to a sandwich shop a couple of blocks from the convention center. She gets the drinks and sits down at an empty table, while he waits at the counter for their food.

Nora watches him standing there, hands in his pockets, rocking back and forth on his heels. She has had the thought in the past few weeks that maybe, eventually, they could be friends. Or at least friendly. But the suit is not doing her any favors. She feels the familiar butterflies. Her brain starts playing the hits on a loop: the first time she saw him, their first date, all the cheese he bought for pizza night. He's walking toward the table with the tray by the time she gets to their breakfast at Jack's.

"Penny for your thoughts," he says as he takes a seat on the other side of the table. He puts the tray down and holds up a finger. After digging around in his pocket, he comes out with a handful of change. "What about a nickel?" He slides it over to her.

Where do men learn this shit?

"I don't think you want to hear them, but I'll take the nickel." She tosses it into her purse, where she'll probably find it later and frame it.

They both unwrap their sandwiches in silence, even though Nora doesn't feel much like eating.

"So," Garrett begins, "what have you been up to?"

Nora snorts. "Oh, this and that."

"I'm serious."

"Okay, well, I guess I've been crying over my breakup. Drinking a lot. Selling caskets. The usual."

"If you're insinuating that it's been a walk in the park on my end, remember that *you* broke up with *me*."

"What have you been up to?" Nora asks, taking a bite of her turkey sandwich. It doesn't taste like anything. Just bread and a hint of mustard now and then.

"I've been working. I had to go to Tuscaloosa, and I couldn't stop thinking about you, so I spent a lot of time in my hotel being sad."

Nora nods her understanding. After a moment of loaded silence, she volunteers: "I've been redoing the store."

Garrett perks up. "Redoing it how?"

"I don't know for sure yet. I got some paint samples. I cleaned out the back room, which took me a whole week."

"You're going to paint it yourself?"

"I guess so. I'm the only employee."

"I'll come help you."

She gives him a look. "Actually, I might take you up on that. It's the least you could do."

Garrett shakes his head at her but decides to drop it. "What made you decide to do that? The painting and stuff?"

"I guess I felt a little like I was working in a crypt, which might be the perfect vibe for a casket shop, but I don't think my parents would want me to keep it exactly how they had it."

"That's really exciting. I'm happy for you." He smiles, and she can tell he means it.

"Thank you. Who knows? I might end up selling it."

His brows furrow. "You want to sell it?"

"I don't know. It's an option. I never wanted to own it in the first place." She opens her bag of sour cream and onion chips, and the smell fills the air around them. Maybe she should have chosen plain.

"Did someone make you an offer?"

"I was talking to Johnny about it. Nothing serious." She pops a chip into her mouth.

He crosses his arms. "He wants to buy your store?"

"He said he was going to look at the numbers. I could keep working there if I want, or I could sell the house, too, and go somewhere else entirely."

"Was this your idea?"

Nora thinks about it. "I'm not sure. I guess it was his. I didn't offer the store to him, if that's what you're asking."

Garrett props his elbows on the table and rubs both hands over his face. "Please let someone else besides you look at the paperwork before you sign anything. It doesn't have to be me. Find a random lawyer. Someone outside of the situation."

"I'll try not to be offended by that."

"You can't trust him, Nora."

"And you aren't the most objective source. I'm a grown-up. I can handle things myself."

He crosses his arms again, preparing for a fight. "Don't sell the store to him just to spite me. Is that what your family would want? For it to go to the Chandlers?"

And with that, Nora loses her appetite. She puts her tasteless sandwich on her tray and moves the tray to the other side of the table. "You know what my family wants? For my parents to be alive. So why don't you sit with that while you go to your perfect job every day."

"I didn't have anything to do with your parents."

"You know what I mean."

"I do, and maybe you should consider what it would have been like if someone hadn't been there for them. I don't know what the situation was like, but I'm glad if it had to happen that they had someone next to them helping them through it. Since I've met you, I've heard so much about your family and what a big part you've all been in your community. You got an award for it today. I think, if it came down to it, you would want to help people in this situation, too."

"Help them die."

"They're already dying. We're all dying. And you can't stop that. You can't control it. If you're not ready to accept that, I understand. I won't push it anymore. But I can't sit here and act like it's a good idea for you to sell your family business to bad people."

"'Bad people'?" Nora laughs. "That's really funny coming from you. What makes them so bad?"

He shakes his head. "I'm not getting into that. I don't want to talk about him."

"By all means, tell me what you'd like to talk about. I try to talk to you in a normal way, and it just turns into a fight."

Garrett straightens up his tray and stacks it on top of Nora's. He starts to reach for her hand out of habit. They both pretend not to notice. "How's your garden?"

"My garden?"

"I remember you were digging it up. Trying to start over."

Nora laughs. "Oh God, I was a crazy person. It's still sitting there. It needs more work. I need to find some ideas. What do normal people plant in gardens?"

Garrett laughs. "Flowers, vegetables, whatever you want. I think you'll have to wait until spring to start planting, but I can help you with that, too."

Everything inside is screaming for her to say yes. Planting flowers, going to hardware stores, making a life with Garrett—that's all she's wanted, since the day she first met him. This whole situation is too much. She should have known it would end this way.

"Why don't you walk me back to the convention center instead?"

He nods, understanding. "Let's go."

They walk in silence, neither of them knowing what to say. They go through one crosswalk, and then the next. As they're strolling down the last block, Garrett shoots his shot.

"Do you remember when we met?"

Nora smiles. "Yes, it wasn't all that long ago."

"Well, that was pretty easy, don't you think?"

"What do you mean?"

"I mean, I liked you and you liked me. We didn't really have to convince each other of anything. It was an immediate thing."

Nora stops on the sidewalk. "Say what you're trying to say, please."

He takes her elbow and guides her out of the way of the other pedestrians. They both notice that this is the first time they've touched in a long time.

"I'm saying I didn't have to do much wooing when we first met. I asked you out and you said yes."

Nora tilts her head. "What does that have to do with anything?"

He takes a gamble and reaches for both of her hands, and she lets him hold them.

"You deserve to be wooed, and I'm prepared to do that. I told you I wasn't going anywhere, and I'm not. Until you give me another chance."

Nora snatches her hands away. "So, what, you're going to stalk me? Showing up here is a little creepy. I get to have a say in my own life."

"The woman I love was accepting an award in a public place."

"Don't act like I'm crazy."

"You're not at all crazy. I hear what you're saying. I saw you with Johnny. I know you're trying to move on."

"You're blowing that out of proportion."

"I see how he looks at you."

"And how is that?"

Garrett looks down at his shoes, debating. "Like you're something to win." He holds his hands in the air. "Please don't yell at me for telling the truth. If you want to go down that road with him, I hate it, but it's your choice. I'm not going to fight over that. It's not worth it."

"You're talking in circles."

He sighs. "You scramble my brain a little. You always have. All I'm saying is that you should do whatever you feel like you need to do. And I will be around."

"What if I don't want you to be around?"

"Well, I've been listening closely today, and you haven't said no once."

She opens her mouth with a rebuttal, but he holds up his hand.

"You don't have to yell at me. I know. I do love you, and I also respect you, and no means no. If you want me gone at any point, say the word and I'll go."

He just had to use the L word. Nora takes a deep breath. "I want to go home now."

"If you'll ride with me, we'll leave right now. My car is in the deck."

"I agreed to ride with Johnny, and my stuff is in his truck already. I'm supposed to meet him at the convention center."

"Can I walk you back to the door, and I promise I'll leave?"

They take the short walk back to the door in silence.

"It was good seeing you," Garrett says. "Thank you for lunch."

"You paid. I should be thanking you."

He shakes his head. "I'd like to hug you goodbye, if that's okay."

Nora can't help but get close to the flame, so she reaches for him first. She wraps her arms around his waist, and he pulls her close, pressing his face into her hair. They both pretend not to notice the tears in Nora's eyes as she walks through the door and leaves Garrett standing on the sidewalk.

Nora walks around the convention center, waiting for Johnny, thinking about her day. She woke up wondering what was going on with Johnny, and now Garrett has added himself into the mix, as if he'd ever really left in the first place. Of course she loves him, but nothing has changed, lunch or no lunch.

Johnny texts that he's almost back, and Nora meets him outside. Once she's in the truck she asks, "Are you drunk?"

"No, are you?" he asks, giving her a once-over.

She rolls her eyes. "I don't know what you've been doing with Larry, and I don't want to ride with a drunk driver."

"I wouldn't pick you up if I were drunk, Clanton."

"Great—let's go home then."

Neither of them says a word until they get out of Birmingham and onto the interstate. Nora is perfectly content with this, because it gives her the chance to overthink the past few days, past few weeks, and, hell, the past year of her life. She figured she would be upset today, but she thought it would be for a different reason.

Johnny breaks the silence: "Do you want to talk about it?"

"Which part?"

"Either the part when you got a miniature tombstone for your father in front of a crowd of people or the part where your ex-boyfriend showed up like a knight in shining armor."

She laughs. "That all happened at once, didn't it?"

"Pretty much."

"Do you think the speech went well? Be honest."

"The speech was great. They'll make kids memorize it for public speaking class."

"Have you ever thought about being serious when someone asks you a serious question?"

"No."

"Why not?"

"Part of the charm, Clanton."

"I can't believe all of those people stood in line to talk to me. My parents would have loved that."

"But you didn't?" he asks.

"I'm just not good at talking to people."

"Not liking it and not being good at it ain't the same."

"Is this your version of flattery?"

"If I were trying to flatter you, you'd know it."

"Oh, right, I forgot."

"I would tell you that even holding a tombstone trophy, you were the most beautiful woman in that room."

"In a room full of sixty-year-old men? Gee, thanks, Johnny."

"Does this mean you don't want to talk about the ex-boyfriend?"

"Nothing to say. I was surprised to see him. But nothing has changed."

"He looked rich."

She rolls her eyes.

"That was an expensive suit."

"So is yours!"

"Well, I don't usually meet people on my level."

"Oh, please. You're not a Rockefeller."

"You can't have it both ways, Clanton. Am I a spoiled plantation owner or not?"

"You definitely are."

"He was good-looking, too. Like James Bond."

"Yes, he's good-looking." No one could disagree with that.

"And still pining after you," he says, glancing across the truck to see her reaction.

She shrugs as if she's never had a care in the world. "It doesn't matter."

"I'm not sure I'm buying that," Johnny says. "But I'm glad he showed up."

"Why?"

"To put a face on the competition."

She narrows her eyes at him. "It's not a competition."

"Well, not for long. I do intend to win." He has the audacity to wink.

"Why don't you concentrate on driving for a while? You're making my hangover come back." She finds the button to lay her seat back and turns to face the window.

"Your wish is my command."

They arrive back in Rabbittown, and Nora gathers her things as Johnny pulls his truck into a parking spot in front of her store.

"Thank you for the ride," Nora says. "And for everything else."

"It's my pleasure," he says, unleashing the full force of one of his smiles on her. "I'd like to call you later."

She hesitates, so he adds, "No pressure."

"That would be okay with me," she says.

When she gets home, she unlocks her front door and walks straight to her room to lie down on the bed. She can't think any more about today. Not about her thoughts or her feelings or the store or her love life. She has no idea what she's doing, and she doesn't expect to figure it out anytime soon.

CHAPTER

17

The sun rises as Grandpa drives through Rabbittown. His old truck has been rattling lately, but he ignores it. He's used to the noise by now, and if it bothers other people so much, they don't have to drive it. Nora worries, but he has been driving twice as long as she's been alive.

He follows his usual route past the church and the cemetery, and around the corner to Jack's. When his wife, the first Eleanora Clanton, was alive, she made breakfast every morning. Now that he lives alone, he realizes how much time and effort she spent in the kitchen. They should have been driving to Jack's every morning and spending more time at Pearl Café in the evenings.

Grandpa picks up his sausage biscuit and coffee from the counter and finds his seat among the other old-timers in the community. The gossip about high school sports and something to do with the church choir gets repetitive, especially with the literal repetition of every other sentence to reach Don Graham's hearing aid. He sips the remainder of his coffee, waiting for an opportunity to exit the conversation without giving the impression that he has one opinion or another about the topic at hand.

The coffee at Jack's is not anything to get excited about, but it has a reliable taste, and Grandpa didn't have to make it himself. He can also order it by saying the word "coffee," unlike the options at the Chat & Brew, which requires a full sentence of an order to make something spurt out of one of the machines behind the counter. On his way out the door, he has the young man behind the counter refill his cup.

Rabbittown Square is still waking up. Most of the businesses open at ten, but the lights are already on at Rabbittown Casket Company. Nora could probably open at ten, too, but she does things how her parents always did them, which is how Anita's parents had always done them.

Grandpa had not agreed with Billy and Anita's choice to keep the store open when Anita's parents died. He had tried to talk Billy out of it. He had tried to talk him into selling it many times over the years. Then the worst had happened, and Nora got stuck with the blame place. Like her mama, she did what she thought was the right thing. Nobody within a stone's throw of Nora had wanted this for her. She was supposed to be the one to get out of here. But here she was. Repeating history.

They had all tried to explain the business to him, as if he couldn't possibly understand why anyone would do that sort of work. Of course, as far as they knew, he had retired from an insurance company. He could have explained everything, but it had always seemed like something they could talk about later.

Then Billy and Anita's names had been on the list, and he knew he had missed his chance. Once you were on the list, there was no changing it. He had tried when he'd seen his wife's name on the list, years earlier. She had understood, and eventually, he had, too.

Grandpa figures Billy and Anita knew a little about Death, even if they didn't realize he had been part of it. They wouldn't have had a reason to suspect it, since he was never in the field. He had worked in one of the local offices before technology had taken over a lot of what he used to do. Maybe the information would have been passed down to Nora if things had been different.

He thinks about telling her the truth from time to time, but he's never been able to go through with it. It would change things between them, and he knows his name will be on the list soon enough.

He hadn't put Garrett and Death together at first. There's no secret head nod or handshake that would give it away. He had started to wonder when Ed mentioned seeing him at the Sanderson boy's accident. The first time he had laid eyes on Garrett had been the night Frank died, after all. Once he had seen the business card, he had known for sure.

He can't say how much Nora knows, but he assumes it's a lot, based on the past few weeks. Maybe it's something she would have learned eventually anyway, working in the casket store. He won't ask her about it. He'll do what he's always done as far as Eleanora Clantons are concerned and keep showing up until she's ready to talk.

"You're out early," Nora says, hugging her grandpa carefully, so she doesn't spill any coffee from the Jack's Styrofoam cup in his hand.

"I wanted to see about you," he says. She sat next to him at church, but they hadn't had a chance to catch up. He's wearing an Alabama hat that has seen better days. Probably in the 1970s, to be exact.

"I'm here," she says. "Want to see the award?" Her dad's tombstone-shaped Lifetime Achievement Award sits on the edge of the desk because she's not sure where to put it. It deserves a place of pride, but it might creep out customers who are already primed to be creeped out when they enter a casket store.

He nods, and she gives it to him. He examines it, putting down his cup so he can weigh it in both hands. "This thing is heavy."

"I think it's granite," she says.

He places it on the counter and sits down in one of the empty chairs in front of the desk. "How was the ceremony?"

"Better than I thought it would be. I didn't realize Mom and Dad spent so much time with those people."

"Well, your dad thought of everyone as family."

Nora resists the urge to point out where her dad had learned that trait. "That's true."

Nora slides her feet out of her Target flats and into the fuzzy slippers she has started keeping under her desk since Garrett walked in on her that very first day with her bare feet on the desk. If she can't trust herself to keep her shoes on, she thinks slippers might be slightly better than walking around the store barefoot. She tries to wipe out that memory and replace it with a memory of Johnny. That's how it's supposed to work, isn't it?

"How was Johnny Chandler?" Grandpa asks.

At first, Nora wonders if he was reading her mind, but his question does make the trip a little easier to discuss without causing some sort of heart malfunction. It's not a great idea to surprise an eighty-five-year-old. "Well, it wasn't what I was expecting. It was surprisingly fun."

He doesn't react right away. Instead, he reaches for his coffee and takes a sip. If he's doing this to make her squirm, it's working.

"I know it's weird," she says. "I'm still trying to figure it out."

"So, nothing from Garrett, then?"

Nora takes a deep breath. "Well, he came to the conference, actually. For the award ceremony."

Grandpa's eyes widen. "That was right nice of him."

"I guess."

He shakes his head, but he's smiling. "I wish your mama and daddy were here, just so I could see the looks on their faces. You and a Chandler."

She rolls her eyes. "I'm sure they know. Maybe they orchestrated it."

"Think they're getting bored up there?"

She shrugs. "I doubt it if they can see what's going on around here."

He turns his coffee cup in his hands, waiting for her to get her thoughts together. Or maybe he's getting his own thoughts together. Either way, they sit in silence for a few minutes, giving her a chance to try to make sense of everything in her brain.

"I was trying to convince myself that I could work things out with Garrett, but it just doesn't make sense. I know Johnny's family hasn't always been that nice to us, but Johnny's been nice to me lately, and he's different once you get to know him. Plus, he understands all of *this*." She gestures to the store, and specifically to the row of caskets in the front.

"I'm not here to judge you," Grandpa says. "If you're sure."

She doesn't owe Garrett anything, but she does plan to keep his secrets. Besides, those secrets are something else you don't just drop on an eighty-five-year-old. "I don't think Garrett and I were ever really on the same page. I just thought we were. Johnny lives here, and he already knows everyone. We've known each other forever."

"I can't tell if you're convincing yourself or me," he says. "But you don't have to be sure right now. Try some patience on for size."

"I'm tired of waiting, Grandpa."

He laughs. "I can see that, even with these old eyes."

"I just want something of my own. Everyone else seems to have it already."

He reaches across the desk between them and pats her hand. "These things can't be rushed. You won't be happy."

"You don't think I'll be happy with Johnny?"

"That's not what I meant. You have to make your own choices."

Nora spends a quiet night at home. She does some laundry and makes pasta for dinner. Well, as much as boiling some spaghetti noodles and mixing them with sauce she found in the pantry counts as making pasta. She straightens up the house while watching a football game. In these moments, she sees that everything is fine. The store is fine. Her relationships are fine. There's nothing she should be doing to make any of it better, at least for one night.

She's in bed watching *Cheers* when Johnny calls.

"I have a proposition for you," he says when she answers.

"I think there are other numbers you can call for that."

"A business proposition, Clanton. Get your mind out of the gutter."

"What kind of proposition?"

"Can you meet tomorrow? At my office? I've been thinking about what you said about selling the store. We should talk about details. See if it's something we want to do."

Nora stares at the frozen image on her TV screen. Sam had sold the bar, and everything turned out fine, didn't it? "Sure. What time?"

"Eleven o'clock. I'll take you to lunch afterward."

She smiles. "I would like that."

Maybe, Nora thinks, she should start going through the motions and the feelings will follow. Some decisions are fifty-one percent one way and forty-nine percent the other, and you eventually have to accept that an answer is an answer. Instagram therapists are always right.

Nora rifles through her closet, looking for anything that will be appropriate both for a work meeting and for lunch with a man she might like. She settles for her least-wrinkly pair of dark gray pants with a wannabe-silk maroon top with cap sleeves. Not exciting, but not frumpy. Nothing she'll fiddle with during awkward moments, although she can always seem to find something to fiddle with, no matter how she tries to prevent it from happening. She dries her hair and applies real makeup, stops for a coffee, and still manages to make it into town a few minutes early for her meeting with Johnny.

The Anniston location of Chandler Funeral Homes was their first location and, of course, became their finest. Giant white columns line the front of the dark-brick three-story building. The first floor is ceremony and visitation space, while the top floors are said to be offices. Nora can't fathom why they would need so many employees to have so many offices, and she certainly can't imagine how they make enough money to pay that many people. In the past few years, the Chandlers had opened locations in Heflin, Talladega, Pell City, and Sylacauga. Nora could tell Johnny was exhilarated by all of the expansion, but the thought of opening another branch of Rabbittown Casket Company made her want to run away. Johnny could probably do more with the store than she ever could. Maybe she wasn't competitive enough to run a business.

She steps into the building, unsure of where Johnny's office is, until she sees him standing on the other side of the foyer talking to someone. As she approaches, she recognizes Larry from the National Funeral Directors Society conference.

Johnny greets her with a hug. It feels a little weird, especially in a business context, but Nora feels weird in most contexts that involve hugs.

"You remember Larry?" Johnny asks.

Larry extends a hand and shakes Nora's with vigor. "Larry Hill. Great to see you again."

"Great to see you, too." She looks to Johnny. "I'm sorry, did I get the time wrong?"

"Nope. You're right on time. Let's go to my office."

They ride in the elevator together, as Johnny and Larry recount a story from their golf outing. Both of them find the story hilarious, but Nora doesn't understand the humor in a grown man throwing a golf club into the woods. She does appreciate the appeal of a well-tailored suit and fancy loafers and the dad-like quality of Larry in a Prestige polo and tennis shoes.

Johnny leads them down the hall, past other offices with people at their desks typing on their keyboards. It brings Nora back to her time in finance, when she would spend all day typing on her keyboard, waiting for a co-worker or a client to interrupt the monotony. Now her daily interruptions are usually tinged with grief, except for the one time someone had come in to ask for directions.

The office at the end of the hall keeps Nora from thinking any further about that. Johnny's office is about the same size as Nora's entire store. The windows overlook downtown Anniston, and she thinks she can make out the steeple for Parker Memorial in the distance. He has a living room set up, with a couch and easy chairs, on one side of the room and a conference table on the other side. His desk is next to the windows, with full bookshelves lining the back wall. Nora hadn't taken him for a reader, but really, how well does she know him?

"Have a seat," he says, gesturing to the chairs in front of his desk.

"You're probably wondering what I'm doing here," Larry says as they all take their seats.

"It has crossed my mind," Nora says, hoping for a whimsical tone but not quite getting there.

"Well," Larry begins, "Johnny mentioned you might be looking to make some changes at Rabbittown Casket Company, and I thought I might kick in my two cents. I've been in this business a long time, and I knew your parents for years. I'd love to help you brainstorm."

Nora glances at Johnny, who shows no signs of being annoyed or surprised by this. He had invited Larry to the meeting, after all. "I'm not sure what I'm looking for, but I'm happy to hear your input," Nora replies. Her face says otherwise.

"You said you never expected to be running your family's store," Johnny says. "There are a few different ways you could go about it, and Larry has *years* more experience than I do—right, Larry?"

"I think that's your way of calling me an old man, but I might as well use all those years of funeral talk for something."

"Seems to me," Johnny begins, "the obvious way to start is selling the store. The different options come in when you think about what role you would want in the future."

"It's really common for smaller funeral homes or casket stores or hearse companies to sell the business and stay on as part of the staff," Larry explains. "I've worked with a lot of those businesses on those deals."

"At Prestige?" Nora asks.

"Yes, I've been there for twenty-five years. We do a lot of this sort of thing."

"I've noticed."

"A lot of these small companies are going under," Johnny says. "With Prestige, the business gets to stay open."

Nora stares at Johnny, trying to piece things together. "Assuming you're talking about me, my store isn't going under."

Johnny and Larry can't get the protests out of their mouths fast enough.

"I just meant to say that they help people who need it," Johnny says.

"A lot of people try to separate business and personal," Larry adds, "but businesses like yours are a family operation, and we want them to still feel like family for everyone involved, even after Prestige takes over."

"Got it. What does this have to do with me?"

"Well," Johnny begins, rocking back in his leather rolling chair. "I was telling Larry I was thinking about making you an offer, and he mentioned that Prestige might be interested, too."

"*Well*," Nora says, "I might not be as successful as the two of you, but I do have a business degree and I've seen a few movies, so it's a little odd that the two of you are here together if you're both trying to buy my business."

Johnny smirks, and Nora isn't as charmed as she usually is. She stares at him, waiting for a response that doesn't treat her like a child.

"You sound just like your dad. He liked to get to the bottom of things, too," Larry says. Nora isn't charmed by him, either. "We think there's something here for all three of us. Johnny and I could go in together to buy the business. You'd get the best of both of our companies, and you could stay on as staff or take that money as a chance to start over, if that's what you want to do."

"Personally, I'd love it if you stayed on," Johnny says. "At least for a while."

Nora nods. This is what she wanted. To get out. The money would be nice. She could live on it until she decides what to do next. "What's the timeline on this?"

"I think that's a question for you," Larry says. "We'd love to start talking about details as soon as you're ready."

"How would that work?"

"We'd have to get lawyers involved," Johnny says. "Which is my least favorite sentence in the world. But we'd have to go through your finances and assets and come up with a proposal for you."

Larry starts talking about lawyers, and Nora tunes him out, turning her attention to the framed photos around the room. She recognizes a few of Johnny's family members and a couple from fancy vacations. What would her parents think of her being here, in this office? Had they ever been here? What had they really thought of Larry? They could either be screaming at her from wherever they are or be completely supportive, and she would never know.

"Nora?" Johnny calls.

"Sorry, it's a lot to think about," she says. "Can I have a couple of days?"

"Of course!" Larry says. "We aren't deciding anything today. Take as much time as you need."

"Great, thank you both for talking with me," Nora says, as politely as she can manage, even though they all know she was ambushed.

Johnny stands, signaling everyone to stand, and he walks them back down to the elevator.

"I've gotta get going to another meeting," Larry says once they're in the lobby. "But here's my card. Let's stay in touch."

Nora takes the card. "Thanks, Larry. I'll let you know soon."

"See ya, Johnny."

They all shake hands, and when the door shuts behind Larry, Nora turns to face Johnny.

"Lunch?" he asks.

"Oh, we're going to talk somewhere."

"Let's take a walk."

Nora follows him out the door and onto the sidewalk. He seems to have a destination in mind, so she hurries to try to keep up.

"Are you sure you can walk in those shoes?" Nora asks.

"Don't start with me, Clanton."

"Where are we going?" The weather is about as perfect as it can get in Alabama—seventy degrees and sunny. No rain. No storm. No oppressive heat.

"Don't you trust me?" He gives her one of his trademark smirks.

"Not after what you just did."

"I just did you a solid."

"Working with Prestige? Are you kidding me?"

Johnny pauses to let a car pass before jaywalking across the street. Nora looks both ways before following him. She might follow him into a lot of situations, but traffic is not one of them.

"Can you slow down?"

He stops to let her catch up. "Can you walk faster?"

"I could run, I guess." She takes his arm to keep him at a calmer pace. "And you could answer my questions."

"Remind me what they were."

"Where are you taking me right now?"

He points ahead toward the old train station, which has been turned into a brewery. "I thought we could get a beer."

"Do you normally drink at lunch?"

"If the situation warrants."

"And you think this situation requires a beer?"

He smiles down at her. "I think there's a small chance you end up yelling at me, so yes."

They walk into the brewery, and he pauses to say hello to the staff working behind the bar before leading Nora to a table.

"You must come here often," Nora says as she slides into the booth.

"It's close to work."

Nora looks down at the menu, pretending to study the options, but her brain is full of everything that happened that morning.

"You want a beer?" Johnny asks. When Nora nods, he waves at the bartender and holds two fingers in the air. After the beer arrives, Johnny sips his and lets out a dramatic sigh. "Okay, let's do this."

Nora rolls her eyes and swallows a sip of her own drink. "You put yourself in this position by lying to me."

"I never lied."

"You told me I would be meeting with you. You didn't mention Larry or Prestige at all. I was blindsided."

"I invited you to a meeting. I knew you wouldn't come if I told you about Larry."

"That should have been enough for you to know not to invite him. I wanted to talk to *you* about it. Not him. This is my family's business, Johnny. It's not a joke to me."

"You think it's a joke to me? I brought Larry into this so you can get a better deal."

"You should have talked to me about it. I could have been more prepared."

"Well, I didn't. I'm sorry. But you handled yourself fine."

Nora sighs. "This is all just a lot to process."

"I know. What do you think?"

She laughs. "I think a lot of things."

"Larry seems motivated. I think you'll get a good offer."

"Why is he even interested in my store? Why are *you* interested?"

"It pains me to admit this, but you're running a successful business. Against all odds, I might add. There should not be a casket company in Rabbittown."

"Everyone dies," Nora says. "Even people in Rabbittown."

"You know, there are people out there who have happy jobs."

"I used to be one of them."

"You could be one of them again. Or stay here and hang out with me and all the corpses. The world is your oyster, Clanton."

"I don't like oysters."

"Choose your own sea creature, then."

"Well, if I'm going to keep the store profitable, I have to get back to it eventually."

"Let's order. What do you want?"

"What are you getting?" Nora asks, flipping over the menu.

Johnny raises his hand to wave at the bartender. "Can we get two burgers, Drew?"

"Sure thing, man," Drew shouts.

Nora hits Johnny with her menu. "I asked what you were getting. I didn't tell you to order for me."

He takes the menu from her and slides it to the end of the table. "If you hate it, you can order something else. Order the whole menu."

"Whatever."

Johnny laughs. "Are you twelve years old?"

"Actually, I'll be thirty-one tomorrow."

"No shit. You weren't going to tell me?"

"I just did."

"Are you having a party?"

"I'm not a party person, but I'm having dinner with my grandpa."

"We should do something this weekend."

"Me and you?"

"And Larry, of course."

Nora tries not to laugh, but she can't help it.

"Yes, me and you. What do you think?" Johnny asks.

"I'm open to it. You have my number."

When she wakes up the next morning, nothing is different. She feels the same. She looks the same. Everything else looks the same. She gets ready like always. She drives to the store like always. She thinks this is one reason so many people are let down by birthdays: you expect everything and everyone to be different or special, including yourself, but nothing ever is. It's just another Thursday, except a delivery man brings two giant bouquets of flowers around lunchtime.

"It must be your birthday," he says. He slides both vases onto the counter. One bouquet is long-stemmed red roses. The other has sunflowers, daisies, and other brightly colored flowers that Nora can't name right off.

"It is," she says. "But I wasn't expecting either of these."

"Good surprises, I hope."

"Can't really complain about flowers."

"Well, have a happy birthday."

"Thank you."

He exits as quickly as he came, and she's left to examine the flowers. She opens the card on the roses first. It says: "Happy Birthday! See you soon." It's signed "J."

She's opening the card on the second bouquet when the delivery man rushes back in the door. "Sorry, I forgot this part of the gift." He hands her a small box wrapped with balloon-covered paper, and then he's halfway out the door again.

"Wait, there's no card for this one?" she asks.

He stares at the box for a moment. "I think it goes with one of the bouquets. Let me call the store and ask."

"That's okay. I'll figure it out."

"Sorry, again," he says, running out the door.

She finishes opening the card for the second bouquet, expecting to see her grandpa's name, or Jean's name, or the name of someone else from the church, but instead it reads: "Happy Birthday! All my love, Garrett."

Nora's brain starts up. She didn't even remember telling Garrett when her birthday was, but he remembered it. She will overthink this later, but first she has a gift to open.

Her heart catches as the wrapping paper falls away, and she knows this gift didn't come from Johnny. She tilts the box, and a baseball falls into her hand. One side of the ball has the *Cheers* logo on it, and the other side is autographed: "Mayday Malone #16."

"Oh my God," she says aloud to an empty store.

She tosses the ball into the air a couple of times and admires the signature. She figures this came from some internet *Cheers* store and that Ted Danson has no idea it exists. She doesn't care. It's perfect. It's exactly what she didn't know she wanted.

She scrambles around in her purse to find her phone.

Garrett answers on the second ring. "Hello?"

She's running on a bit of adrenaline and doesn't feel nervous until she hears his voice. "Uh, hi. It's me. It's Nora." She traces her fingers over the seams on the ball.

"I know." She hears him smile, and it makes her smile, too.

"I'm sorry to call in the middle of the day. I should have asked if you were free."

"I'm free."

"Well, I'm calling because I just got your present." She looks at the bright bouquet beside her. "Oh, and the flowers, too. They're beautiful. You didn't have to do any of this."

"I wanted to. Happy birthday."

"Thank you. The ball is perfect. I don't even know what to say. I love it."

He laughs. "I'm glad. When I saw it, I knew I had to get it."

"It's perfect," she says again. "The internet is a wild place."

"I ordered it from the real Cheers. It's in Boston. We could go. Or you should, at least."

She's not used to hearing Garrett stumble over his words. It adds to the bubbly feeling building in her heart. "Yeah, that sounds cool. I've never been to Boston."

"Me either."

They sit there for an awkward beat, and then they both try to talk at the same time.

"Go ahead," she says.

"I was just going to say, I'll be at home with my family this weekend, but when I get back, I'd like to see you. If that would be okay."

If nothing had changed between them, she would have been

with him in Raleigh, meeting his family, and she feels a pang of regret that they had spent so much time apart. "I think that would be okay. Have fun with your family, and thank you, again, for the gifts."

"You're welcome. Have a good birthday."

She hangs up and starts to pace. Friends get each other presents all the time, right? They've been through the "more than friends" part of it already, and it doesn't work. Nora wants to be with someone who aligns with her beliefs and her values. She can't worry about what he's doing when he goes to work every day. She can't live a secret life.

She tosses the ball back and forth between her hands. It isn't just any present, at least not to Nora. Garrett knows what *Cheers* has meant to her. It's been her constant since her parents died. It's been her comfort. It's been her company through the grief. Sure, that sounds silly. It certainly doesn't make logical sense that a 1980s sitcom about a bar would help her through the loneliness of the past year, but there doesn't seem to be any logic in grief. Even her most elaborate pro and con lists couldn't help Nora cope with the losses in her life. When she feels like she's sinking, she grasps on to whatever might keep her afloat, and *Cheers* has been that thing on so many nights.

Garrett's gift honors that, but how much should she read into it? He didn't seem to get it. He didn't understand why she would be so upset with him about his job working for Death, after all Death had taken from her and others around her. Did this mean he understood now?

Nora stops that line of questioning and takes a drink of water to try to reset her brain. She knows it doesn't have to mean anything like that. It means he knows her well enough to get her a decent birthday present. Expecting something out of nothing is going to get her where it's always gotten her: nowhere.

She puts the ball into a desk drawer to examine Johnny's roses. Now, this is a romantic gift. This gift means something. You don't send roses like these to a random girl. Johnny likes Nora, and Nora likes Johnny. She doesn't need to mess this up because of a fantasy that will never come true.

She texts Johnny a photo of the roses with the caption *Thank you. They're beautiful* and adds a red heart emoji.

After an hour or so he replies: *Happy Birthday Clanton. See you this weekend.*

As Nora pulls her car into her grandpa's gravel driveway, she tries to imagine what the place looks like objectively, instead of what it looks like to her. It's certainly old. Certainly lived in. There's no sod, just normal grass. The yard and the flower beds are maintained by an elderly person, so they wouldn't be on HGTV, but Nora loves it here. This house means a lot to her, cluttered garage and all.

Nora walks in without knocking, as she always does, and she realizes the birthday dinner is more like a party than advertised. Grandpa is in the living room with Joe and Jean, and someone has hung streamers around the room and into the kitchen. There's a cardboard "Happy Birthday" sign tacked to one wall, covering an old family portrait.

"What's all this?" she asks.

"Happy birthday!" they call in unison. Even though Nora didn't want a fuss, she's glad to be spending the night with family.

She's greeting Grandpa, Joe, and Jean when Margaret, Ed,

and Ms. Annie walk in. There are more hugs and hellos before they all try to choose places to sit on the screened-in front porch. Seeing Ms. Annie reminds Nora of Frank, which reminds her of Garrett, and she stops those thoughts before they can get going. Nora sits next to her grandpa on the swing hanging from one end of the porch, and everyone else finds a mismatched chair.

"I didn't expect all this," Nora says.

"Well, it's not every day you turn thirty-one," Grandpa says.

"You just had to remind me."

"You've got a lot of years to go, honey," Jean says. "You don't know old yet."

Nora sees Ed elbow Margaret and knows something ridiculous is coming.

"Now, I know it's your birthday, but I heard something, and I've been dying to ask you about it," Margaret says. "What's going on with you and Johnny Chandler?"

"Well, what did you hear?"

"I heard he's been picking you up at the store in that big truck of his."

"He picked me up *once*," Nora clarifies.

"Oh, here we go," Jean says under her breath, but plenty loud enough for everyone on the porch to hear it.

"There's not much to tell. He drove me to the conference where I got that award for Dad. I'm seeing him sometime this weekend."

"Dating your competitor is an odd choice," Joe says. "But what do I know?"

Nora gives Grandpa a look and hopes no one notices. She knows no one here likes the Chandler family. Maybe that's why Grandpa invited them.

"Well, to be honest, he's interested in buying the store."

After a moment of shock and gaping mouths, Grandpa asks, "What do you mean?"

"Nothing is certain, but I was telling him that I never meant to be living in Rabbittown and running the store, and he thought we might be able to come up with a deal to help us both, if that's what I decide. I could keep working there, if I want. Or use the money to take a break and figure out what I want to do. There are a few different options."

"And you're thinking about it?" Jean asks.

"Yes. I love being so close to all of you, but it's not a secret that it's been a hard year here. I never wanted to sell caskets. I never wanted any of this."

Margaret looks at Ms. Annie, and then they both look at Jean. No one seems to know the right thing to say.

Ed clears his throat. "The way I see it, you're grown. You've gotta make your own decisions."

Nora relaxes a bit, knowing that Ed is the most level-headed of the group. Maybe this idea isn't completely around the bend.

"I just can't imagine Rabbittown Casket Company in the hands of the Chandlers," Margaret says. "What would your Papa Moore say?"

"You act like she's selling out to the devil," Jean says.

"She might get more money out of the devil," Joe says, elbowing Jean.

"I haven't gotten any money out of anybody yet," Nora says. "We're just talking. I'm the one who brought it up. I didn't expect him to make an offer, but here we are. I feel like the most responsible thing to do would be to hear him out. And my Papa Moore isn't here. It's just me." She wants to remind them that her Papa Moore was an old crank who hated everything and everyone except for the Crimson Tide. He would have hated everything her parents did with the store, so really, she was just continuing her family legacy of disappointing the generation that came before.

"There's no rush," Grandpa says, patting her leg. "It will sort itself out."

"I believe we're supposed to be celebrating," Jean says.

"I believe you're right," Grandpa says, standing from his seat on the swing. "Why don't we have some supper?"

The rest of the night goes as well as it can go. Ed and Joe set up card tables on the porch, so everyone can eat in the same room. They have Nora's favorite meal, pot roast and fried okra. Nora gets a few more presents: her favorite candle from Ms. Annie, Braves tickets from Joe and Jean, and a beautiful chocolate birthday cake from Ed and Margaret (mostly Margaret), and then her grandpa gives her a framed photo of the two of them.

"Was this at Frank's?" Nora asks about the photo.

"Ms. Annie took it for us a while back. I thought we could use an updated picture."

"I love it," she says, trying to hold back her feelings. The day has been enough without adding tears to it. It hasn't been her first birthday without her parents, but Nora wonders how many years it will take not to think about her dad's singing voicemails or her mom's macaroni and cheese.

"I have one, too," he says. He points at the mantel, and Nora feels bad that she didn't notice when she came in that he had added a new brown frame next to the old ones.

As it gets later and the gossip runs out, they all decide to call it a night. Nora says goodbye to everyone individually, thanking them for her presents.

When she gets to Grandpa, he whispers, "Be easy, girl. Everything will be fine."

She hugs him tightly, "I know. Thanks for tonight. Love you."

"Love you, too."

As Nora drives into town on Friday night, she doesn't know what to expect. Johnny has invited her over to his house for some sort of birthday celebration, and she assumes it could turn out either mildly awkward and mostly okay or horrifically bad on all levels. They don't know each other well enough for him to plan the perfect birthday celebration for her, which generally involves as little attention on her as possible.

Even though they have a lot of obvious things in common, they've led very different lives. He lives down the road from his parents, near the country club, and she figures he must have a landscaper because there's no way his yard would be this immaculate otherwise. He answers the door in a golf shirt and shorts and leads her to the kitchen, where he presents a table full of Chinese takeout.

"Happy birthday!"

"Who is going to eat all this?" Nora asks.

"I didn't know what you wanted."

"You could have asked."

"Maybe I didn't know what *I* wanted. There will be leftovers. It's fine."

"Thank you for doing this."

"Don't make it weird, Clanton." He reaches into the cabinet to take out two white plates, and he hands her the top one. "Birthday girl goes first."

Nora fills her plate with a little of everything: fried rice, lo mein, two kinds of chicken, and two kinds of egg rolls. She thinks she might have overdone it until she watches Johnny cover his plate with one layer of entrees and lo mein and then a second layer of egg rolls. He pours a glass of wine for each of them, and Nora thinks of Garrett for a moment, before she forces him out of her mind.

They eat at Johnny's dining room table, which doesn't seem like it's ever been used. The house is beautiful and well decorated, but she doesn't get the feeling he picked any of the décor out. There doesn't seem to be a theme, other than expensive. Some of the paintings on his walls could be in a dentist's office.

"Where did you get that?" she asks about an abstract painting of blue and green lines hanging on the wall behind him.

"Some art dealer in Birmingham," he says, barely looking up from his plate. "I don't remember. I'm sure you'll judge me for that."

"I'm not judging. It's nice." It's not nice, but she doesn't know what else to say.

"I'm not that attached to it." He uses his chopsticks to pick up a pile of lo mein noodles and slurps one into his mouth. "How was your first birthday dinner?"

"It was good. My grandpa invited over some family friends, and we had pot roast and cake."

"That sounds nice. My family doesn't really do birthdays like that."

"Not even when you were little?"

"We had big parties when we were kids. One year, my mom rented ponies for my sister."

"And now?"

"We usually just text one another or send flowers or something."

"Maybe you should invite them over for your birthday this year."

He laughs. "That sounds like the worst birthday I can imagine."

"You don't get along?"

He pushes a pile of rice across his plate with his chopsticks. "There are pain points in all families."

"That's a very polite answer."

"I'm a polite guy."

"Well, I'm sorry, for what it's worth."

"It's fine. Enough about them. Have you thought any more about the deal?"

Nora sighs. "I've been thinking about it."

"I'm not rushing you, but you can talk to me about it, no matter which way you're leaning."

"It seems to be happening quickly."

"Nothing has to happen unless you want it to."

"I know. It's a lot to consider." She picks up the last bite of her egg roll. "I can't eat another bite after this."

"You want to watch a movie or something?" he asks.

"Sure."

Johnny takes care of their plates, while Nora attends to the leftover food containers.

"The fridge is pretty full," Johnny says. "Let me make some room."

As she waits, she notices a stack of papers on the edge of the counter and shifts it out of the vicinity of the food to keep it from getting covered in some kind of sauce. One of the pages sticking out of the pile catches her eye, as she makes out the word "Rabbittown" at the top. Her first inclination is to pretend she didn't see it. He hadn't shown her the papers, so she shouldn't be looking at them. At the same time, she did see it. And she's done with secrets.

She tries to pull the page out of the pile, but it's stuck in a folder, so she grabs the whole folder. It has the Prestige logo on the front. When she opens it, she finds photos and drawings of her store. In some of the drawings, the Rabbittown Casket Company sign has been replaced with a Prestige logo.

"What is this?" Nora calls to Johnny.

He peeks his head out from behind the refrigerator door. "What is what?"

"This folder. Did this come from Larry?"

Johnny closes the door and leans against it. "Yeah, he dropped it off."

Nora turns the pages to see more drawings, contracts, and financial figures and reports, all on Prestige letterhead. "I don't see your name anywhere on this. Would it be two separate deals or something?"

"Uh, no, it would all go through Prestige."

Nora closes the folder. "How does that work?"

"You don't have to worry about that part." He walks over to stand next to her. "Larry and I are working that out."

"Well, I do worry about that part. Would I be selling the store to Larry or to you?"

"We're working together."

The rage inside Nora bubbles up before she can stop it. Johnny doesn't necessarily deserve the brunt of it, but she's had about enough of men lying under the guise of protecting her. "Cut the shit, Johnny. This is my whole life. I deserve the truth."

Johnny sighs. "Look, it's complicated. The deal would go through Prestige, but I'm part of it, too."

Nora tilts her head. "How are you part of it? Are you getting paid?"

"Yes, I'm getting paid. My name just isn't on it."

"Are you getting fifty percent?"

"We haven't worked out the details."

Nora runs the situation through her mind. It's not fully adding up. She can come up with only one answer, so she spits it out before she can talk herself out of it: "Are you getting a finder's fee? Did you orchestrate all of this so that Prestige can buy my store?"

"It's more complicated than that."

"Then explain it."

"Look, Nora, you told me about the situation at the store, and I mentioned it to Larry. I didn't think much about it at the time, but he's like a dog with a bone, and Prestige could get this done a lot faster than I can and for more money."

"And you get a cut."

"Yes."

All of the air has gone out of the room, and Nora is having trouble breathing. Her hands are clammy. Her face is red. Her first instinct is to run out the front door, but she resists.

"So that's what all of this is." She gestures at the counter of Chinese food in front of her. "You try to kiss me and send me flowers and invite me for dinner. You encourage me to talk to you about how I'm feeling. All this time, you're just waiting to make money off of me. Off of my dead family."

"It's not like that."

"It's exactly like that, Johnny. I can't believe I trusted you. I knew better."

"You *can* trust me. I'm trying to help you."

"Then why wouldn't you just tell me?"

"Because I know how much you hate Prestige."

"And you thought misleading me into selling my family's business to them would turn out fine? That I wouldn't notice?" She pulls out one of the drawings from the folder and points at the Prestige logo at the top of her building. "Was any of this real between us, or was the whole thing an act?"

"Of course it was real. Do you really think I would do all of this to get some money out of you?"

Maybe it's intuition. Maybe it's a message from above. She imagines her parents having to watch this whole thing with their hands over their faces. Maybe her grandpa was right, and she just needed time for things to work themselves out. But now she knows. She can feel it. All of this is wrong. Selling the store. Moving away. Johnny.

This was never about Johnny or Garrett or her parents or anybody else. This has always been about her. What does she want to do? Who does she want to be? She can't expect anyone else to know the answers if she doesn't know them herself.

While she's not experiencing a miracle of biblical proportions, she has figured out exactly what she doesn't want. She doesn't want to be Nora Chandler, running a branch of funeral homes for Prestige. She doesn't want holidays at the country club. She doesn't want abstract paintings or housekeepers.

She doesn't want to sell her family's store. Not to Johnny. Not to Prestige. Not to anybody. Nobody knows how hard her family has worked to build that business. Nobody else helped her parents pick out the carpet. Nobody watched her dad get those four model caskets through the front door. Nobody knows and cares about the community like she does. If someone is going to be selling caskets in Rabbittown, it's going to be a Clanton. It's going to be her.

She knows what she wants, and as much as she hates to admit it to herself, it doesn't involve Johnny Chandler.

"Thanks for dinner, Johnny. You can tell Larry no deal."

"Don't be like this. Give me a chance. Let's talk about it."

She could spend some more time avoiding the truth, but she decides it's time to be honest with everyone, including herself. "I don't want to talk about it anymore. I tried, but none of this is what I want."

"You mean I'm not what you want. It's James Bond, isn't it? The guy from the conference?"

"It's not James Bond. It's me. That's the truth."

He nods. Then, the corners of his mouth curl up in a smirk. "Never thought I'd get my heart broken by a Clanton."

She takes a step toward the front door. "I know my way out."

He follows her to the foyer. "Can I just say something first? I know I'm not good enough for you, but neither is he, or he wouldn't have let you go in the first place."

"I think maybe you've got that the wrong way around."

ONE MONTH AGO

"About time you got here," Mrs. Dooley says, closing the magazine she had been reading.

Garrett steps into the room without comment. He has gotten used to old people and their confusion. "My name is Garrett Bishop. I'm here to have a quick conversation with you. It won't take long."

"I know who you are. I'm Violet Wheeler Dooley, but you know that already."

He nods. "I do know who you are, Mrs. Dooley."

"I thought you'd be here sooner. I've been stuck here with all these old people for years."

Garrett looks down at his watch. "In the next few minutes, you're going to feel a change in your body. You'll feel some pain, but it won't last long—"

"You don't have to explain dying to me, young man. I'm sure they teach you all this at angel school, but you can save the speech."

"I'm not an angel, but I am here to be with you during the process. I'll be here the whole time."

"When I was seven, my dad died. He had always been a drinker. A woman was there. She had dark hair. She gave me a piece of candy and told me everything would be fine." She holds out her hand. "Where's my candy?"

Garrett reaches into his pocket to retrieve a handful of hard candy. "What color do you want?"

"Red."

He places the red piece in her hand, and she peels apart the plastic wrapper. She plops the candy onto her tongue. Her eyes widen, and she reaches for her heart.

"Here we go."

Garrett sits down in the chair next to the bed. "Everything is going to be fine, Mrs. Dooley. It will be over soon. I'm right here with you."

She winces. "My husband is waiting for me. My mama, too."

"What's your husband's name?"

"Leo."

He reaches over to take her hand. He's held so many hands like this over the years—delicate, wrinkled, cold. "I'm sure Leo is waiting for you. Think of his face. You'll see him soon."

She forces out a sentence: "He spent his whole life waiting on me."

Garrett smiles. "Then you shouldn't keep him waiting any longer."

Her eyes flutter, and her breath slows. She squeezes Garrett's hand, and alarms start to fill the silence. Garrett checks his watch to note the time, as the alarms get more earnest.

"Nice to meet you, Mrs. Dooley."

He pats her hand one final time and slips out of the room.

CHAPTER

18

Nora has no idea what she's doing. After much ado, her brain has finally given up at 7:37 A.M. on a Saturday morning. Or maybe a few hours before that.

She's in her car. She's driving east on I-20; then she'll head north on I-85 and east on I-40 until she hits Raleigh.

Is this a good idea? Probably not. But Nora can't see anything but Garrett.

She called her grandpa as she was getting on I-20 to let him know she had set off to Raleigh without a plan. He didn't try to stop her. When she pointed this out, he said, "I know better than to get between you and whatever you've got in that head." Not exactly a vote of confidence, but it is the truth.

Last night, Nora spent an hour or two crying. Mostly, she was crying about her own choices. She never wanted to work at Rabbittown Casket Company in the first place! Why was she suddenly making a big deal about it? She could sell the store. She could sell her parents' house. She could sell everything that has ever given her any trouble. She could buy new clothes. She could get a new name. She could leave Rabbittown. But she would still be the same person. She would still have dead parents and the weight of trying to carry everything they left behind.

All of those separate pieces of her life: her old job, the plans she used to have, her family, her future, all the futures she didn't get to have, and everything else—they all keep shifting and overlapping to make more room for every new thing she adds in. She can't become one thing or another without the rest of it. She has to carry it all. She has to accept life as it is, not as she wants it to be. She can see that now.

All of these thoughts keep leading her back to Garrett. They couldn't work it out before, because Nora wanted to meddle in his life, too. She wanted to take the Death part out of his life, but if she can't even take the Death part out of her own life, what sort of sense does that make? Is there anyone on the planet who doesn't have Death lurking around somewhere? Isn't Death a part of everyone's life? Garrett tried to tell her this, but she wouldn't listen. She wasn't ready to hear it.

She knows there's a chance that he won't be ready to pick up where they left off. She thinks this surprise road trip might increase those chances, but she just couldn't wait another second to talk to him in person. If he turns her down, she won't be any worse off than she already is. If he calls the police, she'll see if Jean can come get her out of a North Carolina jail.

As Nora was wrestling with this decision last night, she ran through all of these details. Of course she made a pro and con list. The biggest con was definitely jail time, but maybe she could talk him out of that. Another con was not knowing his parents' address, but the internet helped. The last con on the list was breaking her own heart again, but she's survived that before.

Nora tries to listen to the radio to pass the time in the car, but she ends up spending most of the eight-hour drive overthinking and reviewing the legal pad in the passenger seat. She stops twice for caffeine, which makes the overthinking worse, but it keeps her from turning around. She makes it to Raleigh and into the suburbs, and her heart starts to beat faster. As she gets closer to his parents' neighborhood, she tells herself if she can just lay eyes on him for a moment, it will calm her racing heart and the butterflies banging around in her stomach.

Nora turns into his subdivision, because of course Garrett Bishop grew up in a subdivision, and she scopes out the houses. They seem pretty normal—slightly worn siding, newly painted shutters, vibrant flower beds, and children in almost every yard. She sees some people in the street ahead, because of course people run here on a Saturday afternoon. A woman in neon colors waves as she passes by going in the other direction. Nora sees a man running ahead of her in basketball shorts and a T-shirt.

Maybe Nora doesn't recognize those shorts and that T-shirt, but she definitely knows the man wearing them. She would know him anywhere. Her heart beats faster, disproving her earlier theory; she really had not considered a situation like this in all of her overthinking. How had she missed a scenario in eight hours of hashing through the possibilities? She considers turning back because she is not properly prepared, but she didn't drive this far to change her mind in the end zone.

When she catches up to him, she rolls down her passenger window and yells, "Hey!"

He has headphones on, so he doesn't hear it. Maybe she should park the car and run after him? That is a terrible plan. She tries again to get his attention, but this time she drives a few yards past him and stops in the middle of the street. She sees the confusion on his face in the rearview mirror, and she waves at him through the back windshield.

He takes out his headphones and leans down into the passenger window.

"Hi," Nora says.

"Hi." He almost smiles, but he's having a hard time breathing. He bends over to catch his breath.

"Are you okay?" she shouts across the front seat and out the window.

He puts his hands on his knees so he's eye level with her. "Not really, no."

"Do you want a ride?"

"I'm kind of gross," he says, looking down at his shirt.

"Some people don't care as much as you do about the cleanliness of their cars."

He smiles as he opens the car door and sits down next to her. "As I'm sure you can imagine, I have a lot of questions."

"I have answers." For once, she's telling the truth.

"Don't take this the wrong way, but what are you doing here?" He's still trying to catch his breath. A drop of sweat runs down the side of his face.

Nora holds in a laugh. "I wanted to see you."

"So, you drove to Raleigh?"

"Seems that way." Even though he's covered in sweat, she is

absurdly attracted to this man. She doesn't know how she ever thought she could have these feelings for anyone else.

"You know, I would have been home on Monday." She hears the humor in his tone, so maybe the jail scenario is becoming less likely.

"I'm not good with patience."

"Well, you're here. Now what?"

"I want to talk." All of the overthinking that brought her here, and she can't remember anything she planned to say. "I know we've had our differences or issues or whatever you want to call them, and I know I told you that I couldn't get over them."

He nods, and her brain tries to figure out what to say next. She decides she might as well be as direct as possible. What does she have to lose?

"I was wrong. About all of it. I can get over all of those other things, but it doesn't seem like I can get over you. If there's a chance you would want to try and work things out or see where we go from here, I want to do that."

"I thought you had moved on," he says, staring out the windshield. He doesn't give anything away.

"I tried. It didn't happen."

"How would this work?" he asks.

"What do you mean?"

"How would we work things out?"

"I don't know. You said you wanted to get together to catch up. Maybe we could start there? I know we have a lot to talk about."

He nods as if he's thinking it over. "I think that's a good idea."

"Really?" Her eyes widen. She thought for sure it would take more convincing. Or at least some convincing that she isn't completely insane after stalking him to his parents' house.

"Really."

"I mean, I don't want to change your mind, but I know I hurt you, so if you need some time, I would understand. Or we could talk about all of it first."

"I'm actually extremely sick of talking about it, and I would be fine if we never talked about it again."

She tilts her head to consider this for a moment. "I can stop talking."

"I can't believe you came all the way to Raleigh. I probably don't even want to know how you tracked me down."

"Probably not."

He smiles at her, and she smiles back, with those same slightly nauseating emoji heart eyes they've always had for each other. She reaches across the console to grab his sweaty hand, but to be fair, hers is a little sweaty, too.

"If it's okay, I would like to kiss you now," Garrett says.

Nora nods, because she's lost the ability to speak.

He leans over and presses his lips against hers so gently that Nora thinks he might be giving her the chance to change her mind. Then he takes her face in his hands and kisses her the way he used to kiss her, the way that conveys all the feelings they have for each other without them having to say a word. He stops long enough to say, "I've missed you," against her lips.

"I missed you, too."

They don't kiss for much longer because they're sitting in a car in the middle of the street where he grew up.

"What now?" he asks.

"Whatever you want," she says.

They're both smiling like the biggest idiots on the planet, and maybe that's what they are.

"Can you stay for the weekend? I want you to meet my parents."

"Are you sure?" she asks. "I don't want to make things weird with them."

He laughs. "If my mom ever finds out you were in this city and didn't stop to meet her, we will both be in a lot of trouble."

"I'd like to meet her. I'd like to meet all of your family."

"Let's go, then."

He points at a two-story a few houses down, and she pulls into his driveway behind the other cars. His house is gray with dark blue shutters, but she already knew that from Google Maps.

"Really, though. How did you find me?"

"The internet. I invaded your privacy. I'm sorry."

"Don't be." He leans over to kiss her again before they get out of the car.

"This was a really crazy thing for me to do, Garrett. You should be freaked out."

"I spent a ridiculous amount of money to see you at a conference, so I understand." Her heart flutters at this admission. Somewhere, deep down, she had known he had gone to that conference for her, not for Death.

"I should have left with you."

He smiles. "There are a lot of things I should have done in the time we've been apart, so maybe we're a good match."

Nora follows him up the sidewalk and through his front door, and she tries very hard not to have a panic attack. She didn't think about what would happen after she talked to him. This scenario is brand-new to her brain, and her brain does not care for brand-new scenarios.

"Mom?" he calls. He motions for Nora to follow him into the kitchen, where she comes face-to-face with Garrett's mom. Nora would know those eyes anywhere.

She looks from Nora to Garrett, waiting for an explanation.

"Mom, this is Nora," Garrett says. "Nora, this is my mom."

Nora sticks her hand out because it feels like the polite thing to do. "It's nice to meet you, Mrs. Bishop."

When Garrett's mother doesn't take her hand at first, Nora assumes she's in trouble. Instead, Mrs. Bishop squeals. "Oh, my god! It's Nora!" she says to Garrett. She steps forward and takes Nora into a full-on mom embrace, knocking some of the breath out of her, literally and emotionally. It's been a long time since a mom hugged her that way.

"You can let her go now," he says.

"You didn't tell me she was coming!" His mom swats his arm. "You obviously haven't told me anything!" The more she talks, the more Nora hears her southern accent, and the more at home she feels.

"He didn't know," Nora says before Garrett can explain. "I just sort of showed up. I'm sorry. I promise I was raised better than that."

"Well, what's going on?" she asks. "Tell me everything."

"Mom, give her some space."

Mrs. Bishop rolls her eyes, and Nora recognizes her exasperated face from seeing it on Garrett so many times. "I'm trying to understand, and you are not helping."

Now feels like the time to tell the truth. "Well, honestly, I came here to apologize and to beg him to take me back."

She turns to Garrett. "And what did you say?"

"I brought her here to meet you, so what do you think?"

She claps her hands together and squeals again. Then she hugs Nora. "I knew it!" she shouts. "I told Garrett you were the one. I knew it! Didn't I tell you?"

"Mom, please," Garrett says. Normally it's Nora blushing, but she doesn't mind letting him have a turn. His hands fidget with the hem of his T-shirt.

"Please tell me you're staying. Did he ask you to stay? If not, I'm asking you, and I'm not taking no for an answer." She turns to Garrett and grimaces at his appearance. "Go take a shower. I'll take care of Nora while you're gone."

Garrett huffs, "Well, she just got here, and if she leaves, I'll know it's your fault, so please stop acting insane."

"I think it's the two of you who have been acting insane, but what do I know?"

"That's probably true," Nora says.

"Please don't leave," he says. His eyes say a lot more than that.

"I'm not going anywhere."

They spend the rest of the day with his family. Nora meets his dad, sister, and brother-in-law, and they all seem pleasantly surprised to see her. Nora figured they would be mad at her, but she knew Garrett had to keep things from them, so maybe the family didn't know much about the time they had spent apart.

He brings out a photo album to show Nora pictures of his brother, and they start to talk about the stories behind the pictures. They're all too happy to tell Nora about Garrett playing basketball and falling off his bike and being obsessed with Power Rangers.

She had forgotten what it was like to have a family like this. Asking for details about one another's lives. Making fun of one another. So much talking at once. Garrett's mom never lets Nora out of her sight, and Nora and Garrett can't seem to stop touching each other. After dinner, Nora and Garrett are in the kitchen, doing the dishes, when Garrett wraps his arms around her waist and kisses the side of her neck. She spins around to face him and says, "You're driving me crazy."

He kisses her quickly on the mouth. "I can't help it. I just have to make sure you're real."

"I'm real."

"I'm happy," he says. "This is better than I thought it could be."

She laughs. "I think your mom is happier than you are. I'm going to have questions about that later."

"She was tired of me moping around. She kept telling me to call you, and I wouldn't. She threatened to send you flowers for your birthday herself if I didn't."

"I thought they might be mad at me."

He shakes his head. "They just want me to be happy. I'm happy with you."

Nora kisses him right as his brother-in-law walks in and tells them to get a room.

They do get a room. His parents don't ask any questions, and Nora doesn't protest about sleeping with Garrett in his child-hood bedroom. It's covered in basketball memorabilia. She's never seen so many basketball posters in her life. She reads all of the ticket stubs and autographs while he watches her, as patiently as he can, from his full-size bed.

Nora changes into one of his T-shirts and climbs into bed next to him. She runs her hand over his bare chest for about two seconds before he rolls over on top of her. He kisses her, and all of their feelings rush to the surface. His hands travel all over her body, and she doesn't think it's possible for her to get as close as she wants to get to him tonight. He starts to pull the shirt over her head, and her conscience steps in.

"Wait," she whispers.

"Is this too fast?"

"God, no. I just don't think we should have sex in your parents' house."

He huffs, but he rolls off her. "Please don't do this."

She laughs. "I'm trying to be respectful."

"I know."

"Are you mad?"

"No."

"Are you sure?"

He kisses her neck. "Yes."

"Garrett?"

"Nora?" He keeps kissing her neck.

"I love you."

He moves to kiss her lips. "I love you, too."

They lie there for a moment, until he slides as far away from her as the bed will allow.

Her brow furrows. "I thought you weren't mad."

"I'm not. I just thought this would be the perfect opportunity to talk, since we're not doing anything else."

She laughs. "I thought you were done talking. What do you want to talk about?"

He sighs. "We have to talk about how you feel about my job. I still have the same one, and I don't want you to change your mind."

"I'm not changing my mind. I've decided not to care about your job."

"What do you mean?"

"I mean, I love you, not your job. I'll get over it."

"It really didn't seem like you would get over it, though. Even if I quit today, you'll know I spent years helping people die. We need to talk about it."

She sighs. "I think the expensive death conference helped me realize that I don't have a leg to stand on. I wasn't okay with Death because I wasn't okay with all the death that has happened to me. That's not your fault, though. It has nothing to do with you. And you were right. I make money from Death, too, in my own way."

He tilts his head. "So, you're okay with it now? After all that?"

She laughs. "I wouldn't say I'm okay with it. I would say I'm working through it. I get why it's important to you, and I respect that."

"I'm really trying to understand."

"I don't know, Garrett. I guess I just realized I can't be mad about my parents dying forever. I think the conference reminded me that death is the reason my parents met so many people and impacted so many lives. How can I sell caskets every day if I'm so mad about death? What good would it do anyway? Everyone dies, right? It's not like I can stop it."

"That's logical of you."

"I'm not mad about it anymore. My parents wouldn't want

me to be mad. They would want me to let it go. They would want me to help people if I can. Didn't you say you were helping people? Then you're doing a good thing, right?"

He rubs his hands up and down his face. "My head is spinning a little, but I'm glad you see it that way. It seems like you've done a lot of thinking since I saw you last."

"Maybe I'm not explaining it right, but I promise I'm not going anywhere. Can you just trust me for now?"

"I trust you," he says, taking a deep breath. "This is going to sound stupid, and I already regret saying it out loud, but I don't want you to ignore what I do every day. I want you to be proud of me."

She runs her fingers through his hair. "I am proud of you. You're a good man. I think I've always known that."

He pulls her toward him until they're nose to nose. She takes his face in her hands and tries to memorize exactly what he looks like in this moment, the joy radiating from his face. As he kisses her, Garrett slides his hands up her body, and Nora can barely handle it. She climbs on top of him to feel him against her.

He groans. "I've missed you so much."

"Me, too."

"I can't wait to be far away from my parents' house." He kisses her neck and down to the edge of her T-shirt.

"We have time," she whispers.

They kiss for a while, letting their hands wander until Garrett can't take it anymore. He asks her to talk about something boring, like the paint colors she's been thinking about for the store, and he listens to every word. She falls asleep against his chest, hoping that life and Death will cut them some slack, at least for a little while.

EPILOGUE

Nora stops by her grandpa's house on the way home from work to give him an extra bag of soil she didn't need for her garden. Really, this is just an excuse for her to check on him, and they both know it.

Nora and Garrett have almost redone the whole garden in Nora's backyard. They've gotten rid of all the weeds and solidified the border around it. They're going to have food and flowers year-round if she has her way, and Garrett usually lets her have her way. He's all but moved into her house, so they've been making a lot of changes together, and she's gearing up to redecorate her parents' bedroom. She and Garrett need more space if he's ever going to live there for real, and using only part of the house doesn't make sense. She thinks her parents would be happy that she's finally making the house into a place she wants to live.

She's keeping the store, too. Honestly, it's making money. It's a good financial decision. Nora keeps asking Garrett if he's bringing her business by being in the area, and he usually rolls his eyes. Really, the increase in clients is because she started social media accounts and created a functional website. She also used her degree for once and got the store's finances in order.

Johnny comes by from time to time; they're back to being friends one day and enemies the next. His new girlfriend looks like a swimsuit model, so Nora is sure he's happy with how things turned out.

Nora drops the bag of soil in the garage and finds Grandpa and Joe drinking coffee on the back porch. Her grandpa and Joe had worked at the same company for a while, until Grandpa retired. Once Joe reached retirement age, they started spending considerable time on each other's porches.

"Is the baby here yet?" she asks. Joe's about to be a grand-father again.

"Nope, we're still waiting. How's that man you got?"

"He's good," she says. "Working late."

"Y'all ain't got no babies planned yet?"

She puts a hand to her chest. "Don't even joke."

Grandpa smiles. "I think we could handle a baby, Eleanora."

"I don't know about that."

"We handled you, didn't we?" Joe asks.

"I'm not sure I'm the example we want to set."

They've just started in on the community happenings when someone rings the doorbell, and no one in Rabbittown rings doorbells.

"Are you expecting someone?" Nora asks.

Grandpa moves to get up, but Nora raises a hand to stop him. "I'll get it."

When she opens the front door, Garrett is standing on the welcome mat. He's wearing a dark blue suit and dark blue tie, which sticks out like a sore thumb in this neck of the woods. Nora keeps telling him this, but he can't imagine looking any less than professional.

"Hey," she says, but it comes out like a question. "I thought you were working."

He nods. "I came to see your grandpa."

"Come on in," Grandpa calls from behind her. "You're right on time."

"Right on time for what?" Nora asks. Garrett kisses her cheek as he steps inside the house. Joe joins them in the kitchen, and they all crowd around the kitchen table. She looks at her grandpa and then at Garrett, waiting for one of them to say something.

"Well, Eleanora," her grandpa begins. "I guess it's time we had a talk."

"What kind of talk?" One glance at Garrett's solemn face answers her question. She had known this was coming, that eventually her grandpa's name would wind up on Garrett's list and she would have to face it.

"It's my time," Grandpa says. "Time to move on. I've gotta go see what your grandmother's been getting up to."

"No." Nora steps toward her grandpa, and he takes her hand into his.

"There's nothing to be done about it now. My heart isn't what it used to be."

"Your heart is fine." She turns to Garrett. "You can fix this. This is a mistake."

"There's a time for everything," Grandpa says. "A time to be born and a time to die. There's nothing to be fixed. Garrett did what I asked."

"What is he talking about?" she asks Garrett.

"I called your grandpa this morning," he says. "When I found out."

"And you just told him everything? Without even talking to me about it?"

"He didn't tell me anything I didn't already know," Grandpa says.

"You knew? How?" she asks, suddenly angry at everyone in the room. At everyone in the world.

"Nora," Joe says gently from across the table, pressing pause on the swirl of feelings about to take over her whole body. "Your grandpa and I didn't work at an insurance company."

She takes a deep breath, unsure if she's going to scream or faint as the truth settles into her bones.

Grandpa steps closer to her, squeezing her hand. "I wish I had told you earlier and explained everything, but none of that matters now. What matters is that we're both taking a step forward. We're both moving on. Together."

Her breath comes out in a huff as a sob catches in her throat. "I'm not ready."

He reaches forward to hug her, and she winds her arms around his neck, reminding him of the little girl she used to be. He had expected this to be the hardest thing he has ever done, to have to leave her behind like everyone else has. His own truth had settled in his bones as well: this is how it's supposed to be. "You have the rest of your life ahead and good people who love you. You're going to be fine." He nods at Garrett and Joe.

They had both promised to take care of her, and he had re-minded them that she's perfectly capable of taking care of her-self. She's a Clanton, after all.

"We're not going to talk about that now," Grandpa an-nounces, handing Nora a handkerchief from his pocket. "Why don't you come into the living room with me? I want to hear about your garden. We've got a few minutes yet."

"You cannot be serious," she says, wiping her eyes and blow-ing her nose.

"You might say I'm *dead* serious, Eleanora."

"Grandpa!" She gapes at first, but she can't help the laugh that escapes her.

She will remember this. This last bit of kindness as he spent his last moments caring for her. She will carry this with her, carry him with her, next to the others she lost over the years. She will remember the way they held each other's hands until the very end. Her surprise when she realized he had purchased the brown casket from the showroom. The breeze that wound around her in the cemetery as she stood, wrapped in Garrett's arms, and looked down at the fresh dirt.

ACKNOWLEDGMENTS

This book does not exist without the help of many, many people. Please allow me a moment to say thank you:

To Sophie Cudd, the best literary agent around. You changed my life when you took a chance on my query letter. I'm so grateful for your support and the support of everyone at The Book Group.

To my editor, Hilary Teeman, for loving and believing in this book. Your guidance has made it better in every way.

To Caroline Weishuhn for sharing your ideas and for keeping things moving forward.

To copy editor Bonnie Thompson for your attention to detail and for helping me remember the correct order for the days of the week.

To everyone else at Penguin Random House who had a hand in making this book a reality.

To my foreign rights agent, Jenny Meyer, for loving this book and for sending Nora and Garrett out into the world.

To my UK editor, Sanah Ahmed, for your enthusiasm and kind words. I'm excited to be working with you and everyone else at Orion.

To my film/TV agent, Berni Vann, for loving and championing this book as much as you do.

To Trevor Worthy and Woe Wednesday. Can you believe our jokes live on in print?

To Monica Halka and Nicole Leonard for listening to me talk about this book from the first moment the idea entered my head. I'm so grateful for your friendship.

To my friend Sarah Bode, who has been involved in every step of this whole process. Thank you for reading the very first draft and every draft that came after. Your encouragement over the years has kept me writing even when it would have been easier to quit.

To my beta readers and friends Molly Graham, Katja Huru, and Candice Temple for listening to all the updates and for agreeing to read a messy draft about someone falling in love with a middle manager who works for Death. Looking back, that was a pretty big ask.

To Lara Plishka for listening to me talk about Death at so many Taxco dinners.

To Victoria Taylor for your support and reassurance through this process. I'm grateful to have you in my corner.

To my sister, Kelsey Wilhoite, for taking my author photo and for figuring out what I need before I figure it out myself. Thanks to you and Kevin Wilhoite for handling my website and other things that involve internet expertise.

To my parents, family, and friends for celebrating this book and for buying a copy. I promise not to ask if you actually read it.

To my grandparents George and Elizabeth Evans. I wish they could be here to read this book because it would not exist without them.

To the best beagle writing partner, Lucy. I know it's time for dinner, and I swear I'm almost done typing this.

To everyone who read this far. I know how many books are on my own TBR list, and it means the world that you would choose to read mine.

CASKET
CASE

LAUREN
EVANS

A BOOK CLUB GUIDE

DISCUSSION QUESTIONS

1. When we meet Nora, her life has been turned upside down by unexpected circumstances. What did you think of how she chose to handle the situation with her parents' store?

2. Like many folks from small towns, Nora always dreamed of moving to a bigger city. But when she comes back home to Rabbittown, she realizes there's a lot more to life in a small town than she gave credit for. Would you rather live in a big city or in a small town, and why?

3. Garrett isn't looking for love when he stumbles into Nora's store, but he finds it anyway. Have you or anyone you know ever stumbled upon the right relationship when least expecting it?

4. What did you think of Garrett's job? Did you find the idea comforting or difficult to grapple with? Did you understand Nora's hesitations about it?

5. Much of the novel revolves around the theme of grief and the way different people handle it. While there is no one right way to grieve, did you find yourself relating more to Nora's grief or Garrett's?

6. While Nora often feels alone, she has a tremendous circle of friends and family around her in Rabbittown, all rooting for her and wanting the best for her. Which of these characters was your favorite, and why?

7. How did Johnny and Garrett differ in the ways they viewed Nora? Which character do you think more accurately saw Nora for who she truly is?

8. When Nora is offered the chance to leave Rabbittown and get back onto the path she'd always planned for herself, she realizes some of her priorities have changed since coming back home. Have you ever had a similar experience, where something you thought was an ending was actually a beginning?

9. What did you think of Grandpa's revelation at the end of the novel? Were you surprised by it?

10. If *Casket Case* were to become a movie, who would you cast as Nora, Garrett, and Johnny?

DEATH DOES A SURPRISING AMOUNT OF BUSINESS IN RABBITTOWN, ALABAMA. . . .

GARRETT BISHOP
Regional Director of Logistics

Rabbittown
CASKET COMPANY

Nora Clanton
OWNER

CHANDLER FUNERAL HOME
a Prestige Funeral Home Partner

Johnny Chandler
Manager

A PLAYLIST OF SPOOKY LOVE SONGS

FOR WHEN YOUR LOVE STORY IS ONE OF A KIND

"Magic Man" by Heart
"Love Potion Number Nine" by The Searchers
"If You Ever Did Believe" by Stevie Nicks
"Crystal" by Stevie Nicks
"I Put a Spell on You" by Nina Simone
"Witchcraft" by Frank Sinatra
"Black Magic Woman" by Santana
"Gloomy Sunday" by Billie Holiday
"I'm Your Boogie Man" by KC and the Sunshine Band
"Spooky" by Classics IV
"Dancing in the Moonlight" by Olive Klug

NORA'S "MEETING THE GRANDFATHER" DINNER RECIPES

BBQ Chicken

1½ pound chicken breasts or thighs,
   depending on preference
1 teaspoon seasoned salt of choice
1 teaspoon garlic powder
4 tablespoons secret family recipe BBQ sauce
   (or store bought)
3 teaspoons mustard

Season chicken with seasoned salt and garlic powder, marinating overnight. Throw chicken on the grill, covered, and turning often, until cooked through, 15–20 minutes.

While the chicken cooks, combine the BBQ sauce, mustard, and water to thin until preferred consistency is reached.

Brush the sauce mixture over the chicken and return to the grill, turning a few more times to avoid burning. Remove after about two minutes.

Mashed Potatoes

1 pound Yukon Gold potatoes
⅓ cup sour cream
1 clove garlic, finely chopped or grated into a paste
Salt and pepper to taste

Medium dice potatoes and place in a pot of salted boiling water for 16–18 minutes or until tender. Drain thoroughly and return to the pot. Add sour cream, garlic, salt, and pepper, mashing until they've reached the desired consistency.

Green Beans

1 bunch green beans, preferably fresh from the garden
Red pepper flakes, if desired
Salt and pepper to taste
2 tablespoons olive oil
Shredded Parmesan cheese

Preheat oven to 425 degrees. In a medium bowl, toss washed green beans with red pepper flakes (if using), salt, pepper, and olive oil. Place on a prepared baking sheet and sprinkle Parmesan over the top. Roast 15–18 minutes, flipping the beans halfway through.

Mother's Plain Angel Biscuits

Recipe courtesy of Genevieve Cobb, the author's great-grandmother! (Okay, we know Nora used freezer rolls, but if she'd had more time, she would have made these.)

1 package yeast
¼ cup warm water
2 tablespoons sugar
1 teaspoon salt
1 teaspoon baking powder
½ teaspoon baking soda
2½ cups all-purpose flour
½ cup shortening
1 cup buttermilk

Dissolve the yeast in warm water and set aside. Combine dry ingredients; cut in shortening until mixture resembles coarse meal. Add yeast mixture and buttermilk to dry ingredients. Mix well. Turn out on floured surface and knead for about 1 minute. Roll and cut out into biscuits. Let dough rise for about 15 minutes before baking. Bake in preheated oven at 400 degrees for about 15 minutes or until golden brown.

Nora's Four-Layer Chocolate Birthday Cake

Another family recipe from the fabulous Genevieve Cobb.

1 box white or yellow cake mix
2 cups sugar
1 tablespoon Golden Eagle syrup

¼ cup cocoa

1 teaspoon salt

½ cup milk

1 stick butter, room temperature

1 teaspoon vanilla

Prepare cake mix and bake as directed on box. Allow to cool completely. When layers have cooled, split each layer, making a total of four layers.

ICING

Combine sugar, syrup, cocoa, and salt. Add milk, butter, and vanilla. Cook for about 2 minutes or until a soft ball forms when dropped in cold water. Ice cake immediately while icing is still warm. If icing begins to harden before applied, add a few drops of water and reheat.

Lauren Evans grew up in Anniston, Alabama. She has a BA in English from the University of Alabama and an MA in liberal studies from the University of North Carolina Wilmington. She lives in Atlanta with her beagle, Lucy. *Casket Case* was long-listed for the Cheshire Novel Prize in 2022 and is her debut novel.

laurenbevans.com
Instagram: @laurenevanswrites

ABOUT THE TYPE

This book was set in Electra, a typeface designed for Linotype by W. A. Dwiggins, the renowned type designer (1880–1956). Electra is a fluid typeface, avoiding the contrasts of thick and thin strokes that are prevalent in most modern typefaces.